I0612993

Trinkets in Love's Lost and Found

By

Donald Owen Crowe

W & B Publishers
USA

W & B Publishers

For information:
W & B Publishers
Post Office Box 193
Colfax, NC 27235
www.a-argusbooks.com

ISBN: 9780692371930
ISBN: 0692371931

Book Cover designed by Danielle Crowe
Author photo by Rescma Bhargava (copyrighted)

Printed in the United States of America

Acknowledgements

I would like to offer a very special 'thank you' to all the dedicated people at W & B Publishers, particularly to my publisher and editors William Connor and Jonathan Penroc, who believed in my work and provided me with support, incite, direction and creative input, especially in the latter times of finalizing this work when everything seemed a bit overwhelming. They never tired of my questions and concerns, and helped bring a dream to reality.

This book would never have come to fruition without the support and encouragement of my family. I'd like to thank Shirley and Danielle Crowe for their creative ideas and thoughtful suggestions, and for their limitless time proofreading and editing early scripts. Thanks to Danielle for designing the book's cover and to Brent Gayler, my personal computer wizard, who ensured my laptop never actually went through the window. Special thanks to Donna Berg, my first reader. I owe a great deal to Ron for 'subtle' motivation, and to all those close to me who made sure I had hope and support when I needed it the most.

Dedication

For my brother Ron
Missed and loved
Who must be walking with his friend Camus

Courtesy acknowledgements

Thanks to Danielle for creating and designing the covers for *Trinkets in Love's Lost and Found.*

Author photo courtesy of Rescma Bhargava.

Chapter One

The child screamed.

It was dull, overcast and windy, with just a hint of a deepening cold that would make everyone hesitate at the door and wonder if they should wear a jacket instead of a sweater, so Mathew knew it had to be Saturday or Sunday; but early, because he'd only had to coerce her image from his thoughts three or four times since he'd forced down two burnt pancakes at breakfast.

Mathew was standing pensively in front of the window in the room he never used, the *living* room, watching the first few tentative raindrops speckle yesterday's puddles on the sidewalk and wondering what shape his father might assume today, when another bloodcurdling scream prickled the hairs on his neck. It echoed from upstairs. His son.

The child screamed again, a shrill, primordial howl that tinkled the crystal chandelier in the dining room, the other room where he felt like a trespasser.

Stomp stomp stomp along the hall, then *thud thud thud* down the stairs, feet peppering the steps like an Uzi emptied into mud. The boy jumped over the last step and almost fell. He was crying so hard he had trouble catching his breath. Sniffling loudly, his cheeks pale and white, he wiped his eyes and screamed again.

"I can't remember who I am!"

Mathew turned from the window. Yes, it was another Saturday. The children's' programming must have just ended.

"I can't remember I can't remember *I can't remember*," the boy sobbed. Something between a chant and a wail. His hat fell down over his eyes which made his ears look bigger than they actually were.

Joshua wore a black cape, loosely tied at the neck. He'd made the hat from a folded piece of newspaper; it had started out like half a plane, then he'd turned up the bottom sheets and flattened them out. If he wore it on the side he looked like Napoleon, only smaller, which would have pleased the great man to no end. But if it was straight and tipped rakishly down over his forehead, Joshua was the spitting image of Admiral Nelson before the battle of Trafalgar, except *a lot* smaller, which the Spanish would have found quite amusing. Until the first volley of cannonballs ripped giant holes in their sails and snapped a mast or two in half as shrieking scorched sailors fell into the churning sea.

Joshua had found a pair of his sister's old knee socks, red with a hole in one heel, and he'd pulled them up thigh-high over his pajamas. His top was unbuttoned. He'd penciled a sloping moustache beneath his nose with his absent mother's mascara. He had a plastic sword left over from two Halloweens before in one hand, an apple in the other.

A grenade? Some secret weapon with mystical powers? A seer's orb? Or something plundered to eat and keep the scurvy at bay?

"It's okay son," Mathew told him quietly. He dropped to his knees so he could look the boy in the eyes, and was startled when he saw himself in the child's dilated pupils.

"Calm down. Take a deep breath. Come on, breathe with me."

The usual routine when panic attacked. In and out, in and out, in and out, softly encouraging, like a birthing coach.

Mathew listened to the frantic pulse of his son's heart. He knew the fear was there, sensed it pressing in all around him, the fear he would never *be someone* again. The boy had forgotten *who* and *where* he was at that moment, and the entire world was nothing more than an ether mask waiting to smother him.

"Were you watching something on T.V., Joshua? Cartoons?"

"Yes, yes, but that's not it! That's not who I am! I'm not a cartoon person!"

Shivering, he sniffled so hard he coughed and his cheeks flamed bright red. At least the room was slowly coming back into focus, and his breathing was gradually beginning to return to normal. He looked down at his cape and socks. And the apple.

"Do I *look* like a cartoon?" Joshua demanded, with an eight-year-old's indignation.

The first thing Mathew imagined was Mighty Mouse, but Mighty Mouse didn't have a moustache. "No. You don't look like a cartoon."

"I've got a cape and a sword, but I can't remember who I'm supposed to be!"

"Give me a clue and I'll try to help."

Joshua couldn't think of one. New tears. Mathew stood back and gave the child another look. How often had he done this? He knew he had to hurry: although his breathing was stabilizing, Joshua was really getting worked up this time and he didn't want to lose him.

"Maybe you're Zorro." Mathew slashed a giant "Z" in the air with an imaginary scabbard.

Joshua rubbed his nose and shook his head. Another blank "Flash Gordon?"

"Who?" That was well before his time.

"Are you one of those Power Ranger things?"

"*Noooo!*" The boy's eyes leaked with frustration. Tears bled through his mascara moustache.

Mathew looked down at the apple: the stem was gone. Maybe it *was* a grenade. He grasped for straws. "Vin Diesel? The Undertaker? The bullet-dodging guy from the Matrix?"

The child kept shaking his head.

"What about one of the Gargoyles hunched over the castle wall?" Mathew asked hopefully. "Bat Masterson?"

"No, no, no!" Joshua cried, frenetically stamping his little stocking feet.

Mathew glanced up the stairs. Where was everyone else? His oldest son would be able to help, unless he'd already donned his own hat and gloves so that he could work. His wife? No. Lydia was out on the west coast somewhere -- Vancouver? Spokane? -- pretending to be something, and someone else, too. Mother was at a class, and his father -- well, his father couldn't really help, could he? And Carmalitta was conducting an emergency therapy session at her clinic. Like his son, Mathew was all alone.

"What about Sinbad?"

A soft *no* as Joshua shook his head.

"Are you a good guy or a bad guy?"

"Good." He smeared his moustache over his cheeks.

"How about . . . Johnny Quest?"

"Dad!" The boy gulped back more tears.

Oh right, not a cartoon. "Were you being someone who was a crime fighter? Like Batman or The Shadow?"

Joshua wriggled with uncertainty. Something niggled inside. "Not really."

A hat, a sword, a mascara moustache thicker on one side than the other, a sword, a cape, and a piece of fruit that could have been anything.

Mathew pictured himself smaller, and searched through his childhood memories, when he was always looking up and the world just out of reach. Edges undefined, something always lurking behind and beyond him, voices that rumbled down from above.

"What about one of the Musketeers?"

Joshua's frown trembled, then disintegrated like glass in a kaleidoscope. Everything in the house seemed to breathe a collective sigh of relief with him. His smile broadened from ear to ear, showing the gap in his front teeth where he whistled the letters 's' and 'z'. He brandished the sword and took a few threatening stabs at the air, spun around, then bounded back up the stairs two steps at a time.

"It is I, D'Artangne, the greatest of all the Musketeers. Do not despair. I will save you."

He reached the landing and disappeared down the hall, stabbing and parrying intently with some imaginary foe. A gleeful cry slowly faded with his footsteps.

Mathew sighed as he stood up, his right knee cracking, then walked back to the living room window. Joshua was safe. *For now.* The boy knew who he was, and in all likelihood, he would stay in the role for the rest of the day. Or at least until another character emerged to claim his hopes and dreams and desires and draw him into some other hidden, esoteric world.

Mathew wasn't so fortunate. He listened to the rain splatter against the skylight. It frightened him: he'd forgotten they even had a skylight.

His son had found himself again. For Joshua, all was right with the world. *But who am I?* he wondered.

Who am I?

***

Terrible memories that feel like a fist squeezing a heart are often no different than wonderful ones that fill a soul with long-ing and a faint sense of hope. Neither lasts longer than the oth-er, and both are equally elusive. When old age creeps in and fears of death quietly fester as the seasons change, all memo-ries, good and bad and painful and wrenching, simply tumble together like clothes in a dryer, the things that were, or might have been.

So it wasn't surprising now, five and a half years later, that Mathew couldn't even remember where they were going or why they'd been in the car in the first place, when *it* happened: when his son *changed* for the first time. When he didn't *pretend* to be someone else: but when he actually *became* someone else. Or perhaps let someone else *out*.

Joshua was nearing three. Mathew knew they couldn't have gone any great distance because the child had only asked *how much farther, Daddy?* half a dozen times. Mathew clearly re-called driving, though. Lydia was preening in the little lighted mirror on the back of the visor and mouthing some new line or another while Joshua hummed some indecipherable tune in the backseat. Actually, Joshua was helping Mathew drive: he had one of those little plastic steering wheels affixed to the front of his car seat. He bashed the wheel and turned into every corner with his body, thumping the bright red horn and waving his arms around wildly, grinning and completely unfazed by every-thing going on all around him. He drove like his sister, Carmalitta, never signaling or using the brake or checking blind spots. Joshua had a toy phone just like hers, too, so he was nev-er beyond the social network. He cradled it in one hand and steered with the other, his fingers sticky with juice and the remnants of cheese strips and gummy bears. .

Mathew had just scurried off the Parkway, turned along Bloor, then swung up Castle Frank when Joshua yelled. Not really a yell: it was more like a gravely wail, like a harp seal on a breeding island who can't find its pup. The little steering wheel rolled back and forth unattended.

"Are you okay son?" Mathew called, checking the rearview.

"Stop, Daddy; stop, stop."

"Joshua, what is it? Are you hurt?" He turned to Lydia. "He's not choking or anything is he?"

"No, but --"

"Stop Daddy. *Pleaaaase*! Go back go back *go back*."

Mathew pulled over to the curb. The car behind honked and swerved around him, the driver's hand offering the usual obscene gesture. But Mathew didn't bother looking up. He spun around. Joshua's face was burnt red, his eyes wide, and he was caught between a frown and a smile. The child was trying his best to undo the buckle strapped over his chest and twist free of the car seat. He pushed himself up off the chair and strained to look out the back window.

"The house, Daddy."

"Maybe you should back up, Mathew." Lydia snapped the visor closed. "He seems quite distressed."

Mathew put the car in reverse and inched backwards. More honks. Someone yelled to look where he was going. He would have if he'd known where he was going himself.

"Stop!"

Joshua stared out his side window. They were directly in front of the third house from the corner. A sprinkler was on the boulevard. After a moment's hesitation it arched backwards, spraying the car and tap-tap-tapping across the roof. Joshua shrieked with delight and checked to see if he was wet. Nothing. He giggled again when the water came back.

"This house?" Mathew wondered. There didn't seem to be anything special about it at all. Fifty or sixty years old, nicely kept, recently repainted with a well-maintained lawn, although, if it had been him, Mathew would have angled the front garden out a little more toward the driveway. He didn't like the fact that nothing separated this house's driveway from the one next door, because he knew that someone always took advantage of the other person when a shared driveway was involved.

The water from the sprinkler tap-danced across the roof again but Joshua wasn't smiling any longer. He chewed at his bottom lip and quietly watched the house as if he half-expected it to move. He was looking for something. *Or someone.*

"Joshua?"

Nothing. The child cocked his head to one side, then the other. He circled his hands slowly up and down. Mathew was sure his son was actually *feeling* the house, although he didn't really know what that meant. Up one side and down the other, across the roof, and then lightly over the windows, the way a blind man reads a face.

Mathew probed gently. "Joshua?"

But he could see the child was somewhere else. The look on his face was similar to the one he assumed when he evolved into different characters on Saturday mornings, like Bugs or Fozzie or SpongeBob, but it was different, too: this was more intense, serious, surreal. The water from the sprinkler pitter-pattered against the car, smearing the window with streaks. From the car seat, Joshua thought the house looked like it was crying. He almost seemed to be crying, too, except there weren't any tears.

Lydia folded her arms over the rear of her seat and pushed her chin into the back of her hands. It was as close to being maternal as she could get. "Joshua, tell Mommy what it is. What are you looking at?"

Water drummed against the roof.

"My house," the boy finally whispered. The frustration was easing. His body relaxed and he stopped feeling the house with his hands, but his eyes were still tinted with a wary edginess.

Mathew and Lydia both turned together. There was no resemblance to their house whatsoever. Other than the sprinkler.

"That's not our house, Joshua. Our house has a long, long porch and a big garage. And it's all red brick, remember. This house doesn't have --"

"My house," the child repeated. His agitation was melting away faster than an icicle in the late March sun. His face was soft, almost blank, although his eyes never stopped moving. He was accepting whatever it was that had seized him when they'd turned the corner and he'd first seen the house.

"My house," he whispered emphatically. "Here. I lived here."

"We've never lived here, son. Maybe --"

"No no *no*. I lived here. *Before*."

He closed his little eyes, and sighed. A chubby finger played with his curly hair. "Before." The word felt gentle on his lips. He could almost smell it, and if it would have had a color, it would have been blue.

"Before? Before what?"

A little nod, like they were teasing him. "With my *other* mommy and daddy."

Lydia started to speak but Mathew touched her arm. There was something disturbing about his son's eyes. He knew the boy wasn't daydreaming. This wasn't simply make-believe. He certainly wasn't *pretending*. He was actually re-living something.

"What other mommy and daddy, Joshua?"

The child scanned the roof, the drainpipe, the chimney, the wrought iron furniture carefully arranged on the porch. "The mommy and daddy before you."

Lydia shivered.

Mathew forced the words out. "Which ones were those?"

Joshua seemed unsettled again. He shuddered. "You know, you know! The mommy and daddy I had before you. The daddy that died!"

"But you've always been our little boy," Lydia cooed.

The child shook his head. "No, no, no." His face glistened with a sense of controlled exasperation, like he was trying to explain something very difficult to a child.

"Before *now*." He leaned against the window and pointed a stubby finger at the house. "When I was here before. I lived with them. Here."

Joshua reached out a tiny hand and touched the lines of water streaming down the other side of his window. A funny smile creased his lips and he mouthed something to himself.

"Joshua?"

Silence. And then the change, the first one, the one that would affect so much from that moment on, the ones that came in so many shapes and depths and degrees, the ones that Mathew would see over and over again through the years in his dreams and in the time-fragments he felt most lost and afraid. The child's eyelids began to flutter and the color drained from his face. His lips looked unnaturally pale. The tic slowly settled, and when Joshua's eyes opened again they were misted with memories. He smiled reflectively. When he finally spoke, his voice was deeper, more an adolescent's voice; impatient, not overly tolerant, and riddled with self-importance.

"It's a Cape Cod."

Lydia gasped. Mathew felt his chest tighten. "How do you know that?"

Joshua, or at least whoever it was that was speaking from the back seat who'd been Joshua a moment before, sneered. His eyes rolled upwards, his words flecked with hubris.

"That the house is a Cape Cod? Well truly, father, I think that's fairly obvious. Anyone with a rudimentary knowledge of basic architecture would know *that*."

Truly father, I think that's fairly obvious? A rudimentary knowledge? Architecture?

"The architectural signs are unmistakable, although in all fairness, the model is based on a facsimile of a traditional Cape Cod design."

Facsimile? Traditional?

Hands trembling, Mathew felt his blood pound through his neck. The sprinkler beat a mournful echo against the hood of his car. He quickly pictured turning off the Parkway, driving along Bloor, then weaving onto Castle Frank, and he was sure he hadn't noticed anything change from the numerous times he'd driven this way before. No time warp, that he felt anyway. No worm hole. Then again, things like the fourth dimension were just as alien to him as how they got all the information on a flash drive. And how did it actually play back? He hadn't seen a porthole, but he knew he wouldn't have recognized one anyway. He looked at his son. He was three. Who was this manchild in the backseat of his car? And where had Joshua gone?

"Son --"

Joshua haughtily waved the anticipated rebuttal into silence. "Definitely Cape Cod. Look at the positioning of the dormer windows and how the porch juts out to give it a facade of greater depth. The gingerbread lattice work. Come on, father, it's a closed issue."

A closed issue?

Lydia was gulping for air. She put her window down and fanned herself with her hand, just as the sprinkler turned back toward the car. She didn't seem to notice the water splashing on her face. Mathew reached across and closed her window for her.

"No. No, when I said *'how do you know that,'* I didn't mean *'how did you know the house was a Cape Cod.'* I meant, *'how do you know you've been here before*. That you've had another mommy and daddy.'"

The boy replied cryptically. "How does anyone know?"

Mathew summoned up his courage and voiced the question he didn't really want to ask. "Why didn't you stay with your other mother?"

A nostalgic whisper. "Because I died, too."

Mathew took a deep breath and rubbed the tension from his forehead. He was sweating: he felt a bead course down his back. What had he just said? He was talking to his son as if Joshua really was suddenly someone else. Someone else's son. A son who'd already died.

"Why do you think that, Joshua?"

Nothing. The little boy yawned. He stretched back in the car seat and rubbed his eyes. Waves of boredom washed over him and he took a few haphazard slaps at the little red horn on his steering wheel. *Beep. Beep.*

"Let's go, daddy let's go. Much further? I'm *tiirrred.*"

The *old* voice. The child's tone. And *the look* gone from his eyes. He smacked the horn dead on and it yelped like a puppy.

Lydia wondered, "But what about the house, Joshua?"

Mathew shook his head and mouthed *don't bother* to his wife. Joshua was back: he could see it in the boy's face, and hear it in the change in the child's voice. He had no idea how Joshua had come back, or where the other child was, for that matter. But he knew words like *architecture, Cape Cod, rudimentary,* and *facade* were gone. But for how long? And where had they come from? He knew enough not to pry any deeper right now.

Gone, but not forgotten. Like so many memories. Mathew turned around and started the car. His hands were shaking and he fumbled with the key. The sprinkler pulsed once more against the windshield. Joshua pounded the little plastic wheel and rocked forward so the car would go.

Instinctively, Mathew didn't waste any time wondering if the child would do that again. Change into something else. *Be* someone else, from another time, another place. He knew there'd be another time: he could feel it in the very marrow of his bones.

Another mommy and daddy?

He just wondered *when*.

Chapter Two

Hands in his pockets, Mathew struggled to push *her* from his thoughts once more as he scanned the interior of the fridge. It was full, but without substance, like his job, his life, the house; that's why he hadn't been able to get anyone to help when the swashbuckling D'Artangne had come bounding down the stairs earlier. Everything was full and empty at the same time. The outside wasn't as sterile. There was a faded GE nameplate in the top right corner, three little yellow sticky notes ordered in a straight line, a copy of a blog, two frayed e-mails and a text message he could barely decode. One sticky note was from his wife, Lydia; the others belonged to Eleanor, his mother, and his daughter, Carmalitta. His eldest son Michael had highlighted the important parts of one of the e-mails with a light green marker. That's how Mathew's family communicated; dated memos, hasty notes, sticky tabs, and notes written on magnetic pads that could be wiped clean and be ready for the next person. E-mail, texts and blogs were usually one-way communication devices, because only Michael and Carmalitta knew how to send and retrieve them properly. And since Mathew never used the sticky notes, they were really one-way communication tools as well.

Surprisingly, the fridge wasn't plastered with things that screamed *a child lives here*. No art work. No colored-in doodles, connect-the-dot pictures, finger-painted abstracts, or cute little animal magnets. Nothing from school or church or some club: no calendars, project reminders or *need-to-get* lunch notes. Not one seasonal announcement, schedule, or drawing, which was strange for a home with an eight-year-old inside. In a normal household where a child is present, the fridge is one huge billboard, an ever-changing cornucopia of information, a metallic sign covered in advertisements about dates and places and tests and things to do, like the endless barrage of billboards that frame I-75 throughout Georgia. But then again, Joshua wasn't really a normal child. Mathew knew that even *child* was a stretch.

A child is an adult waiting to happen, a part of the thing that will be a whole the adult will always wish he could remember more of. An unraveling umbilical cord. Joshua, however, was something *different*.

Everyone who knew Joshua had written their own symphony about the boy, and they'd struggled to play *variations on a theme* to Mathew.

At each level of his son's education, Mathew had been summoned by a pedagogue in the hierarchy to talk about the boy. He'd never been contacted or asked to come in because the child had done something wrong: it was always simply because Joshua was being Joshua.

Joshua was . . . well special, the nursery school teacher told Mathew conspiratorially. *Unique. Somewhat odd for his age.*

They'd been standing in the middle of the playground, surrounded by rampant hordes of shrieking trolls. Mathew was overwhelmed by the pandemonium the teacher called *recess*. It made him dizzy. Someone rode a tricycle into his leg but escaped before he had time to grab it.

"*Ouch.*"

"Get out of the way," the child yelled, pedaling furiously, his knees smacking against the handlebars and clothes-pinned baseball cards *click-clacking* against the front wheel's spokes.

The teacher was young, too young to realize that most adults would feel unbalanced by the seething cauldron of activity the little demons boiled all around them. She wore a school jacket with ECE emblazoned across the back. A newbie. She covered her mouth with her hand as she spoke, as if she didn't really want the words to escape into the air. Thin hands, preternaturally veined and ethereally white. Mathew had to lean closer to hear her.

He doesn't seem like a child. I'm not sure I know all of the words he uses. Maybe you should have him tested. He is often .... other people.

Tested. Mathew knew the problem with testing is that you find out things, and answers can always go both ways. "Are you sure?"

But Mathew knew the frazzled young woman was right. And that she was afraid. She was whispering again.

"At nap time yesterday, I heard him explaining to the other children how anesthetics were discovered, and when they were first administered for surgery."

Mathew wasn't sure when that was. He didn't think he could even estimate it within a decade if Joshua didn't give him a hint.

"And this morning," the teacher went on, nose wrinkled and her eyes almost pinched closed, "he told them all about the first few explorations on cadavers, when doctors were trying to understand things like how our blood circulates."

Yes, Mathew thought, *that sounded like Joshua*. He'd always enjoyed reading about the Greeks. And he'd been in a real ancient Roman medical-mode recently.

"You really should have him tested."

Mathew nodded and moved just in time to avoid another suicidal attack by the crazed little goblin on the tricycle.

The psychometrist from the public school board had two sessions with Joshua. She immediately confided to her colleagues that two sessions had been one too many for the battery of tests she had at her disposal. Mathew met her in a cubicle in the basement of the Ministry of Education building on Bloor Street. She looked about fifty, although she wore her makeup so thick she might have been much younger. One side of her mouth looked bigger than the other that morning: she probably put her lipstick on in the car while she was talking on the phone about something that could have waited anyway. Brown hair streaked with silver, an oblong face, and an insipid smile that never seemed to go away.

Joshua is a very . . . unique little boy."

She didn't say *child*. No one that knew him ever did.

"I gave him quite an extensive battery of tests - psychological, emotional, intellectual -- and, well -- I'm not really sure where *the boy* falls on a normalcy scale."

Mathew could see that normalcy scales were very important to the woman and that she was deeply troubled by her inability to give Joshua a proper numerical measurement of some sort or another.

Perhaps the psychologist should test him further.

Mathew pictured the cages of lab rats stacked against the wall, their vocal cords severed so they didn't keep screaming, ricocheting like jumping beans across the wired grid every time they were shocked for not pressing the lever some researcher thought was right. But his son didn't have a tail so he took him anyway.

The psychologist had introduced himself to Mathew with a delicate, almost consciously sensitive handshake that said *I'm a gay psychologist, a confident gay psychologist, and the only thing I'm interested in right now is your reaction to my effeminate little grasp.*

Mathew didn't have any reaction whatsoever, which seemed to irritate the psychologist, Dr. Grovenor, more than just a tad. He waved Mathew into a chair on the other side of his desk. It was one of those sloped things that are supposed to be comfortable, the ones ergonomically designed that don't have armrests or enough back support so you always think you're going to fall over. Mathew didn't know where to put his feet. He balanced precariously on the edge. In fact, when he wasn't thinking about *her,* and his heart was throbbing and he had a loving ache all over, he was always balanced precariously on the edge.

Dr. Grovenor fanned a stack of papers and said he'd administered several different advanced psychological tests to Joshua. He paused thoughtfully, weighing the things he'd seen and heard. Mathew waited to hear where he had to go for the next assessment of his son.

Joshua is a very exceptional young man. Extraordinary.

Mathew knew Dr. Grovenor couldn't understand his son and that he definitely didn't think Joshua was a child, either.

"I got the distinct impression he was testing *me,*" Dr. Grovenor admitted softly, brushing an imaginary lock of hair from his forehead. He rearranged some things on his desk.

Mathew wondered what his son had found out.

"Public schooling is undoubtedly not the best place for the young man. But a school for the gifted probably wasn't quite appropriate either, since his needs are rather . . . unique."

Dr. Grovenor obsessed over some private thought. He was obviously troubled by something, but since he was much more acclimatized to his chair than Mathew was, it didn't appear to affect his balance. Mathew wasn't as fortunate: struggling to maintain his equilibrium, he felt like he was riding one of those mechanical bulls western-themed bars find so fascinating.

"When he slips into other *personae*, he has more general knowledge than most adults I come in contact with," Dr. Grovenor said, confirming what Mathew already knew. "And, unlike most individuals I see, he actually understands the things he talks about."

Mathew shifted again but couldn't get comfortable. *Whoa, Nellie.*

"At times he seems like an intelligent, worldly old man in a child's body. I am concerned, though, about his emotional development."

"But a lot of time he's just a child," Mathew offered defensively. *When he isn't being someone else.*

"Yes, exactly. It's most peculiar."

Mathew couldn't remember the last time he'd heard anyone say 'peculiar.'

"The . . . incidents don't appear to be *episodic*, or anything like that, and they don't show any signs of being situationally dependent. Have you ever noticed anything just prior to the times he talks -- how should I put this -- beyond his years, his experience? A warning? An aura of some sort or another?"

"Like people get before migraines?"

"Yes. Or often before seizures."

Mathew tried to remember something that might help. Two nights earlier, just before bedtime, Joshua was telling him about the intricacies of the rigging on old English sailing ships.

"He gets a funny look in his eyes, and they flutter like they do behind his lids when he's sleeping."

"Anything else?"

"He's distracted for a few seconds and doesn't seem to be aware of anything. Sometimes his face goes white."

"And when the 'episode' finishes?"

"I understand something new."

"No, I mean does he go through some type of transition again. Something you can actually see?"

Mathew shook his head, which almost cost him his balance. He rolled around on the chair like a drunken sailor. "No, not really. Apart from his eyes looking normal again, he doesn't change much at all. One minute he's talking about something I wouldn't have thought he'd even heard about, and in the next instant he's Joshua again." *Whatever that means.*

The doctor was puzzled, yet it wasn't an inquisitive sense of bemusement that provoked his curiosity or scientific interest and made him want to press on. He was simply baffled. So he did the only thing he could think of: Dr. Grovenor performed *the ritual* as he leaned across the desk: *the cough behind the hand, and the passing of the card.* Mathew struggled forward out of the backless chair to take it.

Dr. M. J. C. Stallworth, Psychiatrist. And too many letters after that to count.

Mathew groaned and climbed out of the chair, squirming like an insect in a Venus fly trap. He tucked the card into his wallet and left before he had to shake hands again. On the way out, Mathew stuck his palms under one of the canisters that dispensed antibacterial soaps and lotions that that had become so prevalent since the SARS (Severe Acute Respiratory Syndrome) outbreak several years before. Preying on people's fears of the disease, an endless variety of concoctions were quickly unleashed on the market. Some dissipated faster than others, some were scented, others were made without being tested on animals, and a number helped renew dry skin from washing your hands so much.

After the second outbreak had been contained, only one or two isolated cases had resurfaced, but Mathew wasn't ready to take a chance. *One or two* to the government could mean just about anything. And since many people still failed to use the dispensers, Mathew knew you could always contract *something*. There were viruses *everywhere*. He'd often seen men leave the stalls or urinals in public washrooms and not wash their hands. *Eecckk!* That alone was enough for him to risk getting dry skin. He conscientiously rubbed his hands together, half mumbling and half singing *Happy Birthday* like you were supposed to do.

Mathew had taken Joshua to see Dr. Stallworth the following week after he'd almost fallen off Dr. Grovenor's aerobic chair. Dr. Stallworth was buried in the narrow catacombs deep inside Sunnybrook Hospital. They each needed a pass that said *visitor* in order to access the hall that led to the doctor's office. Mathew already knew they would, because Dr. Stallworth had been Mathew's psychiatrist on and off for about seven years. He'd always liked the little blue *visitor* badge because it reminded him he could still leave when he wanted to, but each time he went he checked the back of the card to make sure it didn't say '*inmate.*'

The waiting room was tiny, the soap dispenser a beautiful mauve. Two doors on opposite walls. Just three chairs, one with the vinyl back sliced open. Joshua's feet dangled far above the floor. He was motionless, quiet, and his face seemed determinedly serene. It was the look he always had when he was hard at work thinking about something. Or when he was away, somewhere. *Being someone else. Oh God,* Mathew thought. *Not now.*

The back door closed, the front one opened. Dr. Stallworth filled the doorway. He was too big for a psychiatrist. Broad shoulders, straight back, thick hands, and the sculpted physique of a triathlete. He'd won the Senior's Division in the Toronto Iron Man competition the last two years in a row. Mathew was a bit uncomfortable with Dr. Stallworth at first because he didn't think a doctor, especially a psychiatrist, should be running marathons. He figured Dr. Stallworth should be able to displace his repressed feelings in some other way. Why did he like running down the street in a tiny bathing suit, sweat glistening on his thighs and corded stomach, a number just above his pelvis that unconsciously drew an observer's eyes toward his crotch? And why was it so important for him to win, anyway?

Dr. Stallworth met Joshua with a smile and told Mathew he'd have to wait outside. It was his turn tomorrow.

Dr. Stallworth saw Joshua three times during the following month before he talked to Mathew about his son. Well, not about his son; about Joshua. Apart from Mathew's immediate family, Dr. Stallworth was the only other person that knew Joshua wasn't really Mathew's son. Well, he was his son. And Mathew definitely was the boy's father. Just not his biological one, even though they shared blood and DNA and epithelials. Joshua was actually the third crisis that Dr. Stallworth had tried to guide Mathew through: they were still working on the other two. Although Dr. Stallworth didn't agree, Mathew considered the woman he couldn't stop thinking and dreaming and wishing about a crisis, too.

"One of the strangest and most perplexing cases I've ever seen," the large doctor pondered over a smoothie made of freshly squeezed papaya and orange juice. He had framed pictures of himself all over the wall behind his desk: running, cycling, swimming. He used a little trophy topped with a bronzed running man frozen in time for a paperweight.

"Atypical, to say the least."

Mathew waited politely. He never knew what to do with his hands when he was with Dr. Stallworth. He didn't want to fidget or leave them dangling out to the side. He didn't want to drum his fingertips against the edge of his chair, and he was definitely afraid of letting them rest conspicuously in his lap. So he held his hands out in front of his chest, like a sterilized surgeon who's just scrubbed up.

"Completely uncharacteristic. Not dysfunctional, but -- let's just say unique."

All this time and we're still on 'unique', Mathew thought.

Dr. Stallworth frowned, undeniably perplexed by some of the things he'd seen in the child. He rose from his deep-backed leather chair, lowered himself to the floor, and did fifty slow, purposeful push-ups. Mathew had witnessed this many times before, and tolerantly waited for him to finish. When Dr. Stallworth's purgatory was over and he returned to his chair, his face was barely flushed and not a hair was out of place. Mathew wondered how many push-ups the man could do if he wasn't wearing a suit and tie.

"I should see the . . . Joshua again," Dr. Stallworth admitted, brushing some imaginary fleck of dust from the trophy. "How has he been at home?"

"The same," Mathew said softly. He heard someone wheeze and struggle to lower themselves into a chair out in the little waiting room. It made Mathew uncomfortable to think that when he left a new patient would come right through the same door he'd used fifty-five minutes before.

"The same?"

"Quiet, then talkative. Shy and reserved, then bold and aggressive."

"And he keeps thinking that he remembers being other people?"

"No." Mathew smiled uneasily. "He knows he really has been those other people."

Dr. Stallworth wrote something down in his notes. Mathew wondered if he kept his file with Joshua's now, sequenced in the little pullout drawer by first name.

"Are you still encouraging him when he *thinks he remembers* being someone else?"

"I listen, let him talk. It's hard to tell him he's not who he thinks he is when everything is so clear to him. He looks and acts differently."

"But you don't actually encourage him?"

"No. When he's . . . someone else, he doesn't need any prompting. He tends to lead the conversation."

"Uh-huh." More note-taking and scribbles. "When was the last time?"

"That he acted out someone in another life, or when he talked about adult things using words I had to look up?"

Dr. Stallworth reached under his desk, picked up a dumbbell, and initiated a series of bicep curls with his right hand. "Both."

"Well, Tuesday after school, when he was having trouble with marking the provincial capitals on a map of Canada, he started telling me all about the *courier du bois* and the early explorers, and how difficult it had been for sailors and adventurers to create the first maps without a topographical perspective. I got lost when he started into the fundamental aspects of triangulation."

Dr. Stallworth changed the weight to his left hand but didn't interrupt. He knew that not many people could identify the provincial capitals or mark them on a map. Pity. But that wasn't the issue right now.

"He explained why a topographical perspective would be beneficial, and then he went on to illustrate some of the problems the initial map-makers had and how they were overcome."

Dr. Stallworth put the dumbbell down. "And when was the last occurrence where he acted like someone else?

"The last time he *was* someone else?"

"The last time you *think* he *acted* like someone else."

Mathew bristled, and the lines of his forehead compressed. "The last time I *know* he didn't *act* like someone else but actually *was* a person he'd been before?

"Pretended to be before."

"Who'd lived before."

"That you *interpreted* as acting like he'd lived before."

Mathew was almost spitting through gritted teeth. "That you *interpret* as *I'm interpreting* that he's *acting* like he lived before."

Dr. Stallworth sighed. Stalemate. He just couldn't get through to Mathew on this point. "Yes. Go on."

"Thursday evening. He'd just finished watching 'Wheel of Fortune' and was getting ready for bed."

"Does he still solve all the puzzles after a letter or two?"

"Yes. But that night he turned it off before the last puzzle. He seemed a little agitated. And then it started when he was brushing his teeth."

"What happened?" Dr. Stallworth began a series of shoulder rolls. His muscles strained against the confines of his suit.

"He got that really serene look on his face, and his eyes started fluttering. He drifted away for a moment, like he was lost in thought. When he spoke, his voice was deeper than normal."

"And he was --"

"A bank clerk in county Cork during the potato famine in the 1800's."

"Did he have an accent?"

"A deep brogue. He said 'Aye' this and 'Aye' that. He talked quite slowly, as if he was measuring his words before he spoke. Like an old man telling a tale in front of a crackling woodstove. He was deeply distressed that the people were suffering so horrendously. But it bothered him even more that the bank was using the catastrophe as an opportunity to buy up land at ridiculously low prices when families were forced to emigrate to Canada and the United States. He admitted it was grossly unfair to take advantage of peoples' misery, but he knew that if he questioned his superiors too harshly, he'd be gone. There were many clerks devoid of his sense of morality that would have gladly taken his place."

Dr. Stallworth frowned. "Have you recently seen a documentary about the famine on television? National Geographic? PBS?"

Mathew shook his head.

"Have they had a field trip to Pioneer Village?

"No. It came out of absolutely nowhere."

"I see. And he was --"

"Brendan McCurk."

McCurk, *clerk*, and *County Cork*. Dr. Stallworth wondered if the key could be in the alliteration.

"He talked for almost an hour about the horrible plight of the children who were starving." Mathew suddenly noticed that his arms had become very tired, so he let them drop and folded his hands together in his lap. He noticed that Dr. Stallworth noticed.

"How did he seem mentally?" Dr. Stallworth prodded.

"Frustrated, sad. And angry, too. He said the banks were stoking the fires of despair, and that they were helping to starve their own people."

"He used that phrase . . . 'stoking the fires of despair'?"

Mathew nodded. "He was genuinely upset, and the longer he talked about it, the more depressed he became. He was deeply saddened by his own inability to do something to help. At one point there were tears in his eyes."

Dr. Stallworth wrote down *ambivalence* on his notepad. The page was crammed with notes because he didn't like using the paper up too quickly. Each page had a little inspirational saying at the top, a motivational phrase for marathoners. *Runners run. The wall is only in your head. Swim like a dolphin, run like the wind, cycle like a windmill.*

"And after?"

"Nothing, really. When he came – came out – he brushed his teeth again because he couldn't remember doing it the first time."

"And, as usual, I assume he didn't recall anything specific about what he'd said the following day."

"Not in the least." Mathew frowned.

"What?"

"That's not completely true. Sometimes he does and sometimes he doesn't. The next morning he didn't remember all the things he'd talked about, the problems and situations he'd agonized over."

"But?"

"But he did remember . . . . No. That's not the right word. He *felt* some of the things that had bothered him so much when he was Brendan, although he didn't seem to know where those feelings were coming from."

"When he *thought* he was Brendan."

Or was it when Brendan thought he was my son?

"He was sad and teary and he didn't want to eat his breakfast, especially when there were so many starving and destitute children in the world. He complained nothing was fair: that he had to eat when he was told, that he had to take a bus to school, that he couldn't stay home if he wanted to. That there were children his own age who were working fourteen hour days all over Asia."

"What did you do?"

"What could I do? I told him he was right, that life isn't fair, and sent him off to school."

Dr. Stallworth took a few deep, relaxing breaths. He put his palms flat against his desk and did some isometric exercises while he tried to remember what he could about the Irish potato famine. Where could the child have acquired the information? Where did the voices come from?

"And it's still totally different than when he simply pretends he's some role model or another? Batman, Superman, that sort of thing?"

Mathew nodded. "There's no similarity at all. When he's playing, he knows he's imagining everything. And he doesn't have *the look*. But when he remembers someone, he's conscious of having been that person."

The isometric exercises stopped and Dr. Stallworth checked his heart rate by touching his carotid artery. He jotted something down. "I'll have to see him again, of course. And your appointment . . ."

"Is tomorrow."

"Perhaps I can ask you to write down whatever Joshua says if he has another episode. It might give me a better understanding of his mental state and emotional perspective at the time."

"Certainly." Mathew rose to leave.

"But Mathew?"

"Yes?"

"Don't encourage him to be someone else."

And just what are you doing? Mathew thought. But he nodded and tried to smile. As he left, he heard the other office door open and Dr. Stallworth usher the next patient in. He cringed when whoever it was slipped down into the chair. *His* chair.

Wasn't there any place that was just his? Where he'd feel comfortable and cared for? After forty-eight years, didn't he belong anywhere? With anyone?

Mathew stepped out into the dying light of a late-September afternoon. Layered with sheets of dark clouds, a brooding sky threatened more rain.

Yes, he thought, *he did*. He just didn't know where she was right now. *Or if she'd want him back.* The only thing he knew for sure was that she plucked at his heart strings every single day with every breath he took, a muse singing a silent song.

Could he find the words, the chords, the music that would make their lives one unforgettable melody once again?

Chapter Three

Mathew had been on his way upstairs to check on his father. He didn't remember hearing the phone ring, the shrill cry that could stop the world, but it must have, because he'd jogged back down into the kitchen, picked up the receiver, and was trying to listen. Static crackled, and he wondered if he'd have to go back to his doctor and have his hearing tested again. The hair he was gradually losing on his crown was apparently directly proportional to the new hair that was growing inside his ears. And nose. He speculated how old the person was who'd said 'life begins at forty.'

Static. Muffled voices. "Lydia? Is that you?"

Nothing.

He scanned the refrigerator door for some clue to where she might have been, but there were simply too many proclamations to go through: cutesy emails, notes scratched on empty corners of magazines, and torn of pieces of personalized stationary. Keeping the message board relatively clean and up to date had somehow become another one of Mathew's household jobs. It wasn't any different than changing the toilet paper roll, taking out the garbage, or opening a new box of tissues whenever the current one was empty. Changing the bacterial soap dispensers. Doing the laundry when the clothes started tumbling out of the hamper like lava from a volcano.

"Lydia?"

He thought he heard someone shout his name.

"Can you hear me?"

"Hello?"

The line suddenly cleared and Mathew heard his wife's lilting voice trill his name again.

"Yes, it's me. I'm here, Lydia."

"Oh thank *God*," she breathed. "I do hate these cell phones, but there's really nothing else too close by. Am I coming in loud and clear?"

Mathew pondered what part his wife must be working on. She was trying a bit too hard at whatever it was supposed to be. She didn't usually say things like 'loud and clear,' and 'too close by.' Or even *God*. Lydia was about as religious as most people who say they don't actually have to go to church to show their spiritual side. God knows they're thinking about Him: they don't have to miss a game to prove it. And most of the time, they make it to the Christmas pageant, don't they?

"Yes, I can hear you fine now. How have you been?"

"Oh *God,* simply harried. Been running around all over the place, haven't I? Frank, the darling, got me two more auditions. Imagine! Just like that. I think I've got about another week of work."

Wasn't she on one of the coasts? "Are you still in Vancouver?"

More broken glass. "What?"

"Are you still in Vancouver?"

"On the island, actually." Birds cried out. "I'll have to tell you all about the ferry one day. Between the wind and the rain and the sea splashes, I don't know what I'm even doing here. You can't imagine what it does to your hair."

Her voice lowered. Someone else was there with her. "Yes, oh *God*, that feels fine. Keep going, it doesn't hurt a bit."

"Lydia?"

"Oh sorry, I thought I had the mouthpiece covered."

"Who are you talking to?"

More seagull squawks. Mathew shook his head. It hadn't always been this difficult talking to his wife. For years they'd been as close as any other couple he knew, mired in the trials of living and raising a family, but always wrapped up tightly in each other's existence. But then something happened. *Life happened.* And like a calved iceberg, they slowly started drifting apart into unknown waters.

***

It was difficult to say when everything changed. It wasn't something that could be pinpointed, nor narrowed down to a particular time or place or event. There certainly wasn't a distinct, defining moment that they could look back on and say "that was when everything changed". Like most things, the silent space, the distance that had come between them, had crept up unannounced. On the one hand, it was slow and methodical, a gradual erosion of familiarity, closeness, friendship and faith. On the other, it seemed to have risen so quickly it was like being shoved in front of an oncoming streetcar, without warning, without time to think or move. One minute they seemed to be together and in the next, they were miles apart. Life changes aren't usually catastrophic until they're over. Relationships come apart: either you step on the land mine and watch everything come to end, or you don't.

In Mathew's case, the "drift apart" was so subtle that he wasn't sure if he'd really been there when his life changed or not. When the big questions about his existence that had always seemed so important started to disappear and leave him all alone, he was already just a shell of what might have been, the last vestiges of a broken promise. With Lydia, however, there was an added dimension, because a great deal of the change in her relationship with her husband occurred when she became obsessed with her burgeoning acting career.

The fracture of their life together hadn't been quite as distinct for his parents. Lorne and Eleanor. They hadn't suffered the same blunt force trauma as Mathew still reeled from. Their slippery slide from *us* to *her* and *him* or *Mom* and *Dad* wasn\t as much as a shock as Mathew's denouement had been. Although Lorne and Eleanor still had a *then* and *now*, their transition back from a couple to two singles had only slowly and delicately pushed them apart. Even now, long after the stroke's scalpel sliced Lorne's brain into compartmentalized components that no longer knew each other, Mathew's parents were still – he didn't know quite how to say it – more of a couple than he and Lydia were. Lorne and Eleanor had never reached that dramatic moment of finality, that point of no return. Yet over the last year, they'd wandered closer and closer to the edge of the abyss.

Other than the tragedy that had befallen his father, three major changes had recently affected the core of Mathew's life. One, for some reason he couldn't quite put his finger on, he no longer spent endless hours thinking about all those mind-boggling questions that had never let him have a moment's peace before. The ones that kept him up all night and were always there, somewhere, plaguing his thoughts and niggling the back of his mind. *What was truth? Had he been here before? What was it like before he was born? What is existence? Why am I here? Here, and not there? What happens when I die?* The questions didn't haunt him anymore, but the emptiness didn't give him peace and quiet, either. If the questions didn't exist, did the answers?

The second thing that changed was that Mathew finally realized, and accepted, just how far he'd grown apart from his wife. He still loved her, but not in the way he always had. Or not in the way he could, or ever would, again. And the farther he'd unconsciously distanced himself from Lydia, the more his mind, his body, his psyche – his soul – had gradually been engulfed with thoughts of his university sweetheart, the woman he thought he was going to spend his entire life beside. *Carol. Carol.*

The third thing that changed was something Mathew didn't like to talk about. He didn't even like to think about it now.

Three interconnected transitional events that completely and irrevocably changed what was left of his life. But the subtle exclamation point on his existence had come the day Lydia went out to have her hair done.

Lydia was one of those women who, had she had unlimited resources, would have loved to have their hair professionally cared for every single day. Unfortunately, she had to settle for a wash and set once a week. It was a routine that bordered on an obsession, and she always went to the same salon: *Giovanni's.* So did almost everyone who could afford it.

Giovanni's salon oozed a sense of false femininity. He reminded Mathew of the men you always see on the front of women's romance novels: skin-tight pants, a silk shirt unbuttoned to his waist, a hairless chest, more gold chains than a rapper, a diamond stud in each ear, and long, thick luxurious hair held in place with a velvet ribbon. The eyes of a flamenco dancer, the build of a matador. He was every woman's dream because he treated each one of them as if they were his most important client in the entire world. And they were, from the moment they sat on his altar to the instant they left, and Giovanni heard the sweet sound of the cash register's *ca-ching*. Then someone else was queen of his heart.

As usual, the salon had been packed that fateful afternoon. In the back of the shop where young trainees washed the client's hair, there was a small television. It continuously ran repeats of the week's talk shows and soap operas for those women addicted to the fantasy lives of others. Meanwhile, gossip, leading innuendoes, cloying suspicions, confessions, and the latest secrets burned endlessly through the rest of the salon like a brush fire.

The gaggle of women seemed quite excited about a program that was apparently just coming on. Always raised, Lydia's antennae tuned in. Big mistake. *Bigger* mistake for Mathew. Smiling flirtatiously as she passed Giovanni, she dragged her husband from the safety of a bench outside the salon and deep into the labyrinth of the women's domain. Several women huddled around the television.

"This was the show I was telling you about," Lydia whispered, plunking him down in a free chair. "The one you said was fake." Lydia, in fact, had only seen *part* of the show.

Evidently, it was about a woman who'd been traipsing around some third world backwater on one of those Eco tours that have become so popular recently. Sometime during the night, some *thing* bit or stung her. They flashed a picture of the plant the insect had fallen from -- it looked almost exactly like the spider plants Mathew saw everywhere. He shivered: they had at least three of the long, green and white leafed plants at home. But his anxiety was quickly pacified. The species, it seemed, was only endemic to the country the woman had visited. Even though it wasn't a native plant, it still took its toll on Mathew's life. Re-runs often do.

The site of the bite ballooned in days. Nothing the medical staff did gave her any comfort or reduced the swelling. Seventy two hours later it was the size of a large boil. Twenty four after that it was almost as big as a tennis ball. At least that's when it stopped growing, or the woman may have ended up with two heads.

Stateside, the woman naturally sought out her own physician. After a few tests, the doctor lanced what he considered a huge boil. The moment his scalpel spit the sac, hundreds of tiny baby spiders poured out. The sac deflated as the spiders overran the woman's cheek, her throat, her arms and chest. Her face and hair were covered.

Lydia feinted. Not so much in a dead heap; she just kind of slipped off the chair and down onto the floor. People rushed to help her. One of the women said she was a nurse and immediately took charge. But before she could check Lydia and provide some comfort, a tall, well-dressed man pushed his way past her. Black hair, black suit, black eyes. black attaché case.

Lydia, slowly coming around on her own (which peeved the nurse to no end) looked up. "Are you a doctor?"

"Heaven's no. I'm a talent agent."

Lydia bolted upright, quickly shooing everyone else away with her hands. "Get away from me, I don't need a doctor," she hissed. "I was acting just then. So you liked the way I fainted, Mr.--"

"Wong. Alex Wong." He handed her his card. "Just as I passed the salon I saw you fall. It was perfect. I've been looking for someone who can faint at the drop of a hat for a television commercial for a funeral home. How about an audition?"

The gossip in the salon flared to infernal heights.

"What's your --"

"Lydia," she quickly stammered. She spelled it for him.

"Lydia. Be at this address at ten o'clock on the sixteenth. Don't be late. There just might be a job for you. More if the funeral parlor commercial works out. I have to run. Call if you need anything." He turned back. "This could be the start of something big, Leena --"

"Lydia."

"Lydia. Look at all the police dramas. The forensic shows. They're always showing dead bodies. Cut you up, give you a 'y' incision down at forensics, find your body in a dumpsite. There's literally hundreds of acting jobs on television for people who can play dead. Think about it. I'll see you on the six-teenth."

And the world, as they say, stopped spinning. If there was a time Mathew and Lydia's relationship changed, that was it. Lydia finally realized she could act: and that realization dramatically took over what was left of her entire life.

Meanwhile, while all the attention was being lavished upon Lydia, Mathew was quietly barfing in a garbage can filled with *hair* and *moss* and dyed clumps of *cotton balls* that happened to be right next to Giovanni's chair.

Given his long-standing anxiety about the plants at home, it didn't take a mental genius to figure out there was a slight chance that Mathew might even develop a disorder about spider plants after seeing the army of writhing little beasts pour out of the woman's face. And that's exactly what happened. It wasn't just the plant, of course: it was what might have lived *inside* the plant that caused him so much trouble. And what they could do. Every time he saw a blemish anywhere on his body he kept a vigilant eye on it for days, making sure it never changed. That it never got bigger or darker *or higher*. Moles were particularly distressing, because they were popping up all over his body the older he got. Every mark, every blemish, became a potential breeding ground for the things that could suddenly bleed all over him in the night when their pimple-sized home ruptured.

In their next session, Dr. Stallworth told Mathew he was overreacting, and buried the topic into his patient's deepest subconsciousness by reminding him that there are inevitably thousands and thousands of mites and ticks and crawling things too small for the human eye to see that live on our bodies all the time, foraging for food and clearing away dead skin. That helped Mathew a lot.

Something snapped Mathew from his reverie, and he drifted back into the *here* and *now*. Lydia was still talking. *How long had he been listening and not really hearing?*

***

"Lydia? What did you say? Who are you talking to?"

She sighed demonstratively. *How much had he missed this time*? "A wonderful young thing, really. What's your name again? Oh yes, I see. Her name's Claire. She and her partner Jerrold are doing my back, and since everyone out here is on some sort of schedule or another, they just can't wait. So they're going to keep working while I talk to you."

"On your back?"

"Yes. They've already finished my face."

Mathew massaged his temple. "Finished your face?"

"Well you see, it was really Frank's idea. He knew someone, Richard Cormier, or something like that, who seems to be a good friend of Sam Marshall, and Sam, the little sweetie, does the extras for most of these Vancouver scenes. He can make anything here look like any place in America they want him to."

"Why does he do that?"

"Oh *God*, really, Mathew. Whatever they film out here has to be made to look like something in the States or the people in the U.S. won't watch it. I thought everyone knew that."

"What does he do?"

"Sam? He can take a small town, or even part of a street, and make it look exactly like some little bayou backwater, or some forgotten cross-roads in a Midwestern farming state. He reinvents places every day. He can use the same building over and over again, and make it anything he wants. One morning the street can be in Chicago, and the next day it's a suburb in Seattle, or the main business artery in Toronto. He's really amazing. He changes everything: post boxes, flags, offices, statues, house fronts, cars, street names. He can take a storefront, throw on a patio, add a few rod iron touches and regional knickknacks, and make it look like a bakery in Maine or Vermont. He can use the same storefront the next day, cover the tables with checkered cloths, put on an awning and a sandwich board, then stick one of those accent things over the word Cafe in the window -- "

"An aigue."

"Pardon?"

"The accent. It's called an aigue."

"Well, whatever. And the place looks like a bistro in Paris or old Montreal. It's all quite exciting to watch. But I'm usually so busy working that I don't have the time to *really* get behind the scenes."

Mathew had to yell over another burst of static. "Why don't they just shoot the scene where it's actually supposed to take place?"

"*God*, Mathew. Cost. Everything here is time and money. Change a few license plates around and put a tag on the screen telling them where they are and most people will believe they're practically anywhere. We can use one little neighbourhood for five separate scenes from different parts of the U.S. and the audience will be none the wiser. As long as they think the place is in the U.S. and they have *some* concept of where it might be, the viewers are happy. You don't think they really shot *The Titanic* out in the middle of the ocean, do you? Or that there's really a Hobbit shire?"

"No. I guess not." *Another fantasy place to escape to ruined forever. Yes Virginia, there is a Santa Claus . . .*

"Wow. Be careful Jerrold. *Really*."

"What?"

"Sorry, not you. You'd think they could be a little more sensitive."

"What are they doing?"

"Cutting me up."

"I beg your pardon?"

"Cutting me up. Stab wounds, slices, that sort of thing."

"I thought you were an extra in some crowd scene?"

"Oh Mathew, you never listen! That was simply days ago. I told you Frank got me something else, didn't I? You know, because of Sam Marshall."

Mathew's head was spinning. He watched two fire trucks blaze by the front of his house with a paramedic's van in their wake and wondered if he'd ever have to have them called to extinguish what was left of his life if it couldn't be saved.

"But you're still a sweetie for remembering," Lydia purred with the seductive, breathy little tone Mathew had always found so enticing. "I was an extra back on Monday. Just a silly little street scene. You know, walk back and forth, nodding, looking around. I was supposed to be hurriedly window-shopping on Fifth Avenue in Manhattan during the lunch hour. Some office orphan hustling back to work, but dreaming about better things in the middle of the crushing throng. I must admit, I had a bit of trouble *really* getting into the part."

"And now?" Mathew was almost afraid to ask. He listened a little impatiently as an ambulance careened down the road.

"Well this one's really wonderful! I couldn't believe my luck when Frank called. He's such a dear. I'll probably have about fifteen or twenty seconds *right on camera*. Imagine! And I didn't even have to audition for the part."

"Is it a commercial?"

"*God* no, don't be silly. This one's *real t.v.* It's scheduled for next fall. I think it's called *The Aftermath*, or something like that."

"I haven't heard of it."

"That's because you're always too busy reading to know what's on. This is going to be really big, I can feel it. It's one of the spin-offs from *Millennium*, which was kind of a spin-off of *The X Files*. It has something to do about what happens to the transplanted brains of serial killers in the future."

"And you . . ."

"I'm a horribly mutilated victim. Knifed all across the back and then shredded with a razor. That's why Jerrold and -- what's your name again honey -- oh yes, Claire, that's why they're here, putting the make-up and bloodied wounds all over my back. I'll tell you, the latex smells absolutely wretched."

"Do you get to say anything?"

"Oh Matthew, *God* no! I'm a serial killer's victim. I've been stabbed about a hundred times. They find my body in a deserted area of an inner city park, half-covered in leaves, blood pooling everywhere. It's really kind of creepy. I'm part de-comp so there's fake maggots everywhere."

"*Fake maggots*?"

"So the coroner can make a better estimate of the time of my death, without just using my liver."

"Oh."

"The stars -- two police officers, a man and a woman -- come right in close. The man kneels down beside me, checking for clues, and he calls the coroner on his cell phone while he's looking at the way I've been brutalized. His partner takes a quick look around, then drops down on her haunches. She looks me up and down, studies some of my partial wounds, trying to find out something that might give them a lead. So for all the time they're on camera, I can't twitch or even move a muscle, or even breathe. Imagine!"

Yes, Mathew thought. Imagine. The other face, *her face*, crept back again, luring him away. No blood or maggots or serial-killer slashes . . . just a heart-wrenching smile of simplicity. He struggled to stay focused. "When will . . ."

"Just a second, Mathew. What? No that's fine. Pinch the skin if you have to. What? Oh yes, all right. Listen, Mathew, I really have to go. I have to lie down so they can really cut my stomach up. They have to puff the skin out more or something."

"When will you be coming home?"

"I'm not sure."

"Well, it's Michael's birthday on Thursday, and . . ."

"Who?"

"Michael." *Our son.*

"Oh really, Mathew. You know he just hates *Michael*. Please try to call him Cybernician. He's only asked you about a million times. That's the name he works under and that's what his company is called. Really."

"I still have a little trouble calling my son Cybernician," Mathew admitted.

The fire trucks and the ambulance were framed by the window again. They were going back the other way now, and much slower this time: the crisis was over. Too quick for a fire, so it must have been some personal emergency. No sirens. Either the person was fine or they were already dead, stretched out in the back of the ambulance on the metal gurney the attendants had snapped into place while they pulled a sheet over the face.

"But that's what he is, Mathew. A virtual reality magician. He has talent. And just look at the money that boy's going to make."

The barb left dangling wasn't very subtle. Their son was already making more than Mathew had in his life. More static.

He turned and pointed his antennae in a different direction. Lydia must have been doing the same thing because the line crinkled like foil paper and then was empty for a moment.

"So?"

"So *what*?"

"His birthday. Will you be home?"

"Yes, I almost forgot. His birthday. But really, I don't know if I'll be wrapped up here by Wednesday."

Mathew sighed. "You're a dead body, Lydia."

"A mutilated corpse," she corrected. "Abandoned, unnamed, a horrible product of a despicable culture."

"So you're not sure if you'll make it back, then?"

"No. If I can't make it I'll wire him some money. He can buy something for his computer. Something we probably wouldn't even be able to spell. What?"

"What?"

"Not you. What? Listen, it's Jerrold again. I *really* have to go. I'll try to be back by Thursday. If not, send my love to everyone for me, will you?"

"Of course." It was so easy sending someone else's' love, wasn't it?

"Oh, and how's Mom and Dad?"

"Fine. Just fine. Dad's had three or four episodes this week, and it's wearing Mom down a bit. She's starting to show her frustration. I was just on my way . . ."

"That's a shame. Getting old . . . *that's* the shame, isn't it? Well, listen. Tell them how wonderful I'm doing, and give everyone a big kiss and hug. And Mathew?"

"Yes?"

"I -- I miss you. I really do. You know that, don't you? But you have to understand how important all this is to me. I've waited so long for this chance, and I've worked so hard. There are sacrifices you just have to make if you're going to have a career." *Another barb*?

"Yes, Lydia. I understand. I really do."

"If I'm finished any earlier, I'll try and make it back. Promise."

"Sure."

"Now, I've really got to go and get absolutely *murdered*."

Mathew heard something that sounded very much like a squid being forced through a narrow tube. Had Lydia blown him a kiss through the receiver? He wanted to ask her if she'd given any more thought to what they'd been talking about before she left, but there didn't seem to be much point in doing that right now when she was getting lacerated. Mathew pictured the scars and welts and cuts and slashes that would cover her back and stomach, and shuddered. *Had she been violated again?* He hoped not. At least she'd be face-down in the leaves so it would be a lot harder for someone to recognize her. No questions at work, no more, *Oh, I saw your wife's naked and butchered body on T.V. the other night . . .*

A faceless victim dumped by the roadside, just like always.

Chapter Four

After helping the old man into his favorite chair by the bedroom window and then getting him all settled, Mathew tugged the comforter from his father's bed. The urine had darkened a huge splotch in the middle, and he tried to fold in the edges and ram it down into a green garbage bag without getting his hands wet. Just like he fretted about Joshua, Mathew constantly wondered when his father would change into something else again, too. No matter how hard he tried, he was never really prepared for either transformation.

"Dad?"

Nothing.

Lorne was the second crisis Mathew had tried to work through with Dr. Stallworth. Mathew propped his father up in front of the window, but the old man wasn't looking outside. He'd remain in the exact position Mathew put him in until someone else came and repositioned him into a different one. Mathew pulled a fresh blanket up over his father's legs and tucked a small pillow behind his head. He stared at the shell that was his father and remembered how odd, odd and guilty, he felt trying to explain everything to his psychiatrist after the first few times the old man *changed*. Was it three years ago, or four? He wondered if Lorne knew. He wondered if his father remembered yesterday.

Another session that had supposed to have been Mathew's turned into a fifty minute requiem for his father or son. Mathew didn't really mind: it stopped him from having to talk about Carol. He'd started blurting out the story to Dr. Stallworth before he even sat down.

"My dad watched anything nature-related, and I think he subscribed to just about every magazine there was that had anything to do with animals and the environment. He called them his three F's: Fading flora and fauna. National Geographic, Canadian Geographic, Equinox, The Great Outdoors, Nature's Way, American Pet, Birds and Butterflies, Heritage Canada, and Our Endangered Species of America. You name it, he read it.

"And television, too. Sometimes I think he was addicted to PBS, Nova, Discovery, Explorer, even the children's shows, like Kratt's Creatures. He'd be absolutely beside himself if he didn't get a daily fix of some type of animal program or another. It didn't matter if he'd seen it before, or if he knew everything there was to know about that particular show's focus: he'd curl up in his chair and stay glued to the television, motionless and entranced, as if he was ingesting it through osmosis or something."

"Did it become his sole focus in life?" Dr. Stallworth asked. He moved around behind his chair and took a couple of practice swings with an imaginary ball and seven iron.

"No," Mathew replied, unable to help himself from judging the shot's trajectory. It would have been a hook but he didn't say anything. "Dad was obsessed with learning as much as he could, but not to the exclusion of everything else in his life. He never abandoned his other duties. He loved the whole idea of educating himself about wildlife but he wasn't obsequious about it. He was a sponge that knew when he'd soaked up enough."

"Did he ever work with animals?" Another swing. Dr. Stallworth over-corrected and sliced the shot off into the rough.

Mathew nodded slowly. Just before . . . just before the stroke. But not for long. He did construction on and off after dropping out of school, and he worked as a metal stamper at a fabrication plant downtown for years. A courier, a telemarketer, a shipper/receiver, and one of those salesmen who sells everything under the sun to the little mom-and-pop variety stores. He was even a hospital orderly for a bit during the war. But he never had the chance to work with animals. His schooling was limited, and there aren't many jobs in the animal field for unskilled people that pay enough to live on."

"Quite true," Dr. Stallworth murmured. Beginning to tense with frustration, he moved on to his putter.

"When it came to animals, money was never an issue for Dad. He spent most of what he had on subscriptions, extra cable stations, and yearly membership dues to pretty well every animal rights group you could think of. If there was a foundation for ibexes, he belonged to it. Greenpeace, IFAW, Humans For Animals, The Humane Society, The Sierra Club, P.E.T.A. (People Against Animal Testing). If it existed, Dad had a button or a t-shirt."

"I see." Dr. Stallworth put away his clubs and did a few light side to side stretches. "I assume then, he just didn't support them monetarily."

Mathew hesitated. "You couldn't really call Dad a rebellious activist, or anything quite as glamorous as that. Although I'm sure that if he'd been as committed when he was younger, he probably would have been. Unlike most people, the idea of racing across some Arctic Bay in a little rubber lifeboat so he could bob up and down in front of a Russian whaler or some massive Japanese fish processing ship and scream 'Save the dolphins!' while they pointed their harpoons at his head excited my father to no end. But by the time he was semi-retired and had the chance to do things like that he was too old to keep up. So he helped in other ways."

"Such as?"

"Volunteer work, mainly. He canvassed for resources, delivered pamphlets, helped mail out newsletters, worked on fund raising campaigns, or just tidied up offices if they needed it. Whenever they required it, he could always step in as a placard-carrying protester, too."

Mathew drifted off for a moment. Dr. Stallworth stopped stretching and sat back down. "What?"

Mathew smiled. "Fortunately, for several years, he managed to work as a volunteer at the Metro Toronto Zoo. That faded green shirt with the little logo stitched on the breast pocket, the word 'Zoo' with antlers coming out of the top, was his pride and joy. Nothing pleased him more than the days he spent cleaning the cages or delivering the hay, hosing down the rhinos or traipsing through knee-deep muck to retrieve whatever some idiot had thrown into the elephant enclosure. When most of the animals were kept inside during the winter, he worked indoors showing pelts or skins or shells to tethered groups of preschoolers that exploded off the buses."

"Your father must have built up a fair amount of knowledge over the years."

"Certainly. Their habitat, characteristics, their evolutionary background, where they lived and the main predators they had to deal with. What their daily life was like. He knew why so many yaks are often unruly, why dogs like the smell of horrible things like vomit, or if fish sleep. Why geese migrate in a 'v' instead of an 'x', and what type of birds like what specific kinds of food in each season. If bears dreamed, or why the skeletal differences in various species of ants evolved. Ask him one simple little question and that was it -- he was off and running like a politician at a filibuster, barely slowing down for a breath until he almost fell over from exhaustion."

Dr. Stallworth had to bring Mathew back from the past again. "And then?"

"And then he suffered the stroke," Mathew sighed. "At least I assume he suffered. But since he hasn't ever told us anything about it I guess we'll never really know for sure. It was fairly quick, I'll tell you that. And there certainly weren't any warning signs, any auras or subtle indications that might have tipped you off that something was wrong, that something was going to happen. No convulsions, screams, or seizures. No headaches or dizziness, or problems with his eyes or trouble speaking, or his balance. It was all rather tame, actually."

Mathew wiped away a tear. 'When I saw him later at the hospital in the little curtained-off cubicle and he was cocooned in sheets that looked a little too white and all I could hear was the *beep beep beep* of the monitors and the gurgle of the plastic tubes, he didn't really look all that *bad*. It wasn't like seeing someone for the first time after their heart has exploded and thinking *that's not Uncle Tony* when you're trying to pretend you know the ghost and they haven't changed much at all. He looked basically the same, and since he was in a partial coma and his eyes were closed, he didn't seem that much different than when he was sleeping off a Sunday feast on the couch."

"Sometimes that's even more difficult to deal with."

Mathew gave a slight nod. "But he was different. That tiny weakening in the wall, that teensy, weenie little blood surge that ruptured the tendril of a vessel changed him about as much as the doctor's slap on his bum that made him taste his own air for the first time."

Mathew stared down at his hands. He knew that it was always something tiny, something hidden or unseen, that turned the world upside down and shook your life out into the blackness of the universe like pepper onto a white tablecloth.

"What happened, Mathew?"

"Dad had been watching a new show on 'In the Wild,' a Canadian-directed documentary put together in Toronto that focused on animals from countries all over the world. Wednesday, I remember that. Strange. And the time, too: 7:41. A show on African parks and the day to day problems the rangers face from poachers. Rhinos, baboons, gorillas, elephants -- the poachers murder any animal they can if there's some hint of profit in it. A lot are killed just for one particular body part. A piece of the brain, a penis, a tusk, a paw, a gonad -- and the rest of the poor creature is left to rot. It happens here too, of course. Seals and black bears in particular, since non-traditional Asian medicines use their various parts for remedies and aphrodisiacs. But that program dealt with African parks."

Dr. Stallworth waited patiently for Mathew to go on.

"Anyway, Dad had been watching quietly from his chair, when suddenly, his breath caught. Like when they show some horrible image on the news you weren't prepared for. He lurched forward, reached for the remote, murmured something incomprehensible, clutched at one side of his head, then collapsed back into his chair. He jerked once, then was still. His eyes had closed, but he kept blinking furiously for about a minute."

"And that was the last time he ever spoke?"

"Yes it was," Mathew said sadly. "He was in the hospital about a month before we were allowed to take him home. The doctors told us what we already knew: he'd probably never get any better. The fact that he was alive was about all we could ever hope for."

Dr. Stallworth watched Mathew remember the day. "It's a horrible feeling of helplessness, isn't it?"

Another slow nod. "We did whatever we could for him, but I always had the feeling it wasn't enough, that something was missing. He was almost always with us, but not *really* with us, if you know what I mean."

Dr. Stallworth offered a slow blink of understanding.

"I hate to say it, but it almost seemed as if he'd died and we'd had him stuffed. Like a fisherman who sticks some big Muskie to a board and hangs it over his fireplace. We took him from room to room, place to place. Outside, if we were working in the garden or sitting on the deck. He was like a great big Paddington Bear doll, without the hat. I think everyone lapsed into a state of resigned acceptance. Dad became a fixture, just like everything else in the house. It wasn't until about six months later that the whole animal-thing started."

"No warning?"

"None I ever identified." Mathew took a deep breath. "We were having dinner. Lydia was downtown, working as an extra on one of the Star Trek spin-offs. That was back when American companies, because of the change in the dollar and various tax breaks, started using so many of our studios for their programmes. They started dubbing us the Hollywood of the North. Anyway, Lydia was a dead alien or robot or something, found behind one of the taverns in the intergalactic bar scenes they always have now. Michael -- *Cybernician* -- was in his room trying out his new keyboard, and Carmalitta had been called into the clinic for an emergency appointment with a hedgehog. Its frantic owners were convinced the poor thing was trying to starve itself to death."

Dr. Stallworth tried not to smile. "She's the vet who's also a pet therapist, right?" he asked condescendingly. "Like the dog talkers or the horse whisperers?" He looked up admiringly at the degrees decorating his wall.

Mathew nodded. He ignored the doctor's prominently displayed degrees and thought about his daughter. A doctor and a veterinary surgeon, she had just as many. Despite Carmalitta's rationalizations, he had never understood what it was that had could possibly have been so upsetting, so disturbing, that it could force a gentle animal like a hedgehog to see death as its only way out.

"I forget what we were even talking about now. But whatever it was, it was innocent enough. Mom -- Eleanor -- was pureeing some vegetables for Dad, who was sitting at the far end of the table. I was putting out the dishes, and Joshua was on the other side, coloring. Eleanor turned from the stove, went to say something, then some invisible hand throttled her throat and she coughed. And then one little word, one short syllable with restricted rhyming capabilities changed everything all over again."

"What did she whisper?"

"'I've got a *frog* in my throat.'"

"That's it?"

Mathew nodded. "Apparently, Joshua hadn't heard the phrase before. He dropped his red crayon, scrambled up the back of his chair, and yelled, 'let's see!' He seemed pretty disappointed there wasn't a leg or a foot sticking out of her mouth."

"You're just teasing," Grandmother.

But she was really choking. It almost sounded like she was gargling. She coughed harder, once, and then again. Then harder, her voice raspy. Something mucousy and gross dislodged from her throat and ricocheted into the sink. She downed a glass of water.

"God," she sighed. "That's better." She coughed again, just to make sure the dryness was gone, and took another long drink.

Joshua asked her what '*having a frog in her throat*' really meant.

She told him it was just an expression. "It just means there's something's stuck in the back of your throat. It could be anything, but for whatever reason, people usually used a *frog*. Maybe it was because they were slippery and could swell up or something, and they would be hard to cough out."

Mathew frowned. "I assumed Joshua would probably figure it out himself or look it up later; but I suggested that the phrase might have originated because of the sound. That when you talk or try and clear your throat, it often sounded a little bit like you were croaking."

Dr. Stallworth seemed puzzled. "And that was all there was to it?"

"That was it. I would have thought that at some point in the previous six months since the stroke that someone would have inadvertently mentioned some type of animal or another. Especially Carmalitta. She tried not to bring her work home, but she's always found it difficult not to become emotionally involved with her patients. I'm not sure. Perhaps it was because the word was repeated three times in succession that made the difference. Maybe it was the word itself, or something magical in that extra repetition. I don't think we'll never know for sure. But whatever it was, it pried its way into the deepest part of the labyrinth that was Dad's mind."

Dr. Stallworth absently reached for one of his hand weights. He began a series of controlled wrist exercises that awakened the veins in his forearms. "What happened?"

"Dad leapt up from the table. And I mean that quite literally: he *leapt* up the way a frog does. Hands in front of his chest, head forward, and a springy push from bent legs. I wouldn't have believed it if I hadn't seen it with my own eyes. In two leaps -- *in two hops* -- he was at the kitchen door. There's no way he could've done it under normal circumstances. Not with those bones and muscles, and not without his walker. All he'd done for months was sit."

"So," Dr. Stallworth mused. "The word triggered some unconscious connection?"

Mathew said yes. "That's what Carmalitta speculated."

"What did you do?"

"What could we do? For a second I don't think anyone realized what had happened. But then Dad took another hop and sailed right out of the kitchen and into the dining room. By the time we reached him he was sitting beside one of the chairs. His legs were kind of tucked up beneath him, and his arms were extended out against the carpet in front. His eyes were bulged wide open and he kept flicking his tongue out at something only he was seeing. And then --"

"What?"

"He *croaked*. It was like a long, drawn-out beer-belch. You would have sworn there was a bullfrog right there in the room. And I guess there was. The biggest bullfrog you've ever seen. He hadn't done anything louder than a murmur for six months, then all of a sudden -- *rrrriibbbetttt*. It was unbelievable. And then he croaked again."

Mathew shook his head. The memory was still hauntingly fresh and invasive, like watching a scalpel biopsy some seeping wound. "He just sat there and did . . . well, *frog* things."

Dr. Stallworth didn't ask what 'frog things' were. "How long did the whole episode last?"

"Fifteen, twenty minutes. And then suddenly time stopped and he was just squatting there again. The *frog* was gone and Dad was sitting on his behind staring straight ahead. We helped him up and took him back into the kitchen. He sat back down as if nothing had happened. To him, maybe it hadn't."

Dr. Stallworth changed the weight to his other hand. "It must have been terrifying."

"I don't think I was terrified. No. More apprehensive than anything else. Apprehensive, with a touch of panic."

"I assume you took him back to the hospital?"

"The following week. We might not have, I guess, if it hadn't happened again."

"But it did?"

"Oh, yes. Several times, actually. And often when you least expected it. Animals come up in conversation more than you realize."

Mathew sheepishly lowered his voice. "Well, one of those times was on purpose. Kind of a *test*, you see."

Dr. Stallworth frowned. "A test?"

"To make sure. To see if he was teasing us. I don't know. Anyway, after it happened the second time, we were certain he wasn't faking it. But -- but we had to know for sure. So I mentioned another one. Deliberately."

Deliberately. Mathew folded the comforter up a little tighter and tried to stuff it a bit farther down into the bottom of the green plastic garbage bag. The stench of urine was making him a little queasy. His father stared out the window, unperturbed.

Eyebrows raised, Dr. Stallworth waited quietly.

"It was a parrot." Mathew looked guilty. He started fidgeting with his hands, and his cheeks blushed a strawberry red. "We were in his room. He was looking out the window and I was on the bed. I didn't say anything else to him, just the one word: parrot."

"You think that would be difficult to do."

"No, I could have said lots of different things."

"I mean for your father."

"Oh, right. But, no, it was easy for Dad, too. He was perched up on the chair in an instant. He tucked his arms down tightly into his sides, strained upward, and kind of bobbed back and forth from side to side. He moved his head up and down like an owl and he kept scratching at the chair with his claws. His feet."

Mathew shook his head. The memory was still difficult to digest. "That was originally what we found so puzzling. The fact that he could do things, physical things, like move his arms and legs, or get up and turn around, for example, things that he simply couldn't do normally. It was only when he'd assumed the personae of some animal or another that he had the ability to move around on his own."

"Did you say something else to him?"

"I had to, just to see. Easy words, mostly one or two syllables. He'd squawk and repeat them back to me. Over and over. He even repeated nonsense words when I tried to trip him up."

"Amazing." Dr. Stallworth took a much needed exercise break. A light sweat creased his forehead. "Does it happen every single time? The transition?"

Mathew said, "Yes, and that's one of the strange things. He can hear a particular word on two occasions, and only --"

"Respond? React?"

"Yes, thank you. *Respond* on one of them."

"What did they say at the hospital?"

"The neurosurgeon was hard-pressed to understand for a while, because she didn't change into one of the normal white masks you have to wear at the hospital. She kept her larger surgical mask on when she was talking to us. She put Dad through all the standard tests again, but she couldn't find anything that may have been responsible for his transitions. She told us she'd seen other cases that were similar, but never one quite as *unique* as his. She didn't know why it started at that particular time, or why he responded to some voices rather than others. Why he could make sounds but still not speak, or why he had the physical ability to be able to move around and do the things he couldn't normally do. She couldn't offer any definitive insights into what was happening, and she couldn't make any informative predictions other than *it might affect other behaviors, or it might not*, or *he may stop doing it at some point in the future, or he may just keep doing it forever*.

"And it's never stopped or changed in any way?"

Mathew exhaled a deep sigh and rubbed the back of his neck. "Not that I've seen. Maybe to *him* it has somehow, but not to the rest of us. That's why we have to be careful and use pig-Latin."

Dr. Stallworth had stopped writing. "Pardon?"

"Pig-Latin. Remember, like you did when you were a child. Take off the first letter of the word you want to say, put it at the *end*, and add an extra 'a.'

"So --"

"So, 'bear' becomes '*earba*' and 'bird' becomes --"

"'*Irdba?*'"

"Right. '*Osa Randadga oesn'tda hangeca ntoia naa nimalaa.*' The pronunciation alters the word enough that Dad doesn't recognize it."

"Does it always work?"

"So far."

But they couldn't be on guard all the time, and his father had turned into more animals than Mathew could remember.

So far.

A sudden noise flared outside, a noise so explosively loud the window shimmered. It was just a passing car, radio blaring, the subwoofer turned all the way up, the base beat thudding repetitiously. It jolted Mathew from the past, and he slipped back into the here and now. How many sessions had passed since then? Forty? He couldn't remember. Lately, it seemed like he was always drifting away. Loosing time. Unless he was thinking about *her. And what might have been.* But the *boom*

boom boom was gradually fading, and Mathew was back in the bedroom again, his arms were still in the bag, trying to push the comforter deeper inside so he could close it. All he could smell was stale urine.

His father hadn't moved a muscle nor made so much as a hint of sound. Mathew checked his dad's pillow, fluffing it up a bit, then tugged the blanket higher up over his thighs and chest because the window often leaked drafts.

"I'm going to go and get this washed." He gestured to the green garbage bag. "Mich -- Cybernician -- and Joshua are here, if you need anything. Joshua will keep checking in on you. Okay? And Eleanor should be back shortly, too."

The old man was staring down at something in his lap.

"I'll be back as soon as I can."

Mathew paused by the door, and the image that haunted him night and day stabbed him through the heart and drained the blood from his face. *Carol.* That's what he'd said to her all those years ago, before the children, before Lydia, before his marriage was a stone in quicksand, before his family wasn't anything more than a sticky note on the fridge, before he'd lost the ability to dream. *I'll be back as soon as I can.* But he'd never come back to her.

He hoped the laundromat was closer.

Chapter Five

Eleanor paused at the door. The new room was larger and brighter than she'd expected. She sniffed, and then again before inching in. The forced air seeping from the vents was annoyingly cold and made the joints in her toes ache. No matter. She claimed an easel in the middle of the room but right at the back so she'd be centered and recessed. Eleanor unfolded her stand and carefully arranged her brushes, paints, pallet and cloths, and then adjusted her chair several times until it was at a perfect angle so she'd be able to watch the instructor yet keep the entire easel in easy reach. She stared at the canvas and felt the familiar rush of excitement, the tinge of creative foreboding the blank space always incited. A touch of unease. It would pass: it always did. She smoothed out the creases in her smock, checked her hair, and waited.

She could have been anyone's mother, but she wasn't: she was Mathew's, and there was an unmistakable resemblance that even a casual observer would have noticed with a passing glance if they were anywhere near each other. High cheekbones suggested a Slavic background somewhere down the family line. Eleanor's nose was a little broader than her son's, and perhaps a shade longer, but both their faces were strong and angular. They had the same broad forehead, each etched with different lines of worry, repression, and age. Thin eyebrows that grew quickly, lips that were barely pronounced, and small, grey-green eyes that sparkled when they laughed. Eleanor had been spared the two small birthmarks that marred her son's left cheek. She had an elongated neck that made her seem graceful, like a swan, but the same feature had made her son look somewhat gangly and emphasized his Adam's apple. Both had thick, curly hair. Eleanor had just had hers dyed and set, then tucked into a bun with one of those beautiful Victorian combs. She'd touched all of her intimate body parts, her neck and wrists and elbows and the back of her knees with dashes of her favorite perfume.

Other students filtered in, mostly singles, hidden behind armloads of books, brushes, and supplies. But not many: it would be a smaller class this time. The thought sent a shiver up Eleanor's spine. She smiled noncommittally at anyone who looked her way as they found an unattended easel and performed their own ritual of preparation. Two minutes before the class was to begin the room was still only half full. The rows of blank canvasses made the silence of anticipation even thicker.

It had happened every time, every class, but the feeling still startled Eleanor when she sensed *him* moving down the hall. Her chest tightened painfully, her nipples tweaked erect, and even though she was sitting perched over her easel, her knees shook when the door opened and *his* cologne whispered on the hallway breeze, *he's coming. He's here.*

Carlos Rojas Montoya. But to Eleanor, the spirit of the wind. Sixty-one going on thirty, he was medium in height but well-proportioned with an athletic gait. Smooth, olive skin blessed by the sun, softly sculpted features, and deep, hypnotic eyes a haunting sapphire-blue. A thick mane of wild, chalk-white hair tumbled over his shoulders. If a unicorn ever had to change into a man to escape its enemies, then this is the shape it would take.

Eleanor indignantly sensed the hearts of two young women up near the front melting when the instructor smiled. A man on the other side of the room blushed and hid behind his easel.

"Good evening. Please, allow me one moment to get everything ready. I apologize for the delay."

I apologize for the delay. His voice was like a wonderful memory, tugging at Eleanor's heart and calming her secret fears at the same time. She knew the two girls in front would eagerly have waited for him until the very day the world would begin all over again. The woman on the left, Gabriella, had been in the last class, too. She twisted uncomfortably in her chair and seemed to have trouble swallowing. Eleanor knew the feeling. She stared down and watched her canvas swirl with a thousand shapes and images of the things it could become. If love at first sight was possible, Eleanor had been blinded. She looked up cautiously and recognized the same look in Gabriella's eyes.

Eleanor watched the other young women study every nuance of Carlos' movements as he emptied his briefcase and fanned his notes out across the desk. Bristling with jealousy, she burned a curse into the women's' hearts with a hateful stare until he finally glanced up and saw her.

When he smiled, Eleanor felt more special than she'd felt in a long time. A lifetime ago she'd been in labor with Mathew for over twenty-seven hours, but the feeling she had when he finally left her and the doctor scrambled to loosen the cord from Joshua's neck was not as intense or enthralling as this. To feel his eyes on her, to savor his smile broaden, to sense his aura reaching out, expanding, drawing her in. He stepped around his desk and glided forward with the graceful fluidity of a ballroom dancer, never looking away or letting his smile become fragile, until he loomed right above her and his shadow was a silhouette on her canvas.

"I'm delighted you decided to come back and explore your talent even further."

Eleanor was glad he hadn't said her name, not now, with everyone staring. The blushing young man strained backward to see, unable to stop looking Carlos up and down.

Nothing could have kept me away. "I thought I'd try once more."

"To paint?" He smiled wickedly. "I'm sure you'll do fine."

I will if you just stand there and never, ever move.

"In fact," the instructor breathed, breaking the spell and turning toward the class, "I'm honored you've all signed up to take my course. It's wonderful to see so many new faces." A special smile for Gabriella that made her gulp. "And it's so nice to see people I know, too. Creativity is always intimate."

Eleanor felt her back stiffen when the girl smiled coquettishly behind a flush of crimson.

"I'm sure we will work in harmony, and that together, we'll bring the best out of each other."

A slow, thoughtful glance at the hiding young man. "Trust me, and I will take you to places you've never been before."

Eleanor closed her eyes and tried to slow down her breathing, but she knew he was looking at her again. *Yes, take me there.*

Carlos glided around the room. "I want to see you work, how you begin to get your thoughts down on paper, how you project whatever is inside to that blank wall that's staring back at you. Each week we'll go deeper, further, harder."

Oh yes. If only . . .

"Leave whatever holds you back at the door, the things that won't let you be creative in your life. Fear, personal troubles, the sense of failure. Others that can't let you go." He paused and glanced at Eleanor. "Guilt."

Carlos looked away, a mischievous glint in his eyes. "An artist has no secrets," he whispered, "because an artist is nothing but a secret waiting to be told." Another glance at Eleanor. "To be shared."

Carlos clasped his hands in prayer and stared at something on the floor no one else could see. The room was hushed.

"Draw my voice."

He didn't move. Feet shuffled, and someone coughed self-consciously. Seconds ticked past obnoxiously loud. One student finally lifted a pencil from their case; someone else, a piece of worn charcoal. Brushes and colored chalk. Canvass-scratchings quickly filled the room. Carlos stirred, hands still clasped, and quietly walked behind the easels. He paused by Gabriella's stand and leaned closer, making the girl's hands shake. Carlos brushed his lips close to the soft folds of her ear.

"Close your eyes and listen to my voice. Listen. Hear it inside, in your heart."

A pencil snapped in half at the back of the room. Carlos smiled, but didn't turn and redden Eleanor's face any more. He slipped between the easels like an eel through kelp, watching, wondering, finally stopping behind the young man that couldn't hide anymore. He moved in close, saw the sweat bead on the man's neck. The canvas was blank. Carlos laid one hand on each shoulder and squeezed ever so lightly.

"What is your name?"

The young man managed to mouth *Tristan* just above a whisper.

"Do you like to dance, Tristan?"

"Yes."

"And when you dance, you let the music flow through you, don't you? You let it beat with your heart, your breath."

An uncertain nod.

"Then let your hands work the same way with your thoughts. Don't picture what you want to see; see the picture when you're finished. Relax. Imagine all your fears, all your inhibitions, as giant stalks of ripe autumn wheat, rippling in a morning breeze. Then let the freedom of your spirit be a scythe. Now, draw."

The young man sagged beneath the weight of Carlos' hands. He closed his eyes, felt the long fingers, the curve of the wrists on his shoulders, and then slowly, his pencil started making great arcs of different shades across the paper. His whole body sighed when Carlos moved on.

Eleanor had dipped her hands in the paints and was using her fingertips as brushes. She smoothed her hands across the sheet, swirling the colors together in constantly changing patterns. Carlos peered over the easel and saw she was feeling his voice.

"I hoped you would be back."

She couldn't speak.

"Look at me."

The hypnotic allure of his voice made her legs tremble. Her hands stopped moving and her fingertips looked like they were bleeding tears. She struggled to obey, to look up and see his whole face. It was almost shining, just like she remembered.

"Why did you come?"

You know why.

"And your . . . husband? How is he now?"

No answer. She kept looking at his face, watching the fire dance behind his eyes as her hands swirled across the canvas.

"There will be no turning back this time, Eleanor."

An omen and a warning. The words stunned her like a cattle prod. Eleanor thought she was falling. Falling *up*.

"Leave," he whispered carefully, lips caressing each syllable, "before it is too late."

They both knew how dangerously close she'd come to leaping into the abyss the last time, yet Eleanor wasn't sure what he meant: leave the class, or leave her husband. But she didn't move. She couldn't move.

He's still my husband. Whatever he's become. I can't betray him. What's left of him . . .

When Carlos turned abruptly and walked back to his desk, the spell shattered and Eleanor almost fainted. She had an overwhelming urge to climb up onto the top of her easel, spread her arms, jump, and swirl down to the earth on gryphon wings.

For Eleanor, the first hour of the class was nothing more than a dream. 'Draw this," he said. "Or this." Object after object, feeling after sense. Carlos walked slowly around the room, stopping and talking to each student, studying their work, whispering what could make it better, gently tossing comments and criticisms into the air like petals from a flower girl. He rarely stopped moving, yet wherever he was, no matter what was between them, Eleanor sensed he felt her cobra eyes follow his every breath.

The hour passed in a minute. Immersed in her work, Eleanor was shocked when Carlos announced it was time for a break. After telling the new students where the cafeteria was, he floated back to his desk and began packing his materials into his briefcase. Students quickly milled around, asking questions there weren't really any answers for. Eleanor had done the same thing. Her heart ached. She knew they just wanted to be near him, to be close, wrapped in a comforting warmth they couldn't understand.

Eleanor held back as long as she could, but it wasn't any use: a gaggle of students stayed at his desk, straining to listen, to see, to be seen. She clutched her image of Carlos' voice to her chest and slipped forlornly from the room.

***

The nervous young man, Tristan, was already perched expectantly at his easel when Eleanor returned. The room filled quickly as the big black hands on the old school clock jerked toward eight. Carlos walked in a moment later. Eleanor could feel the warmth through his cardigan from the back of the class, and the scent on his skin made her head swirl like the first jolt of a narcotic. It reminded her of thick evergreens on a cold winter morning.

There was no engaging preamble this time. "Now we will try something different."

He opened the classroom door and ushered two people in. A man and a woman. Both were in their early thirties, tall, athletic looking, with the dull eyes that come with the confidence of denial and distance. Carlos didn't introduce them. He cleared his desk completely and told the students to relax, to be very quiet, very still.

"Pick a medium then close your eyes."

He waited while everyone did. A few moments later, Carlos told them to open them again. The man and the woman were sitting together on the desk, naked, backs to the room, their arms and legs entwined. No one knew where to look. Eleanor gasped and a surge of blood flushed her neck pink.

"Show me what you see," Carlos whispered. "What you want to see."

No one moved. The silence was stifling, like the seconds before a eulogy.

Carlos urged them on. "Show me the beauty of the flesh."

He stared at Eleanor, who was trying to hide behind her easel. Seconds slipped into a minute. Somewhere, a box of pastel crayons rattled like a snake. Tristan picked up a brush but quickly exchanged it for a fresh piece of charcoal, rubbing it between his hands until his palms were black. Gabriella instinctively chose pencils: Eleanor, squeezeable paint tubes. The classroom quickly filled with the sounds of etching, scratching, brushing, stroking, scraping. And the unmistakable sounds of longing.

Carlos walked around quietly, hands clasped behind his back, nodding, musing silently, his steps as light as nascent snowflakes, whispering past the canvases, past the students, to something deeper. Eleanor knew he was speaking to her.

Watch the light on her arm as she breathes. See the veins in his arms pulse, feel the hair on his thighs sway as he tries not

to move. Listen to her heart, her lungs, the softness of her neck.
Think of what might be.

Eleanor watched, stared, thought, listened, felt. Her mouth
was dry, her breath short. She couldn't stop imagining Carlos
up there on the desk, the snow white hair falling over his shoulders, the soft lines of his chin, the restrained powerfulness of
his arms, the gentle slope of his back. But her husband's face
kept infiltrating her thoughts, seeping in like religion into consciousness before death. She'd push it away but it would be
back again, stronger, more insistent, younger, sometimes.

"Now stop," Carlos suddenly demanded. "Turn the page
over and begin again. *See* them again, because they are not the
same people now."

Paper rustled. Eleanor flipped the page over the top of the
easel. When she looked back up the man and the woman had
moved. They were facing her now, embracing, heads tucked
down into each other's neck. The woman's breasts were small
and round and just barely grazed the man's muscular chest. His
penis was soft and stretched down across the inside of his thigh.
Eleanor was sure that if she looked at it long enough it would
harden, but she was afraid to stare. She didn't need prompting
this time: she picked up a pencil and began to draw.

The lines swirled together. In the traces of lead imbedded
on the canvass the model disappeared, and it was Lorne's face
she saw, slowly transforming over the years: young, stern, naive, angry, passionate, parental, secure, soft, forgetful, dull, life-
less. She looked at the man's thighs, the flatness of his stomach,
the strength in his shoulders, the threat in the veins of his manhood. She wanted her husband back, the husband that had been
there before. The man that had stroked her hair and caressed her
breasts and dried her tears and washed her back when she was
pregnant and shoveled the snow from the driveway so she could
get her car out and rested his head on her stomach when he was
laid off that summer and held her hands firmly behind her head
as he thrust his hips harder and harder, pushing his cock deeper
until she moaned as he slipped out limp and wet and collapsed
on top of her. She wanted the unbearable weight of his life
again, but she knew he was there, in front of the window at

home, curled into the chair, the blanket up over his legs, framed by the glass, staring, staring at something she couldn't see.

Chapter Six

Although he'd gradually come to use a variety of them more regularly because of his father, laundromats were still as foreign to Mathew as streetcars or buses or subways. This was another new one. Ducking beneath a little tinkling bell, he didn't know where to look when he first walked in. Feigning disinterest, he studied the layout surreptitiously, like a robber casing a bank. With the green garbage bag stuffed with his father's comforter slung over his shoulder like Santa, he shuffled self-consciously over to one of the last machines lined up against the wall. He recalled the mistake he made at the last laundromat and prayed he remembered to bring some change.

He read the instructions on the underside of the washer lid, then crammed the wet comforter down deeply inside. It was the second time in a month his father had peed so much in his sleep that he'd drenched the mattress protector, too. Mathew hoped no one smelled the urine, but the unmistakable odor was so pungently overwhelming he was sure everyone did. For some reason, it was different washing something soiled by a parent than it was for a child. Mathew felt the eyes on his back, heard the hushed whispers, but knew it could have been worse: at least he didn't have to bend over some dirt-brown river and pound and stretch the comforter against the rocks. He thought about the old washing tub his great-grandmother had, the one with the two rollers you had to feed the clothes through on one side and tug them out on the other, and wondered what it would have been like to get your hand or arm caught between them and have your fingers pressed flat.

There was only a smattering of people in *Fresh To Go* today, so Mathew didn't put on a mask, but instinctively scrubbed his hands with the lotion from one of the dispensers. It was scented with pine, which he assumed was supposed to make him feel like he was in the middle of the great outdoors, and not stuck in some seedy little gossip shop waiting for his stained laundry. Yet pine was pine: it didn't transport him anywhere. With just a handful of women in the place, he was tempted to throw his jeans and t-shirt in with the comforter. But Mathew was shy: the thought of sitting in his underwear for an hour and a half terrified him. He could have used one of the communal robes that were hanging next to the last washing machine so that you could wash the clothes you were wearing, but he had no idea who'd worn them last, or when they'd been washed. *If* they'd been washed. Or *if* they'd been washed in the same tub as someone's soiled-soaked diapers. Or comforter.

When the machine jerked and the cycle started, Mathew sank down onto the nearest bench. He chided himself for forgetting to bring a book. If he didn't have anything to distract him, the only thing he'd be able to do would be to think about *her*, the love of his life. And thinking about Carol was both a curse and a blessing, something that invariably made him happy and sad at the same time. Hopeful and lost. Soothed yet alone. She was a dichotomy in his existence like no other, and lately, the memories he shared with her were taking up more and more of his time. Like the compulsion component of someone fighting OCD. He'd tried talking to Dr. Stallworth about his fixation, but most of their sessions usually ended up being focused on Lorne or Joshua. Granted, they were crises, too. But he was getting to the point that he was obsessing about her whenever he had a free moment. And even when he didn't. She was slowly taking over so many of the precious moments he didn't really have to spare, they were making Mathew feel *timeless*. Like repressed fears, she crept into his thoughts night and day, when even the smallest sliver of a memory opened up and invited her in.

A half hour passed. There was an irritating buzzing noise, and then the washer groaned to a stop like an old wheel on a paddleboat. Mathew packed the bedraggled comforter into a dryer, glad that even if it was soaking wet it didn't smell of urine any more. A moment later, just as he started stuffing the comforter into one of the large tumble dryers, the little bell-chime above the front door tinkled wildly. A brass triangle in the symphony's percussion section. Oozing disdain, one of the women folding clothes spoke loudly to a friend. There were both in robes. The one speaking had her hair in curlers and big fuzzy animal slippers on her feet.

"Can you really believe *that's* someone's mother?"

Everyone glanced up at once. Mathew stiffened. Even though it was a different laundromat, he recognized the new-comer as soon as the door fully opened and the woman, pushing her cart, waddled in from the street. *How couldn't he*?

Mathew remembered the last time he'd seen her this close. He'd been in the little parkette at the bottom of his street, kick-ing through piles of dead leaves beneath a late-autumn sun and wondering why they still bothered having daylight saving time. (Twice a year he had to play with his clocks. Years ago, it was-n't that much of an inconvenience, but now, with all the elec-tronic paraphernalia in the average household that had a clock or some sort of digital display, the job was ridiculously time consuming. All the clocks in Mathew's house were out by about a minute.) Tucked between two main roads, the parkette was supposed to give everyone a breath of green, a touch of wilder-ness, but all it did was make the encroaching concrete that much more oppressive and aggressively overbearing.

He'd wondered the same thing that day as the woman fold-ing clothes in the fuzzy animal slippers had just verbalized. But *'perhaps she wasn't really someone's mother'* had been his next thought. He'd seen her a few times before, sprawled across the grass, or shuffling along the cobbled pathways that dissected the trees. Singing, laughing, raging, stumbling, cursing. He kept scattering the leaves, but he couldn't stop glancing back at the old woman. She was perched on a bench, watching her shadow lengthen over the path. Something made him keep looking. No: he wanted to look. Had he *needed* to look?

Mathew listened to the comforter tumbling around inside the dryer. It had a hypnotic sound, a mesmerizing **clumpity** *whump,* **clumpity** *whump,* **clumpity** *whump* that tugged at his thoughts and started pulling him away. Pulling him *back.* It was last fall and he was transported to the parkette again, strolling through crinkled leaves as the sun browned the grass, and sur-reptitiously watching the old woman from a safe distance. He realized -- too late -- that there isn't really a safe distance from anything. How could he have possibly imagined that the withered bundle of flesh teetering so precariously on the bench could have had the power to change his life so deeply?

***

Enthralled by the scent, a swarm of flies zigzagged in a buzzing cloud around her head. Gnats joined them for a while, then flew off. Tiny flying insects landed in the sparse pockets of wilted grey hair that speckled her scalp, but she didn't notice. After all they were company, and she didn't get much of that anymore. She hadn't in a long time, as long as she could remember. Last week, at least.

As usual, no matter how crowded the parkette became, the old woman had the whole bench to herself. Two lovers strolling by hand in hand inadvertently stepped on the bench's shadow. The old woman gnashed her teeth and growled like a cornered animal. The lovers broke their embrace, took one look at the battered old shrew and scurried away, instinctively brushing at the dirt and disease-laden things they imagined on their clothes.

Beatrice spit a wad of something onto the ground and rubbed her mouth with the back of her hand.

Beatrice Osgoode. 'Bea' to the other bag ladies who always looked away when they met. She often passed them in the back alleys as she pushed her shopping cart through puddles littered with trash, the day's fresh finds stacked in teetering piles atop the other things she'd salvaged.

Batty Bea. No one knew how old she was, since Beatrice didn't know herself. It didn't matter: she was as old and disgusting as people needed her to be. That's why they left her alone, why she always had the bench to herself.

Over the years, Beatrice had shrunk down into a smaller and smaller version of herself. She was almost invisible behind her rickety old cart, especially if her stuff was piled up past the seat where the children had once sat when the cart was used for grocery shopping. She was slender, almost as hauntingly thin as the line between good and evil, and she was hunched over so much it looked like her neck was boneless and her head came right out of her chest.

Beatrice was always dressed the same, no matter what the weather: a winter coat, and long, black, fingerless gloves she'd found inside a pair of panties behind the topless bar on Simcoe Street. She rarely took her coat off. *Someone would take it,* she thought, *and then where would I be when winter came?* She didn't know if she'd be able to scrounge up an overcoat so nice again. She wore a ragged dress two sizes too big and two decades too old, black boots that almost came up to her bony old knees, a tattered scarf. A bracelet she'd made from scavenged pieces of metal dangled from her wrist. It was a charm bracelet, and she never tired of making up new stories about where she'd found this piece or that, or about what had happened when she'd tried to get it. How she *freed it from its owner,* she liked to say.

Yet it was Batty Beatrice's hat that always distinguished her from the other women roaming the streets behind their own carts or lugging bulky shopping bags through the alleys. It wasn't really a hat, but everyone probably thought it looked like one. It was a crown. It was a crown because Beatrice was a queen.

Her crown was too tall for her scrunched up little face. It sat up high on her head, poised on the bald spot that grew farther back every year so she saw more and more of the deep wrinkles that creased her washboard forehead. It was made of some stiff material that was reluctant to lose its shape, like the old magician hats with the tiny folds inside to hide the rabbit or the dove. A mottled silver, the crown was covered in gold tassels that cascaded down its sides like the blonde ringlets of the princess that waited in the castle window for her knight.

Beatrice loved her crown very much. She rarely took it off, even in the winter, when bitter winds whipped the flimsy tassels against her frozen cheeks. She couldn't remember exactly when she'd first started to wear it, but she knew she'd had it longer than her rusty old metal cart. She'd even had it longer than her keepsake bracelet that weighed her hand down more and more as each season passed and something new was added.

There were bird droppings all along the top rung of the bench but Batty Bea didn't care. The shadows lengthened in front of her, half-hiding the pigeons and squirrels that scrounged around her feet for the little bits of bread she threw. A crow landed beside the bench and flapped its wings aggressively. The pigeons held their place and refused to be intimidated, so the larger bird gave up and flew away after a few, threatening squawks.

More people passed, but no one looked directly at the old woman sprawled across the bench; a furtive glance from behind their sunglasses was enough to hurry most people on. Amazed and confused, the children stopped longer. They wouldn't get off their bikes, but teased and taunted her from a safe distance. What they *thought* was a safe distance. Sometimes, after repeated dares and fierce rounds of bitter name-calling, one youngster would dismount and venture nearer. But Batty always saw them before they got too close, and she'd look up quickly and bare her rotten teeth and growl some unholy cry. The child would scream in panic and race back to his fallen bike. The whole group would disappear in a flash, laughing and crying and yelling, their faces flushed with the excitement of dread.

Beatrice never minded them. She tolerated everyone, just like she accepted the flies, the smell of her clothes, and the stench from her cart. She was queen, and whatever happened, whatever foul names they called her or whatever cruel jokes they played, the people were her subjects. Bea knew she had to protect them, regardless of what they did or said.

Beatrice pulled her shopping cart closer to the bench: she was always afraid of losing things or having her treasures taken by people less fortunate. It happened all the time. Yet if someone was really down on their luck, she'd give them whatever she could.

Harriet -- that's what Beatrice called her -- was a stringy, toothless mulatto who was always in and out of CAMH—the psychiatric hospital on Queen. She'd been beaten up pretty badly after she'd found a gun in the dumpster behind the hookers' donut shop on Parliament and shown it to one of the gang members who owned the turf.

Or what about Mrs. Thompson, the disgusting fat old woman who slept under the picnic tables at the other end of the park? She'd found a notebook once. It looked official, and since she couldn't read, she'd taken it to the police station. They'd put her in jail because they hadn't known she couldn't read, but *they* all knew what the officer had written down by mistake.

And look at Dorothy, Dorothy *what's-her-name*, the one who hung around the mission and prayed for food? The weird one that traipsed up and down the street, singing as loud as she could, or stood on the Bloor viaduct screaming at the trucks on the highway underneath? Dorothy had found a shirt in the trash in front of a dilapidated building on Coxwell the previous summer. There was a key in one pocket. She'd shown it around all day, but no one had been able to figure out what kind of key it was. That night, she'd gone to share a bottle with someone in the park, and that was the last time Beatrice had seen her. Or the key.

Beatrice finally ran out of food bits, so she scattered the birds and animals foraging at her feet with a quick swipe of her boot. The pigeons cooed indignantly, and the squirrels scampered up the nearest tree, nattering away through clenched teeth. The sun had moved behind the treetops at the far edge of the parkette and her bench was in shadows. Most of the people were heading to their cars or walking out the exits and back onto the street. Their pace quickened as they passed the bench. They tried not to look but they wanted to, just to make themselves feel a little better about themselves.

Beatrice glanced around and brushed a couple of irritating flies from her forehead. She tilted her crown so it was centered on her head and sat quietly for a while, her hands folded together in her lap. She was a little disappointed that the man who'd been watching her for so long hadn't had the strength to come closer, but she knew there'd be another time. She just hoped it wouldn't be too late.

Beatrice finally pushed herself up with a tired sigh that seemed to come from the bottom of her feet. She checked to make sure the day's findings were balanced properly in her cart and shifted a few items around so they wouldn't fall. Straining, she leaned down and brushed dirt and pebbles from her rusted wheels. She waved to the squirrels that clung to the trunk of a nearby tree and tossed a last chunk of bread to a little chickadee scavenging behind her bench.

The cart seemed heavier all the time. She was beginning to wonder if she really needed all these things. Beatrice leaned against the handrail, and then pushed the cart along the path toward the street. Her crown was slightly askew, her back ached, her steps were painfully slow, and she was a little cold, but she enjoyed listening to the sound of the wheels clattering against the asphalt.

***

Mathew didn't know how many times he'd seen the bag lady since that day in the parkette, but he was sure it was at least three. Maybe four.

The old woman smiled as she steered her cart past the tables of folded clothes, washers and vending machines. She loved the smell of the laundromat. She wished she was a cat so she could curl up in one of the baskets atop a pile of warm clothes fresh from the dryer. People scattered, and a few of the regulars made angry faces at the manager who pretended to be busy separating sheets. The woman looked skyward with a shrug and a *what-could-I-possibly-do* sort of grimace.

The rusted wheels *click-clacked* to a stop, and Beatrice appropriated the rest of the bench next to Mathew. He stared straight ahead and watched the comforter tumbling into itself. Bea carefully chose a machine on the other side of Mathew's. He'd noticed before that for some strange reason, no one ever seemed to choose the machine nearest them.

"Stop looking at me."

The words startled him like a gun blast. The voice was lighter than Mathew would have expected, and he didn't smell any liquor. A hundred other perturbing scents, but no liquor. An accent? He didn't think so, but he wasn't sure. Was she actually talking to him?

"I beg your pardon?"

"You heard me. I said 'stop looking at me.'"

"I wasn't."

"You were. And I saw you looking at me in the parkette that day, too."

Several customers snickered and instinctively started to give Mathew a wide berth as well. He knew what they were thinking: *pervert*.

Beatrice rummaged through her cart and conscientiously extracted all the pieces of clothing she wasn't wearing. Her bracelet clanged noisily against the metal rungs. She had money and soap, which seemed to surprise the manager, although it didn't appease anyone else. All her belongings fit into one washer. After she tucked an old ripped blanket around whatever else was left in her cart, she sank down heavily onto the bench. Mathew surreptitiously moved his coffee cup to the other side.

"I don't drink plain coffee," she mumbled, making him blush.

Mathew wished again he had a book; there's only so long you can watch clothes go round and round and round. He knew that's why they had commercials on television. No one else came near, and the washers on Mathew's side of the laundromat remained unagitated. At least the old woman didn't keep talking. She seemed quite content to read the signs plastered all over the walls.

The change dispenser is at the back. Coffee is now .75. Lost and found is not open after 11:00. Please clean out your own lint. Please put magazines back on the rack. Clothes thieves will be prosecuted. Make sure you dry your own things.

Mathew wasn't sure why he felt so nervous. Perhaps it was because she'd seen him watching her in the parkette. Maybe it was because she'd *remembered* him. Out of all the people she must come in contact with on any given day, why *him*?

The clothes kept tumbling. ***Clumpity*** *whump,* ***clumpity*** *whump,* ***clumpity*** *whump.*

He tried to steal a sidelong glance when Beatrice suddenly started to move. He frowned. It looked like she was putting on a crown of some kind. He prayed she wasn't going to start singing or anything.

"Mind your own business." She looked him up and down. "Besides, I've got a pretty good voice for someone my age." She giggled. "My age."

Mathew ignored her after a self-conscious sigh.

"Just because I live the way I do doesn't mean I never wash my clothes, you know. And if you *must know*, I have my own mini bottle of Purell with me all the time, too, so I don't get anything from people like them." With hubris, she stuck her chin out at the women in the battered old robes and fluffy bunny slippers. "I bet I wash my hands more than you do. So if you don't like me here, too bad. It's not your laundromat. Maybe you should just go home to all your little problems."

He turned reluctantly.

"Oh yes, that's right. I know a lot about you, so don't you worry."

You don't even know what day of the week it is. What year.

"Saturday."

"What?"

"I said it's Saturday. And keep checking that comforter. If it gets too hot in there you'll scorch it."

"How did you know it was a comforter?"

"I'm old and wizened and I don't always eat right but I'm not stupid."

"No, I guess you're not."

"See the crown?"

"Well, yes. I did notice it."

"I'm a queen."

"I see."

"No. No you don't." The old woman watched Mathew's dryer spin.

"Beatrice. Queen Beatrice to you. You haven't come to a laundromat in years. Except lately, when you have to." She gave him a knowing wink and whispered behind her hand so the other women wouldn't hear. "What's this? The fourth time?"

Mathew tried not to show he was startled.

"Someone must've whizzed on it again. Your Dad? Well, of course it was your father, wasn't it?"

He jumped and almost spilled his coffee.

"It's too big for your dryer at home, isn't it?" she asked, shooting the eavesdropping manager a dirty look. "A woman her age wearing those stupid slippers. She's probably got a pierced belly button. Humf."

The manager blushed uncomfortably and scurried away, holding her stomach.

"Yes," Mathew admitted quietly. "It is."

"It's unfortunate, but we old people do it all the time."

How did she know it hadn't been a child? Mathew looked down at the oasis of bench that separated them.

"Don't worry."

He looked back at the comforter. It was deep red, a vibrant, fiery red that dramatically accentuated the bedroom wlls his fther had painted an almost tribal green, then streaked them with tall, waving veins of brown. Like so many other things, it sounded odd but actually looked quite nice, since Lorne had always wanted to live on th edge of a wadi.

"I'm queen."

"You said that."

"So I can't say it again? You're a pushy little prick. No wonder she left you."

He almost choked. "Who left me?" He felt a need to explain. "No one's left. My wife's just out on the coast."

"Goody for you. That's not who I meant and you know it." Beatrice – *Queen* Beatrice, shook her head despondently. "Sometimes you have to tell people something over and over before they understand."

"Okay." He struggled to calm himself down. "Queen of where?"

"Not where. What."

"What?"

"Queen of 'what.' I'm not queen of *where*, I'm queen of *what.*"

"I see."

"Don't keep saying that. People are always saying 'I see' when they don't have an idea of what's going on. How often?"

"Pardon?"

"How often does the old man soak the comforter?"

Mathew looked around at some of the women folding their clothes and lowered his voice. "I think this is only the third or fourth time."

"There'll be more, but at least it's not chronic. That's good. It's degrading the first few times, so get him to wear a diaper. In the long run it's best for everybody. Does his daughter-in-law know?"

How did she know it's my dad, and not Lydia's? "I don't think so."

"She would if she was ever home."

"Why would you think she's --"

"I think your comforter's heating up too much."

Mathew opened the door and checked: she was right. The comforter was just his side of hot. Confused, he realized he'd been watching the wrong dryer. He'd been keeping his eyes on the one next to his, and he'd even put two extra tokens into drying someone else's clothes. He started bundling the comforter back up into a new green garbage bag he'd brought. Beatrice was enchanted by something on her bracelet.

Mathew felt oddly uncomfortable. He didn't want to stay, but he didn't really want to go home, either. Something about the old woman made him feel uncertain, but not uncertain in a bad sort of way.

"You never answered me," he said, carefully avoiding the hot metal zipper as he stuffed the comforter down into the bag. "Queen of what?"

"Your heart." She whispered low enough so that only he could hear.

"Sorry?"

She leaned over conspiratorially. "Don't be. I'm you fairy godmother, so I'm queen of your heart." She stabbed an arthritically crooked finger at his chest. "But I'm also queen of all the other fairy godmothers."

Someone behind them choked on a laugh.

"I see."

"Why do you always say 'I see' when you really don't?"

Mathew didn't know what to say.

"I'm their queen," Beatrice whispered, laying an old bony finger along the side of her nose. "But more importantly, I'm your fairy godmother, too." The old woman's eyes sparkled.

Several of the women snickered, but when Beatrice glanced up they quickly looked away. Mathew gulped. *If you're my fairy godmother you should know my name.* "What's my name?"

"Oh, that's a tough one, Mathew. I didn't use it because I didn't want to frighten you anymore than I have."

Mathew's stammered protest fizzled as soon as it began. He huffed petulantly and wondered whether or not he was going to get three wishes.

"I'm a fairy godmother," Beatrice said coldly. "Not some bottled genie."

The buzzer screamed that the old woman's washer was finished. "And don't worry about that ... that *other* problem. You've got enough to worry about as it is."

Several women stopped folding their blankets and strained even harder to listen.

Beatrice turned to the room at large. "Mind your own business you old biddies. God, you're worse than a bunch of fishmonger's wives."

Huffing and puffing and whispering a few "*well I never*," the women pretended to concentrate on their clothes.

Mathew felt deeply uncomfortable. "What other problem?"

"In the park last fall, when you were watching me. Remember?"

The day came back once more like memories from an old photograph: Beatrice on the bench, the sun just above the trees, the birds, the squirrels, the layers of fallen leaves. Mathew remembered being confused about the whole turning-the-clocks-back-issue, which had led to the why-can't-something-go-faster-than-the-speed-of-light question, but nothing else came to mind.

"The *other* problem," Beatrice sighed softly, with just a hint of impatience. "The *personal* one."

And then Mathew remembered. His whole body blushed. It had been that very morning that his deepest fears had been confirmed and he'd finally realized after months and months of apprehension and worry that he was right: his penis was actually getting *smaller*. It seemed to have started once he hit forty. Not a lot, just a little, but still noticeable, especially since he wasn't humongously endowed to begin with. His friend, but not a threat. He never *measured* it or anything, at least not with a ruler. But he kept inspecting himself regularly, and he was sure that he wasn't quite as well ... well, quite as *manly* as he used to

be. Old age? Diet? Some innate biological predisposition because it wasn't a tool of procreation any longer, just a tool?
Something to do with his testosterone? Some other hormone
that he couldn't even spell? He wasn't sure. The only thing he
did know was that his butt-clackers were stretching down longer and longer, just like his wife's breasts, her behind, and the
clumps of flesh that hung down from under her arm. Perhaps it
was just a use-it-or-lose-it type of thing. He certainly couldn't
check with Lydia, because she didn't see it enough anymore to
know. At thirty-five, when Lydia's desperate need for a career
evolved into an obsession and slowly began to supersede everything else, sex had been the second thing to go in their relationship. Mathew finally admitted something was definitely wrong
when he started thinking about his wife in terms of
'relationships.'

Partly in the sun and partly in the shade that day, as he
kicked through the crumpled leaves, Mathew had wondered if
other men his age experienced the same thing. But it wasn't
something you'd normally ask in the locker room, or when
you're carpooling on the way home from work in one of the
HOV lanes, either. There never seemed to be a right time to
open the discussion.

*Oh, and by the way Glen (or whoever it was you were go-
ing to ask), have you noticed if your penis has been getting
smaller lately?*

Glen would probably redden indignantly and dismiss the
preposterous idea with a glare while he wondered *how the hell
did Mathew know?*

Another imagined friend: *Hey Carl. I was thinking about
your penis and was wondering if you thought it was still quite
as big as it used to be?*

Waiting for an answer, Mathew would feign indifference,
as if the whole issue didn't really matter, as long as Carl hadn't
knocked him out yet.

"Morning, Paul. How's your old penis doing? Mind if I
take a quick look? Just check it out for a second? I've been
wondering . . ."

It wasn't the easiest conversation to broach. There were
ads about feminine itching on the television every night, and

about bloating and headaches during your period, but there certainly weren't any tabloid headlines in the check-out lines at the grocery store screaming about shrinking penises. No disguised talk-show guests confessing their trials and tribulations over the hopelessness of their plight. No documentaries, or questionnaires in women's' magazines, either. No *Run For The Cure*. So, like almost everything else in his life, the whole issue remained unresolved, and Mathew had retreated home from the park more confused and lonely than when he'd left.

"Do you mind?"

Beatrice wanted to use the dryer Mathew had, mumbling something about it already being so nice and warm. Mathew nodded. She spoke as she loaded her things from one machine to the other.

"It's just not important enough to worry about. A woman's body goes south, and so does yours. There's not really much you can do about it. You should be more concerned about *why* you're worried about it in the first place." She nodded down at his crotch. "Almost everything else is more important than that. It's certainly not what makes you a man."

Mathew was just about to ask her what does when the old woman reached over and touched his hand. Her fingers felt so soft and warm, and he didn't even jump. They weren't coarse and wrinkled, like he'd imagined. Her eyes smiled and drew him in closer.

"Love, Mathew. Love."

Silence. Just the agitated water that made the washers bump together, and the *wuummp* of the clothes tumbling over each other inside the dryers. When Mathew looked down he realized he was still touching Beatrice's hand. He pulled away, undoing the twist-tie and wrapping it around the top of the green garbage bag.

"And don't worry about that." The old woman nodded at the plastic bag. "Once in a while isn't too bad. And besides."

Beatrice started the dryer, leaned down closer, and winked. Beneath the crown, her grey hair sparkled in the overhead lights behind her.

"If he hadn't whizzed his bed right down to the comforter, you might not have met your fairy godmother."

Mathew didn't know what to say. She seemed to know too much, while he understood very little.

"How did you --"

But Beatrice was already teetering off toward the bathroom at the back of the laundromat. She appeared to be favoring her left foot. The customers still left quickly pulled their baskets and piles of clothes out of the way so they wouldn't have to wash them again. Beatrice growled at one of the women folding her clothes. Not a *grrr* sound, but an actual animalistic guttural growl.

Mathew reluctantly gathered up the bagged comforter. He wanted to wait, but couldn't. He knew it was a ridiculous idea, and that the old, haggard crow was completely out of her mind. But somewhere deep inside, in a way he couldn't quite verbalize, he felt a little . . . relieved. Even if she was a complete nutbar, he still had a fairy godmother.

Didn't he?

Tinkling the little bells that hung beneath the laundromat's door as he left, Mathew didn't look back. He had the strangest feeling that this wasn't going to be the last time they'd meet. The thought made the hairs on the back of his neck stand on end. But not from fear.

A minute later, the obnoxious buzz of the smoke alarm started wailing. One of the dryers farthest away from Mathew's had been on too long, and one of the women who'd been trying to listen to absolutely everything the queen had said realized her underwear was on fire.

***

Mathew tossed the comforter into the back of the car, then zipped across the street to pick up some groceries. He had a small pile of sticky notes, rather than one list. Half an hour later he was struggling to push the comforter over so he could put the groceries in the back seat of the car when he caught the echo of the most beautiful sounding chimes he'd ever heard. He listened, completely enraptured, like when he dreamed about Carol. He turned around, following their siren pull. Beatrice, crown and all, was coming out of the shop next to the laundromat. She held the door open with one hand and pushed her over-stuffed shopping cart out with the other, the chimes still calling. Mathew ducked down out of sight behind the trunk of his car. For some reason, his heart was beating wildly. Beatrice adjusted her crown, rearranged the laundry on top of her cart, and then waved to Mathew without looking at him. Straining with the weight of the cart, she started off down the street, loudly echoing the notes that floated with the chimes with her own voice.

Mathew waited until she was out of sight and then made a quick dash for the store. The chimes were wooden and carved in different thicknesses and lengths. Their echo sounded like a pan flute, sweet and ethereal. The vibration was so wonderful, he opened the door twice. Again. *Angel's breath.*

His heart stirred. The first thought he had was of Carol -- the chimes reminded him of the softness of her voice. A delicate lilt, coupled with the song of a sea shell. Soothing, relieving, relaxing. The music that gently wafted through the store was the same. Mathew envisioned a seascape, a lonely, uninhabited beach of pure white sand, with wind-bent palm trees reaching out over a receding tide, the sun warming his face and toes.

Carol. Mathew drifted away. She'd been his best friend forever. Long before he'd met and married Lydia. She'd always been more sensual than his wife. At university, Mathew and Carol were always giving each other neck massages or foot rubs with creams or scented oil that smelled so luxuriously sweet and gentle. Rosemary, lavender, strawberry, mint. They'd sit in a bath together for hours, gradually adding more hot water as the tub cooled, warmed by the oils that made their skin so slippery and smooth. And that's when they talked. Talked about all the things no one else seemed to have the time for. They'd slip down so that just their heads were above the bubbles, sip wine, and watch the shadows the scented candles rippled over the walls.

The chimes were still echoing. There was no one around, so Mathew started poking about. Unlike the stores at the mall, the little shop was neatly set out, and there was actually space between the aisles. Everything wasn't simply jammed together on spinning racks and cluttered into bulging shelves lining the walls. You could actually *look* at things. Then again, the store only carried two different items: there were about a hundred of different sets of chimes made from wood, metal, glass and what appeared to be seashells. Apart from the chimes, there were even more hand-carved boxes lining the shelves. They came in a variety of shapes and sizes, and were individually made from specially woods, from polished teak and varnished bamboo, to Brazilian hardwoods and sea-smoothed slices of driftwood.

"May I help?"

Mathew jumped. The sound had come from nowhere. Turning, he returned the young woman's slight bow. He smiled insecurely because the girl was smiling. She'd come up behind him on pixie feet.

"Oh, I sorry if I startled you."

"It's all right," he stammered. His heartbeat slowly returned to a normal pulse.

"I am Mitsu." Another bow.

"Mathew."

Young and petite and delicately tanned, her long black hair hung down her back to her waist. Her features were a tantalizing mixture of Caucasian and Oriental. Everything about her movements showed she was well-balanced, lithe and strong. Not a blemish or wrinkle on her face. She wore a pink t-shirt, stretch pants, and ballet slippers on her dainty feet.

Mathew was momentarily tongue-tied. A deep breath helped. He remembered seeing Beatrice leave. "The chimes are magnificent. I'm sorry, but I couldn't help opening and closing the door a couple of times."

"That is fine. And thank you. Many of them were made by my great uncle."

Mathew was wondering if it was her uncle who owned the store when suddenly his body froze and the color drained from his face. Mitsu quickly guided him to a bamboo chair and helped him to sit. He slumped down awkwardly. He could hear Mitsu's voice, but it was a long, long way away, at the farthest end of a tunnel he couldn't see. A kaleidoscope of spinning images made his heart beat faster and his spine tingle.

Mitsu left, returning a moment later with a glass of cold water. "Sip this and take slow, deep breaths." She turned to see what Mathew had been looking at. It was the large spider plant hanging in the corner, the biggest one Mathew had ever seen. Numerous tendrils drooped over the side of the planter, sprouting long green and white shoots that sprouted other baby shoots that would eventually grow into new plants.

"You are all right?"

He nodded. He couldn't describe the sensation that had so quickly and completely overwhelmed him. He wasn't sure why, but he quickly started telling Mitsu about his spider plant phobia. About the things that could lay their eggs right on your cheek and then explode out their sac and scurry all over your face.

Mitsu gently rubbed her fingertips over Mathew's temples in slow, expanding circles. Her hands were tender, her skin as soft as the wind. Her fingers eased the tension from his forehead. She gently touched his eyelids, the sides of his nose, the line of his jaw. Mathew felt his entire body relax in gentle swirls of warmth.

"You okay now?"

He nodded, teetering when he stood. Mitsu took his arm. The longer she touched him the better he felt.

He looked slowly around the little shop, gently touching the nearest chimes. "What else do you sell?" he asked.

Mitsu smiled beautifully. Some flicker of light danced in her eyes, pulling Mathew in deeper. He could have sworn he saw . . . *a young Beatrice.* No. How could he?

"Peace of mind. Come. I will show you. I think you need some."

Despite the fact that they were different in some way or another, every single one of them, shelf after shelf, was, at first glance, a sand box. Although the central motif was one of stones and sand, many of the boxes sprouted carefully preened Bonsai trees. Like the exquisite chimes, everything in the little shop was a variation on a theme. Some long and rectangular, some small and perfectly square. Some shallow, some deep, but all with the purest sand Mathew had ever seen. They all came with bright, smooth, highly polished stones. A few were decorated with handmade artificial tropical plants: others had little bamboo buildings that were perfectly symmetrical. Many were dotted with little candles.

Mitsu smiled. "They are Zen Gardens. They can be any shape or size you like. We can even have large ones custom built in your backyard. But they take a great deal of time and patience to maintain. Each one comes with a set of rakes, brushes and hoes. The large ones, too."

"But what do *do*?" Mathew wondered aloud. Whatever strange feeling he'd had when he thought he'd seen Beatrice, but *a younger Beatrice*, in Mitsu's eyes, was gone. It made him feel sad.

"They help you relax and meditate," the young woman smiled. A soft and gentle blush. "The owner usually helps explain because it is hard for me to say it in English because sometimes I forget English words." A little bow. "You make the sand perfectly even, then choose some stones and make a scene that gives you peace and calm."

"Peaceful?"

"It is better if I show you."

Mitsu took one of the larger boxes from the nearest shelf. It was about two feet square. Using the rake's tines, she made the sand perfectly level in a few minutes. "Now you add as many polished stones – the ones that make you feel *something* - as you want. You use them to create a design that is soothing to your eye and calming to your soul."

Mathew chose five or six multicolored stones from a large display. Some were so smooth he didn't want to stop rubbing them. Others had ridges worn with time, or soft, soothing little indentations that gave them a personality all of their own. He was surprised at how quickly he could tell them apart without looking at them.

"Where do I put them?"

"Anywhere. Wherever it is that when you look at them, you sense that you're right. That *they* are right. So that the edges of the stones, the ripples in the sand, and you, you are all in harmony with each other."

Harmony. Mathew tentatively put the stones in a circle. It didn't look right. He put two together and three down the far side, but the arrangement still didn't seem balanced. He tried two stones close to one end of the box, one just this side of the middle, then added two more in a straight line several inches away. He sat back and stared. That was how he liked them, how they looked right. *Felt* right.

"Now," Mitsui said quietly, taking his hand and guiding his fingers over one of the little rakes, "you draw the sand into simple patterns around the stones. You can make the lines straight from one end of the box to the other, or you can curve them around the rocks, like this."

She showed him, and then erased their design. "Breathing softly, in and out, in and out, you create your own image so that the sand, the rocks, and the lines all flow together as --"

"One." Mathew smiled. "Like a bonsai tree. I've killed about a dozen trying to grow them."

Mitsu giggled. "Yes. Bonsai is harder than it looks. But these Zen gardens are not easy either."

"What do I do when I'm finished?"

She smiled. Another slight bow. "You are never finished Mathew."

The look in her eyes made him feel calm and sad at the same time.

"They are designed for beauty and for meditation. There aren't any rules when you're designing your garden. You can add a tree or a little house. A pond. Almost anything your heart desires. They're tools for relaxation and meditation, so no two gardens are exactly alike."

Mitsu lightly drew the rake through the sand. Pure white. "You rake the patterns you wish around the stones, constantly changing them until it looks perfect to you. You rake each line over and over again. You draw the lines around the stones until their depth is perfect. It takes concentration. So all the time while you're working you must clear your mind. You must stay focused on the garden, on the sand, the lines, and the position of the stones. You rake it over and over, letting all other thoughts drift gently away."

Mathew picked up another rake and started making a few tentative lines. He brushed them out and started again. He pushed and pulled the sand as lightly as he could, but he couldn't get it even close to being smooth.

"Let go of all the things you're worried about, all your problems, all your fears. Erase anything away that's troubling you. Breathe from your heart. Focus deeply on the sand, the stones, the tines on the rake, forgetting all else for even a moment. Let nothing exist except your mind and that one pattern it sees in the sand. The desert of your spirit."

Mathew kept raking. It wasn't long before he realized his breathing had slowed down considerably, although he didn't consciously *realize* it. It was easy to get lost in the rhythm of the movement. He had a warm feeling in the pit of his stomach.

Mitsu saw the understanding in his face. "It's very similar to many types of meditation," she whispered. "Like drawing mantras, chanting, or performing Tai Chi. When you work on your garden, nothing else matters. All other things slip away. You search for the same feeling or sense of timelessness, of thoughtlessness, one feels in any kind of meditation. You breathe in and out with each stroke, and you let all of your difficulties, all of your daily decisions and upsets and anxieties gently drift away into the formless sand."

Smiling, Mitsu gently took the rake from Mathew's hand. "You change the sand, the patterns of the stones, and the sweeping dunes as often as you wish. You can make it as complex or as simple as it needs to be. Like life." She laughed, a sound not unlike the chimes.

Mathew checked his watch. His breath caught – he had no idea how much time had passed. It was getting late, and he was worried about his father. What if something happened and he'd changed into something uncontrollable? He had to go. Quickly. But he didn't want to.

Mitsu saw the look in Mathew's face. She carefully pried the rake from his hand. "Come back," she offered quietly, "when the owner is here." She waved her hands towards the shelves. "Choose any one of them then, and the owner will help you with the color of the sand, the kind of stones, and your own plants if you need them."

Mathew looked a little surprised. "I thought you owned the store. You seem to know so much about everything."

"Oh no, Mathew. I just work here. But I was taught well. And it's a wonderful place to work. To learn, to relax. The joy of finding yourself never stops."

"I will, then. What's his name?"

"*Her* name. It is Beatrice."

Mathew almost yelled out. His pupils dilated, and he remembered watching the haggard old woman walk off down the street, singing notes that harmonized with the beautiful wails of the chimes. He could feel something gnarling in the depths of his stomach, something writhing, something uncurling, something reaching towards every fiber of his being.

His fairy godmother.

Silence. It suddenly dawned on him that he hadn't told Mitsu his name. She was looking at him with one of the gentlest smiles he'd ever seen, the kind that makes you wish the moment would last forever. The way Carol used to look at him when they were wrapped so closely together as they snuggled under blankets fresh and warm with their love-making.

Mathew knew he had to come back. He needed to tend a garden of his own.

For a moment, he thought he was going to be *sick*, but it was a *nice* sick, which made his whole face smile. He bowed and backed away, the scent of the sands seducing his senses. The chimes tinkled as he left, following him as he walked back towards his car, whispering, whispering.

Chapter Seven

The second floor of Mathew's home.

Except for a few odds and ends, a recent painting job they'd only managed to get started, a splurge of touches intended to make everything more personal, and a couple of physical changes the contractor had insisted would make the space larger, the second floor was probably just about the same as any of the other two-story homes on Mathew's street. It was never the *house* that changed, no matter how many times it was redecorated -- it was the people inside that made all the variation in the world. There were many houses where they didn't change much at all, and you really couldn't tell which ones they were from the outside. Four bedrooms, two closets, a slide of a laundry chute in the master bedroom that sent clothes right down to the basement (which was, quite fortunately, too small for Granddad to fit in), two bathrooms, and a utility closet.

Mathew cracked the first door open, and immediately realized the odds were rather good: D'Artangne was magnificent in his defensive parries, and his daring thrusts were easily keeping the Cardinal's personal guards at bay. D'Artangne was a superb swordsman: the epée merely an extension of his hand and arm. He knew when to advance and when to feint, when to guard himself and when to slip close inside for a quick foray and a strike. He knew the classical moves of the fencer as Mozart implicitly heard the delicate intricacies of a concerto before they were born.

A parry, a defensive ploy, and D'Artangne's blade slashed one of his attacker's wrists. The frilly hem of the man's shirt filled with blood. The other officers faltered: the long peacock feather in the Musketeer's hat quivered impatiently. Another slash and stab caught a blade and flicked it away. Without a moment's hesitation, the Cardinal's men turned and fled. Chivalrous as always, D'Artangne let them go: he only killed when he absolutely had to, or when his own life was at stake. And today, protecting one of the Queen's daughters was far more important than sword play with one of the Cardinal's traps.

Two doors down from the swashbuckling heroics of one of France's greatest heroes, Mathew's father, Lorne, listened to the exquisite dance of blades. *Swoosh swoosh, stab.* But did he really *hear* it? Mathew peeked in. Lorne was still where he'd left him, in his chair by the window, the blanket up over his legs and chest, his face turned towards the world beyond the glass. A chickadee landed on the window sill.

Between the two rooms, two more. Eleanor's was still dark: the art class generally lasted several grueling hours. Unless she had some errands to do, it wouldn't be long before she was home. A soft blue light glowed from under the door of the other room. Highlighted by a bank of monitors, screens, television modules, modems, cameras, tablets of various sizes and digital screens, the light testified that Cybernician was hard at work. His room would be locked for security reasons and contracted issues of client confidentiality, but he would invariably hear his younger brother knock. Like a new mother and father worried about their child, Cybernician was always instinctively aware if Joshua or their grandfather was in trouble, regardless of the hum of the machines, the blip of the monitors, or the incessant *clack clack clack* of his keyboard. It was strange, but he seemed to have a built in baby monitor.

As Mathew passed the door his son's on-line messenger flashed a psychedelic green. He'd been working so hard he'd missed his normal talk-time with Sheila, so as soon as he saw the icon flash, all of his other work was put on hold. Client files floated somewhere through cyberspace, protected by his personal virus scanner. He heard his father walk on down the hall.

***

03:14:18
Sorry I'm late. I had some last minute things to finish up with CompuImage for the Atlanta show. I missed you. I always thought it sounded kind of ridiculous when I'd hear people say

things like *I think about you all the time*, but that was before I met you. Now I know how it feels. I'm always aware of your presence, and I'm conscious of a nagging void in my existence because you're not here. It hurts to miss you that much, but the expectation of watching your words appear on my screen makes me giddy sometimes. Did you have a good day at work?

03:17: 21
Only when I was thinking about you. And you're making me blush, Cybernician. Got home fine. I feel like that too: that something's missing, that something's not quite right, when I'm not reading your text as you type. Sometimes I watch the letters independently without looking at whole words, and they look like a rabbit's paw prints in the snow. There was a severe acci-dent on the Parkway: I feel guilty getting angry at mangled wreckage that makes me late. Work was huge! I'm working on a new program for Animatics and the bugs were really biting today! How are your new gloves?

03:20:02
I thought Animatics did everything through SpectralLaser in Phoenix? Don't worry: everything will be up and running in no time because you're the most remarkable programmer I know. And the most beautiful one. I downloaded your last set of pics. Thanks, and Wow. Your new hairstyle looks kind of Kathleen Turnerish. The gloves are wonderful, they feel like a second skin; thanks again for sending them. My other ones are in the wash as we speak. My palm doesn't sweat if I hold the mouse for 2 hrs straight, and they really let your figures breathe. They'll really help with the Carp-Tunnel. And surprise -- they match the frames on the colored glasses I always have to wear for screen tint. Oh, and Mom probably won't be back for my birthday. She's still a mutilated corpse out in Vancouver.

03:25:39
Sorry about your mom. I hope you like what I sent. It should be there tomorrow.

03:26:55
As long as *you're* here, Sheila. That's what counts. Think we'll have time to talk after my birthday dinner? Huh? After all, that's the present I *really* want. How about it?

03:28:40
You're nasty. I know what you mean by 'talk.' I'm blushing again. I think we can spend some quality keyboard time together. Anything special u want me to wear?

03:29:11
Now look who's blushing! Well, since it's my birthday, maybe you could wear that nice blue dress. The thigh length one with the "v" neck.

03:31:44
You rascal. But it *is* your birthday. Is everyone else taking u out fr dinner?

03:33:01
I think so.

03:33:56
Are you worried about going to dinner, Cybernician? About *going outside?*

03:34:42
A little. I haven't been out of the house in months.

03:36:18
Don't worry, you'll be fine. And I'll be with you, remember. In whatever format you need. Is your Dad doing any better? You were worried about him the other night.

03:40: 21
No. I don't know what's wrong with him. He mopes around like he's just waiting for the end of the world. I doubt if he's left more than two messages on the fridge in the past week. Half the time I see him, he's just staring out the front window, watching

the world go by, or sitting out on the back deck, staring off into the sky. If it's a mid-life crisis, it's a weird 1. And you know Dad. Ever since Mom started going off on these commercial shoots, he's been here basically on his own. I guess that's probably a part of it, too.

03:47:59
That's a shame. Do you talk to him much?

03:49:45
He can't use a board, so probably not as much as I shud.

03:52:10
And how's your grandfather? Any episodes lately?

03:54:00
Yes. And that's got to be putting pressure on Dad, too. But u know, I get the feeling it's something else. Anyway, Carma was upset bout something that happened at work and she let one slip. She called some of the staff at the clinic a bunch of lemmings.

03:58:02
Oh no! What happd?

03:59:31
Granddad was downstairs in a flash. He was crunching his neck down and trying to look small, the way self-conscious tall people do. He looked like a penguin with a spine injury. He didn't walk, he waddled, and his arms hung straight down at his sides. His eyes were startled wide, like a deer trapped in headlights. Every movement was terse, indecisive, ambivalent. He had the frenzied antics of a cornered animal.

04:04:56
O my goodness.

04:06:19

Somehow he opened the back door that goes out 2 the dek. There's just three little steps down onto the grass. They're quite a drop, though, for a distraught lemming caught in the midst of a hysterical horde that's connected by one irresistible thought, one overpowering and innate urge bellowing 'leap to your death, leap to your death!' over and over in their collective heads.

04:09:23

He didn't!

04:11:39

He did. He tore out the back door, shrieked when he smacked his shoulder into the handle, then raced across the dek in pursuit of his brethren. At the edge he lept off the top stair and into the abis. Splat! He fell onto the ground, toppled over, and did a series of awkward somersaults before he crashed to a stop. His eyes were wide, and he realized he was alive! But was he supposed to be? He had presumed he'd been part of a grisly plunge to the death, but the realm hadn't changed. He looked around the yard for some sign, for some omen that would tell him what to do.

04:15:55

O, Cybernician, it must' hv been horrible for him!

04:17:41

Then something stirred in his little body, a spasm that shivered from his feet to his furry head. The others he imagined were there felt it too and were already regrouping. He followed them up the steps and into the house again, circled the foyer, then charged outside and threw himself back into the chasm. On the third suicidal run he banged his head. Not 2 hard, bt hard enof. Carm and Dad got him inside. They tucked him into bed and put a compress on his forehead. He didn't have a concussion, just a nice welt.

04:24:06
How sad. How is he now?

04:26:33
Better. There's barely a mark on his forhed.

04:27:54
Tell him I said hello.

04:28:19
I will, Sheila. And thanks for listening, fr being so understanding. Sometimes I wonder how much closer we could get. I
don't know any 1 who toks more than we do. We shar everything and we have so much in common. I hope I don't say it too
much, but I love you.

04:31:10
I love you, too, Cybernician. My heart akes when you leve.
I've never told you this, but I always sit and run my fingers
lightly over the keys after you're gone. It's like I can still feel
you there, inside the letters, down beneath the keys, under my
skin. And then I always kiss the fingertips of my gloves, just
like I'd love to kiss you.

04:38:00
I'm reading that again, and I don't know what to say. You
make me feel so special, Sheila.

04:40:38
You *are* special. I know I'm not supposed to pressure you,
Cybernician, but have you thought any more about . . . meet-
ing? In person?

04:47:15
I think about it a lot. But we have so much going for us.
I'm afraid that if we go the next stp, Sheila, make that next
commitment, our relationship will change.

05:01:01
It will. We'll be even closer, I know it.

05:03:15
How can u b so sur?

05:04:55
How can anyone b sure, Cybernician? You have to trust
your heart, and my heart tells me I love you more than anything
else in the world, and I want to stay with you forever. I know
how hard it is for you to go outside. But just say you'll really
think about it. You know I'll always be here at the keyboard,
waiting for you. No matter what.

05:08:09
I will. And thank you, Sheila. I think I just need some time.
And speaking of time, I really should go. Will you be home
tomorrow night?

05:10:25
I should be, as long as I get the back-up support I need
from S Diego. Leave a message so I can read something from
you before I go 2 bed. Goodnight, my sweet. Pleasant dreams.
And remember -- I'm thinking about you all the time, and missing you even more.

05:14:11
Be careful driving, and good luck with those bugs! I'll see
you in my dreams. Forever yours, with love, Cybernician.

Chapter Eight

Joshua was at the back door when Mathew came in from the yard. D'Artangne was gone. The metamorphous was complete. He was wearing a new pair of thick, wooly pajama bottoms folded up to his knees, old gray hockey socks, someone's scarf around his head, a plastic sword, a patch over his left eye, and a tea-towel lashed about his waist.

Mathew had seen this devil of the high sea before. "Black Bart?"

The boy smiled and gestured to his room upstairs with a nod. "Me crew's back upstairs, checking the booty. And a fair haul 'tis been."

"Just pulled in to port?"

"Aye. Still gettin' me land-legs back." Joshua wobbled around and pretended to stumble. "Haven't seen any shanghaies about, 'ave ye?"

"No, not I."

The boy squinted. "What were ya doing outside, then?"

Just standing there, thinking about my fairy godmother. "Checking for the King's men."

"Oh aye, there's trouble." He pointed to the green garbage bag. "What's that?"

Mathew lowered his voice. "Treasure from the high seas. Granddad's things." He winked.

"Again?"

"Again."

Black Bart shook his head. "Aye, matey, 'tis a pity." He'd die on the high seas before he turned out like that old, decrepit sailor. He struggled to keep his balance. "He still be in his bunk. Hasn't moved. And da ones you be callin' Cybernician be working. I seen the bluey light under his door when I crept ashore. That wench Carmalitta left us a picture of some devilish hell-hound that says she be stayin' at some clinic, and will be late coming in to port." Black Bart studied his plastic sword and frowned. "Dat old one don't look so good. Scurvy, me-thinks."

Would it have been better to make him walk the plank?

The pirate brandished his sword and took a few stabs at the air. "And me mom hasn't called. There ain't no ransom note on the fridge, neither."

"I see." Mathew caught himself saying that again. Old habits die hard. He knew he had to stop saying it, because there were so many things he didn't see. "And your Grandmother?"

"Out. There's a map to her whereabouts on the fridge." He lowered his voice, but his eyes went wide. "Or maybes it's some kind of treasure map."

"Well then, Black Bart, feel like a little more adventure? A drive? I'm dying for a treat."

"Sure." Joshua rubbed his chin. "I mean *aye*. I ain't eaten yet so's a treat sounds right good. I'll have to make sure me crews okay first." He leaned closer and whispered behind his hand. "You knows how those sea farts can be on shore leave."

Mathew nodded sympathetically. "Tell them to be good, that you've got some ambassador-type work to do. Throw your jeans on and after I hide my loot I'll meet you in the car."

Black Bart was already bounding up the stairs. The blue light was still on. He quietly opened his grandfather's door just enough so he could peek in and make sure he was all right. The old man was sleeping, or perhaps just looking out the window. Joshua backed out and tiptoed to his room, bracing himself for the stern lecture he had to give his men. He'd have to lock the rum chest this time, too.

Downstairs, Mathew left without bothering to leave a sticky note on the fridge. There wasn't enough room for another one, anyway.

***

Mathew sat in the last booth with his back to the wall so he could see everyone who came into the Dairy Queen. There was a fairly constant exchange of customers. The *whhhirrrr* of the milkshake machine ground to another stop, and someone waiting at the counter smiled.

There was something darkly special about ice cream. Mathew couldn't help smiling either whenever his treat left the cashier's hand or he had it safely in his own. It didn't matter what it was: a sundae laden with whip cream, berries and nuts; a cone dipped in chocolate; an ice-cold freezy on a sweltering day that made his teeth hurt so badly he could feel it in the back of his head. Classic brain freeze. Mathew always looked down and smiled as if the prime minister had just bestowed some precious medal of honor upon him before he took that first bite. He often thought it would be much simpler to get world leaders to meet and understand one another if the official vehicle of the United Nations was an ice cream truck. It was hard to be angry, resentful or antagonistic when you heard the tinkling sound of those little bells. He leaned over his sundae: he liked to scoop up the hot fudge that pooled in the bottom of the cup with his spoon and drizzle it down over the curly top of his ice cream. Joshua wasn't quite as artistic. His hand and spoon moved like a back hoe at a construction site.

Mathew watched the chocolate lava course down the mountainside. He couldn't stop thinking about his fairy. . . . No, it was just an old woman. An old woman in a laundromat. But an old woman who knew a great deal about him. How could she know those things? And how many other things was she aware of that he thought were secret? Did she know how much he thought about Carol? About the rapture and the dilemma she put him in? *And what about those Zen gardens?*

"What, Dad?"

Mathew looked up slowly. The fudge framed his son's lips like a clown mask. There was a tiny dollop of whipping cream on the boy's nose.

"Nothing Joshua. I was just thinking."

"You haven't eaten your treat. If I finish mine first I'm having yours."

Mathew nodded and noticed another satisfied customer leaving. He didn't really want to tell the boy about the dirty old shrew he'd met earlier, but he felt the urge to talk. Unburden himself. He always did when he was alone with Joshua.

"Joshua, I was at the laundromat today, washing grand-dad's comforter, and I met --"

But the child's face had turned to stone. Joshua's spoon clattered into his cup. Fluttering, his eyes misted with that far-away look, that visceral aura, that always came so suddenly and unannounced when the woolly mammoth of memory pulled him back into the tar pits of time.

"Joshua?" Nothing. "*Joshua.*" Mathew knew there was no point in trying to get his attention: the boy had already slipped somewhere else. *Some time else.* The child sitting across from him wasn't his son.

"We often don't know what to expect when we meet some-one new. Why didn't you believe her?"

Mathew stirred the fudge around in his cup. He didn't bother asking Joshua how he knew what he was thinking, since there was still a part of him, a small part but a part nevertheless, that tried to deny the boy's psychic gift as much as he could. Sometimes it made everything else just a little bit more tolera-ble, and gave Mathew a sense of control he desperately needed.

"It was just a crazy old woman who thought she was a queen."

"To everyone else. Maybe she was in disguise. Maybe she *was* something different to you."

"Joshua . . ."

But Joshua had completely disappeared. *Whoever was there* stared into Mathew's eyes. "Who was she, really?"

Mathew felt embarrassed. He was the person who's walk-ing along the sidewalk that trips over their own feet then self-consciously looks back to see what they fell over. There was no use trying to hide.

"She said . . . she was my fairy godmother."

"A fairy godmother." Joshua nodded slowly, chewing the image over in his mind. "Did she *feel* like your fairy godmoth-er?"

Mathew shrugged. Who knew what a fairy godmother *felt* like? The hot fudge was only lukewarm now, and clumps clung to the side of his mountain of ice cream like cooling magna.

Lowering his voice, Joshua quickly glanced around. "When I was here before they were called other things. Pixies, spirits, elves, imps."

Mathew asked, "Did you know one?"

He nodded. "I called him my guardian, my messenger from the gods. It was a long, long time ago."

"Here?" Mathew spoke without thinking. He knew it was a ridiculous question to ask because there weren't any ice cream stores a long, long time ago. But he was flustered. It always unnerved him a little to realize he could slip into conversations like this so easily with Joshua. Or with whomever Joshua had become.

The boy shoveled half the whip cream into his mouth. "Carthage. I was a Roman Legionnaire. The others knew me as Octavius."

The people in the next booth stopped eating and leaned back, trying to hear. Mathew stretched forward across the table.

"A Roman soldier?" He pictured the guards holding the citizens back when Liz Taylor makes her triumphant entrance in *Cleopatra*. Better a soldier than a slave.

"Of many battles. I was almost thirty, at a time when the life expectancy of a civilian was twenty-five. That's why I knew I had someone looking out for me."

"Did you ever see your guardian?"

"I didn't have to; I knew he was there. I'd survived many times when I shouldn't have: a faulty bowstring of an archer I didn't see; a lance that broke just in time; an enemy who fell from a horse and took a spear meant for my heart." Octavius stared straight at Mathew. "Never underestimate the power and knowledge of the spirits that watch over you. Your fairy godmother could save your life. She's made herself known to you, and they never do that unless there's a reason."

The boy finished the whipped cream and looked outside at the parking lot, but Mathew knew he was really seeing some distant time again, some other life he still carried with him. Speaking slowly, Octavius couldn't hide a burgeoning uneasiness.

"The glen was still, the sloping forests on either side eerily quiet, except for a lone crow cackling somewhere in the trees.

The sun inched over the horizon, sparkling the grass with morning dew. The air was warm, the bugles silent. Behind me, horses whinnied nervously, stamping and pawing at the ground.

"The enemy marched slowly over the crest of the hill. The sun glared off their helmets as they jostled into formation. Row upon row of men massed together with practiced precision until they'd joined the sides of the glen with a glimmering ribbon of bronze. They were well equipped and had seasoned horses. Their armor appeared finely made, their weapons forged with care.

"Our regiment was interspersed with archers, and right behind me was a thin wall of horse-mounted soldiers and lancers. But not many: our captains had studied their parchments well and had hidden most of our mounted divisions in the trees on either side of the glen. They'd charge when the time was right, and the lancers would stab everything in their way. Swords would fell swatches of men like scythes through wheat."

Octavius shifted closer, his hands fidgeting with the ice cream cup. "Their first two lines wedged apart and four rows of archers moved in to fill the gap. The first ones knelt; the ones behind stood, bows drawn, quivers at their sides. Another row of foot soldiers moved into place and tightened the formation again.

"As I watched the first few columns take their places I knew something was wrong. I shifted anxiously back and forth, and I was already sweating beneath my helmet. A burr on my nose guard from a past battle irritated my skin. The laces on my sandals were too tight. My armor felt deceptively light and I couldn't slow my heartbeat down. I felt completely alone, vulnerable, full of dread. I knew he wasn't with me."

Mathew sensed his son's distress. "Your guardian?"

Octavius answered with a glazed stare. It was a minute before he continued. "Until then, he always appeared right before battle."

Octavius shuddered, frowned. "A shape, a feeling. A premonition perhaps, that briefly let me see it as a man. He was a presence, nothing more, that I felt as much as saw. But that morning I couldn't feel a trace of him."

Octavius pushed his ice cream container away and stared across the battle field. The man in the next booth stopped eating and whispered to his wife not to slurp her drink so loud so he could listen.

"The soldier on my right was new; I'd met him the night before while our captains studied battle plans. He'd replaced a good friend, Salerius, who was felled in a previous attack by a lance that pierced his neck. Big and strong, the new man was too young to bear many scars. He might be the bravest soldier I'd ever met, but that could change the instant the standard-bearer's bugle cried across the glen. I prayed he'd remember my warnings from the night before while we polished our weapons and used our daggers to scratch out battle formations in the dirt."

"Such as?" Mathew asked uncertainly.

"I told him archers fired in arced volleys, that arrows will fall like pounding rain, so he wasn't to lower his shield until they were too close to unleash their arrows without fear of striking their own men. I warned him of the horses that would trample anything underfoot, and the lancers that would stab indiscriminately when the battle raged hot and close. I said he should be wary of our own men, their hatchets and swinging swords, lest he take a blow meant for another. I told him not to get separated, to stay shoulder to shoulder in tight ranks, and to fight on if he was wounded. There was no other choice. And I reminded him again and again to never believe a man dead because he lies upon the ground.

"My cousin Claudio was on my other side. I'd stood shoulder to shoulder with him many times. He tapped my shield with his lance as he stared across the field. He was lean and wickedly strong, unforgiving and merciless in battle. He'd saved my life more than once but I'd always repaid the debt. He was good with a lance and fast with a dagger, and in close he wielded his sword with uncanny precision and speed. His blade tasted many deaths and his shield was marked with cuts and stabs and bloodied dents. He looked at one man, one man among many, who stood across the field, and whispered that man would be the first to die.

Mathew shuddered.

"The soldiers across the field finally stopped moving. Their standard bearer galloped down the front line, then took his position at the far end of the first row. Their archers readied their bows. A horse in the back reared up and clawed at the air, its mane braided tightly beneath its helmet, its flanks covered with layered metal. The first line stepped forward; lances raised, weapons were drawn, hatchets unsheathed.

"I knew the time was close and smelled the bitter stench of choked-back vomit; it was the new man."

"Josh -- Octavius?"

When the boy looked back from the window, Mathew could smell his fear. The child's eyes were old, his face lined with grief.

"I palmed the steel of my lance. The first line of our archers dropped to one knee while the ones behind drew their bows. I heard the clatter of metal on metal as the men echoed orders and unfastened their weapons. A line of lancers stepped past the kneeling archers and took their place in front.

"I remember muttering a hurried prayer to the gods because I knew what was coming. Bloodshed. Unimaginable bloodshed. But I knew no one was listening this time. I could feel it in every pore. I checked the strap on my shield, the edge of my dagger, the blade of my axe. The new man did it too, but without the superstition that comes with survival. It didn't help. The terrifying sense of unease was eating a hole through my insides. He hadn't come, and he wasn't coming."

Mathew swirled some fudge through the decaying pyramid of his ice cream. He was afraid to ask, but he had to. "How would it start?"

"The standard-bearer would tilt the flag as a signal and the bugler's cry would echo across the field. The kneeling archers would release the first volley, the men behind them the second as they restrung their bows. The foot-soldiers would follow the lancers' attack, each line moving forward together in relentless waves, shields raised as arrows rained down. The first casualties would cry out in pain, but the thudding rumble of the horses' hooves would cut their screams into silence.

"Orders would be shouted and trumpets would blare. Screams, curses, taunts, the rattle of metal, and whispered prayers. The fierce and ignoble sounds of death. But all those sounds would quickly be overwhelmed by a tumultuous roar when the lines finally clashed and intermeshed completely. Time would stop; nothing in the world would exist except for the battle."

Mathew shook his head. "It must be utter chaos."

But Octavius wasn't listening. He was leaning over to the side, talking again to the new man, trying to prepare him for something impossible to describe.

"The whole thing is uncontrolled, wracked with confusion and laced with panic. You hack and slice and stab at anything you can find: a horse's flank, its rider's leg, someone holding their guts in place as they struggle to their feet. Maces mutilate shields and armor, helmets and skulls, severing limbs and men from life. And the sounds are deafening: shouted commands; the pounding of hooves; the crack of shields and pierced metal; the horrible sucking sound when a lance is jerked back out of bone; the cries of the dying; the gurgle of men choking on vomit and blood. In a matter of minutes the ground is strewn with mangled bodies. And all the time the arrows fall like razor-sharp lightning bolts.

"On and on. As soon as you pull your blade from a stomach another man appears. Then another, and another, until you can't lift your arm up to parry a blow with your shield."

"Octavius?"

Joshua's hands were shaking.

"What happened?" Mathew couldn't picture himself there, laden with armor, covered in blood, face to face with death. But it was even harder envisioning Joshua on the battlefield.

Octavius's eyes narrowed. "Their first few volleys were long and did little damage so we moved in quickly, jamming through their lines and wedging them apart. I was back to back with Claudio, stabbing and hacking at whatever came near and careful not to trip over the dead."

"How long?"

"Who knows? Hours? Minutes? The sun was high, I remember that, and the glare off helmets was strong. Claudio fell once but wasn't hurt badly. Just a small gash to the shoulder and neck."

"And your new friend?"

"Skewered with a lance in the first charge of the mounted soldiers. He died bravely, with barely a sound. I slayed the man that dispatched him, cleaving my sword through his chest. But that's the last thing I remember clearly."

"You . . . you were hit then, too?" It was hard to picture a son dying, even if it was a son from a long time ago and even if *you* hadn't been born yet.

"A horse knocked me to the ground. I rolled away before its hooves trampled me. But another volley of archers' rows fell and one was lucky enough to find my thigh. A second pierced my breastplate but I knew the wound was slight. I gained my feet and stumbled toward Claudio: he'd have to draw them out. But then I heard the *whhoooosh* of a mace chain swinging through the air. I felt the first spike sink into the back of my head, and I'm sure I saw my helmet falling slowly to the ground before me, into my own blood. Then everything went deathly black."

The people in the next booth leaned so close together their heads touched. They whispered excitedly back and forth, and gestured toward Mathew, but they were afraid to turn right around and look. The man across the aisle with the slurping wife was deathly still.

"And you --"

Octavius nodded. His forehead was creased with an odd sense of pain and detached abandonment. "I know I never regained consciousness, yet sometimes I think I remember little things after. But I'm not sure."

"Little things like what?"

"Sounds. Horses and screams, things like that. The clanging of metal, which seemed a bit like church bells. Someone calling out my name. Claudio perhaps, but it sounded like his voice was echoing out of some deep fog. Sensations, too. Being rolled over, because suddenly, everything was so incredibly bright. And water. Lots and lots of water."

"Water? From where?"

Octavius shrugged. "I had the feeling I was *sinking*. Maybe it was just because there was so much blood. Or maybe I was being baptized again, sometime later. Who knows? Many things are still foreign to me, hidden by the veil of mystery that's life."

The people in the next booth left their trays on the table and scurried toward the exit doors. The man made a big show of adjusting the collar on his sweater and risked a surreptitious glance back. Octavius turned at the same time and stared right at him. The man blushed crimson and hurried after his wife.

Octavius watched the last little bit of his ice cream melt into a chocolate-laced pool of smooth vanilla. He wondered if Claudio survived. He knew his cousin would have sent word home to his parents back in Rome that he'd died honorably in battle. They'd be proud but deeply saddened by the loss.

"The worst thing was that I never got to speak to Lucreatia again."

"Lucreatia?"

"My wife. She was a wonderful woman, even though she was a little headstrong and set in her ways. But I never met a more loving and giving person."

Octavius looked sad. "We argued before I left on that campaign. About what, I can't remember. But no argument is worth it anyway. The last words we had were harsh." Octavius closed his eyes and listened to the sounds of the battlefield. "I'd do anything to have our last time together back. I never stopped loving her, but we left each other on angry terms. You never know when you'll get a second chance at love, do you? A chance to take things back or start over."

Octavius opened his eyes. "So even before the first bugle sounded, I knew that battle would be my last."

"Because you never saw your guardian angel?"

"Yes. I was still hoping against hope he'd make himself known to me, even when the first few rows started their descent. But he never did, and that was message enough. Whenever he'd appeared, I'd survived. His absence told me there wouldn't be anyone looking out for me that day."

"Why then, do you think? Why that particular battle?"

"Who knows? Why is it anyone's time? It just is, because every battle could be your last. But that's why you shouldn't take your meeting at the -- what did you call it?"

"A laundromat."

"A laundromat so lightly, my friend. For some reason it's an important event. It certainly wasn't simply a chance meeting. A whole world of interrelated occurrences and events transpired to bring you both together at that particular time, in that particular place, on that particular day. You'd be wise not to underestimate her power. Perhaps she's forewarning you about something. Maybe she's an omen, and she took the guise of a fairy godmother because she knew you'd have an understanding of what that was. Her true self might be beyond your grasp."

"An omen of what?"

Octavius didn't answer. "Tell me everything you talked about, the things she said."

Mathew recounted the conversation as best as he could. The whole thing sounded even more ridiculous when he said it aloud. When he finished, he waited impatiently for his son to say something. Anything.

But Octavius' breathing lightened noticeably before he answered. His eyes fluttered uncontrollably for a moment, and when they stopped, the heavy-lidded, glazed expression was gone. Octavius was lying on some forgotten battlefield long since overgrown with weeds, and *Joshua* -- Joshua was back. Puzzled, the child looked down at his ice cream cup. Lines of chocolate swirled through what was left of his liquefied treat.

"Hey, who finished my ice cream?" He checked inside the cup and underneath but the culprit had vanished. The cherry was gone, too. Hands on hips, he looked up guardedly at his father.

Mathew held his hands up in surrender. They'd been through situations like this before, when Joshua underwent some transformation or other. "You ate most of it yourself and the rest melted."

The child nodded uncertainly. He knew he often lost time, that he *suddenly woke up* and couldn't remember falling asleep, that sometimes he did things that he couldn't actually recall doing. But he also knew how much his father loved sundaes. He stared into his cup: still nothing. He looked at Mathew, but his father was dreaming now, too.

Mathew was staring at his fudge-smeared spoon. The chocolate residue seemed to make an image, but he couldn't tell what it might have been. Was it an omen too? It was his turn to stare off at nothing: he was back at the laundromat, listening to the *creak clack* of the old woman's cart and watching the clothes tumble around and around, and for some strange reason, realizing that the ice cream wasn't any different than his life.

Chapter Nine

Mrs. Tomlinson was obsessive compulsive, and she'd undoubtedly show up for her appointment exactly five minutes before the expected time. Not late and not early. Not six minutes before her scheduled time and not four, either. Five. Always five. And no, the woman wasn't anal: people liked to use that word because it made them feel like they knew something about psychology and its related disorders. They also just liked to use the word anal. Mentioning that someone else was anal gave them an air of hubris and authority so that other people who weren't sure what being anal was like wouldn't challenge them, because naturally they wouldn't want to be anal. Elizabeth certainly wasn't a veterinarian like her idol, and she wasn't a pet therapist, either. But she'd come to understand some things just by watching the patients and how they interacted with the animals they brought, and she was quite certain that Mrs. Tomlinson's problems with her cat were indubitably a function of the woman's own neurotic behavior. She didn't know, however, if she was anal or not. She didn't particularly like the word anal, but she always loved it when Carmalitta used it when she was explaining something to her. Anal. Then it sounded right.

Ten minutes to two. Elizabeth tugged a tissue from the box left out for distraught owners and carefully, almost reverentially, cleaned the bronze name plate that sat on the corner of her desk. *Carmalitta.* She wiped the fingerprints off the pictures of some of the various dogs and cats and horses Carmalitta left on Elizabeth's reception desk, the ones that she was particularly proud of, the ones who'd taxed her the most but had eventually given the ultimate meaning to her profession, bonding people with pets who never dreamed they'd end up having such a wonderful relationship again.

Three minutes left. Elizabeth took a soft cloth from her top drawer that promised to get the dust off of anything without a mark or a streak, and ran them over carefully over Carmalitta's degrees and certificates: her Bachelor of Science, her Masters, her Doctorate of Veterinarian Medicine, and her Surgeon's Degree. She also had certificates for training a variety of different breeds to become working animals for the disabled, and for dogs to be companions to people, especially seniors, who didn't have anyone left in the world and desperately needed something alive and breathing and loving around them as much as possible; something that would never pee or bark in a senior's residence or adult condo. The most important certificate for this clinic's practice was her Degree in Pet Therapy. Few veterinarians went on to become pet therapists and handlers/trainers as well. It added at least two years onto her education, and one year of residency. But there were few things more important to Carmalitta then helping to dissolve the issues plaguing their relationships and bring parents and pets closer together once more.

There was a light knock at the front office door. It was exactly five minutes to the hour, and Mrs. Tomlinson walked in carrying a small tabby. Elizabeth didn't have time to run her cloth over all of the pictures of the various exotic animals Carmalitta had helped over the years that lined the walls. She'd have to do it later. She walked back to her desk, pulled out Mrs. Tomlinson's file, re-checked all of her pertinent health and pet insurance, and then asked the woman to have a seat.

Mrs. Tomlinson never said a word. She seemed anxious and distraught. The cat stayed on her lap but she wasn't petting at all, and the sleek little yellow and beige Tabby wasn't purring, either. This was her fourth visit in the last two weeks alone. You could feel the angst in the air. The insurance she purchased only covered so many appointments and consultations, but Elizabeth knew that Mrs. Tomlinson was one of those people who'd spend their live savings on their pet. No amount of counseling, surgery, medication, rehabilitation or aqua therapy would ever be enough to keep her pet alive and well. Elizabeth had seen it a hundred times.

There were moments, however, when it seemed odd and difficult to rationalize. While half the world was starving, pet owners and lovers would invariably spend more on their dog or cat or parakeet then they'd donate to Third World children so that they might have food and fresh water and some kind of sanitation to help prevent disease. Yet they'd keep their own pet from contracting some intestinal or anal virus even if they had to borrow the money from their savings to pay for the medication right now. They'd see a filthy child mired in the muck of some distant backwater Hell-hole who had a horribly distended belly balanced on boney legs, yellow eyes, and a cleft pallet who'd throw up everything if there'd ever even been a teensy bit of food to eat. But television commercials bombarded pet owners with ads that made them feel inferior if they didn't buy a special brand of food for their aging dog or cat, or punish them psychologically if they didn't give their pet the new, scientifically proven proper vitamins for their pets' age. Sometimes, it just didn't seem fair.

Carmalitta opened her office door so her next patient could be ushered in. She glanced quickly at her secretary. Dressed in a nicely matched ensemble of blouse, skirt and scarf, the woman sat forward on the edge of her ergonomic chair behind a glass partition that definitively delineated the patients as *them* and *us*. It was a little like sitting beneath a sneeze barrier at a buffet. Elizabeth gestured to the owners with a nod, then looked up at Carmalitta the way puppies do when they know they've been good.

"Any messages?"

"Two, Doctor. But I'm sure they can wait." A polite smile. And something more. Much more.

"Have you reached Dr. Emerson yet?"

The young girl's eyes narrowed apologetically. She had a pleasant face, although it was a little small. An upturned nose that would only seem cute for a few more years, freckles, and a long, graceful neck that other women often envied.

"He's still in surgery, Doctor. He'll call as soon as he can."

She obviously liked to mouth the word *doctor*, as if the status of her employer affected her own value in some way. As if the title itself effused subconscious worth.

"Keep trying, Elizabeth."

A coquettish smile, like they were sharing a secret. *Oh, I will.* She blushed and her skin tingled. Carmalitta hadn't noticed but the girl always reddened when she used her name. Elizabeth didn't mention the ones messages from *her*. Those could *really* wait. The three from Miriam had already been filed under 'g.'

Elizabeth turned to the glass, the smile gone, and through her own reflection, summoned in the next patient. Rory.

Carmalitta prevented Mrs. Tomlinson, the patient's mother, from rising and leaving the waiting room with a definitive hand gesture that looked like a police officer stopping a speeder. Mrs. Tomlinson hesitated but sat back down.

She was a tall woman with a head much too large for her body, and bottle-thick glasses with ridiculous frames that sloped up and out to the side like peacock feathers. When she wasn't reading they dangled down over her chest on a gold chain. Slumping forward, Mrs. Tomlinson immediately began to fidget, picking at the skin around her nails until it started to bleed. An agitated cough. She tried to peer into Carmalitta's office, wincing as the door closed with an ominous thud. Mrs. Tomlinson stared up woefully at the glass partition but Elizabeth ignored her completely. She was writing down cancellations and referrals, but all she could think about was the delicious, delicate scent of Carmalitta's perfume. The gentle slope of her jawline, the perfect nose, the blue eyes, and the shoulder length hair she teased in under her cheeks. The soft, sensual rise of her breasts. She shuddered.

Rory immediately leapt up onto his chair. He sat on the opposite side of Carmalitta's desk, far off to the right, completely ignoring her and looking toward the window. *Defensive,* Carmalitta noted on her little pad. *Isolated. Hostile?*

Rory was six years old. Nicely proportioned, with long, finely kept hair, clean white teeth, sea-green eyes, and light, almost gossamer whiskers. A beige and orange coat that glistened with care. A dangling choker for a collar, studded with fake diamonds. Carmalitta quietly watched the cat preen and wrote *nervous* down on her little scratch pad.

It was her fourth session with Rory, but the first time she'd seen the cat without Mrs. Tomlinson. During their initial meeting, Mrs. Tomlinson outlined what she conceived to be the main problems in their relationship. Carmalitta gathered as much information as she possibly could about parentage, upbringing, feelings, fears, anxieties, illnesses, phobias, needs, and wants. And then she'd asked about the cat.

Experience told Carmalitta that communication was often the instigating problem in the interplay between pet-and-people dynamics. It was by far the most prevalent reason so many people came to the clinic. But Carmalitta never let her opinions be swayed by expectations. She allowed Mrs. Tomlinson to completely unburden herself for over an hour. While the poor woman went through a gamut of emotions, Carmalitta watched the cat out of the corner of her eye. Rory pretended to be unconcerned with the attention. He seemed enthralled with a postcard on the corner of Carmalitta's desk: some fisherman was displaying a swordfish he'd snatched from the sea.

"He just won't listen." That, in a nut shell, seemed to be Mrs. Tomlinson's presenting problem. She expressed the sentiment in a variety of different ways, but that was the crux of her dilemma, the reason she needed professional help.

"He won't come when I call him, or let me pet him, even when I really want to. He won't eat the same food two days in a row. I'm at my wit's end."

She wrung her hands sorrowfully together. Her eyes were red; she'd obviously been crying earlier. Carmalitta knew she'd been right about the first thing she'd noticed; Mrs. Tomlinson's head was definitely too large for her body. If she wanted to be catty, she'd say that Mrs. Tomlinson kind of looked like a balloon squeezed through a narrow tube.

Despite Mrs. Tomlinson's emotional turmoil, the cat had been extremely well-behaved throughout the session. He purred when Mrs. Tomlinson stroked his back and nuzzled her leg when she stopped. When she told him to get on the chair, he leapt up without a moment's hesitation. When she told him 'lie down,' he did. The perfect cat. Like taking a car to the garage because it's making a 'funny noise;' it will never make the same sound when the mechanic is there. Carmalitta had written down *unconscious hostility* and *obsessive desire to please* on her notepad. Then an *R* for Rory.

This time, without the distraction of Mrs. Tomlinson's presence, Rory was much more aloof and condescending. He licked his paws rhythmically, yawned, then stretched out fully across the chair and tried to disregard his therapist completely. Carmalitta framed a question in embellished parenthesis in her notebook and underlined it several times. *Is his hostile avoidance situationally dependent?*

Carmalitta let him be. She knew she had to win the cat's confidence slowly, as well as his trust. It would take time and effort, but if she was patient, the results would come. The office shrank with a strained silence. Carmalitta stared at the cat, but Rory refused to meet her eyes.

Passive aggressive, classic in cat psychology. The clock on the corner of her desk beat a stoic pulse into the stillness. And then Rory moved so suddenly Carmalitta was caught off guard. His head twitched from side to side, he licked his lips, and then slumped back into a regal pose, paws outstretched, tail curled into his back, head erect. A butterfly had landed on the edge of the window sill. Carmalitta sat back too, and waited. Nothing.

"It's a monarch. They migrate almost three thousand miles a year, from Canada all the way down to Mexico."

The cat made some sound like a quietly revving engine and looked the other way. *He's crying out for help*, Carmalitta thought. Just like everyone else.

Two patients followed Rory; a dog and a hamster. Like Dr. Stallworth, Carmalitta had two separate doors in her office, so that the patients and their owners could enter and leave without ever coming in contact with one another. The secrecy encouraged them to think the doctor was there just *for them*, which made them feel special, and they needed to feel special if they were to regain their mental and spiritual health.

Carmalitta had been seeing the dog for almost two years. Mr. Gumbel was a small, sleek dachshund with gray-green eyes and a shiny black coat that was almost seal-like in its smoothness. Floppy ears, and stubby little legs so that he always had to run to keep up when he went for a walk.

Their sessions had been a difficult and slow journey, like blind mice in a maze struggling to find their way, and results had been minimal. Carmalitta was obfuscated by Mr. Gumbel's pressing condition; she still hadn't been able to find an appropriate way to stop him from chewing the baseboards every time his significant others went out. The house was filled with teeth marks, and the poor dog was plagued by a numbing sense of repressed hostility it couldn't express in any other fashion than to chew even more.

Carmalitta was mildly frustrated by the therapy's inertia, while Mr. Gumbel had trouble concealing his own sense of disappointment. He didn't like to chew and get into trouble, and he was especially sensitive to the *bad dog* tone his parents used when they came home and his mouth was lined with splinters. But he just couldn't stop *chewing*. Carmalitta was seriously contemplating medication, although she didn't believe Mr. Gumbel's treatment required so drastic a measure. *Yet.*

The last patient for the day was a fuzzy little dwarf hamster. Nero had long, pink ears, a flesh-toned tail prickled with fine hairs, and delicate paws that rarely left the front of his face. At first glance he seemed contented and well-adjusted. He loved the cage, the wheel, the interconnected tubes that were his home, and the see-through ball he could get in and roll all around the house just by running. But the problem was that he seemed to like those things just a little *too* much. Nero was almost the size of a small guinea pig when the Trelawns first brought him in. He never stopped running, climbing, or doing stops-and-starts throughout the entire session.

"He never stops," Mrs. Trelawn confessed through her Kleenex as she blew her nose. "For us, or the children." The hamster's wheel spun so fast the *clackclackclack* became a screeching whine and kept the entire family up all night.

Keeping an eye on Nero while she jotted down notes, Carmalitta was amazed the rodent never did actually stop to rest. She couldn't figure out why he wasn't hyperventilating, but then again, she'd never encountered a hamster that had bulked up to these proportions before.

"Diet?"

Mrs. Trelawn sniffed. "Those little pellet things. Carrots, celery, and sometimes cheese."

"He won't eat treats," Mr. Trelawn added.

"Sleep cycle?" Carmalitta was having trouble hearing over the *whirrr* of the wheel.

"Just a few hours during the day, and then he's up early in the afternoon. I can hear him running around long after we go to bed."

Carmalitta delicately cleared her throat. "And has that affected your –"

"No," Mrs. Trelawn answered quickly.

"Yes," her husband intervened, just as fast, his lips pursed.

Carmalitta made a mental note to check for antihistamines or steroids when the blood work-ups were done. She wondered if Nero could have attained his physique through exercise alone. Or had Trelawns actually wanted a larger pet, and unconsciously projected those feelings to the little rodent?

"Does he play with the children?"

"No!" Mrs. Trelawn cried. "He won't run up their hands, or around their necks, or anything at all like that. No eating from your palm or chasing bits of food."

Mr. Trelawn hurriedly nodded his agreement. "He doesn't come when you make that calling noise with your tongue that sounds like a baby woodpecker." He took his wife's hand. "It's very distressing."

Carmalitta opened a fresh box of Kleenex and surreptitiously slipped it across the desk towards Mrs. Trelawn. Nero was busy doing laps in the maze of tubes that were connected to his cage like spokes. His fur glistened with perspiration.

Carmalitta wrote down *inferiority complex*, and *obsessive personality disorder*, circled them both, then tied them together with a little squiggly line that went up to the word *dwarf*. Once again, she lamented the power of stereotypes. She knew the road to recovery would be strewn with stones of despair. She hoped the Trelawns had proper and sufficient medical coverage for the animal.

This was the third time she'd seen Nero and he hadn't slowed down a bit. She checked her notes; the lab confirmed no presence of antihistamines or steroids. *No traceable presence.* But she knew most athletes rarely tested positive either. She watched him run back and forth through the plastic tubes for almost the entire fifty-five minutes allotted to his weekly session. He slowed down to change direction, slurp up some water from the inverted dropper, or to give the wheel another brief spin for a change of pace, but he never actually stopped. His upper body was even bigger than last week and slightly more hirsute, and Carmalitta realized it wouldn't be long before he'd be unable to make it safely through the interconnected tubes. Some of the elbow joints were narrow and quite treacherous: it wasn't difficult to imagine him stuck somewhere *between* tubes, wrenched in the plastic so tight he'd eventually suffocate.

Carmalitta understood prompt intervention was not just a matter of psychological well-being but an element of physical safety as well. There was no other choice; the rodent would have to be medicated until the symptomatology was under control. Thinking of Ritalin first, she checked her compendium to reconfirm the levels normally considered safe for a hamster. She verified the rate for small guinea pigs too, and calculated what the proper dosage should be. It wasn't an avenue she liked to take, but she couldn't see any other way of preventing Nero from obsessively exercising himself to death. She scribbled down *Thantos*, and then made a note to call Mrs. Trelawn's pharmacy with the prescription. The wheel clicked on. Nero was running so fast the cage shook. The little metal bars sounded like tuning forks.

The patients had been back to back, and Carmalitta was mentally and physically exhausted by the time Mrs. Trelawn packed up all of Nero's cages and tubes so she could cart him home. She buzzed for her secretary, never thinking for a moment what that simple summons always did to the young woman.

Startled by the intercom, Elizabeth quickly regained her composure and shuffled an array of governmental remittance forms together that were fanned out across her desk. She tried to take a deep, relaxing breath, then reluctantly reached down and retrieved several pieces of paper from the garbage. Her stomach gurgled. She scrambled through her purse for her little make-up mirror, wishing when she saw her reflection she hadn't found it. She was still there, just like she always was, compartmentalized and framed in plastic, some small, rather nondescript part of a whole she couldn't recognize. Elizabeth shuddered. This was the face she showed the world, the one Carmalitta saw. *Was it enough?*

Elizabeth's heart thudded expectantly against her chest. This was the moment she'd been waiting for; the one she'd been dreading. The fear of rejection tightened around her throat like a hangman's noose, choking off her breath. All the planning, the thinking, the anxious nights of wishing, hoping, praying, the nausea, the fear, the ruthless constipation and the images of linked hands on a moonlit beach surged back in waves, pounding the shores of her memory and flooding her senses with a tide of possibilities. She thought she was going to faint and reached out for the edge of her desk. It seemed a long, long way down.

Elizabeth had the desire, the hope, the dreams. And safely tucked away in her drawer she had the airline tickets. But did she have the courage?

The buzzer cried again. Elizabeth smoothed the wrinkles from her skirt and brushed her hair back. Conscious of the blood pounding through her temples, she gathered up what was left of her tenacity, gently ran her fingers over Carmalitta's brass nameplate, turned, knocked, and went in. She closed the waiting room door behind her.

Rooted like a statue in the center of the room, *what ifs* swirled through her thoughts, stabbing her heart like needles in a voodoo doll. Her legs grew weak but she didn't want to sit down. Not yet. She wanted to speak, to say *it* first. To let go. That's what Carmalitta was always saying. *Forget repression: let it go.*

Carmalitta was checking over a file and didn't look up. "Did Dr. Emerson call back yet?"

God, your hair is so beautiful. "No, Doctor. I tried him once more, but he was still in surgery on that Rottweiler. A hip replacement. He said he'd call when he could."

Elizabeth fidgeted nervously while Carmalitta jotted something down. She desperately wanted to speak, but the words wouldn't come.

Carmalitta looked up. "Is there something else, Elizabeth?"

Her mouth was parched. The little voice that floated through her head urged her on. *Tell her the Rottweiler's owners should have asked her to do the surgery, since she was the best.*

"Any other messages?"

Silence.

"Elizabeth?"

"Oh, I'm sorry. Yes. Dr. McMichaelson called about the convention dates." *She's so slender, so graceful, so perfect. What would she ever want with . . .?*

"And?"

"And Mrs. Tomlinson called back to ask for an appointment without Rory."

"Interesting," Carmalitta mused, closing a folder. "Why don't you sit down, Elizabeth. You seem a little pale."

Because if I move I'll fall and if I fall I won't be able to see your face, the strength in your eyes, the roundness of your chin. The little voice that was always in the back of her mind cried out to *say something, for Christ's sake!* There was never enough time for love.

"Doctor? I was wondering . . ."

"Oh, I'm sorry. Did Miriam leave any messages? I'm supposed to meet her after work."

Elizabeth felt the world crumble and fall away beneath her. Jelly knees, and the breathlessness that comes with panic. One crushing word. Just three small syllables that sounded the death knell for her dreams. *Miriam.* That's who needed surgery. And Elizabeth wanted to be the anesthetist. She unraveled the scrunched up papers she'd retrieved from the garbage.

"Elizabeth?"

"Yes?"

"Are you sure you're feeling all right?"

I would be if you spent the time with me that you did with your animals. "Yes. Sorry."

"You don't have to apologize. Is something bothering you?"

The little voice, louder and more insistent this time. *Tell her! Say it now!* She gulped. *It's just that I'm afraid to tell you how much I want to be with you, that I want to be by your side, waiting for you when you came home . . .*

"No. No Doctor, I'm . . . I'm fine."

Carmalitta eased the file closed, aware of the tension strangling the room. "Is there something you'd like to talk about, Elizabeth?"

Elizabeth couldn't speak. She shook her head.

"Are you --?"

"No, I'm fine," she blurted out louder than she meant to. She knew she had to hurry, that she had to get away before her carotid artery pulsed right through the skin of her neck.

"Miriam said she'd pick you up downstairs in front of the clinic around five o'clock."

"Good." Carmalitta checked her watch. "I'll give Dr. Emerson one last try."

But she was still looking at her young secretary. The poor girl's eyes hadn't changed and her little freckles seemed to be on fire. She folded her hands together, her fingers in a steeple.

"Can I help you with anything, Elizabeth?"

There, screamed the voice. *She said your name again. That's the signal. Go on! Tell her what you're feeling.* But the words wouldn't come. *She could never want to be with me.*

"Elizabeth?"

The young girl was shivering. Perspiration beaded on her forehead. She wrung her hands together to stop them from trembling and her breath came in spastic spurts. Her ankles felt like cement blocks. She knew that if she stayed any longer she'd break down and start to cry. She forced herself to breathe, then waved a quick dismissal that everything was fine, the way people do at funerals. She lugged her feet around so the blocks were pointing the other way. Retreating.

How could I have been so stupid? Elizabeth missed the door handle on her first grasp. Another quick grab. The little voice droned on like helicopter blades. *Stop, stop and say something tell her how you feel let her see you tell her what it is!*

Elizabeth leaned back against the door as soon as it closed. She was panting and trying not to cry, but the tears came anyway. Cold tears, ice cold, tears that stung her cheeks like a hundred little bee stings.

***

The first thing that caught Carmalitta's attention when she stepped out into the street was a young man with short hair, featureless skin, an ape-like gait, and biceps bulging through a muscle shirt who was yanking a German Shepherd puppy along the sidewalk. Every time the dog tried to stop and sniff a parking meter or garbage bag waiting curbside for the morning pickup, the man tugged the choker chain so hard it snapped the puppy's head back like a crash test dummy hitting a wall.

Miriam was doubled-parked directly in front of the clinic's door. Carmalitta knew she would have been there at ten minutes to five. The passenger door opened as she approached and a waving arm beckoned her in.

"Waiting long?" Carmalitta asked, slipping down and crinkling into the plush leather.

"Five minutes, here or there," Miriam whispered, leaning closer and kissing Carmalitta warmly on the cheek. She searched for the softness of her lover's lips with her own.

"Not here," sighed Carmalitta, her nipples already erect.

"I know, I know, but I missed you so much today."

They held hands down between the seats, and Carmalitta noticed Miriam's palms were warm. She'd obviously just showered and changed at work, and the car was filled with the luxurious scent of lilac. Her hair hung down thick and straight over her shoulders and her eyes sparkled mischievously. In the deflected light of the car her skin seemed unnaturally soft and smooth. Flamingo-pink nail polish that matched her lipstick, just retouched lashes, and a new pair of skin-tight black jeans. Carmalitta felt her thighs flush with a shiver of anticipation.

Miriam hadn't stopped smiling since she'd seen her lover glare aggressively at the young man with the puppy. It was a disarming smile that had first brought them together, but it was her persistence and her need that had slowly pried Carmalitta apart from her former companion. Song Lee.

"You're warm."

"I am now that you're here," Miriam said. "Come on, I've got a surprise for you."

Miriam let Carmalitta's hand go, brushed her cheek with her fingers, and revved the engine.

"What kind of a surprise?" Carmalitta gave her a slow, wistful look up and down. She could almost feel the muscles in Miriam's thighs straining against the newness of the denim.

"A nice one and it's not far," Miriam teased, slipping into traffic. She saw the man with the puppy waiting at a light just ahead. "Want me to run him down before he pulls that little dog off the curb?"

"I wish," Carmalitta sighed. "But there'd just be another abandoned puppy down at the Humane Society."

They drove for about ten minutes, weaving in and out through tangled lines of commuters, cutting off trucks, scattering pedestrians, and ducking past idle buses so closely they practically touched bumpers. Carmalitta shook her head. She was no angel, but Miriam's driving always made her nervous. Her lover was two different people: one, a professional sports physiotherapist who was erudite, cultured, emotionally well-balanced and intelligent; and two, a psycho-driver.

Miriam was consistently impatient behind the wheel, but rush hour inevitably brought out the worst in her. She expected people to let her in, *demanded* they let her in, but she never extended the same courtesy to anyone else. She only merged at the very last second, and expected everyone to know that her car was nothing more than a weapon. Traffic lights were an imposition, corners something to be straightened out, squeegee kids neurotic speed bumps. Miriam didn't like to leave a slice of space between her front bumper and the next car that someone else might sneak in to. Defensiveness was something left outside when the door was locked and the rally began.

They flew along Queen Street. Carmalitta watched the little shops whiz by in a colorless blur, saw the signs above the doors change from one language to another.

"Where are we going?" She unconsciously checked the side view for flashing lights and frantically pumped a foot at her imaginary brake.

"It's not far now."

Then again, nothing was very far when you were travelling at the speed of sound. Carmalitta's fingers were imbedded so deeply in the edge of the leather seat she couldn't pry them open. But then, for some strange reason, Miriam actually stopped at the next light. A thin young girl in ripped jeans and someone else's' sweater danced towards the car like a drunken fairy, her squeegee raised like a wand, the evening light glistening off her nose ring. She stopped when she recognized the vehicle and scrambled back for the safety of the sidewalk like a giant crab.

"Miriam," Carmalitta began as the light changed. But she couldn't speak. Her head snapped back and her cheeks were pulled up toward her ears.

"It's just up here."

Miriam took the corner on two wheels, grazing the curb. She cut off a delivery van that had the temerity to share her road, forced a taxi to swerve out of the way, then slammed to a stop so hard Carmalitta felt the front bumper dig into the pavement.

"We're here!" Miriam cried. She jumped out and ran around to open Carmalitta's door.

'Here' was a great big empty yard sprinkled with chunks of broken concrete, pipes, nail-studded lumber, defiant weeds, and bales of shredded wire. Years of blown papers and Styrofoam cups splattered a tall wire fence at the far side of the barren field. To someone on the Arts Council who controlled the grant funding it was probably some kind of living abstract sculpture worth millions. Especially with that battered and rusty chain link fence.

Carmalitta whispered her usual prayer of gratitude that they'd survived again. Miriam helped her from the car and led her toward the center of the field as the color slowly drained back into Carmalitta's fingers. She glanced around at the emptiness.

"What am I looking at?"

"Heaven."

"Heaven?"

"It could be."

"Miriam, isn't this --"

"The lot next to the old race track? Yes. It's been empty for years. But not for much longer." She smiled and spun around on her tiptoes.

This was where the sulkies had trotted to victory for so many years. The thoroughbreds still raced at Woodbine, the track out in the west end near the airport. The sulky venue had been one of the last prime real estate properties inside the city core that had a sprawling view of Lake Ontario. An Olympic sized pool was right across the street. So was one of the largest sand beaches in the area, a yacht club, bike path, playgrounds, and a century old boardwalk. It wasn't long before builders snatched it up. Much of the land had already been used for condominiums, townhouses, low-rise apartment buildings, a uniquely dated bandstand, and English-style row houses that had inside elevator parking. There was only a small quadrant left, which had already been designated for two more condo complexes and a parkette that overlooked the lake.

"I don't --"

Miriam touched her arm. "Only one parcel left. The groundbreaking ceremonies are in two weeks."

Recent headlines flashed through Carmalitta's mind. "Twin condos, right?"

"With a full rec complex, indoor and outdoor pool, a terraced garden, two-story lofts, full security, the whole nine yards."

Miriam grabbed her lover's arm and turned her slowly around. "Quick access in and out of the city. Right on the main bus routes. Across from the beaches. Close to everything. Still *downtown*, but with a little space. And --"

She turned Carmalitta toward the south. "Ta-da. A view of the lake." She spun her around in the other direction. "And shopping galore."

***

Carmalitta was tensely still, but she could still hear her heart pounding. "I thought the whole development was presold, that none of the units were even offered in the local papers."

Miriam nodded. "They weren't. Every condo was grabbed up by Hong Kong speculators within two days. But –"

She wrapped her arm around Carmalitta and pulled her close. "Remember Paul Wu?"

"The sports psychologist? The one you worked with at the National Swimming Championships?"

"Uh-huh. He bought three. One for his parents, and one each for some uncle and aunt. But the aunt changed her mind and isn't coming now, and he'll let us have it for what he paid." She leaned closer, whispering in Carmalitta's ear.

"It's one of the largest lofts there is. And it's lakeside. Just think: a short drive from work, lots of space. We're just up from an evening swim. Sitting out in the solarium with a glass of wine, a fire on, sailboats shimmering on the water, our own double-sized bedroom room a few steps away . . . "

"Miriam . . ."

"Don't 'Miriam' me!" She spun away and folded her arms around her chest. Her right eye was twitching. "This would be perfect! And you know it."

Carmalitta stepped closer but Miriam backed away. She brushed her hair from the side of her face and looked up at the spot in the sky where their imaginary unit might be.

"I know it would. But that's not the point."

Silence.

"Is it?"

Miriam kicked a weed, scattering something that almost made Carmalitta sneeze. "You have to make a commitment, Carma. You have to."

Over the last several months, most of these conversations had been the same. Shared thoughts and feelings, but nothing ever resolved. Carmalitta still believed she needed more time before she embarked on a step like this. She was unsure of her feelings, her needs, her wants. She loved Miriam with all her heart, but that didn't seem to be enough.

She glanced back at the lake. Sweeping gulls and terns squawked by overhead. The terns, of course, were smaller, and had distinctive white and black markings on their shorter little aerodynamic bodies. Sunlight rippled off the glass windows of a nearby condo. How long had she been with Jordan? A year and a half? No, almost two. And with Sebastian? They'd lived in that nice apartment off Dan Leckie, so it was a quick jog to the Rogers Center for a game, or a ten minute walk to the lake on a sun-blessed Sunday. They'd shared a bed for just under a year.

Interspersed with the men, there'd been two women Carmalitta had become lost with, two wonderful, gentle women who were about as far apart in looks and needs and desires as anyone could have possibly imagined. She'd loved those relationships as much as she'd loved Corrine and Song Lee, experimenting and living in different condos in different parts of the city in different life-moments of her existence for about twelve months each. She'd almost married Song Lee, and she'd actually been engaged to Jordan.

Carmalitta glanced around the lot, imagining everything. She'd seen pictures of the completed towers, the glass pool, the bar and movie theatre. She tried to keep pace with her thoughts. It certainly wasn't the end of the world. Everything could always change again; there was nothing new about that. It wasn't as if by virtue of buying the condominium, she was falling in the water and treading her life away forever. Perhaps more than anything else she'd done in a long time, the move that she was contemplating, buying the condo with her lover, would ultimately swing the pendulum of her ambivalence into motion, and finally force her make a decision about the breadth and depth of her own sexuality. Once the inertia had been set into motion, would that pendulum ever oscillate back towards a different lifestyle, and let her become something new again?

Living together meant something more, much more, and more than having her own place and being able to come and go as she wanted. It was the ability to change her mind when she pleased, or the sex of her lover. Her body's needs. What could she do? For Miriam, marriage meant forever. It certainly didn't to Carmalitta. She thought about her parents and her grandparents, people waiting to change, to start a new life with someone else. Why did she have to go through all this first? The ownership. The sacred promises. The endearing, unending relationship, when it probably wasn't going to last forever. Most marriages lasted until the children were either finished school or old enough to be on their own. How long would it be before she was bored, before her needs and wants left Miriam in the dark? Was it fair to give her a ray of hope, a piercing sentiment of light, and then let her live in the darkness when the best years of her life had come and gone?

***

Pages and pages of an old shredded newspaper blew by, a kite without a string trying to fly with the wind. She'd had numerous other short-lived affairs and live-in lovers with both men and women over the years; she had to admit that none of them were as intense or exciting and comforting as the one she was involved with right now. She didn't know how, but Miriam was different than the rest. It was somewhere in the bottom of her heart where she'd heard that little voice, the one that sits behind your thoughts that's always questioning who you are and what is it that you're doing, that kept telling her she would never share the same intensity with anyone else that she had experienced with Miriam.

She'd been alone for the better part of a year before she'd met Miriam. It had always felt different, being alone. Hadn't it? What was it that made her moments with Miriam so different than all those other lifetime commitments, those precious affairs and obligations?

Deep down inside, she knew that each delay pushed Miriam a little farther away. And there's only so far you can push someone before they can't come back. She didn't want that. But even if she did go along with Miriam and make some sort of marriage commitment, it wasn't as if that completed the equation of *a lifetime*, either. After all, they were simply getting married, weren't they? And marriage certainly didn't mean *forever* anymore, did it?

But by leaving her apartment again, just when she was used to living alone, she'd be surrendering the last vestige of a secure port in the storm. She'd be leaving security behind. There'd be no place to hide. No place to go when the world began to cave in all around her.

That was it and she knew it. Carmalitta had fought the stress and strain of her bi-polar depression for as long as she could remember. Right now it was under control, a nuisance more than a disorder; she knew it and could feel it. On those days when she cycled so badly, so completely and suddenly, that reality seemed nothing more than a distance promise, she'd managed to find her own little hole of light in the darkness

Up until now, she'd always had a place to escape to, a place where she could retreat and suffer in when the vampiric fangs of her despair tore into her neck and bled her into a deep depression. She could crawl into bed and let the blood pound and stay in a fetal position until she could finally unfurl her own gryphon wings. Could she become what she could be if Miriam was always there?

The traffic whizzed by. The ferry that went back and forth to the islands just offshore unleashed an enormous *hoonnnkk* that seemed to stir the waves crashing across the lake. Tires squealed against the asphalt and horns blared a symphony of resentment. Seagulls raided a garbage can.

"Miriam --"

She put up her hand dismissively, tears welling behind her eyes.

"Why don't we go out for dinner? Somewhere quiet. We can talk and --"

"And what? You can tell me how much you love me, how deeply you feel, but that you're not ready to live with me? I've heard it all before, Carmalitta. The echo hasn't even faded from the last time. And we're not getting any younger, Carma."

"I'm not saying it's not going to happen. It's just --"

"That you need more time, I know. You need time more than you need me."

Tears glistened in the corners of Miriam's eyes. "I don't understand what you're waiting for, Carmalitta. I really don't."

Neither do I.

"You can wait too long, you know."

A threat, or just fear? Carmalitta slipped her arm around her lover's waist. Miriam was shivering.

"Come on. Let's have some dinner and work through this together. When did Paul say we have to make a decision by?"

"The end of the month."

"Then we will." *One way or the other.*

"Promise?"

"I do."

A deep breath. "I can't keep going on like this, Carmalitta. Waiting, dreaming, hoping. Worrying."

"Shhh. I know. Come on, it's getting cold and I'm starving."

Carmalitta tried to smile and squeezed Miriam's hand. "The Keg. My treat. Do you have any floor plans? We'll look at them together over dinner, and you can show me everything you've got."

Miriam wiped her eyes with the edge of her hand, a smile threatening. She slipped her arm through Carmalitta's, gave her a reassuring squeeze, then started off across the vacant, dust-bowl-of-a lot. She talked almost non-stop all the way back to the car.

"Oh, it's really gorgeous, Carma. Did I tell you they have a full spa center as well?" She turned back quickly, envisioning their life suspended up in the air somewhere. "And did I say it has a fireplace? And an eat-in kitchen with a pantry?"

They walked back to the car, shoulder to shoulder and hands closely linked. The sun had sunk halfway into the lake, but the last filaments of its dying light were wrapped in clouds. The water was cast with a black sheen. Miriam kicked a chunk of stone into a broken piece of rusted pipe, and Carmalitta's thoughts were filled with a sickening, dull *thud*.

Before she opened the door, they both stopped and looked up their imaginary love nest in the sky.

Oh, Carmalitta admitted, *it would be wonderful not to have to commute anymore, to be able to save almost three hours every day. Fifteen a week. Sixty a month. Delicious!* But even though she was still relatively young and just thought she was old and wise, she knew that there was never a decision that came without a price.

And this time, the price would be psychological freedom.

Chapter Ten

Everyone except Lydia had read the sticky notes on the fridge and had made it in time for Cybernician's birthday celebration. The restaurant was on King Street, right in the center of the mayhem known as the Theatre District. Thick crowds choked the sidewalk, talking and shouting and pointing in scores of different languages. Pedestrian traffic coagulated behind the people who kept stopping to look at the menus each restaurant had pasted in a little box beside their front door. There was a second sign that announced the city's grade score for cleanliness to potential patrons. Soap dispensers were placed prominently nearby. Bikes whizzed in and out through stalled traffic with taxis in hot pursuit. Exhaust fumes were thick and heavy. A Japanese man across the road, seriously intent on a photograph of the CN Tower, had erected a tripod and was busily fastening a camera to the top plate with the thickest, fattest lens Mathew had ever seen. A mounted Metro Police Officer in bright red and blue *clip-clopped* past the window and bounced out of sight, but not before he coaxed the beggars away from the metal bicycle racks that lined the curb, and checked the men sleeping under cardboard boxes to make sure they weren't dead yet.

Small and quaint, the restaurant was stamped with the impressions of an owner who had never been out of the province of what some Mediterranean seaside port must surely have looked like. Sandy-pink walls, fishing nets draped from the ceiling, red-and-white-checkered tablecloths, waiters in black bow ties and starched white aprons, and a stand-up bar that was ostensibly designed to look like the inside of a cave. For some reason that went completely over Mathew's head, a flock of pelicans dominated a mural that covered the far wall.

An androgynous maitre d' directed them solemnly to their table. Mathew wanted to sit at the back. He scurried along the bench behind the table, skillfully ducking under a hanging spider plant Carmalitta thought he hadn't seen but hadn't had time to warn him about, either. Dangling tentacles of green and white striped leaves waved eerie shadows over the table. Long, vine-like tendrils reached down from the edge of the basket and festered into little balls beneath the host plant. *Spider plant babies.* Shivering as he ducked past them, Mathew brushed off any imaginary little hitchhikers that might have fallen from the plant. He took a few slow, deep breaths and tried to ignore the fact that he'd have to run the gauntlet on the way out, too.

Mathew couldn't remember the last time he'd been to the restaurant, or if he'd ever been here at all. They all looked rather the same now, years after the novelty of dining out had worn off and become nothing more than just another diversion. He couldn't picture the last time he'd been out with Lydia for a romantic dinner. In his heart he knew that with Carol, they would have all seemed brand new, exciting, a shared experience he'd never forget. Everything with her had been. Whispers across a quiet table for two in the corner, hands almost always touching, fingers feeling each other out like ant antennas, smiles that wouldn't fade.

The restaurant was relatively quiet for a Thursday night. But that had been Mathew's choosing for his own piece of mind. He'd carefully reserved a specific cusp between surges: eight o'clock. The patrons dining before the theatre had already left, and the ones that would feast after the shows were still a merciful two and a half hours away. Mathew and his family shared the little restaurant with twenty or so other ticketless strangers.

He turned and squinted outside a narrow window as the others took their places. Across the road, sheathed in layers of speckled smog and smooth concrete, was the C.N. Tower, the largest man-made structure in the entire world that the picture-taking Japanese man was so focused on. Well, it had been the largest, until The Tokyo Skytree had soared into the stratosphere, which, Mathew recalled, in a rather uncharacteristically and demeaning crude sense of the ultimate pissing-contest, had itself been superseded by the Abrajal Bait Towers in Mecca.

Higher and higher, farther and farther. Bigger and bigger. Then, naturally, just to put the 'Mecca Monster' back in its place, along came the Khalifa Building, which momentarily gave Dubai the title of superstructure in the entire world. Mathew wondered how many travel brochures and information booklets and things on the Net had to be changed when the Tower was only the *second* tallest man-made structure in the world. And then *the third.* The only good thing that the travel and tourism brochure industry really had in its favor was that regardkess of its height, the CN Tower was still the largest structure in the *Western world.* All the snow in all the cheap bars behind Canadian watering holes would still be the yellowish the farthest. He tried to picture a new 'biggest one' constructed that didn't look quite so much like a penis with a cyst, but he couldn't.

Something else bothered him even more as he watched the multi-colored flashing lights warn errant planes away. Canada has the lugubrious claim to having the lamest security in the world. Just ask the Mossad or the C.I.A. It's definitely the easiest country to sneak in or out of. And no matter how politely you're asked to leave, anyone can hide in Canada for a decade while they're waiting to file a refugee claim. Despite the majority of the world's best attempts at eradicating terrorism, Mathew knew that no place was immune. So he wondered: if some transplanted radical hiding in Toronto had brought his country's political battle here, and if that very same gutless troll had decided to plant some incendiary device somewhere in the base of the structure's shaft, would the Tower be long enough when it dropped to the ground like a stunned cow in a slaughterhouse to reach their little red-and-white-checkered table? Would the revolving restaurant that swirled around the head of the great phallus actually fall right on top of all the unsuspecting patrons dining or watching the new A.L.Webber musical at all the venues throughout the theatre district? He brushed a baby from the spider plant out of the way and tried not to think about it.

The lake was there too, right behind the Tower. He couldn't see it because of all the buildings that fought for space along the edge of the shore, but he knew from his youth that it was there, somewhere behind them. He guessed that if the Tower fell the *other* way, out onto the lake, it wouldn't be long enough to reach Centre Island, but he wasn't sure. If it did it would make a nice ready-made pier. At least it would miss the Japanese man who was still setting up his camera.

Across the road, and thirty parking meters and just four or five squeegee kids to his left, was Roy Thompson Hall. The Hall was home to the Toronto Symphony, and looked a bit like a glass Bundt cake pan turned upside down. A man in a tuxedo with a bag over his head strummed a guitar before the front doors, nodding gratefully when someone tossed coins into his open case. The huge, egg-shaped Roger's Centre was to the right, its roof retracted to the night and glowing with television lights. Someone was playing someone, in some sport or another, in the endless series of games that never seemed to stop, even when someone won.

A young man ran past the window, thighs as large as tree stumps and a ponytail that touched his behind, pulling a sightseeing couple along in a little covered contraption based on a rickshaw. Despite the effort, the young man was barely perspiring. Did the people in the carriage have a little whip they could crack over his head when he slowed down? Did the man have to stop and urinate in the gutter like the horses did?

Eventually, Mathew's family settled. Everyone started looking around, pointing out this and that, as if they'd never had the pleasure of dining out before. Joshua was the first to notice the glass sculptures that decorated many of the walls in the Mediterranean seaside port. Although they weren't thematically relevant, they were beautifully designed and quite unique. He leaned forward, scanning the room for more, nodding appreciatively.

"Look at the stained glass. Neat, eh, Dad?"

Carmalitta interrupted in a whisper. "Well actually, Joshua, they're not stained glass. They appear to consist of highly polished segments of mirrors pieced together. The artist has put little prisms of cut crystal behind the designs. That's why they reflect the overhead light and make the different parts of the mirror assume transitory color patterns. If you look closely, you'll see the images and the shades of light are always changing."

Eleanor huffed and patted Joshua on the head. "It looks like stained glass to me, too." She didn't ask what Lorne thought. Like Mathew, Granddad was wearing casual pants, a dress shirt, and a matching cardigan. He'd never liked ties.

Carmalitta nodded. "Well, yes. I guess it does. Perhaps the artist was trying to show the fragility of perspective."

"They're all different," Joshua admired, glancing around the restaurant. "*Coool.*"

Mathew pointed at the far wall. "That one over there looks like the Gooderham building. You know, the one shaped like a piece of pie."

Other buildings appeared more foreign, stucco white and sea-bleached. There was a large work that incorporated placid outdoor scenes of mountains, lakes, and fertile hillsides. A small cityscape in terra cotta beige, and over there, an antique automobile with a rumble seat and spoked tires. Obviously, the Mediterranean-wannabe didn't see anything incongruous about them at all.

Carmalitta saw one that reminded her of work. Of Rory. A long, slender piece of interconnected glass fragments that looked like the regal cats the ancient Egyptians revered.

"Isn't that one lovely." She lowered her voice in deference to her grandfather and switched to Pig-Latin. "The '*atca*.' The Persian. It would be perfect in my office."

Joshua nodded. "It's even got little whiskers."

"Yes, and for some reason, that's the only one without colour," Carmalitta remarked. "The glass is clear. It reflects everything."

Eleanor had been studying the menu and had lost the thread of the conversation. She craned forward to look but didn't see the design. "A mirror? Cat?"

Mathew started to say something -- *oh no*, or something equally banal and woeful at the same time -- but by then, it was too late.

A *mirror cat.*

Granddad was already rising.

He was on the savannah, guarding the burrow while his companions fed. His turn would come, but someone always had to stand watch while the others were vulnerable. The monsoons were still months away and the land was parched. A warm evening breeze rippled through the acacia trees on the edge of the plain, blowing dust up from the wadi. A black dung beetle scurried through the sand behind him.

Granddad's elbows were tucked into his ribs and his hands looked as if they were curled around some imaginary bar in front of his chest. His body was painfully erect, his head straight, his chin angled down toward the ground. He pricked his ears to the night, his chest heaving with the dryness, his nostrils flaring in anticipation, and his eyes darted relentlessly back and forth. He sniffed the air in every direction, constantly vigilant for even the slightest sign predators were near. He scanned the horizon, searching, wary, tensely alert.

"Oh God," Eleanor mumbled, hiding behind the menu. Then, a disgusted "*Ooooh*". There was a ketchup stain over the word *appetizers*.

Mathew leaned up and touched his father's arm. "Dad, sit down now. Come on, everything's fine."

Perhaps to the untrained eye or the ears of the inexperienced. No, the savannah was never safe. Death lurked behind every rock.

Granddad sniffed, pawed the air, and swung his gaze over the bushes and sandy anthills. He'd watch his brethren feed. One of them would finish soon and another sentry would relieve him so he'd have a chance to eat, too.

The people at the tables nearby seemed intrigued by what had startled the old man. There were hushed whispers and muted giggles. Numerous phones came out, snapping up pictures and sending them away in the blink of an eye. Mathew put a hand on Dad's elbow as the waiter approached to see what was the matter. But he came too close. Granddad's body became breathlessly rigid, his head jerked back and his eyes narrowed.

Danger!

"It's all right, Dad. This one is coming to relieve you. He'll stand watch while you have your turn eating with the others."

The waiter looked around, wondering who the *others* were. *Stand guard over what?*

Granddad didn't move until the waiter was at his side. Mathew waved the man into silence and put a bit of pressure on his father's elbow. He nodded, winked, and tried to draw the young man's attention to his father's hands. The waiter tucked his menu under his arm and raised his hands in front of his chest like granddad was doing. He stretched up, straining his neck erect, and glanced slowly from side to side. Several people behind him did the same thing.

Granddad took one last look around, lowered his paws, and slowly relinquished his position as temporary overseer. He was starved, exhausted by the demands of being the sentry. This one would watch over the others now so he could feed, drink, rest, then relax and gnaw the fleas from his fur. The waiter waited for some signal from Mathew that he could lower his hands, that the savannah was clear.

"Is everything fine now, sir?" the waiter asked. He didn't take his eyes off the old man.

Mathew nodded. *Yes*, he thought. *My father's a meerkat but it's safe to eat now.* He quickly tried to explain, but the waiter wasn't listening. He heard *stroke, National Geographic, Nova*, and *some nervous condition where he becomes different animals*, and *he thinks he's a meerkat*, yet the poor young man was at a loss to string the disjointed sounds into a cohesive whole. He just nodded politely and slowly breathed the colour back into his face. At least he didn't have time to effuse "good evening, my name is Albert and I'll be your waiter tonight." The old man was completely still and bent over his place setting.

Can I get you something from the bar? seemed a ridiculous query to the waiter, but he whispered it anyway. Whatever these people were on, they certainly wouldn't want to drink anything that might bring them down.

"Perhaps we should order now," Carmalitta suggested. The waiter seemed relieved. Another one of them could speak.

"Mother?" Mathew prodded.

She kept her head down. "The penne arabriatta and a glass of your house red, please."

The waiter paused as he looked at the old man beside her, unsure of what to say. *And for the meerkat?*

"My husband will have a salad. Please have the vegetables cut into bite-sized pieces."

The waiter cocked an eyebrow. *Naturally.*

Carmalitta lowered her menu with practiced flair. She liked every movement she made to have a purpose, a significance that transcended the situation.

"A glass of your Bernkastler Riesling, and the linguini in the clam sauce."

"Very good. Sir?"

Mathew checked to make sure his father was still preoccupied with his empty plate. "A bottle of your house white, please. And I'll try the manicotti. Does that come with *oatga* cheese?"

Mathew drew the waiter closer and whispered. "That's goat in pig latin."

The waiter didn't know pig latin. "Yes sir, it does." He turned toward Michael. "And for you, sir?"

The waiter tried not to smirk. His attention had been captivated by the life and death struggle unfolding on the savannah, and it was his initial look at Michael. The first thing he noticed was the hat tilted forward at a rakish angle; second, the muted glasses; and third, the gloves that looked like a surgeon's second skin. Was the young man some mutant offspring of a genetic experiment with Michael Jackson and Humphrey Bogart gone awry?

Keeping the bottom half of his face hidden with the menu, Cybernician realized he was having a mild panic attack, he was starting to perspire. He spoke into the *appetizers and breads*. Barely breathing and afraid someone else might hear, he ordered the macaroni in a muted whisper. The waiter could barely hear him and leaned closer.

Suddenly, Cybernician felt the table starting to move and the whole restaurant was closing in. He tried to relax again when the man stopped writing, but it was several minutes before the talons of some huge, invisible beast released his heart. His face was blotched crimson and red. Mathew reordered again for his son.

"And for the young man?" the waiter asked, gesturing to Joshua but looking back at Mathew.

"A grilled cheese?" Mathew asked his son.

Joshua nodded excitedly. "And a chocolate milk, please."

The waiter backed away from the table, afraid to let the family out of his sight. The old man was right: the savannah was indeed a strange and deadly place.

The waiter seemed to have recovered some of his composure when he returned with their drinks. His breath reeked of gin. At least the meerkat was still resting. Joshua sniffed the chocolate milk and smiled.

There was a moment of uncomfortable silence when the waiter left again. Mathew knew they were being stared at, but for once he didn't care. It was his son's birthday after all, and he was pleased the young man had even come, since he couldn't remember the last time Michael had ventured into the world beyond their house. Beyond his room. He was actually *outside*. Mathew knew Cybernician was terrified. His face was red, the veins throbbed in his forehead, and he was scrunched up into the corner so hard it seemed like he was trying to merge with the wall. He was sorry for his son and sympathized with his fear, since he still suffered the same kind of debilitating panic attacks that besieged Michael, too. They'd lessened over the years to an infrequency he felt he could control. But they'd come back again for the last several months, stronger, more protracted, hauntingly frequent, and they came with a suddenness that added to his fright. The only thing that helped him calm down were thoughts about Carol. He missed her more than he thought he could have ever missed anyone. So much had been right about their relationship? What had gone wrong?

Mathew poured the wine. "To Mich -- Cybernician," he said, raising his glass in a toast. Everyone clinked their glasses together.

"To a wonderful birthday and a great year," Carmalitta added. Another clink. She watched her brother slink down farther into his chair. She was glad she'd decided against buying him a pet after all. Granddad kept staring at his plate. He seemed to be wondering how the others had eaten everything so quickly.

Everyone exchanged snatches of small talk. It was like the burst of conversations that erupt when distant family members gather for some special occasion, like Thanksgiving or Christmas, and no one really knows what to say. Everyone plays catch-up.

Mathew was pleased when their dinners arrived. There were the obligatory *oohs* and *ummms* and *oh my, doesn't this look nice*, and the conversation quickly evaporated into a metallic din of cutlery against plates. Mathew watched the others eat. He was still worried about Michael. In fact, he was concerned about his whole family. Studying them covertly, he tried to listen and understand the things they *weren't* saying. Unaware of his father's scrutiny, Joshua turned his sandwich around awkwardly in his hand and busily ate all of the crust off first.

Halfway through dinner, a telephone trilled an obnoxious cry. The sounds of the restaurant disintegrated into an anxious stillness as everyone stopped eating and checked their cell phones. Many patrons appeared noticeably upset the call wasn't for them, but at least everyone else realized they carried a phone all the time, anyway.

Cybernician knew it was his before the first ring withered. He checked his watch and straightened his hat. It wasn't a watch: it was a combination of a cell phone, a pad, a tablet, and an infinitesimally small laptop. The *'next big thing.'* Only a handful of people knew that he'd been a part of the original design process. Few individuals had even seen the prototypes, let alone one of the actually working models. They weren't expected to be released for months. And then the world would buy them up faster than the parts could be sent to China. There was an electronic buzz at most of the other tables as people strained to at least get a look. It was everything Jonny Quest or Dick Tracy had ever imagined. And soon, everyone would have one. Until, naturally, *the next big thing* came along. Some people nodded: they realized that the old man gnawing at the vegetables was nothing more than a diversion.

They were equally frustrated when Cybernician pushed his plate aside and opened up his laptop. He plugged in the ear phones, hooked it up to the little portable monitor and donned a headset with a small microphone. Adjusted the volume, and waited. No-one felt affronted, not even Eleanor, because they knew how hard it had been for him to come out of the house, and they understood that he still had to hide behind something.

Sheila's picture was on the screen a moment later. She smiled nervously, glanced from side to side to see if anyone else was with him, then sang 'Happy Birthday' to her lover. Her face reddened deeper with each bar but she managed to get through the whole thing in one breath. Cybernician seemed just as embarrassed as she was. He knew *he* couldn't have sung a note if he'd known there was a room of real people behind *her*.

Sheila's face took up most of the little monitor, and for some reason, the color wasn't as sharp and defined as it should have been. Cybernician wanted to switch to his 'watch.' But at least she was there with him. She looked a little tired, weary almost; the programming must have been going a lot harder than she'd anticipated. Cybernician turned the monitor just a little more so that his father couldn't see the screen.

Cybernician typed furiously for several minutes, blushing a burnt crimson every time he read whatever was on his own screen. Mathew didn't know where to look so he glanced back out the window. The C.N. Tower was still standing, but its looming shadow was always a threat. The Japanese cameraman was gone. Was that good or bad? A plot, or an innocent photo? In the bowels of the kitchen, someone dropped a tray. Silverware clattered to the floor like hailstones against a metal roof.

A few moments later, Cybernician disconnected the equipment, packed everything up, and tugged his plate of wilted macaroni back in front of his place. He speared three or four noodles then pushed it away again.

Albert had been watching the drama unfold by the kitchen doors. He inched toward the table and cautiously broke the silence. "And how was everything?"

Mathew said *fine* through his last forkful. Why did servers always wait to ask you something the instant you put something in your mouth? Carmalitta suggested the noodles could have been a little more *al dente*, but Eleanor thought hers were just right. Granddad pawed at the last carrots on his plate and didn't look up.

"May I bring you the dessert menu?"

Mathew could see the nervousness in the waiter's eyes. He obviously hoped they'd say no so he could shoo them out sooner. Once their dishes were cleared away and the leftover crumbs brushed to the floor, it would be like they'd never even been there.

Everyone shook their heads. "No, I think we're all right," Mathew said. "Just some coffee, please." He turned to his son as Albert slipped away. "So, Cybernician, what did Sheila give you for your birthday?"

It was a harmless question, but since it focused everyone's attention back on him, it threw Michael into a frenzy. His breath caught in the back of his throat. He though he was going to be sick. He struggled valiantly to stay in control. His knees started knocking together beneath the table and the fingers of his gloves showed moist patches of perspiration. He hated speaking out loud, even to his family. Pressure came from everywhere at once. He felt like the world was shrinking and expanding at the same time that the air was being sucked away and his body was being compressed so hard he thought his blood would boil and he'd explode.

"A new processor," he whispered between clenched teeth. He wished he'd worn larger sun glasses. He wished he hadn't come. He wished he could be someone else, even for just a little while.

"Great." Mathew wasn't sure what else to say. He didn't know any specific questions to ask because the inner complexities of a processor were as foreign to him as brain surgery was to a salmon. Even if he had, he wouldn't have asked them anyway. Sensitive to his son's fear, he didn't want to keep him the centre of attention for too long: he didn't want him to pass out.

Fortunately, Michael had opened up his birthday presents from his family at home before they'd left. In fact, he'd already used his new watch to make up personally customized little thank you cards for everyone's thoughtfulness. His grandparents had bought him a new hat. Lightweight, he'd be able to use it next summer when it got warmer in his room. Even with the air conditioning it was always toasty in front of the monitor. Lydia had sent him a check, and Mathew had given him an ergonomic mouse he hoped was compatible with his son's other equipment. He couldn't remember the last time he and Lydia had bought a gift together. From Carmalitta, a marble bust of

Gates, and Joshua had depleted his allowance to buy his brother a lined mahogany box for his floppy discs.

Silence. Someone reactivated the small talk button when the waiter brought their coffee, but Mathew had a difficult time staying focused on what was being said. The restaurant noises were distracting and he kept drifting away to other family gatherings when he'd felt more . . . more what? More a part of everything? More contented? More hopeful? He wasn't sure, but it was more *something*. Maybe it was just that a long time ago he thought he had a family. Something he belonged to, that he had a place in. And not just on the fridge.

He looked at his eldest son. A man now, a man who lived in a computer, a man who rarely ever went outside who endured such severe shark bites of panic attacks that he might not ever physically meet the woman he'd met on-line and wanted to marry. What would happen to Cybernician if Mathew died tomorrow? Or tonight, on the way home from the restaurant, if he was struck and run over and trampled under the feet of the man-horse with the huge thighs pulling the rickshaw? His life probably wouldn't change. What did that say about him? About Mathew himself? About the thing they thought was a family? *Wasn't there something more?*

Carmalitta. Bright, energetic, compassionate. But a veterinarian that opted to be a pet therapist. Yes, it paid well. And yes, she was providing a great deal of help to people and animals alike who had trouble dealing with the ever-present difficulties that arose in their relationships. Mathew stared at the graceful, angular lines of her face and sighed. Like Michael, he didn't see a chance of having grandchildren from her, either. He loved Carmalitta as much as any father loved a daughter, and he'd always been comfortable with her sexual orientation. Or her *lack* of one. Admittedly, he was shocked at first, but his daughter's *outing* hadn't been any more of an issue than anything else in his life. She seemed comfortable and happy, and he knew he had no right in asking for anything more. But the idea of being left without grandchildren and abandoned in some pigeonholed home for the aged broke his heart every time he thought about it. So he worried about other things instead.

Mathew sipped his coffee. Everyone else seemed equally transfixed with something in their cups while the conversation ebbed and trickled. Eleanor kept blowing imaginary steam from the rim. Art had become her life, and the more she painted the deeper she became immersed in her own canvas. They rarely spoke any more, just in passing or when something had to be said. What happened? Beside her, Granddad gnawed a ripped piece of lettuce that was just beginning to brown at the edges. They used to be so close, all those years ago. Where was he, when the meerkats were gone? What use was living life if you didn't remember it?

And Joshua. A boy without a childhood and a man that was still a child. Mathew wondered how many lives his son could actually remember, given the right circumstances and the time to meet the people he'd already been. How far back did his history go? And whose history was it, anyway? He loved the boy but he was afraid of him a little, too.

The waiter brought the bill on a tray like he was carrying John's head into Herod. Carmalitta leaned over and told him what the amount should be before Mathew picked it up. The waiter was out a penny: concerned with writing his name and a little happy face with a flourish, Albert had made an error.

Mathew finished his coffee while he waited for his receipt. How did he get here, he wondered. It wasn't a bad *here*, and every time he forced himself to watch the news he realized how many countless souls were far worse off than he was. He had food, clothing, fairly decent health (other than that *little* problem), and a home with a manageable mortgage that didn't keep him awake at night. He didn't have to beg for leftovers, or wait in line all day for a chance at a bit of menial work so he could bring some food home to a tent of dirty, starving children. Joshua wasn't exploited in a child labor factory, and there wasn't any chance of being eaten alive by a tiger or squashed under the feet of a marauding herd of elephants at night. No crossing green or other colored lines to get to work, or being stopped at an endless series of hastily erected checkpoints by youths in balaclavas brandishing semi-automatics. No earthquakes, mud slides, or ferries constantly sinking because they were carrying too much weight. Mathew had as much freedom as he needed.

But then why did he sag beneath the weight of his chains?

He looked around the table and saw a little portion of himself in everyone else hunched over their coffee. He wondered if the old woman -- his fairy godmother -- always managed to find enough to eat. He wondered what Lydia was doing right then, at that exact moment, and he tried not to think about what would have happened, where he would have been, and what he would have been doing, if he'd married Carol.

What ifs could drive you crazy.

And the drive didn't seem very far.

Mathew knew his speedometer was whirling out of control, and he was careening faster and faster in a car that couldn't handle the curves.

Chapter Eleven

Lydia cursed again as she stabbed her fork down into the plastic container. The little pimento-eyes were staring up at her, the Brussels sprouts goading her, the wizened olives defying her to eat them. She rammed another leafy bale down her throat, half gagging, chewing it like she was masticating acacia thorns. Knowing it was good for her didn't make it any easier. New girls were always there, waiting, watching, clutching at any chance to take her place. Younger girls who were prettier. Lydia knew she couldn't lose her edge that she had to stay ahead of them. If the latest self-help book screamed her skin would stay soft and smooth if she covered herself in yak dung every night, she'd do it. She skewered another glaring eye, closed her own, and ate it. She wished Mathew was there beside her. She missed him, missed him dearly, missed the way he'd hold her and brush the hair from her forehead and tell her everything was going to be fine. She wondered if Mathew really knew how much she'd sacrificed to get this chance. And deep down inside, she knew he had as well. Gossip in the business told her that few spouses would have stayed as supportive as her husband had over the years. Missed income from a regular job, birthdays or anniversaries forgotten, vacations that never materialized because of overlapping commitments. She kept telling herself that she'd make it up to him one day when she was an acclaimed actress. But, just like the smoothness of her skin, time was slipping away . . . .

The sides of the coffee truck slammed closed and the driver peeled away to another set on the film lot. Most of the other extras sat together in little groups, but Lydia rarely joined them. They thought her aloof; she saw them as trite and nothing more than extras, while she was an aspiring actress. Two men wheeled a large swinging boom light by on a battered dolly, while a young woman struggled behind a long rack crammed with clothes and various costumes. Tow motors whipped back and forth between the false-fronted buildings, while security guards hitched up their pants and listened to lines being rehearsed.

Another forkful disappeared.

"Lydia, my love. There you are."

She hadn't heard him approach. "Frank. Really, hello."

A kiss on each cheek and a smile neither wanted to be the first to let go. Frank held on until his mouth started to hurt.

"Salad again?"

"It's dreadful."

"But it's what Meryl has for lunch every day."

"I know, I know. But really." Lydia pushed an olive down under a tomato half.

Frank sat down beside her and lit a cigarette, then waved to a couple of people riding past in a golf cart. "Grant Mostioche," he whispered behind a smile as the men waved back. "Such a dolt. I just finished reading his latest script. It'll be another bomb but he's still under contract. Hopefully this will be it and I won't have to see his shallow little face around here again. What are *those* horrible little things?"

"Artichokes."

"So how did it go this morning?"

"Fine. But I'm still stiff from lying there so long."

Frank saw the pout coming. "There now, it's almost over. And I told you right from the get go it wouldn't be easy. And we didn't know they'd have to shoot the scene again and again, did we?" He leaned closer and whispered. "That insipid little rodent Delilah Morrison! Did you know that's her real name? Delilah? I just don't know why she doesn't take the time to learn to say the medical terms properly. How can anyone mispronounce internal hemorrhaging wrong so often? They wouldn't have to shoot the same scene so many times if she'd only learn to read. Well, I guess I do know why." He gave Lydia the upward eye like a teenager. "I think she'd do the script girl if she had to. But you played dead just perfectly." Another air kiss. "How's your back?"

"Sore." She pulled her dress down from her shoulder.

Frank gasped. "Oh, that's simply awful."

Lydia smiled, feigning indifference. "Yes, it takes them hours. My whole back is like that. I was supposed to be stabbed dozens of times. *Really*."

"I was talking to Werner. He says the stills are done."

"For the board in the police room, where they put up all their notes and photographs and connect them with little lines?"

A nod, and half the cigarette crushed out. Frank immediately lit another after a quick cough. As usual, his suit would have looked much better if he'd spent a little more money, then had it properly tailored. He had an off shape to begin with, and his paunch seemed to be getting bigger every time Lydia saw him. The pinstripes hadn't helped make him look thinner. He'd started a goatee, which was just totally wrong.

"You look good." He leaned over and kissed her lightly on the shoulder before she pulled the dress back up.

"Frank, --"

"Your body looks nice even when you're dead."

Lydia pierced an artichoke heart. "Do they still need me this afternoon?"

"One or two more shots."

"I can't move at all, you know. God, death makes you tense."

"No problems though? You're sure you can finish?"

"Of course. But that new lighting man makes my skin crawl."

"The guy with the funny hair? Long on top with the sides shaven?"

"Uh-huh. *Really* Frank. He waits around and just gawks until I'm on the set and I take off my robe and lie down in the grass. It's creepy."

"Never mind him."

"You'd think he'd never seen a naked woman before."

"Probably not one as beautiful as you." Frank waved at someone else walking by who didn't seem to recognize him.

"Have you heard anything about the other parts yet?"

"You know everything takes time, Lydia. But I keep after them, you know that. You wanted a good agent, and you got one."

She nodded.

"The *'People's Verdict'* thing is a done deal, though. Did I tell you that already?"

"Yes. First row, right?"

"Now remember. You'll have to look really interested and serious. That's what they need. But don't take anything away from the plaintiff or the defendant. Nod a lot, like you're weighed down by the evidence that you're struggling with the momentous responsibility of what's happening all around you."

Lydia imagined herself in the role. She'd only made it to the back row before. This time she'd be sitting up right in front of the camera.

"And I've got something else on the go, too." A quick wink.

"What?"

"Two things, actually."

"Come on, what?"

"I don't want to say yet, in case it doesn't all come together."

"No." Lydia was adamant. "Tell me anyway."

"Lydia --"

"Please Frank."

He made a show of checking his watch. "Well actually, I should hear something later this afternoon about one of the parts. Maybe we could have some dinner, talk about it then."

Dinner. Lydia knew what that meant. Cloying talk, over-priced food she couldn't eat anyway, too much wine, and a constant battle to parry his officious groping attempts.

"They'll want to meet you first."

Lydia knew what that meant, too. "Sure. Sure Frank, that sounds fine."

"'Anthony's? Tonight, say eightish?"

"Yes, they should have all the scars off by then." *Just in time for some new ones*, she thought. For some reason she was feeling quite bitter.

"Great. Got to go now, so I can straighten everything out."

Lydia looked down at her salad.

Frank paused theatrically. "This could be a big break, Lydia."

When he said that before her eyes used to brighten. But there was always one more part, one more crowd scene, that had to be done first. She was getting tired of all the waiting now, and as the days passed and her part didn't change, she was thinking more and more about going home. For good. Could she salvage what was left of her marriage?

"Do you really think so?" Lydia asked wearily. She'd reached the point where she never really wanted to let the promise of the next opportunity gain too much of a foothold. It was less of a fall that way. Frank leaned over conspiratorially like he always did whenever he wanted to impart great importance to what he had to say.

"This one's a good piece, Lydia. Three or four clear shots of you, facials, with lip-synched dialogue. And Leo Gorman's sitting in the director's chair."

"Gorman? So it's a music video?" Her eyes really did begin to sparkle. She'd always wanted to do a music video so she'd have a chance to *act*. "What's the part? Is there any dancing? I'm not the *mother* or anything like that, am I?"

"I'm not sure about the dancing. All I've been told so far is it has something to do with sea nymphs or sirens, that sort of thing. The band playing on some deserted island after a shipwreck. I think there's a monster or two as well."

Lydia sat back with a sigh and pictured herself as a half-naked nymph coming out of the water, pulling back her long, flowing hair, the sun glistening off her breasts, the camera in so close it practically touched her skin. Suddenly, the salad seemed appetizing again, but she didn't want to eat it. She touched her stomach: if she hurried, she could spend a half hour on the incline board over at the gym before the afternoon shooting.

"But that's not the big one." Frank threw his cigarette away and gathered in his breath. Lydia's heart skipped a beat.

What could possibly be bigger than a rock video?

"Michael Cordel."

Lydia didn't remember the name.

"D . . . T . . . T," he whispered. Frank enunciated each letter so slowly he almost wheezed. "Day time television. Maybe something recurring."

"No!"

He nodded.

"You're serious!"

"But don't say anything or get your hopes up too much just yet. There's still some details."

Details. That meant other girls could do the part. She glanced up as another golf cart whizzed by using the stage hands as pylons. No. Not this time. *Focus*, she thought. There were no other girls. It was *her part*, and only *hers.* No one was going to take it away from her this time. *Day time television!* She thought about Mathew, how proud he'd be. Lydia absently speared another forkful of salad but she was too nervous to scoop it up from the container. Her hands were shaking, and for some strange reason, the cuts on her back almost seemed real.

"Lydia?"

"Oh, I'm sorry."

"So eightish?"

"Yes, I'll be there, Frank. And Frank. Thanks."

She kissed him on the cheek, and then watched him walk hurriedly away. He talked and shook hands with as many people as he could but never stopped moving. Lydia stared at the remnants of the salad, then crunched up the little plastic container and threw it in a garbage can that was supposed to be just for bottles. She didn't have to eat it now; there was always an endless hierarchy of other sacrifices that were much more important.

What was one more?

***

10:00:21

It seems like ages since we talked. I luv u I luv u I luvvv u

10:01:17

Any time I don't hear from you is 2 long, Cybernician. The project's done. Don't know how much more I could have pt into it.

10:02:02
I'm glad yur finly finished. Maybe you can relax a bit.

10:03:01
Right! They'll have me snowed under by nex wek. The powers-that-be dont think nerds sleep. Stop worrying, Cybernician. No. On second thought, keep worrying. Just not 2 much.

10:05:37
I always worry because yur *out* so much. It frightens me. I wish ther was somthin I cud do to make you safer.

10:07:06
Pretty soon we'll have micros implantd fur satelite tracking anyway. How's everyone there?

10:08:10
Hard to say. Grandma's acting weird. Don't se her much and hr notes are all scrawld. She's frustrated about something. Mom's well . . . mom. Joshua was telling me about being an architec again, how he was just getting interested in feng-shui before he di -- well, you know. And something's up with Dad. Talk about weirded out.

10:08:58
Why?

10:09:13
Not sur. But hes not riht. He just passes thru the house, lik hes ther, but not ther, if u kno what I mean. He stares out the window like before, just longer. You can see the ache in his eyes.

10:10:22
Mybe its becuse yur moms awy so much. Or it's some kind of mid-life crisis.

10:10:59
Posibly. But I think its mor than that. He's so preoccupyd. He misses notes. Meals too. He spends alot of time with Granddd.

10:12:01
Have u tryd to get him to talk?

10:12:45
I wouldn kno what to say.

10:12:55
Try. Mabe he just needs somone to listen.

10:13:33
Mabe. But I have this funny feeling, Sheila, that something's going to change. I think --

10:14:10
What?

10:14:22
I think he's thinking about leaving mom.

10:14:51
No! Rely?

10:15:18
Well, shes rarly home any more, and wen she is, shes alwas rehersing for the nex part that will make her famous. They don't do anything together, and they never share anything like we do. She misses everything. I'm not sur whats left in the relationship fr either of them.

10:15:59
What a horrible price to pay stardom. But wanting to leve. That must be a hard decision for your Dad to make. He pretty well runs the household. When do you think it starts?

10:16:17
What do you mean?

10:16:50
When do you start thinking you should leve a relationship? Is it one litle thing after a whole lot of litle things, or is it 1 big catastrofe that changes yur percepshun of everything?

10:17:29
I guess it depends on the relashunship. But it must be terrible the first time you start thinking about ending a long term comitment. The first moment u admit 2 yurself that something's wrong, that life has to change. There's no erasing that thoht. No 'going back'.

10:19:00
Do you think there's a moment when you actually fall out of love?

10:19:59
No, I don't. I think it's more of a realization, an understanding, that hadn't been there before. I hope you never come to that moment with me.

10:20:55
O, Cybernician! Don't even think about such a thing. You know I love you with all my heart. If your parents separate, where will you go?

10:21:37
I dont kno.

10:22:52
Mybe that would be the perfect opportunity to take the nex step. The time fr us 2 meet . . . in the world.

10:23:29
I don't want to meet you in the world just because I'm afraid of being by myself

10:24:29
We'll have to meet one day, Cybernician.

10:29:02
I know, Sheila, but it still frightens me. The world. At the same time, thou, I cant imagin a day withot u. I dont kno how 2 pepel cu ever b closer without actually *being the same person.* I keep thinking about the image in one of John Donne's poms where he symbolizes two lovers as points on a compass.

10:31:31
A sundial? I don't understand.

10:31:59
No, not that kind. The kind you draw circles with in math. The ones with thin, adjustable, pointed legs. Donne saw two lovers as the legs of the compass.

10:33:33
Because they had parallel lives, and he saw that as parallel existences? Parallel loves?

10:34:01
Partly. But one foot of the compass always stays in one place while the other circles it endlessly. The same path, the same arc. They can never be separated; there's a finite distance the legs can be apart. Symbolically, they can never be completely separated because they're two parts of a whole. Each completes the other. And the *circle* is obviously a symbol of eternity.

10:37:39
And a symbol of love.

10:38:15
Sure. But the image of the compass also captures the inherent loneliness of the individual, the separateness of the human condition, since the compass legs can never share the same

point. They can't be separated, but they can never be in the same place, at the same time, together. They can be close forever, eternally dependent, but never be completely *one*.

10:41:51
That's kind of sad.

10:42:17
Life is sad, Sheila. But I don't see Donne's image as negative. The compass legs signify one of the main goals in life. To be as close and supportive as we can to the person we love, to be as close as we physically and spiritually can without sharing the exact same point in existence. I've never loved anyone as much as I love you. If something happened to you, Sheila, I'd be one half of a compass. Handicapped without your love.

10:44:03
Plese dont think lik that. Nothing's going 2 hapen to me. Or 2 u.

10:44:50
It still makes me queasy.

10:45:22
O, Cybernician! Then come and meet me in the rel world while we stil have time and its not 2 lat.

10:46:20
Im afrad.

10:47:13
Then be afrad with me, Cybernician.

10:48:00
Il try.

10:49:55

Pleas. Listn. Id luv 2 talk 2 u more, but I have 2 go. I have a meeting at 9:00 to revu the Datascope projec. Will u think abot me tonit, Cybernician? And think abot hw much I luv u?

10:50:59
I always do.

10:53:13

And try nt 2 fel sad. Everything will wrk out, youl se. Now dont go sitting there and thinking bad thouts in the drk. Put your glasses on the se table, take your gloves off, and think about all the wonderful times we've shared and how much we love each other. And think about us together, out in the real world.

10:55:00
I will.

10:55:24
I love you, Cybernician

10:56:01

I love you, too. Maybe that's it though, Sheila. Maybe I'm afraid of loving you too much. And it hurts. And I'll bet you that at some point or another, everyone says something almost the exact same as that. *I'll love you forever. I'll never leave you. You're my one and only.* And yet so many relationships die out. What comfort is there in that?

10:59:59
O my Cybernician, all we can do, all we can –

11:02:03

I saw something the other day by Orson Wells that I just can't stop thinking about, my love, and it seems so wonderful and so horrible at the same time.
We're born alone
We live alone

We die alone
Only through our love and friendship
Can we create the illusion for
Just a moment
That we're not alone.

Chapter Twelve

"What do *you* think, granddad?"

Perched in his chair by the window, Lorne stared down at another time he saw in his lap. Another *Lorne*. His dark blue flannel pajamas were imprinted with little designs Carmalitta couldn't quite make out. Animals? Impossible. Abstract sketches? Maybe, because wasn't he one himself? Dinner was long past, the meerkat was gone, and he had no idea what had happened to Eleanor. Someone had combed his hair across the top of his head so he looked wind-blown. Or like Jack Nicolson in *The Shining*. For the hundredth and second time, Carmalitta wondered what it was like living everywhere else but here. Or living here, but not knowing it. In the here and now. She tugged her legs up beneath her on the edge of the bed.

"Were you ever jealous of Grandma?"

His nostrils flared. A thought, or a dust mote swirling on some unseen current?

"Hasn't she ever given you cause for concern, something to worry about, in all these years?"

His reflection was frozen in the window. Outside, early evening darkness rippled shadows over the backyard. Somewhere off in the distance, but not too far away, a couple of dogs barked back and forth, with obviously unconcerned owners.

"If she had been unfaithful, do you think you would have wanted to stay with her? *Could* you have stayed?"

Was he answering, somewhere?

"And if she never actually cheated on you, what kinds of things would have made you jealous, anyway? Her friends? The things she wore? The things she did or didn't do?"

Granddad was resolutely still. One of his nose hairs was so long it had started to blend in perfectly with his moustache. Carmalitta got the little pair of cuticle scissors from his bedside table drawer and deftly removed the offending hair. Lorne didn't so much as blink.

Carmalitta leaned back onto the bed and closed her eyes. A few labored breaths and she was back in the shower at Miriam's little apartment after dinner the other night, the water steaming off her skin and her lover's arms wrapped tightly around her stomach and chest. They stood together without moving for several minutes as rivulets of warmth coursed between them, thinking, dreaming, imagining. Miriam's hands never stopped moving. She kissed Carmalitta's shoulders, her back, along her spine, and then buried her face softly in the sweetness of her neck.

"Why not?" she purred. Her fingertips traced circles through the soft, silky hairs on Carmalitta's belly. "Look how long it took us to get back here, to the burbs. If we lived there, right downtown, we would have been home hours ago. Sitting out on the solarium with a glass of wine, staring out at the lake." Miriam's hands moved up higher as she pictured them in the imaginary condominium in the sky that was waiting for them to be built. "Naked."

Carmalitta arched back and let her lovers' hands mold to the contours of her breasts.

"We could slip down for a swim later or play some squash. Exercise in the training room. Read in the library. Park *underground,* and let the concierge worry about security."

Miriam squeezed Carmalitta's breasts together and held her nipples up to the pulsing water. Token resistance, nothing more. An almost soundless *aahhh.*

"No more paying rent or board. No quick dashes along the hall so obtuse, ignorant neighbors don't have anything to gossip about. All the shopping we need just a short walk away, and core gay clubs we can go to and hold hands and do whatever we want without everyone staring." *Whatever we want.*

Miriam played her trump card. "Minutes to work, so tomorrow we could *sleep in.*"

Carmalitta managed a murmur as the warm water pulsed against her nipples and slowly filtered down between her breasts. *Sleep in.* A siren's irresistible song.

"Oh, it sounds wonderful, Miriam. And I know it makes financial sense, and that it would give us so much more time together."

Miriam knew there was a caveat buried in there somewhere.

"But I'm not sure --"

"You're still not sure you want to make a commitment to me. Isn't that it?" She flicked her fingers lightly over Carmalitta's nipples so they harden painfully, then pulled her hands away.

Carmalitta gently pulled Miriam's hands back up to her breasts, and sighed. "You know how much I love you."

"Oh, I know you love me. You just don't want to share your life with me."

"Miriam --"

But she was already sliding the shower door back and stepping out into the foggy coldness of the bathroom. The steam occluded the glass, but she watched Carmalitta's shadow stand beneath the water and wash her fear away. By the time the last trail of water swirled down the drain, Miriam was out in the living room, wrapped up warmly in her robe, and was on her third martini. The night was over.

Carmalitta opened her eyes and leaned up on one arm. She stared intently at her grandfather, but she couldn't remember him as he used to be. *Would she ever?* He used to take her to the park and push her on the swings. They'd hunt for stones at the little pond's edge, and he'd always be ready to catch her at the bottom of the slide. He walked her to school when she was little, and never missed a play or band recital in all the years Carmalitta had a part. What part did she play in his life now? Her thoughts drifted back to Miriam. Finally, their own home. It sounded wonderful and stifling at the same time, with the stability that can give so much comfort, but make you age so quickly, too.

What was she afraid of? The commitment and all the things it meant? Or was she simply still jealous, still unable to reconcile her fears and insecurities? She thought about all the young, beautiful women that Miriam came in contact with every day. How she saw them, touched them. She wasn't sure if she'd ever feel completely comfortable with that. Is possessiveness something you actually outgrow, or does it simply change and become something else, something less aggressive and controlling? Like over-protectiveness, perhaps. Or do you reach a point where you're just numbed by so much incessant worry that it doesn't matter anymore? The nagging doubt she'd fought so often before crept back. Was it her own jealousy she was afraid of, or did the real fear lie deeper? *Did she really want a man?*

For an instant, Carmalitta had the unmistakable and unnerving feeling that her grandfather had moved. She shifted forward and waited. Nothing. She waited a little longer. She must have seen his reflection in the window. She was always waiting for something. Something she couldn't even define in her weakest, most frustrated moments. How long, she wondered, would Miriam wait?

Carmalitta knew she could rationalize herself into a stalemate. She was sure she could trust Miriam, yet she had enough training and psychological expertise to know that doctors and psychologists weren't immune from falling from the pedestal of objectivity and into the labyrinth of emotions and fears that confuse any relationship. Priests, jail guards, police, teachers. Physical therapists. What you are doesn't change when you put on some uniform. She couldn't help wondering what Miriam was thinking when she massaged the graceful, powerful legs of some gorgeous swimmer, or kneaded a cramp from some beautiful Olympic hopeful's chest or thigh.

Carmalitta remembered a slice of time long ago. Her best male friend in grade six was Maurice Jacobean, a small, wiry child with unruly hair, features that bordered on effeminate, thin lips, and hazel eyes that were always hiding something. They met at the chess club a teacher ran at lunch time. Maurice didn't like the rough and tumble play that defined his peers, and despite his father's repeated attempts to force him to play something physical, he abhorred any sport that required teams or the potential of being hurt. A bright, motivated child, he was a natural at chess. So was Carmalitta, although no matter how often she played, she was never comfortable sacrificing a pawn for some future, undetermined greater good.

Maurice had two goals in life: one, always deep inside, was an overwhelming desire to become a doctor. The second would take longer: he wanted to get laid. Both things clung to his mind like maggots on a decaying body; feeding, eating deeper, festering and growing larger.

It was Maurice who blurted out the ins and outs of sex to Carmalitta one lazy lunch period when they were both hunched over the board, and a half-dozen men on each side were recalcitrant on-lookers. Carmalitta couldn't recall why they'd even been talking about it in the first place. But then again, it was just about the only thing other than stethoscopes and diseases on Maurice's mind. He was absolutely amazed Carmalitta's parents hadn't imparted the wondrous, secret knowledge to their daughter.

He tried to explain things as best he could without laughing or teasing, but Carmalitta wasn't getting the *whole picture*. Health class obviously hadn't helped prepare her for the *granting of knowledge*, the *passing of the big secret*.

The job of health education was given to Miss Rogerson by default, since the part-time nurse the school had originally hired seemed to get quite . . . well, quite *agitated* when she used the anatomically correct dummy. And whispered comments over coffees in the teachers' lounge suggested she liked to use the dummy to a point that wasn't deemed appropriate. She'd even given it a pet name. Everyone assumed the name referred to the *whole* dummy, but no one knew for sure.

Miss Rogerson had probably never done *it* in her life. At the same time, with someone else. She was forty-eight but already pushing sixty, with loose skin on her face that hung in folds that made her look like she was melting. Thick glasses, grey hair, and more wrinkles than a Shar-Pei. Worst of all, she had heavy, muscle-less arms, and great huge bags of jiggling fat trembled uncontrollably each time she wrote something on the board.

She was uncomfortable but tried her best. She used diagrams, overheads, books, pamphlets, guest speakers, movies, video shorts, hospital footage, and blurry chalk drawings on the green blackboard that she erased as soon as they were finished so the janitors wouldn't come in at lunch and embellish them with officious little doodles. Miss Rogerson wanted to help the children as much as she could, but she didn't want to tell them *everything*. She felt that was a job for the parents or older siblings. She did explain the miracle of birth, how the egg grows, how many sperm die on their long journey of hope, how young boys' and girls' bodies change as they get older. None of the girls could imagine Miss Rogerson with hair *down there*. Did it hurt? Tickle when she pulled her panties on? If everything their older brothers and sisters told their underlings that people actually did couldn't that kind of hair poke you in the eye?

Although Miss Rogerson categorically refused to acknowledge the more guttural references many of the boys ascribed to body parts and their functions, it was important to her to ensure that her charges were aware of all the proper names of the things she talked about. This troubled some parents to no end. But she knew that it was usually those same parents that used words like *wee- wee, thing, privates, do-do,* and *love nest* that never seemed to have time to talk to their children about procreation, sexually transmitted diseases, or condoms. The girls in those families often believed a baby came right after she lay down on a couch with a boy. Later, when that proved untrue, that if she swallowed semen she might get pregnant *because the sperm things are still getting inside her, aren't they?*

So Miss Rogerson always said *penis, vulva, vagina, labia, scrotum,* or *glans*, which titillated the students to no end and reduced the shyest ones practically to tears. Maurice loved it. He chanted the words like a mantra, rolled them diligently over his tongue, held them in his mind's eye, caressed them with his very being. They were the last thing he thought of at night and the first words that broke through the shadowy veil of his sleep.

Miss Rogerson wanted the children to understand the words, but she never actually told them how the words were figuratively *combined*. Like many sex educators back then, she felt it was enough that the children understand what happens *before* and *after*, but not *during*. The sperm fertilize the egg: fine. But the process of the sperm's introduction was better left unsaid. Besides, if she started talking about *during*, then the dummy invariably started becoming more interesting to Miss Rogerson, too.

Maurice leaned closer over the board. In a Freudian slip that would remain in the nether world of his unconscious and haunt him dogmatically for many, many years, Maurice almost picked up the king and a bishop, but he corrected himself just in time and grabbed the king and queen. He held them together, face first, then rocked them up and down. The frown stayed on Carmalitta's face.

Maurice pointed to the place the king's *penis* would be, then ran his finger over the queen's *vagina.* He held them back together again, and this time, he even added moans and grunting sounds between breaths. But Carmalitta just sat there, still feeling rather incomplete, and stared down at her own king and queen.

Maurice quickly became exasperated. It was his favorite subject of all time, and Carmalitta wasn't saying anything. He took the queen in one hand, the king in the other, and gestured to their sexual organs with his eyes.

"The man's penis gets hard," he whispered, feeling an odd pulse somewhere below his waist. "He puts it right inside the woman's vagina."

Carmalitta's face contorted into a painful grimace. And then Maurice did something she never forgot. He made a circle with the first finger and thumb of his left hand, then extended the middle finger on his right. He held them aloft for a moment like a magician confirming to an audience he's holding *two separate rings,* then rammed his finger furiously back and forth through the hole. Then he turned the chess pieces together again and banged their bottom halves together.

Carmalitta knew the sperm came out somewhere from the man's penis (the side? directly from the testicles? osmosis?), and that the woman had eggs somewhere deep inside her body (like a hen?), so it wasn't a great leap of understanding for a bright young girl to finally assimilate the disparate parts she'd understood before and put them into a unified whole. She nodded appreciatively and noticed her mouth had become painfully dry. Truth inflamed her eyes like a lighthouse beacon. The men who'd been half-heartedly watching the match backed away in stitches, hands over their mouths, tears in their eyes.

"Get it?"

Another slow nod. She *got it*. But Carmalitta knew at that moment that she never really wanted to *get it* at all. Ever. Period. Maybe once, just to see, but that was it. Nothing seemed more disgusting and gross.

The old *finger-stabbing-through-the-circle* gesture was something Maurice loved to perform. He did it all the time, whenever or wherever he could. He used that little action the same way many people use *fuck*; as a noun, verb, point of exclamation, a command, a warning, an adjective, a threat. Instead of saying *fuck off*, Maurice would show his target his hands, and then perform his little ritual. Rather than say *I'd like to get into her* when some older woman who was at least twenty-five strolled past a group of his friends on a Saturday morning at the mall, Maurice jabbed his finger through the magic hole and rolled his eyes upward. He did it so much he was fortunate that he never broke his finger.

As the school years faded by, Maurice's preoccupation turned into an obsession, and, like many unconscious conflicts, was eventually acted out in a more socially acceptable way. *Sublimation*. Although he never managed to get laid even when he was at university, even though he was in a co-ed dorm, Maurice fulfilled his primary desire and became a doctor. In fact, he went on to become one of Toronto's leading gynecologists.

Carmalitta pictured Maurice: clean shaven, white coat, tie, just dry-cleaned slacks, stethoscope, his breast pocket filled with script pads, lights and pens.

"Yes, and how are we today Mrs. Keever? Good. Now lift yourself up a little higher, and keep your feet right there in the stirrups. I'm just going to have a little look."

Every woman who came to see Dr. Jacobsen knew they never had to be embarrassed when he looked and probed *down there* because he was a doctor and it didn't mean anything to him at all.

So, knowing what she knew about Dr. Jacobsen, how could Carmalitta really believe that Miriam was always objective and consummately professional in her work? Carmalitta didn't care in the least that her lover spent a great deal of time with men. Pool side, watching their sleek torsos skim through the water. Hairless for speed, strong shoulders, flat stomachs, their bums tight and muscular in the tiny Speedos, their bulging manhood framed in front. And then later, glistening in the hot tub or up on an examination table, barely covered with a small white towel, as she massaged the cramp from a shoulder or stretched out a tightened tendon in a calf.

But what did Miriam think when she was with the women? What did she feel? Miriam didn't just see them in the pool, or stretching from side to side on the deck, their slim one-piece suits tight and almost transparent over their shaven sex. She saw them in the change room too, and in the showers, laughing and joking with each other, their taut bodies covered in a soapy lather, their hair sleek and wet, their nipples hard beneath the warm pulse of water streaming down their skin.

And after she'd seen them there, naked, exposed, vulnerable and unaware of her darting glances, Miriam would be waiting for them when they wandered into the fitness and rehab room, tussling their hair or retying a towel around their waist.

Tense shoulders? Stiffness in the lower back? A strained muscle beneath the scapula, or a hamstring that refused to loosen? A pulled groin? No problem. Just lie there and relax, let the warm oils start to work. Let me run my hands all over you, up and down the soft contours of your body, kneading, probing, exploring. Spread your legs a little more so I can loosen those knotted muscles of your inner thighs.

Carmalitta felt her body tighten. She looked up at the statue that was her grandfather.

Was she afraid of making a commitment to Miriam because of her jealousy, or was she right, and her jealousy was just one doll inside another, hiding something deeper? Buying an apartment together meant two things to Miriam: permanence and the expectation of children. Carmalitta didn't know what she feared more.

She stretched back down onto the bed, and listened to her grandfather start to snore. Quiet at first, then louder, more strained. What was the difference when he was asleep, or awake? Did he really hear things, or think about people or times or fears or things that still hid in the past? Or were they lost to him, forever? Carmalitta didn't want to end up sitting in a chair by the window. But she didn't want to live a life where jealousy constantly crept in to everything she did.

She thought about her parents. About the lives Joshua had lived. About Mich – Cybernician never being able to meet the person he thought was the love of his life. She wished to God that she knew for certain whether she'd ever have another chance at life or not.

Carmalitta started thinking about Rory, and hoped Mrs. Tomlinson's cat wasn't deliberately provoking the old woman or giving her any problems. Everyone had a breaking point, and Mrs. Tomlinson wasn't far from reaching hers.

Chapter Thirteen

Everything had started out so perfectly.

Mathew hated the Don Valley Parkway, the main artery that wound its way into downtown Toronto. Early planners must have thought 'one city, one main road', which, unfortunately, didn't work over an extended period of time. The lanes seemed overly close together and there was virtually nowhere to go if anyone swerved out of control or had a heart attack at the wheel, because the winding little speedway didn't have shoulders. One little mistake and the Parkway could be tied up in knots for hours. Construction on the Don Valley Parkway was normally heavy, especially in the spring when the damage that the long Canadian winter had done to the asphalt with intermittent attacks of ice and snow finally became apparent. Yet today, the traffic had been minimal, especially for a Friday morning, and the drive was mercifully short.

Mathew had also managed to find some parking fairly near the museum. The lot was just off a narrow side street north of Bloor on Avenue Road, and since the cost would be under twenty-five dollars, Mathew believed he'd come away relatively unscathed. Joshua and his father were dressed in jeans, moccasins, and matching denim shirts, a sense of familiarity Mathew found quite comforting. There hadn't been the usual chain-gang of school buses parked out front, and the lady in the foyer kiosk had graciously offered to put his coat *and Joshua's* on the same hanger and only charge him for one. When Mathew thought about it later, he knew he should have had an inkling that something was wrong when the security guard stopped them on their way in. They'd lathered their hands with a lightly scented lotion from the ever-present canister when the guard told him he had to wear the little pin he received when he'd paid for the admissions.

Mathew argued his right to go pinless, but the security guard simply shrugged. He obviously couldn't understand the problem. It was just a little circular pin shaped like a miniature frying pan with the first initials of the Royal Ontario Museum emblazoned on the front. The handle on the frying pan folded back so it could clip to just about anything. But wearing the pin wasn't the problem for Mathew; it was the fact that someone else had worn it before. There was a large glass container in front of the museum's exit doors where you could throw your pin on your way out. The frying pan handles would be re-straightened and the pins could be reused another day.

Mathew had always been pro-recycling, and was aware that most of it made sense. But he also knew he'd never know who had worn the little pin before he did. Or how many times the thing had been used. Anyone could have used it. Maybe their shirt was dirty. Perhaps they didn't wash their hands after they used the bathroom, then touched their pin. What if they had some communicable disease? Or head lice? Didn't use the dispensers? Under the steady gaze of the security guard, Mathew finally clipped the ROM pin to the cuff on the bottom of his pants. The man glared indignantly, garbled some warning, and finally stepped aside.

No matter how often he came to the museum, years melted away and Mathew was a boy again the instant he stood in the central foyer and looked up at the ornate cathedral ceiling that seemed to go on forever. But Joshua wasn't interested in ceilings: he wanted to find the dinosaurs. He tugged on Mathew's arm, then bounded up the broad staircase that twisted skyward from the main floor. The steps spiraled around a huge totem pole that went up and down for several floors like some giant vampire stake stabbed through the museum's heart.

Mathew followed Joshua as quickly as he could, but the winding steps and the irresistible urge to stay focused on the intricate patterns carved into the totem pole confounded his balance and made him nauseous. He almost fell. He grabbed the railing and waited for the sudden dizziness to pass, then joined the boy at the top of the stairs.

Joshua was a babbling tour guide that chain-smoked questions: the instant he finished one he fired up another. *What's that? When did they live? How'd they get so big? Do you have to dig real deep to get that kind of stuff?* Mathew wasn't concerned that Joshua didn't wait for his feeble replies, because he didn't know many answers anyway if he didn't have time to read the little information cards imbedded in glass alongside the displays. But Joshua loved the museum's unanswered secrets just the same, and scurried from room to room with unbridled awe and excitement. Mathew thought he'd slow down eventually but there was simply too much to see. As soon as Joshua stepped into one room he was anticipating the next. They crossed epochs and continents, sciences and peoples.

When he finally paused long enough to take a breath, it wasn't the little boy in the matching jeans and denim shirt who stopped near a collection of broken pots and cups carefully sequenced through time, it was someone else. "Joshua" was gone. The change happened so fast that Mathew hadn't had time to react. One minute they were looking at an early Mesopotamian burial site recently unearthed and rendered before them with life-size figures in a glass case, and the next, Joshua swayed as if he was going to faint, screamed, and took off so fast a toddler nearby fell in the *whooosh* of his wake. Joshua zigzagged hysterically through Ancient Egypt, the Pleistocene period, half of the new Arctic explorers exhibit, and then along a narrow corridor that immortalized the predators and prey of the African savannah before he finally collapsed behind a makeshift wall that enclosed something 'under construction.'

When Mathew found him, his son was laying on the floor in front of one of the little windows that looked out onto University Avenue. Joshua wasn't gulping for air any longer, but he was still out of breath. His face was red and perspiration beaded on his neck. Although he'd taken a less circuitous route as frightened bystanders directed him on with quickly pointed arms, Mathew was huffing and puffing as well when he slumped down onto the vinyl bench. He waved an inquisitive little child away and tried to help Joshua sit up beside him. The boy was a dead weight, and it took Mathew ages to drag him onto the couch. When Joshua finally slumped back against the glass, Mathew looked outside while he waited for his heart rate to return to normal. An idling truck belched black smoke into the air. Behind it, an orange school bus jerked to a stop. A rampant horde of frenzied children was already pouring out before the frazzled driver had time to fully open the doors. Joshua watched them too, but Mathew could see they'd become something else for his son and that Joshua was really looking past them. Way past them. Beyond them. His eyelids fluttered – his *other* eyelids.

Mathew spoke carefully, trying to remember what they'd been looking at before the boy disappeared. "What did you see, Joshua?"

Joshua stared blankly at the waves of children besieging the museum's steps. He spoke without blinking, his voice deep and resonating, his words uttered with the cadence of someone unhurried. "They stick together and attack like the marcher barons."

"Who?"

Silence. Then softly, "The marcher barons."

"Who were the marcher barons, Joshua?"

"Rich landowners who controlled the border lands between England and Wales, from Chester in the north to Chepstow in the south. Usually they were independent, but many were trying to lay to rest the petty feuds that had long divided them. We knew if they united together and linked their lands they'd be able to stop the flow of supplies into Wales. They'd strangle us."

Mathew whispered. "Who are you?"

"Owain ap Rhys."

Mathew gulped and glanced around to make sure no one was listening. "ap Rhys?"

Joshua looked proud and sad. "Owain. Son of Rhys."

So, Mathew thought, he had another father. "Were you at war? When was this?"

Owain looked tired and exasperated. "Ever since the 1300's. We'd fought for years, harassing them with sudden attacks and hide-and-seek ambushes they couldn't counter. The tactic had always favored us, since the barons were reluctant to be dragged into battles that were nothing more than an endless series of short skirmishes and secret attacks."

"And you?"

Owain sneered. "The English branded me a Welsh rebel, but I was just one man, an aspiring bard, one man in many who only wanted freedom."

"And the barons? They were trying to stop you?"

Owain nodded. Mathew glanced around the museum alcove, wishing he'd had more of an interest in history at school. "So they succeeded in banding together?"

"Yes. The invasion was being directed by a more patient and determined court in London that wanted to crush the rebellion once and for all. The marcher lords jumped at the chance to rally behind the King's call for an all-out war. They were to move slowly, piercing through our defenses, then mass together for a full assault at Llangollen. Once they combined their troops on our side of the border, they'd lay siege to the Welsh stronghold of Mount Snowdon without fear of counter attack. The English would control the supplies coming into Wales and could easily wait us out. The death knell of the uprising would sound, choking the song of Welsh freedom from the heart of the forests and valleys."

"Why were you there, Owain?"

Another bus rolled to a stop behind the first one. More children oozed out onto the street, flowing up the steps like a multicolored amoebae.

"My father was killed at Llandudno, near the castle at Conwy, where the land juts out into a gentle point in the sea. That year, the English forces had been striking out from Wrexham, deeper and deeper into the Welsh North Country. My Da led a small group of men to a hilltop post overlooking the town. Hidden behind the rocks, they watched the ships that plied the coastal waters between the seaside ports of Rhyl and Bangor, ferrying men and supplies to the English troops. He knew the English were preparing something big, that he had to get word to the Council. But they had a traitor in their midst. A small band of English troops overwhelmed them as soon as they left. They all perished."

Owain clutched the edge of the couch until his knuckles were bone white. "I grew into a fierce fighter, loyal to Prince Llewellyn and Wales. I was good with a dagger and better with a bow, but my speed with a sword struck fear into the hearts of men throughout the valleys. Even the English knew me well, since the rebel band I led in my father's place took many of the barons' men."

"Were you getting ready to fight?"

Owain shook his head. "I carried a letter for our defenses. I'd slain a secret messenger and fled the guards defending Sir Rutherford's castle at Shrewsbury several nights before. Sealed with wax by the King himself, it detailed the English troops' plans and movements for the coming months. I had to get it to the Prince."

"How far did you have to go?"

Owain's eyes misted and his voice was barely above a whisper. "I was still a day away. The forest was so thick with trees it was hard to see the sky. I remember running, the kind that takes your breath away and makes you think your heart will burst. I was soaked in sweat. Branches scratched at my face and arms, and I kept tripping over tangled vines and rotten logs. But I didn't slow down. I finally stopped when I was sure the barons' advance regiment was still back on the English side of the river. The scouting party would be closer; I figured I had about a half day's grace.

"There was no time to rest. The scouting party would fan out once they crossed the river, and it wouldn't be long before they found me again. My only hope was to keep going, to reach the castle at Mount Snowdon, our main fortress.

"I'd ridden for days, racing through the thick glens from Llanfyllin in the Middle Country and up to Bala in the North, pushing my poor steed as hard as I dared. But the pace had been too much for Pendar and she'd come up lame trying to claw her way out of a river I used to cover our tracks. Some of the lords' scouts were Welsh born and bred, and they knew those secretive lands as well as any. They picked up my scent again just south of Swallow Falls and caught up easily, creeping close as I rested under the cloak of night. The stars and moon were hidden with clouds and their weapons didn't fire true, but their arrows found Pendar's flank and neck. He'd flailed and thrashed his legs wildly as he fell, kicking one of the scouts and breaking his leg."

"The poor thing."

Owain nodded. "But Pendar's death saved me. I drew my own bow as the soldiers scrambled for cover, striking two and killing one for certain. I slipped away while the others hid, but not unharmed. One of their arrows pierced my arm just above the elbow. My tunic was covered in blood, and I knew they'd follow the red-black trail in the morning when dawn's light pulled the shroud of secrecy back from the forest. I had to keep on.

"I stopped a few miles north of the Falls. I went there once with my Da when I was still just a chicken-feeder and sword-sharpener to my older brothers. We'd gone to the market in Betws-y-Coed to do some trading, since I was the only one that could do some figures and read a bit, too. We ate by the side of the river as the water splashed over the rocks. Da talked about the rebellion, the battles already waged and the wars that were sure to come. I'd never seen him so intense and afraid. We talked long into the afternoon, then sang songs of old, of castles and kings and queens and dragons that I'd always dreamed about beneath the stars."

Mathew shifted uncomfortably. He never liked hearing about the child's other fathers. "Were you wounded badly?"

Owain shrugged. "The forest was cold and damp despite the morning sun, and the steep hills that framed the valley were covered by a thin grey mantel of fog. I checked to make sure I was still alone, then leaned back against the trunk of a towering oak. A rabbit darted through the underbrush. I unsheathed my dagger and sword. I laid the sword against my knees and balanced the blade between my legs. My shirt tore easily. I remember staring impatiently at the wound, like it was someone else's arm. The arrow had pierced the muscle but the hole seemed clean. If it hadn't been for the feathers the arrow would have gone right through. I snapped the shaft in half."

Mathew felt the nausea coming back. He wanted to reach out and touch Joshua but he couldn't move.

"I sliced off my tunic sleeve and tied it tightly between my elbow and the wound. I braced the sword against the ground so the tip pointed toward my face and squeezed it between my knees. I held my arm up so I could see both sides of the arrow sticking out. I used my dagger to widen the wound further, then probed the exit hole to find the arrow's barbed end."

Owain grimaced and braced his back against the wall. "I leaned forward and took the sword's tip between my teeth. I bit down hard and thought about Geraint, my eldest brother. The King's guards caught him destroying a huge cache of weapons in the castle at Warwick and he'd been beheaded. I held him in my mind and grabbed hold of the broken shaft. With a long, slow push, I rammed the arrow right through until the tip broke free. I yanked straight down and tore the rest of the arrow through my arm."

Owain coughed and stared down at his sleeve. "I was dizzy and weak and my arm was numb below the elbow, but I knew the worst was over. The pain was already throbbing into the past. I was incredibly thirsty, and another scurrying rabbit reminded me of my hunger. But when I wobbled up to my feet, something snapped in the underbrush behind me. I froze."

"More scouts?" Mathew asked anxiously.

A quick nod. "My blood had given them a trail. No horses, so they were on foot. I heard it again: a branch, or the crunch of dead leaves. The sound stopped almost before it began, but I knew it had come from the right, toward the river. There were two, circling from each side, cautious and slow. I couldn't outwait them or fight them together. I leaned out to the left from behind the tree, keeping low. Nothing. I crossed myself quickly and leaned to the right. The man had just started to move.

"He must have seen my shadow because his bow was raised and he released his arrow in a second. But his aim was off and the arrow whizzed past and struck a massive knot above my head. As I rolled to my feet he yelled to his companion and I heard the other man start running. I threw my dagger while the first man drew his bowstring back again. It caught him cleanly through the chest, just below his neck. He quivered and fell forward without a sound, clutching his heart.

"The other soldier saw his partner fall. He screamed a curse of vengeance and charged, his sword brandished above his head. My left arm was bleeding badly and I had no shield. The man attacked in a rage, swinging his sword in vicious broadsides at my head. I felt the puff of wind as the blade tore by, and narrowly managed to thwart the first few blows with my sword. But the man was quick and caught me on the arm before I could drag the useless limb away. It cut deeply, right to the bone, making me scream. I stumbled backward and parried his savage swipes and thrusts, but tired quickly. I couldn't strike back and I knew he smelled my death.

"His next thunderous strike sent me to my knees. I kept my blade raised, but each blow pinned me closer to the ground. He raised his sword for a last strike that would cleave me in two. I grabbed the bloodied hilt of my own weapon and leapt up before his blade fell. I turned as I jumped, exposing my dangling arm as a target. The blade sliced into my flesh, severing the bone beneath my shoulder and tearing the arm apart. There was too much pain to even yell. But I struck the instant the blade fell, stabbing him as hard as I could through the ribs. The sword twisted as it found flesh and I buried the point into his heart. His eyes glazed, and he stared down in horror and disbelief as his weapon fell to the ground. When he clutched at his stomach, blood and pieces of ripped flesh clung to his hands. He stumbled backward and crumpled against the tree.

"I swooned with unimaginable pain as my severed forearm bled into the thick grass, and stared up at the swaying treetops while I listened to the English soldier die. My eyes closed, and I sank into darkness."

Mathew gulped the dryness from his throat. "But ... you lived?"

Owain's lips curled into a half-grin, half-sneer. "I had to. I had the letter. And I could never have let Gwen down."

"Gwen?"

"My love of all time. Twenty-three I was, but I would have given it all back just to see her face before me once more."

"She was your wife?"

Owain ap Rhys' eyes reddened. "She was. And the most wonderful woman in the valley. A voice, oh a voice you had to hear. I loved her as I loved Wales. I was always fighting, planning, going on secret missions deep into England, but she never once left my thoughts. I never regretted what I had to do for my country, but I was always saddened by the times we had to be apart. You usually only have one chance at love, and she was mine."

Mathew shifted uneasily and wondered what Gwen looked like. A love of all time. Wasn't that how he'd always thought about Carol? Had he ever been on some far off battlefield, in a different time or a different place, dreaming of her? Did he have the love that his son knew was more than love, that kind of love that was a very part of his soul? Is that why she was always in his thoughts? Why he'd never been able to let her go?

"When I finally awoke, the glen was shrouded in blackness and a light rain had begun to fall. I struggled to my feet and quickly threw some underbrush over the dead soldiers. I made a fire and let the coals glow orange and red. I laid my dagger in the fire until the blade glistened with sparks, prayed to St. David, then touched the burning blade to the severed end of my arm. The smell was putrid. The blood bubbled as the metal seared the skin, and I struggled to stay conscious. A while later, I tied and flattened the stump of my forearm against my side with a piece of torn cloth, then tucked it tightly inside my tunic. I gained my feet, and using my sword like a staff, started off through the woods. I couldn't run but I loped on as best I could, stopping every few minutes to see if I was being followed. Nothing gave them away, but I knew I wasn't safe.

"It was early morning when I reached the crest of a hill that sloped away to the foothills of Mount Snowdon. It was still raining. I could see the grey stone walls of the outpost tower on the far side of the valley, but at that painful pace it was still a couple of hours away. I bowed my head and thanked our patron saint again. All I had to do was make it down the hill to the edge of the valley where the tower guarded the pass. A runner would take the letter on to the castle, to Llewellyn, and the Welsh defense would be set in motion. If luck was with us we'd have two days' leave before the English troops arrived.

"I stumbled down the hill. It was too late to worry about pursuers; there was no time to hide, no time to wait or move defensively. The edge of the forest was just ahead. All that separated me from the stone sanctuary was a grassy plain littered with rocks and boulders. When I reached the bottom of the valley there'd be no cover at all. No matter what it took I'd have to make it across the grassy knoll as fast as I could. Once they saw me, my companions would give me cover with their bows, but first I had to make it across the uncovered plain.

"I stopped and checked the letter was safely in my tunic's pocket, took one last look at the trees, mouthed a prayer to Gwen, then lunged down the slope toward the outpost. Behind me, farther up on the hill where the fog met the sky, English archers appeared from the trees. I never saw them, but somehow I sensed their presence."

Mathew was rubbing his own arm. He couldn't imagine the pain. Had Gwen felt it, too? "The other scouts must have kept tracking you."

Owain ap Rhys nodded glumly. "I heard the feathers slicing through the air, the arrows twisting on unseen currents. I ducked and weaved, making the first few miss. But then one went cleanly through the left side of my back, the barb poking blood through my chest; the next buried itself just above my waist. A third missed, but it didn't matter. The shock almost lifted me off the ground and I fell spread-eagled into the grass. It was wet from the rain, and softer than I'd ever known it to be before. A partially hidden field mouse hole was just ahead; a small cluster of wildflowers to the right.

"And then I had the strangest and most wonderful feeling that Gwen's lips were on mine. I looked up through the blood. She was always with me when death was close, when I fought, when I slipped through the forests for a melting dawn's raid, when I pierced another man with my dagger, when I loosed my own arrow into the heart of a king's man who was just lifting his own bow towards me. She'd be a pixie, a Welsh sprite, a butterfly. She could take the form of anything magical and blow new life into my heart and soul the moment fear unfurled. An arrow flew past my head, stabbing into the ground of my homeland. And then I saw her more clearly then I'd ever seen her before. Not a dragonfly, but two, entwined, hovering together on see-through wings, humming softly in the wildflowers before me. Her wings, her lips, brushed mine again, softly, softly. I heard another arrow dig into the ground, but the next one found its mark in the center of my back, twisting and digging, making my legs go numb. I thought I saw someone running towards me, so I tried to pull the paper from my belt, but I couldn't move. All I could feel, all that I knew, was my Gwen. But time slowly wrenched her face away, and the morning mist grew so thick I couldn't see the heather in front of me. But oh, the lilacs smelled so wonderful."

Owain ap Rhys' eyes closed and rippled beneath their lids. He coughed like he was trying to spit up blood. Mathew wrapped his arms around his son's shoulders, squeezing him to his side. Where was he when the boy had fallen? Had he been there in the rock-strewn outpost, watching the messenger being cut down, not knowing who he really was? Had he been one of the Prince's runners, and tried to save him? Had Carol been there too, shivering with Gwen behind him in the tower, changing their forms together, one, last, time?

Mathew closed his eyes and waited for Owain ap Rhys to stop shaking and come back from the distant field. If he saw Gwen tomorrow in the street he knew he would know her, just like he'd know Octavious's Lucreatia. He blinked the tears from his eyes, eyes that felt the gentle puff of the dragonflies' wings.

He could smell the wood of the arrows, the heather, the lilacs, the blood.

Chapter Fourteen

The small, round, checker-clothed tables at Anthony's circus were packed with boisterous clusters of animated performers caught in an endless struggle to eclipse each other for attention. It was continuous movement beneath a cacophonous din, like penguins scrounging for mates on some icy promontory as the iceberg floats away and carries them to who-knows-where. Handshakes, knowing winks behind half-closed eyes, secret fraternal gestures, mouthed innuendoes. Names were shouted back and forth as white-aproned waiters hurried by with large scalloped plates barely contaminated with food.

Lydia heard someone call the three stark syllables she was always expecting, and offered a monarchical wave toward the far corner of the room. Her mantra kicked in instinctively: *Slow down. Don't look needy, for God's sake. A seductive reserve. A seductive reserve.*

Frank started to rise as Lydia weaved between the gauntlet of waiters, but he only got halfway up before his knees caught the underside of the table. He managed to grab his wine glass before it toppled onto his companion's plate.

"Lydia, my *love*. You look *absolutely* wonderful!" He ushered her to the empty seat beside him, admiring the new dress. Cinched at the waist, dark black for power, and a plunging neckline that elegantly proffered the soft curves of her breasts that had cost her a small fortune.

"Romero! Another bottle." The waiter nodded dully and Frank sank back down.

"Mike, this is the incredible woman I've been telling you about. Lydia, this is Mr. Michael Cordel."

Cordel was smaller in person than he looked in the tabloids and media releases, but Lydia recognized him instantly. The blotchy redness of a perpetual drinker, too-tanned skin that made him seem wizened, a high, blank forehead, hair cut like Nero, and a three thousand dollar suit that must have made the tailor cringe to see him wear it.

Lydia offered a gloved hand and a charming smile, but she felt like a female tarantula watching a suitor's parrying approach. The director held her hand firmly and pulled her closer across the table. He studied her face the way a medium examines a palm, and then kissed her lightly on each cheek. His eyes lingered on the plump contours of her breasts as he released her into her seat. Frank's arm was around her shoulders before she was settled comfortably.

"Your portfolio pictures don't do you justice, Lydia."

Then why don't you look up at my face, she thought.

The director turned to the woman beside him. "Nicole Germont." He smiled and slipped a hand beneath the table. Early twenties, teeth freshly done, professionally applied make-up, collagen, Botox and implants. *If she's French, I'm Sri Lankan.* Lydia hated her instantly.

The women exchanged syrupy smiles. The conversation faltered with the new arrival for a moment, then exploded in a free-for-all that left Lydia's head spinning. The two couples enacted the same, tautologous ritual at their booth that was being rendered, in one way or another, at all the other tables. Talk, drink, laugh, look around the room, wave, kiss, squeeze, wink, say hello, see who's looking, feign indifference. Talk, drink, laugh, look around . . .

The feverish pitch slowly dulled. Mouthfuls of requisite small talk quickly evaporated into even smaller crumbs as the next bottle of wine was emptied. Lydia was careful to pace herself: she knew nothing was more pathetic than an aspiring actress who got drunk before she was supposed to be. She smiled when it was appropriate, looked concerned when the men frowned, and did her best to restrain herself from diving across the table, grabbing Cordel's throat, and forcing whatever it was he was *really* trying to say from out of his lungs like a python around a calf.

There was a brief altercation at a nearby table that the maître d' quickly resolved without having to remove either man. After another hour, Lydia was beginning to think this was just another waste of time. She'd been reeled in with the promise of day time television, and once again she'd have to struggle to get off the hook without being devoured when Frank escorted her to the car. It was business: she was certainly mature enough to know that. But Lydia despised wasting time: at forty-three, it was one of the only things she feared letting go. Probably the only thing.

But then the mood shifted. Michael Cordel leaned forward and looked her up and down again with an appraising eye. Nicole shifted uneasily. She knew there was something about this new one, something *reserved*, that stirred Mike's passions in a way she couldn't appreciate. The bitch was twice her age for God's sake. Nicole poured herself more wine because Mike's hand was busy under the table scrunching up the bottom of her leather mini skirt. He winked at Lydia, then nodded at Frank, which was the cue to the agent that the secret could finally be shared.

"I've been looking for someone to fill a particular gap for quite a while. Frank thinks you'd be ideal for the part."

Lydia smiled graciously. Frank self-importantly refolded his napkin over his lap, and Lydia felt his hand resting against her leg. She didn't move: no one had actually mentioned the part yet, and she didn't want to cut her wrists before someone else did.

Frank cleared his throat. "Michael wants you to come in Friday for a screen test, Lydia. He thinks . . . *we think* you have what it takes for a three or four episode commitment to *"Raphael Santoriago Investigates."*

The floor opened up behind the table and the restaurant fell into some soundless chasm. Lydia teetered on the edge of the abyss. Speechless, she looked back and forth at each of the men. Waiters moved in slow motion, the tinkling glasses were more of a color than a sound, and Frank's hand moved up an inch and touched the bottom of her dress. Lydia didn't move. She felt guilty, but she knew she needed him completely on her side if this part was going to be hers.

Raphael Santoriago. The name tore Nicole from some problem with one of her nails but she knew enough not to interrupt. She snuggled in closer to Cordel.

Frank mouthed the name once more, pleased with the aftertaste. All that was missing was the drum roll. "I don't need to tell you, Lydia," he sighed indulgently, telling her anyway, "that Santoriago has got one of the hottest daytime talk shows around."

"The hottest."

"Frank's right. The hottest."

Lydia's head was spinning. She tried to stay calm, to stay focused, but all she could think about was sitting on the same set and sharing the same camera with Raphael. There was a God after all. Her body flushed with warmth.

"What we're . . . what Michael is looking for is a guest who can play a couple of different parts. Someone who can change dramatically. Be what he needs on different shows. That's why I showed him the diverse looks in your portfolio."

Cordel eyed Lydia's cleavage and nodded. "The guest changes because of the audience's expectations. And because of Raphael, of course. His incisive comments, his empathy. His struggle to bring out the best in everyone, no matter how hard he has to search for that kernel of goodness."

Lydia finally broke her anxious silence. "I'm flattered you're considering me for the part, Mr. Cordel."

I'm flattered you're considering me for the part, Mr. Cordel, Nicole mimicked behind a sneer. She thrust her hips down hard against Coredel's hand. *I'll make sure it's the only part you'll get, bitch.*

"We've run the whole gamut, just like everyone else. Transvestite hookers, teenage prostitutes pregnant again, infidelity, marriage break-ups over gay lovers, and lots and lots of racism."

"Spin-off of spin-offs," Frank added.

Cordel silenced him with a glare. "We need something fresh. So we want to go back to what Raphael did best in the beginning; ambush journalism at its finest. Provoke, attack, humiliate. Let the audience feel good about themselves. Then let them be flushed with pity, and be instrumental in helping the thing they destroyed. Nothing affects the ratings like a good denigration and resurrection."

"So I'd be one of the guests?"

The director shook his head. "*The* guest, Lydia. *The* guest."

"I've showed Michael the way you can change, Lydia. You're hard to recognize in some of your photos."

How many ways can you screw up being a dead body, Lydia thought? For some reason she couldn't put her finger on – *Nicole?*- she wasn't overly hopeful at this point. She thought about closing her legs, but just pushed them a little tighter together. She'd been in too many of these situations before: close, but not close enough. Too many Mike Cordels.

"And that's what I need," Cordel added with a flourish as his fingers curled into the edge of Nicole's panties.

Frank tossed his hair back. "You see –"

"You see," Cordel interrupted, "I need someone who can be introduced to the audience as the epitome of despair, of sociopathic indifference. Someone so conceited and arrogant that everyone will hate her. I want the audience filled with rampant loathing and hostility."

I can do that. "And then?"

"And then Raphael will guide you to the light. Naturally he'll tear you apart first. Brutally, without care or concern. But then he'll redirect the audience's scorn and help them find their own compassion. Seeing the error of your ways you'll be remorseful, and after you've suffered enough you'll become desperate for clemency, for penance and rebirth. I've seen your portfolio, Lydia. I think that as you repent and change spiritually under Raphael's selfless guidance, you'll metamorph physically as well. The effect will be overwhelming."

Frank squeezed the inside of Lydia's leg but she didn't feel anything. "How many return shows to do all that, Mr. Cordel?" she managed to blurt out.

"I see three anyway."

"But it could be more, though," Frank announced magnanimously. Lydia pressed her thighs together, reached down, and eased her agent's hand away.

Cordel agreed. "It will depend on the audience and what direction we think we can get the most mileage out of."

"We'll play it as it goes," Frank echoed.

"So what do you think, Lydia? You up to a screen test tomorrow morning?"

A screen test! Her mouth was painfully dry. Could this really be it? Finally, after everything she'd been through? Could she handle the pressure? Would she crack when her microphone was hooked into her brassiere, Raphael called her name, and the audience greeted her with a guttural chorus of *boos*? After all, she'd never done a live rehearsal in front of so many people before, even though they'd all be extras at first.

"What time, Mr. Cordel?"

"Michael, please. Nine o'clock sharp."

"I'll be there, Michael. I'm sure you won't be disappointed."

I hope not, he thought. Frank had the same look in his eye. He'd screen test her before Frank did, that was for sure. The hierarchy was always there.

Cordel raised his glass. Nicole followed suit reluctantly and wrapped her legs tightly around the director's hand, squeezing his first two fingers so *he* knew where the hierarchy *really* began.

"Lydia." He smiled. "To her next step."

The glasses tinkled together. Frank didn't waste any time. He took Lydia's glass as soon as she sipped her own toast.

"That's enough now, my love. You've got to be fresh for tomorrow. Mr. Cordel will want to see you at your very best. Perhaps it's time to get you home, let you relax and have a good night's sleep."

He was already signaling someone for her coat.

"Frank's right. It's going to be a big day for you, Lydia. Don't worry about us. We'll be going soon, too." He stroked his hand roughly against Nicole's pressing mound: there was still another part to finalize tonight.

"See you at nine. And don't be late." He dismissed them both with a wave.

Lydia wanted to say something, but Nicole was already coiling herself around the director's chest. She whispered *nine* and left, dragging Frank in her wake.

***

Shaking, Lydia hung up the phone. No answer again. What time was it back in Toronto?

"Do you usually check in during the week?"

Frank was at the little bar-fridge pouring them each a drink. Neon from the sign across the road flashed intermittently through threadbare curtains covering the window: *Bail and Bond - Cheap Rates.*

Lydia called out from the bathroom. "Once or twice." But she couldn't remember if she had this week or not. She didn't bother checking her lipstick or touching up her hair because it wouldn't matter anyway. She looked herself up and down, smiling. Finally, after all the years of groveling, dieting, weight-training, cosmetics, eating leftovers with the 'extras,' and haunting memories tied with an endless chain of cheap hotel rooms, the chance of a lifetime beckoned. One last obstacle to overcome. Another shiver. She would have rather done anything else than this. But acting was acting.

Lydia smoothed out the seams in her nylons. Just one more job and all the pain, humiliation and sacrifice would end. She pictured Nicole pouting and slithering around Cordel at the restaurant, and admitted that one other performance might have to be made as well. She'd get out of it she could, but what difference did it make after this?

She didn't say anything when Frank called out that he was going down the hall for more ice. It certainly wasn't going to take much, she knew that. She'd rewarded Frank for all his work, the despicable amount of sucking up he had to do, a few times before: a quick feel here, a flash there; a slow strip down to her panties when she was drunk last Christmas at some director's farewell bash. And a hand job once for getting her the yeast infection commercial (*Ladies . . . friends, I'd like to talk to you about feminine itching*), when he'd exploded before she'd even had time to find her rhythm. She'd never felt such guilt, and yet she'd still agonized over the experience for weeks. Lydia never told Mathew what happened, never confessed, and it scarred her deeply as the first real secret she'd ever kept from him.

Lydia checked her purse: two condoms, but she was sure one would be enough. She'd send him back to his scrawny little shrew of a wife with a smile he couldn't hide. They'd fight, Mona would yell, cry, rant, rave, Frank would threaten to leave her again, then they'd screw. Frank would be asleep before he rolled over, and Mona would lie there staring at the ceiling, wishing with all her heart that she was smart enough to get a job, that she should have married Neil Schlansky who had his own accounting business now, that she should have let Frank ski *The Devil's Tail* on his own that night in Aspen when a bunch of them had rented a chalet and he was absolutely plastered.

Lydia heard the door close, the ice tinkling in the bucket, half a whistled song. She took a vial from her purse and tapped a couple of lines onto the counter, then rolled up a bill. A hundred, because snorting with a twenty made Frank feel banal and commonplace, a non-player just like everyone else, which is exactly what he was, and why he liked using hundreds. She looked in the mirror for one last chance at regret, but she couldn't see any. What was she really losing, anyway? Parents that didn't exist, a son that lived inside a keyboard, a daughter that understood animals better than people, a husband that . . . well, she couldn't really think of anything actually *wrong* with Mathew. It wasn't what he did or said, or what he *didn't* do or say, for that matter. It wasn't one particular thing or another: there was just a hole in her heart where the longing should have been. She still loved him as much as she could love anyone now, which made her feel extraordinarily sad. But she was chasing a different dream, and nothing would get in her way. Especially love.

And Joshua? If dad was a centaur, Joshua was a phoenix, caught in the ashes of a man and a boy. A tightrope walker through time.

Lydia leaned down, sniffed hard, and brought the world into focus. Her nose was numb by the time she looked back up in the mirror. She thought of the thousands and thousands of women all around the country that were lying on their beds, eyes fixed on the ceiling, their hearts in some book or t.v. show, half-thinking about the article on 'keeping passion alive in your marriage' they'd read when they were getting their hair done, reminding themselves to murmur and move when some man they had trouble recognizing now masturbated inside them.

Frank called out impatiently just as Lydia snapped her purse closed and checked her watch again. Finish this quick, have an even quicker, cleansing shower as soon as she could, do some yoga, lay her things out for the morning, have a another shower, dial in a wake-up call for six. In less than eleven hours she'd be on the very same stage as Raphael Santoriago. Shuddering as she steadied herself against the counter, Lydia looked in the mirror, crossed herself, and mouthed *forgive me* at her reflection . . . but she didn't really know who she was asking forgiveness *from,* or *to.*

A deep breath, an enchanted smile, and she stepped out of the bathroom, ready for her turn on the altar.

Chapter Fifteen

Queen Beatrice said, "You'll die if you keep doing that."

Mathew wished he had a dollar for every time he heard that warning during his life. Forty-seven years of 'you'll die if you keep doing that' and all the other similar admonitions that were half- threats and half-warnings knotted with 'or.' Parents, teachers, friends, lovers, co-workers: they'd all used the fear of *not being* to make their point at one time or another. And why wouldn't they, if God used it too?

You'll catch your death of a cold if you don't keep that jacket done up. Eat your vegetables or you'll get sick. Don't bother, or you won't live to see your next birthday. Don't swing so high or you'll fall and crack your head open. Don't you dare go riding without your helmet. What if you get hit by a transport truck and they have to hose your brains off the side-walk, how would you feel then? And if you do get crushed by a transport truck, make sure you're wearing clean, unripped underwear. Don't touch a toilet seat or you'll get a disease: you never know who might've used it right before you.

('The person who might have used the toilet seat before' Mathew knew, was invariably worse than any bogeyman imaginable. Who was the vile creature who peed on the seat and splashed the floor and didn't rim the edge with strips of paper before he squatted down and never, ever flushed? Mathew pictured him as some unshaven, unwashed ogre with hair down to his feet, his face covered in blistering sores, his mouth flecked with black teeth; Howard Hughes nails and flea-infested clothes shredded with holes; a Cyclops, pus oozing from his one eye.)

After school, shithead, by the portable. You'll die if you eat too many eggs. Eat foods light in fat but heavy in sodium but don't get too much sodium. Don't eat unwashed vegetables that haven't been organically grown or are served by the mutant thing that might have used the toilet before you did. If you don't study you won't pass so you won't get a good job. If you don't wear your seatbelt then bang! *you'll go right through the window and everyone will stand around gawking at what's left of you and they'll make the accident into a sleazy movie. Maybe if I did it in the bathroom tub there wouldn't be so much mess and they wouldn't feel so bad.*

So it wasn't really surprising anymore that Mathew wasn't all that afraid of death, since dying had slowly lost a lot of its importance over the years. If death cast a long shadow, Mathew was just a sundial.

He looked down at the salted fries stuffed into the greasy little paper bag and thought they looked like children's fingers after all the skin and muscle had rotted away. Maybe Beatrice was right, maybe this type of food would eventually kill him. But Mathew always hoped that one day he'd leave the shuffling little line-up after the cashier reminded him to 'come back soon' and be pleasantly surprised when he opened up the container: miraculously, he'd have a hamburger that looked just like the culinary masterpieces on television that barely fit on the screen, and not the usual squished pile of rubbery beef the abomination that used the toilet before him had already half-eaten and retched back up.

Beatrice didn't want any fries, which made Mathew feel even more guilty each time he munched one down. Beatrice said she wasn't hungry, but accepted Mathew's offer of a hot chocolate topped with whipping cream. It was like a cloud: every time she blew on it Mathew saw a different image in the foam.

The one thing Mathew liked about eating with his fairy godmother was that regardless of how cramped the mall's food court was, he still had enough room to lounge across four seats. Even though numerous people were standing around, shuffling from one foot to the other and trying to eat while they balanced little Styrofoam boxes, Mathew was given a wide berth, a luxurious aura of untainted space he'd never experienced before at the mall. He couldn't deny it: there was a small part of him that was secretly pleased. He knew it didn't really have anything to do with him, but it still made him feel important in some way or another.

Normally, Mathew never liked the mall. It was unsettling and it frightened him. There was a sterile blandness that always made him hopelessly uncomfortable. It was the same feeling he had on those one or two occasions he had to go to the emergency department at the hospital. The mall wasn't unlike the highway: disorientingly filled to overflowing, mentally exhausting, nerve-wracking, and choked with impatient hordes who wished they were somewhere else. It didn't matter if the aisles were narrow or wide: Mathew felt like he was running a gauntlet when he had to go in and buy something, so he rarely did. Besides, there was so much choice there wasn't really anything to choose *from*.

Mathew often wondered how the clothing stores stayed in business since they all sold basically the same clothes to the same type of people at about the same price. Row after row of jeans and t-shirts, blouses, sweaters, accessories. How different could they be made, anyway? How creative were the people who stitched them together, the little children hunched over sewing machines in sweltering sweatshops all along the Pacific Rim? Were the under aged children ever allowed to wear the rejects, or use the extra pieces of discarded fabric that were too small for anything else? Did the jean companies ever rip the legs off the pairs that couldn't be sold and give them away to the little workers that had been foolish enough to step on a landmine?

Electronic stores, sixteen banks, variety outlets, housewares stores, stores that just sold knickknacks so people could constantly collect things, magazine stores, toy stores, music stores that were virtually identical, right down to the vapid, gum-chewing clerks that couldn't stop toying with their hair or nose ring as they mumbled 'if we have it, it's on the shelf,' the huge, multilevel stores that sold everything the smaller stores did, and lots and lots of shoe stores. Hair salons and movie theatres, a shoe repair shop, and a travel agency that told you where you should be instead of at the mall.

And, worst of all, the cluttered dollar stores that sold pretty well everything that could be manufactured for less than a nickel but lasted a long, long more time. In the last few years, they'd exploded across the retail landscape like a pimple against a mirror.

Mathew gnawed another fry. He stared across the food court and watched the gnarled gnome of an old woman jerk alive and smile that officious little smirk that prefaced the 'good afternoon and welcome to Wal-Mart' speech that greeted everyone who walked by. Mathew was amazed that some crazed, disgruntled shopper -- a postal worker perhaps, or a jilted lover who'd been abused as a child -- didn't smile back as he took out a knife and went so berserk it would have taken *Criminal Minds* two episodes to explain his outrageous behavior, and why he wasn't actually responsible for what he'd done because of what had transpired earlier on his life, and the way we, we as a society, had stoked the fires of his blazing ending. Responsibility knew no bounds – they were only victims now.

Yet no matter how pointless he felt in the mall, because he rarely carried a cell phone, let alone a tablet, Mathew knew the food court was even worse. There weren't very many things more depressing than watching a crowd of strangers cram down food substitutes at little Formica tables while bored immigrants swept away what was left after the feeding frenzy. He didn't like thinking about it, but he couldn't help remembering what Mr. Flood, his grade ten Latin teacher, had said about the Roman feasts where the diners would leave after each course and go into a secluded little room to barf so they could keep on eating. Vomitariums or something. It was like watching fat people forage at a buffet. Why did they pile their plates so full? Why did they stack the food groups on top of each other until they could barely carry their plates, even though they *knew* they were at a smorgasbord and could go back as many times as they liked? Were they really worried that the even fatter people were going to eat everything before they staggered back for another load?

The smells in the food court were hard to differentiate since they all oozed together into something indecipherable, like other victims' blood when you're bitten by a vampire. Smells so thick you could almost touch them, like the ones that emanated from the hideous mutants who didn't wash after going to the bathroom and left all those diseases on the toilet seats.

Mathew watched the man beside him dive into some kind of pasta that writhed obscenely on its way to his mouth. His fork didn't stop moving and he never seemed to come up for air. His cheeks were splattered with sauce and he gulped greedily at a Coke with his mouth half-full. Half-empty to the Roman party-goers.

It hadn't been the 'parting of the crowd' that had done it, but Mathew had sensed Beatrice was there long before he'd actually seen her. He wasn't really surprised, just a touch bewildered. He couldn't believe she was following him or anything like that. *Was she?* He had a funny feeling that whatever transpired with Beatrice didn't happen by chance.

She glared at a couple of passers-by that seemed a little too interested in something under the top sheet of her cart. She tugged the cover down tightly over her scattered possessions. She was the same as the last time Mathew saw her: ragged, unkempt, the crown slightly askew, a hodge-podge of bracelets jangling from her wrist, sweating under the weight of her winter coat. The first thing she'd done was chastise him for the fries and warn him death was imminent if he kept eating them. He had to choke the next few down like a python around a piglet.

"How did you know I was here?"

"Don't flatter yourself," Beatrice snickered. "You came because I wanted to see you."

She appeared quite disgusted that he still ignored her warning and continued to gulp down the salt licks. Mathew felt the other people watching them, but it didn't bother him as much as it had at the laundromat.

"What have you got in the bag?"

There wasn't any point in pushing it under the table and shrugging *what bag*, so Mathew tugged it from behind his chair and showed Beatrice.

"A new comforter," he said. "This one's a little deeper red."

"You didn't wreck the last one in the dryer, did you?" His fairy godmother clicked her teeth reproachfully. *Were they real?*

"No, it turned out fine."

"Yes, they're real." She didn't tell him about the fire at the laundromat after he left. "Then why a new one?"

Mathew stuffed it back down into the shopping bag. He whispered sheepishly, "The other one was ruined."

"By your father?"

He nodded.

"What happened? What did he become?"

Mathew stopped cold, a fry suspended between his teeth.

"Stop it," Beatrice warned. "I know he changes because I'm your fairy godmother. Deal with it and get on with your story."

Mathew ate the fry, wondering why he felt so self-conscious. He didn't know anyone close by, and didn't care if they heard him or not, but felt he had to whisper.

"A duck. I didn't think he heard. We'd been talking about one of Carmalitta's patients over dinner."

Mathew envisioned the scene again. Upstairs in his room, Lorne threw off the blanket and lurched from his chair. He crouched down on his haunches, raised his knees, and pressed his bum close to the floor. He pinned his hands against his hips and pushed his elbows up so they looked like wings. Bobbing from side to side, he moved one leg forward, then the other. Teetering back and forth, he almost fell twice, but quickly mastered the technique. If he could have felt something, he would have known his disintegrating knee joints were already starting to swell. He wobbled like a drunken sailor, his neck weaving backward and forward, ready to peck at anything that looked like food. Every few steps he ruffled his feathers and shook the water from his crown.

Quack quack quack. Quack quack quack.

He picked at something on the carpet (a fish? a crust of bread?), threw his head back, and gulped it down. The bones in his knees and ankles creaked painfully, but he was still able to pick up his pace. He went around and around the room, ruffling his feathers and sniffing at the air, squawking to keep his territory free of intruders.

And then he stopped so suddenly his head bobbed like those dogs people used to stick in the rear windows of their cars. The scent was overwhelming. An inquisitive sniff, then another. The duck looked excitedly around. He waddled up closer to the bed, strained up on his little webbed feet, and then started quacking for all he was worth. The pillow and the comforter -- that's where the enticing smell was coming from.

He tried to fly up onto the bed but his wings weren't working properly. He craned his neck toward the enchanting scent but he couldn't reach the comforter with his beak. He tried another attempt at flying but crashed awkwardly into the side of the mattress, falling heavily onto the floor. Inflamed by the beckoning aroma, he was back up in an instant, flapping his arms aggressively at the air.

More quacks, hard and insistent. The duck backed up, aimed, tore off, and took a running leap at the head of the bed. He hit the corner of the mattress and the wall at the same time and kind of *ricocheted* up onto the covers the way a giant, dying whale breaches on shore. The blow startled him for a moment and he seemed flustered and disoriented, but the smell impassioned his most instinctive urges and he recovered immediately. After a triumphant quack, he threw himself upon the comforter in a frenzy of sexual abandonment. He held the pillow tightly between his wings and ravaged it for all he was worth, until finally, his quack turned into a mournful cry and he toppled over, exhausted and relieved.

Beatrice whispered. "Eiderdown?"

Mathew nodded glumly. "By the time I realized what was happening, he'd shredded the pillow and the comforter to pieces."

"That's a shame." Beatrice fussed with her crown. Mathew didn't want to think about his father for too long today, so he quickly changed the subject.

"I told my son about you, after we met at the Laundromat the other day."

"We didn't meet at the laundromat. I told you before I saw you at the park. Following me. Watching me."

He couldn't help protesting. "We never actually *met* there."

"You just didn't have the courage to speak to me. I guess you could've left a little sticky note on my bench."

Mathew shivered. He noticed something new on Beatrice's bracelet: a broach with a simulated diamond in the centre.

She saw him looking. "A little bauble I found outside the bank." She touched the fake stone. "It looked like it had been there a long while."

"The bank?" She must have been just passing.

"Why not? Where do you keep your money?" But Beatrice waved him into silence before Mathew had a chance to reply. "Probably blue chip mutual funds. RRSP's. I don't think you've got the stones for real investing. Humpf. What did Joshua say when you told him?"

"Joshua?"

"Your son. You said you told your son. How does my crown look? And hurry up and finish those things. The smell's making me queasy."

Mathew figured that Beatrice being sick at their little table would have undoubtedly irritated the other patrons just a tad. He ate faster. "I don't remember telling you his name."

She sighed exasperatedly. "Once you get over this teensy, weensy, irritating problem you have about not believing I'm your fairy godmother, you'll just accept I know a great deal about you and leave it at that. What did he say?"

"He said he'd known guardians before, and that they usually appear for a particular purpose. He thought --"

"Yes?"

"He thought I should listen carefully to whatever you tell me."

"Bright boy. But you probably won't listen to him either. There's a part of you that's never quite believed he's been who he says he has. Who he *is*."

Another shiver. "You know about all that, too?"

"What's he told you?"

Mathew scrunched up the rest of the fries. They were cold and rigor mortis was already setting in. He pushed them aside. What has he told me? What *doesn't* he tell me? How can you possibly sum up a life of memories he'd been told about in a couple of sentences? His son had recounted numerous lives since that first day in the car all those years ago, when they'd passed the house that Joshua *knew* had been his, his house *back then* when he'd been on his way to becoming an architect, just like his father. His *last* father. Tales of adventure, woe, horror, painful deaths and uneventful lives that passed without a whisper. And what had he been? A farmer, an Irish clerk, a stable boy, a Welsh rebel, a Roman Legionnaire, a Portuguese slave trader, more than one infant who died early, and at least one criminal without ethics.

Mathew poured out the things he could remember and some of the things he'd tried to forget over the years. Like his son sprawled across dew-laced heather in some distant field, legs quivering, the arrows' feathers shimmering in the breeze. The more Mathew talked the more he remembered, and the more he remembered the sadder he became. He told Beatrice about the boy's problems at school, how he was always dressing up as some character or another, how he'd suddenly start talking about people and places and things that it was inconceivable he knew anything about. Architecture. How the South American Indians made rope bridges that spanned gorges wider than a highway. What herbs and plants were used by mystic healers. The difficulties in crossbreeding crops. The design errors in the first microscopes.

Beatrice didn't speak. Fiddling with her crown and bracelet, she let Mathew purge himself of the things he'd repressed for so long. When he finally stopped, he was covered in perspiration and the food court was almost empty. He had no idea how much time had passed.

"You know he was there, don't you? That he's been the people he says he has?"

What a difference from Dr. Stallworth. "It's hard not to believe."

"So you believe his stories about his past existences, but you can't accept that I could be your fairy godmother?"

"That's different."

"No it's not."

"I've lived with Joshua. I know him. I'm part of him."

"And how do you know you haven't been a part of me before?"

Mathew stopped before he opened his mouth. Suddenly, he felt quite nauseous. He was in the middle of a spinning vacuum, a vacuum without an end or a beginning.

Beatrice fiddled with something sticking out of her cart but Mathew couldn't see what it was. She glared at a couple of teenaged boys who strolled too close, backing them away with an unnerving scowl.

"Tell me about her."

Mathew looked around the food court. "About who?"

"The one you're always thinking about. The one you can't stop remembering. The one that makes your stomach hurt."

Mathew felt his chest tighten. He forced himself to take a long, deep, breath.

"And don't be so dramatic. You're fine. You'd be a picture of health if you stopped eating those stupid things." Beatrice pointed at his crumpled up fries with her nose. "And if you stopped trying to hide." She smiled. A warm, thoughtful, enticing smile.

"I don't know what . . ."

"Time's short, Mathew."

How did she know? Was he really that transparent? She was like Dr. Stallworth, without the push-ups and exorbitant fees to pay for his summer cottage in Muskoka and his condominium in Estero that was on the western coast of south Florida, practically right on Barefoot Beach. Mathew flattened the salt-laced paper out, and then carefully folded the rest of the fries up into a little square. He could have been thinking about anything, but he wasn't. And Beatrice knew. There was no point in being evasive. He'd spent half his life doing it and it hadn't helped him one bit.

"The love of my life, when I was younger."

"Forget the 'when I was younger' part. What's her name?"

"Carol. Carol Davidson."

"You love her very much, don't you?"

"I did. But that was quite a long . . ."

"You still love her. When was the last time you saw Carol?"

Mathew watched a stressed young woman try to get two infants settled at one of the nearby tables. Restraining the twin yo-yos while she emptied out the fast-food bags, cleaned the table, and tried to get the straws and napkins out, she looked like a sheep dog corralling the herd.

"I think it was about a year ago."

"You know it was a year ago."

"I was coming home late from working," Mathew continued. There was construction on one of the Expressway's on ramps --"

"There's always construction on the Expressway," Beatrice said. She leaned closer. "I could tell you what's really happening down there where they're supposed to be shoring up the highway supports, but it's a secret." She laid a finger alongside her nose.

Mathew frowned and made a mental note to use the Lakeshore from now on. "So I had to take a detour, and ended up on Kingston Road."

"And that's where you saw her?"

He smiled. "Walking to a car. She was carrying something, a small shopping bag."

"And you didn't stop?"

Mathew choked indignantly on his coffee. "Of course not. I hadn't seen her in years. And everything else that happened between us was a long time ago. I saw her by chance and . . ."

"Stop saying that. Nothing ever happens by chance. My goodness, you don't like opening your eyes, do you? You worked late on a Friday. Was that normal?"

"No, not really. But how did --"

"And there was construction on the Parkway and the Lakeshore?" She said construction with a wink and held up her fingers like little quotations marks.

"Yes, there's always --"

"So you went a different way home which was probably longer?"

Mathew shrugged.

"And you went through numerous lights, traffic slowdowns, delayed turns. But you passed a certain spot just at the precise moment the woman you think about all the time just happened to be walking out to her car?"

"Oh, come on."

Beatrice dismissed the protest with a curt wave. "Yes, and you met me by accident, too. Right." She rolled her eyes toward the glass ceiling like an insolent teenager. Mathew followed her gaze and wondered how they got all the bird shit off the windows that peaked over the mall.

"Tell me about her."

Mathew started sitting back and folding his arms across his chest but stopped in mid-motion when he looked into the old woman's eyes. "We met in high school."

"Yes, yes. Go on."

"We just passed each other in the hall. I was talking to someone -- I can't remember who it was now -- and something made me look up. When I did, I saw her."

He paused.

"And the funny thing was?"

He smiled at the prompting. "And the funny thing was, she happened to have looked up at that moment, too."

Beatrice smiled. Mathew wondered just how much of the story she already knew. Bits and pieces, at least. He had the singular sensation she was simply getting him to say it out loud.

"Why didn't you talk to her?"

Mathew shrugged. "I did, but it was a few days later. One of my teachers had an appendicitis attack. He curled up like an armadillo and was rushed to the hospital. There wasn't anyone else free to fill in, so the VP had us go in to the study hall. Another class was already there, and she was in it."

"And you don't see anything significant in the appendicitis attack, the lack of any other teachers at that exact moment, the empty chair?"

"What empty chair?" But as soon as he spoke Mathew pictured it again. He'd been the last one coming into the study hall and there was only one seat left that hadn't been taken: the one next to hers.

"Stop hiding and trying to think everything through. What was she like?"

Mathew leaned forward, braced his elbows on the table, and cupped his chin with his palms. The noises in the food court melted away with the years. A cleaner came by and scooped up his tray and he thanked her. Startled, the woman frowned and quickly hustled away.

"She was a little like me, I guess. Shy, reserved, quiet. Friends, but certainly not the most popular person around."

He looked at Beatrice and smiled, yet the memories hurt. "I thought she was absolutely gorgeous, but I'm sure everyone else figured she was a little plain. I wasn't Romeo either, of course."

"She was beautiful in your eyes and that's the only thing that's important."

Mathew gave a slight nod. "She had --"

"Don't say 'she.' Use her name so I can see her more clearly."

"Carol. Carol had long brown hair that was so thick and straight she couldn't curl if she'd wanted too. Grey-green eyes with little lashes you could barely see. She -- Carol -- had a small mouth and nose and the neck of a swan. She hardly ever wore make-up, and her skin was so soft. She was about as tall as me and fairly slender. Neither of us were athletic in the least. And --"

"And?" Beatrice waited for a moment and then drew Mathew back. "And?"

"And she always blushed when she smiled. I thought that was so wonderful."

"So you sat down beside her in the study hall and that was that?"

"What do you mean, 'that was that'?"

"You knew she was the one. The one you wanted to be buried beside. You saw your whole life entwined with hers in a way you couldn't even begin to imagine."

"Well, I --"

"Mathew."

He returned her stare.

"Think back. Close your eyes. What did you see?"

Something made him shiver. One of the youngsters at the nearby table was crying. The other one stuffed fistfuls of French fries toward his face, grinning when one or two managed to reach his mouth. There was ketchup everywhere. When

Mathew opened his eyes the food court seemed different, but he couldn't really say how.

"Not see. Felt." Beatrice waited patiently.

"I felt -- I felt like I'd already known her all my life." He searched for the words. "I know it sounds silly, but I felt closer to her than I'd ever felt to anyone else before and I'd only seen her twice." His face creased with a troubled frown and he shook his head. "But 'felt' isn't even the right word." The sense of being in a vacuum had softened and drifted away without Mathew knowing. *Where was he?*

Beatrice's eyes twinkled. "Say it."

"I knew right away that Carol was the other part of me."

Mathew fell silent. He was there, back in the study hall again, searching Carol's eyes, afraid to look away, the entire world a halo suspended over their two desks. He started massaging his heart again, kneading his flesh, ensuring he was still at the table with the crying children, the sterile lights, and the people rushing nowhere and the hint of roasted garlic on his fairy godmother's breath. He finally looked up. Beatrice toyed with one of the keepsakes on her bracelet. Her face was muted in shadows, like a light behind a veil, but Mathew couldn't tell where the glow was coming from.

"And we fell in love," he finally whispered.

Beatrice pulled the world back into focus with a smile. "No, Mathew. You were already in love."

Some invisible fist squeezed his heart. He looked up, unsettled, unsure, and glanced quickly under the table. Nothing. He scanned the food court. He didn't know what he was looking for, what he expected, but he felt like something was there with him. That he was being watched. He knew he had to move, to do something. He cleared his throat twice before he managed to speak again and asked Beatrice if she wanted a hot chocolate.

She shook her head. "But a double latte would be nice. With chocolate and cinnamon. And maybe a shot of caramel."

Mathew felt dizzy when he pushed himself up from the table, but he'd calmed down a little when he returned with their drinks. He wiped the rim of his cup with a serviette, cracked a gap in the lid, then put the cover back on.

"I don't believe in love at first sight."

"Neither do I, Mathew." Beatrice tongued the whip cream castle in her cup.

"But you said I was already in love."

"And you were. You just remembered it again when you saw her."

"But I'd only seen her once."

"This time."

"This time what?"

Beatrice smiled. "I love cinnamon." She flicked several little chocolate shavings into her mouth like a frog skewering flies. "You're right, Mathew. There's certainly infatuation at first sight. Rapture at first sight. Lust, too." She giggled, her eyes sparkling. One of the children at the next table sneezed so hard he almost fell over backwards. "But those things fill a need, a space where we're not quite whole. You can see someone and feel your heart race, your knees buckle, your stomach gurgle and roll like the sea, but that's very different than sensing who and what they are to you."

Mathew frowned and shook his head. Somewhere behind him, a crackling voice in the ceiling punctured the musak to tell the bustling shoppers that one of them had lost a child. Several women looked down before they hurried on.

Beatrice licked a dollop of foam from her lips and fidgeted with her charm bracelet. "Think of all the things that might normally go through your mind when you see someone you feel attracted to."

She didn't give him a chance. "Oh, she's cute. Look at that. Whoa! Check that one out. Well, *hello*."

Mathew smiled. "Physical appearance always influences who you're attracted to."

"Attracted to, yes. But you knew you were already in love, didn't you? You weren't swept away with her beauty, learned what she was like, and then fell hopelessly in love with her. There was already something there between you, something that bound you both together, right from the moment you saw her. From the moment you *recognized* her."

Nodding, Mathew looked uncomfortable. "But I didn't really recognize her."

Beatrice shrugged. "Not consciously, no. And not with your eyes. But you did with everything else that makes you who you are."

"I don't understand."

"Then stop trying to analyze it so much. Don't try to put everything you think and feel into separate little compartments like a hypochondriac's pills. When you met Carol, something deep down inside you stirred that you've never been able to put into words."

Mathew sipped his coffee. The smells permeating the food court were clinging to his clothes and starting to make him nauseous. He wondered if the lost child had been found. It hadn't been his name the disembodied voice had called, had it?

Beatrice finished her latte. She started daubing up the chocolate slivers that stuck to the bottom of her cup with her finger. "There's something inside you that recognizes things you can't normally see or comprehend, Mathew."

"Like a sixth sense?"

"No. But close. More like an essence. The thing inside you that tells you the things you can't ever figure out how you possibly knew them in the first place."

Mathew thought about the voice in the back of his head that was always commenting on whatever he did or wanted to do. All the words and concepts from his introductory psych courses flooded back like a swollen river through a cracked levee, but none of them seemed right.

"Like a soul, then?"

Beatrice shrugged and wiped her mouth with her sleeve. Mathew winced. "I don't know that much about souls," Beatrice said. "But I do know there's something deep inside that's a part of us and everything we do, but that's also a part of everything that's all around us."

Beatrice paused, gesturing to the mall with a circular wave of her arms. She leaned over and tucked a tattered blanket around the wire rungs of her buggy. Turning, she stuck out her tongue at a security guard standing at the edge of the hallway that led to the pay phones and washrooms. Braced with one foot raised against the wall, he'd been watching her for awhile.

"I don't think I know what you mean." Mathew shot the guard the dirtiest look he could muster but it didn't seem to phase the man in the least.

"Go back."

Mathew looked confused. "To Carol?"

"Farther. Much farther. To a sunny spring morning in a beautiful vale deep in the heart of Wales. A waving sea of grass, shadows, trees, a distant castle, the scent of heather, a circling hawk, lilacs. The *whoosh* of arrows."

Abject horror creased the lines of Mathew's face. His breath caught in the back of his throat and he squirmed self-consciously. "How did you know about that? About Joshua?"

"I'm your fairy godmother."

This time Mathew didn't argue.

"Go back. If you were one of the riders sent out from the castle to help retrieve the young man the arrows felled, would you have had the feeling that you knew him in some way or another? Would you have sensed a bond?"

Mathew's head was spinning. The two little coyotes at the next table were fighting over the bloody remnants of some leathery animal.

"How could I possibly know something like that?"

Beatrice didn't say anything.

Mathew imagined himself there, centuries before, crouching down as his horse shielded him from the attacker's arrows, reaching for the weathered scroll the young man had been carrying in the breast pocket of his tunic, turning him over, seeing the eyes, feeling the last wisp of breath leave the body. Would he have known him in the way the old woman meant?

"I'm not sure," he mumbled uneasily. He shook his head and wondered where the feeling that he was *falling up* was coming from.

Beatrice waited without speaking. Mathew gulped.

"I don't know."

"Yes you do."

"Maybe. I might. I'm not sure."

"Are you going to tell me that when you looked down into his eyes and watched his life flicker away you wouldn't recognize something that would touch you here?" Beatrice laid her hand against her chest, the charm bracelet jingling.

Mathew didn't answer. He thought about the time long ago when he was driving downtown with Lydia and his son, and Joshua started telling them about living in the Cape Cod house near the subway station. He thought he heard the sprinkler drum its metal beat against the roof again.

Beatrice shredded her serviette into strips and watched the children next to their table cling defiantly to their chairs as their mother tried to pull them away to the washroom. Ketchup-measles splattered their faces, and no matter how many times the frazzled young woman slapped his hand, one of the little heathens kept his finger firmly entrenched in his nose.

"Why didn't you stay with Carol?"

The boa curled around Mathew's chest and squeezed again. Why did anyone ever leave someone they loved so deeply?

Beatrice wagged a gnarled finger at him. "And before you start wasting my time and saying silly things like 'we needed to see other people,' or 'I didn't really know what I wanted,' or 'we simply drifted apart,' just tell me the unaffected reason you admit to yourself when you're all alone and it's raining and you're standing in front of the window wondering about what might have been."

A challenge flashed in her eyes, and then Beatrice calmly started picking at the rim of her coffee cup, tearing off little pieces of the edges so it became smaller and smaller. The security guard whispered something into a hidden radio and kept watching. Mathew drifted away. He'd agonized over that same question so often he thought he'd actually spoken and already answered the old woman, but he hadn't. He watched a grubby young teen lean over the condiments lining the counter of a fast food stall and paw the box of straws. Was this the son of the hideous thing that used the washroom before he did?

"Mathew?"

He sensed her there beside him again. Smelled her hair, felt the fragility of her skin, the warmth of her smile. He could have put his hand right *through* her.

"Yes."

He looked startled. "Yes 'what?'"

"Yes," Beatrice repeated. "You would."

Mathew watched the woman's gnarled fingers belittle the coffee cup a bit more. *Yes, I would.* He'd been wondering whether or not he'd recognize Carol after all these years if something horrible had happened, if she'd been in some atrocious car accident and been badly maimed and the reconstructive surgery had completely altered her voice and appearance. Yes, he'd know her anywhere, any time. He thought about Joshua pricked with arrows and stretched out on a bed of heather in a distant field.

"I didn't have the strength to stay with her." The words were coals on his tongue. "I loved her with all my heart. When she went away to school, I couldn't believe she loved me as much as I loved her. The longer we were apart, the less I believed in myself and the more jealous I became."

Mathew glanced up just as the young woman was dragging the squirming tag-team back to their table. She looked exhausted. They obviously hadn't used the SARS dispenser.

"The jealousy ate away my trust. And I guess after a while, there wasn't anything to be afraid of losing any longer."

Beatrice unraveled the last piece of paper from her cup. All that was left was the disc that was the bottom.

"Is that why all your memories of her hurt so much?"

Mathew nodded.

"The memories will always be a part of you, Mathew. No matter what happens, you haven't lost Carol."

The words didn't feel reassuring in the least.

"Sit back," Beatrice said. "Close your eyes."

Mathew did.

"Now take a deep breath. Let it out slowly. Good. Now take another one. Again."

She waited while Mathew calmed his heart down. He wished he had one of those Zen boxes he'd seen in the store with Mitsu. *Beatrice's store.* Something repetitive, something that would let him clear all of the thoughts away from his mind. Help him let go.

A voice. Beatrice's? "Now let your mind wander until you find something from the past."

He went to speak but she stopped him. "Not that. Something else. Farther."

Scenes floated by. Mathew remembered a time long ago when he was in public school. Legs tucked underneath a wooden desk sloped down toward his stomach, he was busily scrawling out the answers to a surprise math test. Beside him, Tommy Morton's pencil was still. A few moments of fierce scribbling later, Mathew felt Tommy lean closer. Straining his neck but still attempting to keep his head over his own desk, Tommy stole anxious glances at Mathew's paper. Indignant, he didn't have time to waste on Tommy. He kept jotting down the answers while the clock ticked on. When he looked up again, Tommy wasn't even trying to hide the fact any more that he was cheating. Perched on the edge of his seat, he was leaning halfway over Mathew's desk.

"Get out," Mathew whispered angrily. He put his arm across his page.

"Come on Matt, let me see."

"No. Do them yourself."

"Matt --"

A ruler slapped against one of the desks at the back. "Mathew! Tommy!"

Mathew jumped and spun around, his face white.

"Both of you, turn your pages over this instant."

"But Mrs. Lancaster, I --"

"I won't have anyone cheating in my classroom."

Burning red, he did as he was told. Later, when the two boys were called in after school, the real story of what happened came out and Mathew was vindicated. Unlike a lot of teachers, Mrs. Lancaster was kind enough to absolve Mathew of his guilt in front of the class the following day. But it couldn't take the experience back. He'd felt humiliated when she'd branded him a cheat in front of the others, and nothing was ever going to mollify the hurt and frustration he'd felt at that moment.

"At least she tried," Beatrice said, twirling a charm on her bracelet.

Mathew wasn't surprised his fairy godmother knew what he was thinking about.

"Feel what you felt back then. See every detail: what you were wearing, what the day was like, the colors of everything around you, the smells, how your body felt."

Mathew kept his eyes closed and swam back through the years until he was ten, much skinnier, his teeth were slightly bucked, and, even though it was only early June, his mother had already offered him up to the barber for his summer brush cut. He smelled the chalk, felt the scrapes on each knee, saw the brightly colored map of North America beside the one of the world that had been rolled down like blinds, heard the faint buzz of the long, overhead lights, and shuddered from the coldness of the metal rung that fastened his chair to his desk. He felt rather than heard Mrs. Lancaster's staccato cry and seethed beneath a heated blush. His throat was unbearably dry as he fought back tears.

Mathew heard Beatrice's words like they were coming from the bottom of a well.

"Be there again. Make it happen all over. Remember everything. Become what you were."

Silence.

"Feel everything. Remember how the room seemed. The other children. How you felt. And keep breathing. Deeper, deeper. Slower."

He did. He was sure he was going to cry.

"Now take another breath and let all those feelings go. All the pain, all the worry, all the concern. The humiliation. You're there, but only an observer. You can feel and remember everything that's happening but you're not a part of it any longer. Let your body relive that moment, but without the things you felt. Watch and listen."

Mathew tried. Minutes passed. And then he started to feel a little better.

"It cleanses your body, Mathew. And your mind. All the things you remember are a part of who and what you are, but they don't have to control you. Or the way you feel. If something hurts, relive the entire experience, then let it go. Enjoy the memory, but let the pain seep away."

Mathew saw the young boy at his desk. For the first time in as long as he could remember, he didn't feel hurt or angry or embarrassed. It was simply another one of the memories that made him who he was.

Beatrice smiled. "Do that every day, Mathew."

He looked up, unsure.

"With everything, with every little thing you remember. Sit, close your eyes, breathe, bring it back and all the things that came with it, then let it go. And slowly, you won't react so strongly when you recall something you've tried to forget from your past. You won't feel like you did back then, and your body won't tense and your stomach won't tighten. You'll have the memory: it won't have you. And you'll be closer to Carol again, too."

Mathew thought about the younger Mathew. Beatrice was right. He could look at the whole experience all over again now without the anger, the frustration. He seemed pleased. Carol. He'd try the same thing with her later at home.

"And it's not any different for your son."

Mathew looked up, confused, but more relaxed than he'd felt in a long time. "In what way?"

"Joshua does the same thing. But instead of reliving memories, he relives lifetimes."

Mathew didn't think that was as strange as it first sounded.

Chapter Sixteen

06:10:21
Hey Cybernician, what's doing? Get all that stuff finished for CompuImage? That dweeb of a client nevr showed, so the second bossman's door closd, I did a roadrunner.

06:11:02
Comptroid plays, when the cat's away. I figured you and Mouseman would be hedin down to the Trade Centre 4 the computer show. The gloves Sheila sent me r grat. Skin tight, and mor flexible than anything I've evr usd.

06:11:59
Mouseman's piking me up at 8:00 so we're ther when it opens. I shud get a new par of gloves 2. I got anothr script 4 pain. The nw char helps but the docts rnt sur what mor they can do. I dont want carp tunl surgry agin. Hows eveybody?

06:12:33
I red doctors calculate a 400% rise in computer-related in-jures within the nex five yers. Hands, bak, neck, tendons - - u name it. Evrybody's oka.

06:13:13
Did Mouseman tel u about Dream@Fangs?

06:13:40
No. Whos that?

06:13:46
Not sur yet. I followe her thru 7 chat rooms the othr nite. She lost me a couple of times but I got arond her blok. I stayd with hr 4 ovr an hor. She's some surfr.

06:15:01
Whered u start?

06:15:12
Cant tel or youl get al parenty. Tel me Il get in truble agan.

06:15:57
I thout ud b mor carful aftr what hapend last time.

06:16:46
With Keystrokestalker? Shes shut don completly. Got a yer 4 threatnin. Doin 1 of thos hos arest programs. They took her computr awy. She wud hav been better off 1n jal. At lest in there she'd have access to their stuff.

06:20:21
So Comptroid, wat mad u folo this 1?

06:20:59
The way she spoke. Hr quicknes.

06:21:16
Yur goin 2 gt in truble, Comptroid.

06:21:55
Wev ben frends 4 eve, Cyb. Trust me on this 1. I learned my lesson. Il wach th info giv out this tim.

06:22:19
Thats wat u sad las time be4 Dream@Fangs wormd eveythin out of yur aconts.

06:22:58
Il b carful. Wer meetin agan 2nit. Hy, did Sheila figur ot that problem with Animatics?

06:24:11
Shes stil workin on it.

06:25:00
Hav u talkd agin yt? Abot hookin up modems?

06:25:39
I cant do it.

06:25:51
Com on, man. U luv hrr. Uve ben on-lin 4 ovr 2 yers nw.
Dont tel me yur stll 2 afrad of th world 2 tak a chanc.

06:27:50
Its a bg stp 4 me. A bg 1, Compy.

06:31:19
Thn let it ride. Dont forc anythin. Th nex thin u no, ul b
surfin th librares 4 self-help books r somthin.

06:31:50
Nothins evr that bd.

06:32:01
So tak a brak 2nitet an get ur mind of thins. Wanna folo me
in2 the *forbidden zone*? Il b on arond elevn. I use th third bak-
up on that list I gav u. Revers ordrd letring, decoded.

06:34:30
Il thnk abut it. If I dont tag along, b carful. Remember . . .

06:35:55
Wat hapend las tim. I wil. And Il b cool. Se u soon, Cyb.

***

Mathew stood before the big front bay window in the room
they never really used anymore. A cleaning company had come
the day before to do all the outside windows of the house with
soapy squeegees, and he had to reach out and touch the pane to
make sure it was still there. If *he* was still there.

The sky was a dull, insipid grey, raked with cloud tendrils wrung dry that morning. The pavement glistened, and little rivers of rainwater gurgled along the curbs and tumbled down into grate-covered sewers. Worms, worms that would probably be dead soon, wriggled in the final throes of life, trying to make it across the last few feet from one side of the asphalt to the other. Their crushed brethren, the ones who had had started their long, arduous trek across the driveway at first light, been rolled into a mashed mess by tires or been picked off by early birds. So what was the point again in being early?

Across the road, an old man in a coat that had obviously been someone else's before shuffled through the puddles. Head down, neck bent painfully forward, hands deep inside what was left of the pockets, he seemed to be dragging his left foot, forcing it to keep up. He stopped every few feet, coughed, spit, limped on. *Was he shivering?* Another month before the holiday, but already the colors were changing and people were entranced by the beauty of death clinging to the trees.

The phone summoned Mathew back from a moment long ago at school when he was a much younger Mathew everyone called *Matt* or *Fatty Matty* who was standing in Miss Prockter's room, all alone at the front of the class, redolent and afraid, (somewhat like *Marquez's* Colonel Aureliano Buendia who, blindfolded, awaits the firing squad's volley in the first sentence of *One Hundred Years Of Solitude,* although Mathew definitely didn't possess the deep, magical existentialism that foreshadows that masterpiece's cerebral drama, nor was he thinking about ice), yet still he was trying, trying so hard, but woefully unable to remember the next sentence in his speech he'd written down so neatly on the little lined index cards he shuffled back and forth in his hands. Now, as this *Mathew*, he was trying to breathe like his fairy godmother had shown him at the mall, trying to inhale an exhale away the things like that moment that still bothered him, the things that still pricked his heart after all these years and made him feel sad or lonely or hurt or insecure or simply unloved, the things in his life he still obsessively held on to, the heart-stings Queen Beatrice had told him to regurgitate and expunge like bones from a pelican's throat. *Let go,* she'd whispered. *Let them go. Breathe them in and let them go. Let your heart make more room for love.*

But the next ring shattered the image of his shaking hands and the bored banality of Miss Prockter's impatient face.

"Hello."

"Good afternoon. Would Eleanor be in, please?"

"Who's calling?"

"Her art instructor, Carlos Rohas Montoya."

"Can you wait for a moment, Mr. Montoya?"

"Carlos, please. Of course."

He turned to start the search, but Eleanor was already there at the kitchen door, standing behind him, her antennae raised. She pointed at the phone with her chin.

"Is that for me?"

"Yes. Mr. Montoya."

Mathew heard his mother's breath catch.

"I thought it might be. I'll take it in the family room."

Mathew didn't really want to, but he hung the receiver up when his mother answered. When he passed the kitchen which was next to the family room – a room they *did* use - she stopped talking until his footsteps echoed on the stairs. Mathew felt like he did when Carmalitta was twelve and some mysterious caller with a breaking voice and acne you could almost feel asked to speak to her, *if it was alright, sir.* Where was *Dylan* now?

"Carlos?"

"Eleanor, how wonderful to hear your voice. Listen, Eleanor. I need to see you."

Her heart beat faster. "What? Now?"

"Do you know Bogart's? The piano lounge on Queen Street?"

"Yes."

"I'll meet you there in an hour."

She almost dropped the phone. "But . . . "

"Eleanor. Peter Garfield. You know the name?"

Eleanor frowned, then nodded excitedly. "He owns a gallery in Yorkville, doesn't he?" She'd seen his picture in the paper just the other day, an informal snapshot of the owner exquisitely dressed at some black-tie charity event that was meant to help the rich feel like they were helping the poor.

"Two, actually. And one in New York and Milan as well. He's thinking of having a small showing at the one here next summer. What he wants to do, and what I've discussed extensively with him already, is a charity show and auction for new and aspiring artists. It would help everyone. People would purchase the newcomer's work for well above the prices indicated. The artist would receive the actual proceeds previously established for their works, but the additional funds would be designated for some charity or other. I believe you would like to show some of your work, yes?"

Eleanor gasped. When she started to answer, her words banged together like the clangs of a blacksmith's hammer. "Well, I, I guess so. Yes. Yes, of course. But Carlos, I'm not --"

"Sorry, I didn't mean to frighten you. Not your own show, naturally. But your work would be included. Peter and I would like to give more exposure to the myriad talent that lies so close beneath the surface of the art world, the new and inspiring work that's always threatening to break through and change its direction."

Eleanor hoped her blouse wasn't rippling where her heart pounded against her chest. Part of an art show! With Peter Garfield and Carlos! She couldn't believe it.

"We're still in the planning stages, of course. There's a great deal of time and effort that has to be invested first. But I've mentioned you to Peter, and he's quite anxious to examine a few of your pieces. Eleanor? Eleanor, are you there?"

Barely. The room was spinning so fast that Eleanor had to lean against the wall to steady herself. Her hands were shaking, and she felt a bead of ice-cold perspiration trickle down her back between her shoulder blades. She pictured Yorkville's tree-lined streets in her mind: the trendy restaurants, the upscale lofts, the sidewalk cafes, the specialty shops that catered to the city's elite, and Peter Garfield's gallery, *Herodotus*, tucked inside a secret court safely off the main avenue. Eleanor almost choked on a gulp. And *her* art on *his* walls, beneath the same lights that accentuated the work of so many wonderful artists.

"Eleanor?"

She didn't hear Carlos ask her to bring her portfolio. She couldn't hear anything because she was gone, gone from the house, the city, the problems at home, her husband's room, gone and going up, breaking free from the emotional chains that bound her like the ropes that fasten a hot air balloon to the ground, and floating away through gossamer clouds so beautiful, so beautiful she wanted to weep.

***

Eleanor scrawled out a quick message on one of the little yellow hasty notes, plastered it to the fridge, and then hurried upstairs to change.

Mathew was just coming back down. "Anything wrong?"

"No. Of course not." She glared, then her eyes softened. "I'm going out for a bit. There's a note on the fridge."

There are a hundred notes on the fridge, Mathew thought.

When Eleanor pushed her bedroom door open, Lorne was still sitting in the glider by the window. Why wouldn't he have been? But Eleanor was uneasy. She almost wished he *had* moved, that he *had* been somewhere different. It would have made everything so much simpler.

She glanced in the mirror: hair fine, dress fine, but she decided to change anyway. A fresh disguise never hurt. She talked as she laid her clothes out on the bed and retouched her makeup at the little dressing table. She watched her husband in the mirror. It was getting harder and harder to remember him the way he used to be. Was the *other* Lorne still inside *this* one, somewhere?

"I'm going out for a little while. I have to see my art teacher about some of my work. Will you be all right?"

He never spoke, but she always waited for an answer, just in case, even when she was in a hurry to leave, or when she didn't really want to hear.

"I'm sure I've mentioned him before." She had no idea why she even bothered to say that. She waited, listened. Nothing. Not a blink.

"Mathew will be here if you need anything." *Why that? For what?*

She checked her lipstick, her blush, looked down at the crinkled skin on her neck. The creams still weren't working.

Why did she have to get older? Why *now*? Why now when everything could have been . . . .

And then she caught her husband's reflection in her mirror. A yellow finch streaked with black landed on the window sill, but the old man didn't seem to notice. From the angle in the mirror, it almost looked like the bird was sitting on his nose.

Eleanor liked to make sure Lorne was clean and well-shaven, and that he changed his clothes into fresh ones every day. This morning she helped him into one of his favorite shirts, an old, stone-washed denim one with long sleeves that he'd had forever. The stitches were coming apart at the bottom, and both of the elbows were so thin you could almost see right through them. The cuffs were frayed and far beyond cleaning. But it was cozy and warm, and always smelled of Lorne, even after the cat had slept on it when it came out fresh from the dryer, and Eleanor liked it as much as he did. The sleeves were rolled back, and she could see the bottom of the tattoo that adorned his forearm.

A tattoo.

Another sudden surprise, just like his earring, the little diamond stud that used to sparkle like his eyes when he laughed. Joshua was more than pleased, because, especially if he hadn't shaved for a few days, it made his granddad look like a pirate. And Eleanor, when she'd had a glass or two of wine and they were dancing at one of the small piano lounges downtown, had to admit she found the little diamond stud rather sexy, sexy in a secretive sort of way. Now it just reflected the overhead light, partially hidden by the tufts of hair that mushroomed out of his ears more and more as he aged. If Eleanor didn't trim it the hair sprouted out like purple loosestrife along a highway's edge, and since she'd started the art classes she had less and less time to worry about grooming her husband. Did he care? Where was he going anyway?

And then a couple of years later, at sixty-four, he wanted a tat. *Everyone else was getting one*, he'd said. He'd gone to An Inkling Of Paradise, a little narrow shop fronting Yonge Street that his physician had already gone to for his own little snapshot of life and knew the place was sterile and hygienic. Lorne had gone in covered in naked skin, but when he emerged from the little shop of gargoyles and flowers, of mantras and stylized symbols, his forearm was covered in gauze. Lorne had the cutest pair of otters infused with the grey hairs on his forearm. They were floating on their backs in some stream, heads together and their furry feet pointing up, snuggling into each other in their thick wet coats the way only otters can do. Their beady eyes sparkling, the little otters' paws were entwined. They were holding hands. Eleanor peeked under the bandages and smiled. She felt the tears welling up and gently laid the dressing back down, hiding their secret.

She went to her husband and pulled his blanket up farther over his lap. And there they were, peeking out from under the edge of his rolled up shirtsleeves, the two little otters entangled in a grey mist of hair, almost smiling, their heads turned in towards each other, their paws touching, their bodies floating as one on a dream of blue water.

She thought about the art class. About Carlos. His long white-gray hair, his gentle, beautiful eyes, the slope of his Mediterranean jaw. That quiver of a smile, the warmth of his hands when they trailed across her shoulders while he studied her work. Studied *her*.

She looked at Lorne. Years flashed by, a kaleidoscope of fractured images almost forgotten, but not quite, not completely. He didn't move. His soft forearm hairs held the little otters afloat. Was he here, or there? *Then*, or *now*?

"Be back soon," she whispered. "Be a good d . . . . She was relieved she hadn't said 'dear' because she didn't have time for another change, and if he would have morphed he could have taken off just about anywhere. At a good pace, too, alert and pouncing, and knowing how to hide.

"Can I get you something?" she whispered.

A memory? Consciousness? A feeling? The sense of skin? A razor?

"Be good, and don't stay by the window too long." *What difference would that make?* "Mathew's downstairs, so you're not alone."

The little finch ruffled its feathers and flew away.

"Need anything before I go?" She'd already asked him that. Twice.

She looked down and saw the otters swimming on their backs through tangled grey strands of kelp. Paws in paws. Eleanor leaned down and brushed her lips so close to the top of his head she practically touched him, then left, closing the door quietly behind her.

Lorne listened to her steps fade into silence. Eleven stairs. He heard the closet open, the front door close, the car door slam, the engine rev to life, the tires flatten out over the asphalt. The finch came back in a flapping blur of yellow and black, but he didn't seem to notice.

***

Sitting at a small table with her back to the pianist so she could see outside, Eleanor had only been at the lounge for a few minutes when Carlos stepped from the world outside and into hers. He signaled the waiter as he sat down, mouthed *the usual,* and then brushed a straggling strand of snow-white hair from his forehead.

He smiled warmly and took her hand. A gentle kiss that almost touched her skin. "I trust you haven't been waiting long."

Sometimes I think I've been waiting forever. Eleanor shook her head.

Carlos didn't speak until the waiter poured the wine. "To you," he toasted, clinking her glass. He looked at both sides of the table and frowned. "Eleanor, where's your portfolio?"

Her heart stopped. "Oh God, I'm so sorry. I completely forgot about it." She blushed and took a long drink, shaking her head. "God, I feel like an utter --."

"Please, do not worry, Eleanor," Carlos smiled. 'I can show it to him another time. I've told him so much about your work already he'll know it before he even sees it.'

Eleanor's heart started again. "So, you and Peter Garfield--"

"You didn't come here because of art," he whispered.

She started to contradict him but stopped when she realized how absurd it would have sounded. Carlos leaned back, laughed softly, and nodded at the man adjusting the piano bench. A few gentle trills, and then his hands began to dance, together but apart. Siren-memories wandered through the lounge looking for a soul to seduce.

"Eleanor, you're wasting your life," Carlos said sadly

She leaned back, surprised, but more angry and hurt. "That's a terrible thing to say."

"Not if it's true."

"Especially if it is."

The pianist began a medley of songs from the Second World War, and a gnarled, one-armed man on the other side of the room started humming. He was seconds off the tune but didn't try to catch up.

"You should be drawing and painting all the time."

"What?"

"You heard me."

"Oh, that's what you mean. I'm wasting time not working enough?"

"You thought I meant with your husband. With your life."

"No I --"

"Yes you did. And that's a shame, too."

She hid behind her wine glass. "He's still my husband."

"Your husband is a meerkat."

Eleanor's face reddened and she sputtered. "That's deplorable. He's --"

"And a coyote."

"Stop it!"

"A rat, a yak, a dear, a chicken."

"You're despicable. I hate you!"

"No, you just hate what he's become. What *you've* become. What you've *let* yourself become because he isn't what he *was* any more."

Eleanor softened. *Hate Lorne? Impossible.* "He's still in there, somewhere. I can't help remembering that."

"But not the husband you know. Not the one you married, the one you lived with all those years. He's not the same man."

"I know." She cleared her throat and whispered. "But every time I see him, every time I look into his face --"

"What? You think it's him? It's not, and you know it. Stop deceiving yourself. He's not in the same world you and I are. With the same feelings, the same thoughts, the same – desires."

"So? Look, Carlos. I hope you didn't bring me down here just to --." Seduce sounded so horrible, and yet so wonderful, at the same time.

"You feed him, change him, help him move. Put him to bed. Help him with anything personal. He just sits there, in some other time and space we can't understand. A dimension we can only dream of. When we have to."

"He's my husband."

"But he makes you feel angry. Lost. Hopelessly alone. You blame him for how you are." Carlos stared into her eyes. "You feel guilty because of some of the things you think."

Eleanor took a long drink of her wine and was suddenly irritated by the song that floated through the lounge. A melody from her youth, when she was dating Lorne.

"You haven't lived through something like this. You're on the outside, and believe me, on the outside everything is easier."

An apprehensive silence hung between them, like fear between virgins.

"Eleanor --"

"What?"

"If he wasn't here. If he had already . . ."

"Say it!"

Carlos leaned across the table and took her hands between his own. He said it so gently, like the soft flush of a butterflies' wings. "Passed." Silence. "Then what would you feel?"

Sadness. Loneliness. Relief. Freedom. And because of freedom, guilt.

"That I'd lost something."

"But it's already lost. What's the difference, when you really look at it, between *then* and *now*? Tell me."

Eleanor couldn't answer, and the wine stuck in her throat. The pianist's song had changed again but the mournful melody was still there. The one-armed man over on the other side of the room stopped humming and stared down into his glass. The bubbles looked like unearthed body fragments covered in lime.

Carlos stroked the back of Eleanor's hands. "Do you think he always loved you?"

"Yes!"

"And do you think he'd want you to spend the rest of your life looking after him?"

"Of course not. That's why I golf, go to card nights, dine out with friends, do yoga. That's why I took your classes to begin with."

"It's not enough. Art is your passion. It should be your career." He held her hands tighter. "You know it. You can feel it."

"I'm too old for a career."

Carlos' eyes sparkled in the half-light of the lounge, his skin smooth and warm, his lips full and blessed with wine. "No-one is too old for a career. Or for love. And I could be the canvas that takes you on that journey."

Eleanor slipped her hands away and quickly gulped her wine. The lounge was spinning and the music suddenly gratingly loud. The beat pulsed with the obnoxious regularity of a heart monitor.

"Carlos --"

Sensing her discomfort the way a horse feels a rider's fear, Carlos leaned back and whispered something to the pianist. The monitor was unplugged, replaced by soft, mournful ballads. The one-armed man over in the corner pushed his glass to the side and rested his head down on the table against a folded arm. He sobbed softly.

Carlos took Eleanor's hands again, smiling at the token resistance, at the tears bubbling in the corners of her eyes. "Let go," he whispered. He brought one hand up to his face and lightly kissed each of her fingers.

Their thoughts drifted with the music. A couple came in and sat near the back of the lounge just as another couple left, stuffing an array of notes in the little glass on top of the piano.

"I'm not asking you to leave him. I'm not asking you to be unfaithful to him, either. I just want you to let yourself have the opportunity to be in love again before that chance is lost forever. There is nothing wrong with loving us both."

Eleanor couldn't pull her hand away, but she knew she didn't really want to. She looked past Carlos, through a small gap in the hair that tumbled over his shoulders, and she saw the first few drops of another rain slap against the window. Rain bordering on sleet bordering on ice. Lorne would be at home, watching the rain come, too. But what was he really seeing? Anything? Nothing?

She pictured herself coming into the bedroom, tiptoeing closer, pulling the blanket up over his thighs, bending down to kiss the dry skin of his forehead, wiping the drool from the corner of his mouth, seeing if his chest was still moving, listening to his bones crumble, moving in front and seeing her reflection in the glass, feeling the same rain she'd heard in the lounge rap at the window, but not seeing or feeling anything within the darkness of his eyes.

Oh God, is it so wrong to need something more? I give and I give and I give. What about me?

She pulled her hands away and covered her face. Her eyes filled with tears, and lines of mascara rippled down her cheeks. She rammed her chair back, almost knocking it over, and ran from the lounge before Carlos could rise and stop her.

She hoped she'd drown in the rain.

***

"Lydia?"

"Mathew?"

"Lydia? Where are you?"

"Mathew? You keep breaking up. Maybe it's because I keep going up and down."

"Up and down?"

"I'm in a car on my cell. It's quite hilly here. Hilly and rainy. Can you hear the rain on the roof?"

"No."

"Oh."

"Well, maybe a little?"

"Oh good."

"What?

"Where are you going in the car?"

"Dinner. What's the place called?"

"How should I know?"

"Not you. I'm asking what the place is called. What?"

"To who?"

"Michael. He says it's called Monnet's. Like the painter but with two 'n's."

"Michael or Monet?"

"What?'

"Who has one 'M?"

"No, two 'n's, not 'm's.' God. Fuck these stupid hills. Mathew, I'm with Michael Cordel. You know, Raphael's producer. The one I told you all about yesterday."

"What?

"Sorry. Just another dip. In the road. We have to do some serious talking while we do dinner. No other chance. It's the strangest thing: I always seem to be running out of time."

"You have to talk about the show?"

"Yes. And you'll never guess. Michael, the love, wants me to do another spot or two. Imagine. Really Mathew. This time I can feel it. I'm on my way. You'll be so proud of me."

A loud honking sound drowned out the world. What was left of it, anyway.

"Lydia? Lydia?"

"Sorry. Another hill. And some idiot passed us on the way down and another car was coming from the other direction. My moment of fame and *poof*! I could have lost it. Imagine. You're always closer to death than you think, aren't you? That was Michael honking."

"Do you know when you're coming home? I know this probably isn't the best time to talk about it, but we really have to get together. I need to talk to you. About some serious things."

"We are talking."

"I mean face to face. There's some things that I think are very important and --"

"Fuck you." A man's voice.

"I beg your pardon?"

"No, not you Mathew. That was Michael. The idiot who passed us deliberately keeps touching his brakes so his rear lights come on which makes Michael keep braking and backing off, and I don't think Michael appreciates it very much. He's a little tense about the show."

Yes, you don't want anything to go wrong on day time television when so many people depend on it. Mathew rubbed his forehead. That awkward place behind his eyes was starting to hurt again. "When will it air?"

"The air? Oh, it's fine. It's pretty damp and dull here all the time though. I think I'm beginning to understand why Duchovny wanted out. It wasn't just to be with Tea."

"'Tea' who?"

"Really? Tea Leoni. Then again, the gossip in Hollywood says he might be having an affair with Gillian. Imagine! Anyway, when they got married he wanted out of Van and back down to Cali. God."

"What?" Mathew just couldn't keep up with the code. Then again, he didn't really want to anymore.

"No. I mean when will the show air?"

"Oh, the show air. I'm not sure."

"Well, it's important I talk to you personally, Lydia. Everything seems to be falling apart."

"What?"

"Everything seems to be falling apart."

"I didn't hear you. You broke up again. This is impossible. It's like driving on glass. Are you ill, Mathew? I hope you're not coming down with something."

Just life. "No, I'm fine." *Fine fine fine fine fine fine.* "We need to see each other, Lydia."

"Can't Cybernician fix it up on his computer thingy some way? We could have a conference call or whatever they call it nowadays in computer lingo."

Hoooonnnkkkkk.

"My God. People pass by each other at the most inopportune times."

Yes, they certainly do, Lydia. They certainly do. Mathew inhaled a long, deep breath and let it out as slowly as he could. He tried to time the inhalation with the exhalation. He felt a piece of his heart tighten and then open up again a little, tiny bit more.

"We almost crashed again."

We are crashing, Lydia.

"Mathew. I can't hear you again. And it's not as hilly here. Mathew?"

He started massaging his temples again, but the pain was severe. "So you'll be staying out there for a while, then?"

"Yes. It all depends on Raphael. Pardon. Oh yes, and Michael. He's been an absolute dream. Everything's going swimmingly." She gently pushed his hand farther back down her thigh. He pushed it right back up and smiled a producer's smile. "You should really come out to the set and watch how the show's produced. The lights, the audience, the cue card guy, the tele-thingy. God, it's utterly fantastic."

"Almost as good as real life."

"I really can't leave right now with everything that's happening. But why don't you come out here?"

"To Vancouver?"

Michael frowned.

Lydia shook her head knowingly. "Sure. We could spend some time together when I'm not on the set. See the sights, go to dinner -- that kind of thing."

"I'm not sure if I can get away either, Lydia."

She winked at Michael. "Well, call me if you change your mind. No, he won't."

"No, he won't what?"

"Michael wants to make sure you know you can't actually have a part."

"Oh, I know I don't have a part, Lydia. Not even a little one. One that might make a difference."

"Good, that's settled. Thanks for being a dear. Listen, Mathew, I better go. There's more hills ahead and lots of those yellow, diamond shaped signs that have squiggly curves painted on them which probably means there's curves ahead. So say 'hi' to everyone for me, will you?"

Mathew looked up at the refrigerator, but there wasn't any more room for magnetized greetings or messages on the front door. So he lied.

"I will. And everyone here wants me to say hello. Have a nice dinner. And --"

"Sorry. Can't hear you."

"And be careful."

"Of course. What a silly thing to say. I'll call you when everything's in the can."

"What can?"

"The movie can. That's what everybody says when the shoot's over. *It's in the can.* Movie-speak."

"I see." *Oops.* "Lydia?"

"Yes?"

"I miss you."

"More hills. Sorry. My God, I think that asshole behind us is trying to ram us now. What a turd. What, Mathew?"

"Never mind."

"We're coming into another part of the road that winds up and down. I'd better go. Give my love to everyone, will you"

"Sure. That's what his fairy godmother asked him before he left the mall. What good is love if you don't give it away?"

"Bye. Call you soon."

But Mathew was already gone. He slid down the wall like a clump of pabulum thrown from a highchair. He was sitting on the floor, knees to his chest and hands cupped over his face, wondering. But he didn't even know what he was wondering about. Dangling beside him, the coiled extension cord on the phone bungeed the receiver up and down. Up and down, up and down.

Chapter Seventeen

10:01:07
I nu ud folo me, Comptroid.

11:01:55
Ur hard 2 resist, HeavensDick@RealDeal. But who's folloin who?

11:02:31
Dont flater yurself. Think ur man enuf? Cn u kep up withot ur kybord getin coverd in swet?

11:03:22
Sonds lik a chalenge. And her I was woried abot u.

11:03:56
Did u bring a frend? I told u I can handle 2 men at the sam tim.

11:04:44
U havent shown me 1's enof. And bleve me -- Im a lot mor than 1.

11:05:18
Yu haf no idea how many times I've herd that. Afrad?

11:05:59
Wy wood I b?

11:06:34
Ur th 1whos been trapd b4. An u lost.

11:07:00
Ho did u no that?

11:07:39
Ur not niev enuf 2 thers crets in Cyberspace, ar u?

11:08:09
She was difrent.

11:08:33
Im difrent. Wat r u realy in 2?

11:08:56
Helples. I lik 2o feel helples.

11:09:59
Helples? Or vulnrabl?

11:10:22
Both. Wat r u lookin 4? Wy r u here instad of *out in the world*?

11:10:50
Out ther cant giv me wat I ned.

11:11:11
Wat r u whering?

11:11:32
Latx. I alwas wer latx on first dats bcos it keps litle boys in lin. A catsut, blod-red, that covrs me from my ankls 2 my throt. Zipers down th sid, th front and underneth.

11:12:00
Wat wood u want me 2 do?

11:12:192
U haf 2 b told? I thot u biled yrself as a rel stud.

11:12:30
Evry womans difrent.

11:12:49
No ther not.

11:13:08
Wat colr is yur har?

11:13:21
Drk bron. Sholder length, with jus a litle bit of a curl at th botom. Jus long enuf that if I len forwrd it covrs my fac. So if I slithred up yur legs, and th latx startd teseng yur thighs, an Id tak u in my mouth . . .

11:14:02
I coldnt c yur fac. Bt I'd want 2, so Id rech down, pic u up, an thro you on yur bac.

11:14:35
Id fite u off. Jus by tuchin u. Squezing u . . .

11:14:56
Not 4 long. Id hold yur arms bak bhind yur hed an pn yur legs stil with my feet. Id let u ly ther 4 a fuw minits, ovrpowrd an afrad, until u startd wonderin if I was goin 2 touch u at al. Thn Id len down, start licing u al ovr, kisin an bitin u thru th latx. It wod get warm insid that soot prety quikly.

11:15:44
Ud be hot 2. Id push my thighs up aganst ur legs an grind my hips in 2 ur pelvis. I'd fel u uncurlin, strainin, startin 2 push aganst my leg. Tel me abot yur cok.

11:16:20
Id lik ech of the zipers that garded yor brests. Id peel them down slowly with my teth, 1 at a tim, huk by huk, until yur niples finly sprang up thru th metl slits. Id flic my tong ovr th tips until thy startd 2 throb, scratchin them bac and forth with

the ziper. The blud wud be starting to pound through my thick, eight inch cock. The veins would pulse harder and harder, and my bulging head would be glistening wet.

11:17:41

Ud b tryin 2 control yurself, bt u coudnt, bcose Id let u undo th zipers completly and suc my tits. U shud c my tits. Theyr big an hard and push stra8t out. I always sunbathe nude, so my tits r a soft bron with dep red aoreolas Im squezing them togethr rit now and rubing my niples aganst each ohtr thru th latx.

11:18:19

Id rip th ziper btwen yur legs opn an spla yur thighs apart with my nees. Id roll up on top of u an neel don btween your legs. You gasp when u saw my erectshun. It wood scar u an mae u wet at th sam tim. Id keep yur arms pined bac as I leend down. My hed wood stay ther, tesingly clos, jus barly insid, an thn Id start rubing yur sx aliv with th undrside of my cok.

11:19:33

Id b rithin aganst u, an the latx wood inflam yur skin. Id star up in2 yur eyes and lic my lips with my tong, bt I woodnt let u kiss me. Id kno wat u want an what u coodnt haf. My niples wood b strainin up thru th slits in the ziper. Id len my hed down and tast them. I nevr kis on my frst date.

11:20:16

Id push my hed in an ud wimper. A litle length, thn Id stop an pul bac ot. Ud buk up an don 2 met me, so Id push in a litle mor th nex tim, srchin farthr, probin deper. Thn Id sloly dra myself bac agan, riht ot so my thic, pulsin hed was jus barly bobing btwen yor lips, an them Id plung in agan, slowly, but deep and hard. In and out, in and out, until you could finally take my whole shaft.

11:21:02

Id squeze u so hard with th musles of my pussy yud beg me 2 let u go, let u mov, so u coud slid in2 my wetnes. Yur body woud b shakin an ud b covrd in swet. Th latx woud mak

my skin on fir, bt Id b completly in control. I woudnt let u orgasm until I was redy, until my clit was raw-rd.

11:22:00
Wen I new u coud tak it Id start 2 mov fastr. Hardr an fastr,
deepr thrusts that woud impal u 2 th bd. Ud b rithin bac an
forth, bt Id keep yur arms pined bac. Ud b monin, begin me
with yur eys.

11:22:59
Id let u rech a feverish pitch, thn Id clamp down so hard it
wold tak yur brath awa. Ud let go of my arms so you culd grab
my legs, try 2 mak me mov. Bt Id hold u stil with my pussy. Id
rech bac bhind u an grab yr har, eas up my muscels insid jus
enuf that u cud start 2 mov agan, an then squeze u so tite agan
ud gasp. Id look up in2 yur eys, smile, lic my lips, feel u squrm.
Id len don and suc gredily at my niples, ignorin the pain of yr
ned, yr desir.

11:24:06
O ys!

11:24:24
O baby! Thats so nic!

11:24:39
O Comptroid. Strok yurself hardr. Hardr!

***

Cybernician scrolled back and read the last few lines again.
At first he'd felt guilty about tagging along and not telling his
friend, but not anymore. Comptroid had asked him to.

The pulse from the screen made Cybernician's skin an
ethereal blue, but he felt bloodless and completely flushed. His
temples were pounding and his hands shook so badly he could
barely press the keys. His gloves were damp. His friend's coded
Internet name had been deciphered and he hadn't even realized
it yet. The woman called him Comptroid -- not the reformulated

password he'd logged on with HeavensDick@RealDeal. Cybernician knew the complex code couldn't have been broken that easily. He'd known his friend's code name, of course. And so did Mouseman. The only other person that could have figured it out would have been Sheila.

Chapter Eighteen

Mathew knew the drive wasn't going to be a slow, unhurried respite through the countryside the moment he first backed out of the driveway and was almost t-boned by a garbage truck driven by a young man smoking a reefer, a young, dirty man with a long, unruly beard with a birthmark on his forehead who was listing to a set of earphones and arguing on his cell phone at the same time about all the things he heard the government was spraying on the marijuana crops to make dopers sick. To compound matters even further, Mathew knew it was going to be an inauspicious drive when he glanced down and rechecked his dashboard, confirming his worst nightmare: that the numerical reading on his odometer was three kilometers past where it was supposed to have been.

Mathew always seemed to be three kilometers behind everything.

And yet he'd planned it so well. After driving around the neighborhood for almost half an hour the night before last night, he should have been at 28,482 kilometers, which should have meant he would have reached the highway's on-ramp at an even 28,500 kilometers. But he couldn't. He was already at 28,487 kilometers -- practically a full 1.8 miles short.

Joshua, however, had been practicing driving up and down the driveway ever since breakfast when he'd found out where their adventure was going to take them today. Unfortunately, he forgot to tell his father about his little escapade, which completely skewed Mathew's sequential timing of his odometer. Which was far more important to him than people would ever have thought.

He was late, just off the mark, like he always seemed to be. *Just* behind where he wanted to be. But then again, everything's relative. If he'd been on time and the odometer was where it should have been, he would have backed up earlier, and if he'd backed up earlier the long bearded man in the garbage truck's twin, the one with the birthmark on the other side of his forehead who threw the bags and emptied the canisters into the back of the truck, would have cared a lot less about the things they spray on pot: he would have cared far more about how this big truck compounded, compressed, reused, and recycled whatever was tossed into the back. *Like him.*

Although he couldn't completely account for the discrepancy, Mathew knew that in some way, Joshua had probably saved one of the two *toker-look-a-likes* from certain death. Either way, the odometer reading had played an important part in his life again.

Mathew knew there was unquestionably a component of superstition, or perhaps obsessive compulsion, involved in his fixation with his odometer, but, nevertheless, he'd always known that the unending, slowly passing of the numbers on his odometer meant something, something personal, to him, a prognostication of something in his own life, an historical landmark that defined *what might have* happened to him, or *what might happen* to him, in some esoteric way. Mathew had always known that the digits on his odometer were really more than mere random numbers scrolling down on a dashboard; something far deeper, far more arcane or even cryptic then they were for practically everyone else. Each time one rolled by, another sacred number that was actually a milestone in his life showed him just how far he'd come, or perhaps how far *he hadn't* come: a numerical sequence that was reminiscent that nothing had really changed. A redolent reminder of what – and who – he was still missing, just one more turn of numbers or tires in a long, endless journey of moments that had come and gone. *Without him. Without the Grim Reaper of Odometer Readings.*

The old *life is a journey, not an ending* kind of thing.

The changing numbers had always had some special, mysterious meaning to Mathew ever since he'd first started to drive. For some reason he couldn't quite explain, he needed to watch the numbers when the odometer rolled to a brief stop at some historic landmark or another he deemed important. With his attention fixated on the rolling figures like some slot machine addict, Mathew had barely escaped accidents on three separate occasions. *Three that he could remember.*

Once, stoned in his old Pontiac Parisienne, the rolling, gas-guzzling boat he'd inherited in high school. He'd been watching the odometer because as one more mile passed by the reading would show an even one hundred and fifty thousand miles, and he'd almost rear-ended the only person in the entire city who actually stopped as the green light changed to amber, instead of just booting it through the intersection like everyone else.

Then later, after a few lines and in a more sedate sedan after he'd graduated from university, he'd been looking up at the traffic and down at the dash (oh, how things like that foreshadowed cell phones and texting) when the numbers were about to morph from twenty nine thousand, nine hundred and ninety nine, someone had almost slammed into *him* just as all the digits in all the slots changed into new positions.

And then, several years later when he'd lost the love of his life and he'd married Lydia - the Lydia before the acting bug bit her in the face and left a dormant horde of acting spiders just waiting to be unleashed - and they'd bought their first car together, *with a sunroof,* and they'd opened it up so that hash oil smoke wouldn't ruin that special *new car* smell . . . . No. He didn't want to think about that again. That *almost.* Not now.

Mathew pushed the image away and looked down. At some point today he'd undoubtedly reach another pioneering obituary, a reading of all *threes, four of them,* including the decimal place, and he didn't want to miss it. He passed the garbage truck and waved.

When Mathew finally managed to beg his way over to the exit ramp and crawl off the Parkway, he felt a momentary spark of freedom when he saw the '401 East' sign looming above. The highway swerved sharply to the right, immediately dividing into separate collector and express lanes. He had to choose quickly because no one really slowed down on the ramps any more, even in a blizzard: you could tell by the mish-mash of paint stripes and dents lining the guardrails. It wasn't a difficult choice -- not quite *the road not taken,* or anything as serious as that -- since the express lanes ultimately merged with the collector lanes anyway, but it was a daunting decision nonetheless because Mathew rarely ever went east. But that's the direction their journey laid today: The Metro Toronto Zoo.

Mathew usually stayed in the city core or went west, toward Wonderland, the Wild Water Park, Woodbine Race Track so he could lose a few dollars, or long ago, a really long time ago, when he and Lydia went on their yearly pilgrimage to Niagara Falls. They'd stay for a weekend in the off-season in one of the scrunched up little hotels on Clifton Hill when most of the tourists were drying off at home. Sometimes, if the sun was just right, the sky was cloudless, the traffic wasn't heavy and the pollution index wasn't hampered by the endless smog that rolled up over the lake from the Ohio Valley, he could catch a glimpse of the majestic Falls through a small gap between the wax museums, restaurants, and tourists shops. He hadn't been to Niagara since Joshua was born. It hadn't changed anyway. Just more constricted, gaudy, confusing, and with signs that announced everything in more languages than he realized existed. The new casino didn't interest him in the least because the crumpled *Depends* packages dotting the parking lots like seagull droppings made him uneasy and sad. One day, he thought, the seats at the slot machines would actually be commodes like they have in hospitals and palliative facilities so the older players didn't have to wait to get all the way out to the parking lots to get rid of their diapers.

The 401 was always jammed and today wasn't any different. Cars whizzed by in tinted blurs. But Mathew was going east and that made him feel relaxed somehow, and he felt the adrenaline rush that comes when you start out on the first stages of an adventure. The only thing that bothered him was the speed of the cars, their closeness, the angry faces of the drivers. He didn't know what he was more afraid of: smashing headfirst into the car in front of him or being rear-ended by someone from behind. He couldn't imagine being thrown over the steering wheel and catapulting through the front window, but the thought of having the steering wheel lance through his chest wasn't any more comforting. Lying on the road, shivering, and blood everywhere, hurt more than angry at the rubberneckers who slowed and gawked at his mangled body. And all of them trying to take photos of him with their smart phones so they could send them to their friends. Or just to anybody. What if the windshield did a Jayne Mansfield? Would he look back and see his own body stretched out on the pavement several feet away, his arms and legs jerking like a slaughtered chicken? He tried not to think about it and determinedly attempted to keep a buffer of space between his car and the ones around it. The problem was, though, that every time he tried to give himself more space, someone swerved recklessly near and took it away.

The race lasted less than an hour and was well worth it. Joshua absolutely loved the zoo. He'd been on an adrenaline high since breakfast when Mathew had first suggested going. He slammed the door closed and was off and running like a gazelle before Mathew had rolled to a complete stop at the far edge of the huge parking lot. Joshua slipped into another world when he walked over the wooden bridge that spanned the river just outside the main gates. Below, barracuda-sized orange goldfish drifted through the currents, waiting for food. Geese wandered nonchalantly over the bridge with him; a monkey howled in the distance. Joshua waited for Mathew to catch up. When he did, he took his father's arm. He sensed something was wrong because Mathew had been unnaturally talkative during the drive, but he wasn't sure what was bothering his father. He'd try and remember to ask him later. He didn't realize it wasn't some*thing*: it was some*one*. Carol. Mathew hadn't stopped thinking about her for days. Days that made everything else hurt.

Tickets in hand, Joshua and Mathew shuffled through the turnstiles. Weaving past the clumps of bystanders that invariably gathered right in front of an entrance or an exit, Joshua stepped into a parallel dimension. Everything was happening all at once. Bestial scents drifted on a light breeze, wrapping them in a comforting smell of hair, fur, sweat. Little social dramas unfolded all around. Some creatures were stomping, nattering, preening, snorting, scuffing at the ground, braying, scanning for intruders, while others scrounged and fought for food. Mating season had obviously begun, and pairs tentatively approached each other, searching for some smell, some clue or esoteric invitation. The males strutted ostentatiously about in ritual displays while the females mulled in nervous groups, eyeing the competitors. There was a nervous sense of controlled confusion that Mathew knew would become even more prevalent when they left the main meeting area and went deeper in to see the animals.

Numerous paths wound away from the main gates and up into the surrounding hillsides. Each one would take them to a different pavilion, a different continent of animals. The routes were marked with painted footprints so the intrepid gaggle of camera-toting hunters knew what animals they were moving toward: polar bear paw prints led one way, elephant hooves and tiger tracks another.

It was a warm, sunny afternoon, and as Mathew followed Joshua up the footprints, he wished his father would have been able to come along too. But that was completely out of the question. His father and the zoo mixed as well as water and the Wicked Witch of the East. The last time Mathew had been cerebrally strangled and had invited Lorne on a summer outing to the zoo had been nothing less than an unmitigated disaster. For someone with an unconscious reaction to animal names that was manifested psychologically and physically, the zoo wasn't an appropriate place to see how well he could control himself.

It had been a Friday morning, early in the season. Dirty, disheveled, his clothes torn and his eyes glazed with fright, Lorne was bathed in sweat before they'd managed to make it up the hill and into the North American pavilion. Unsuspectingly, everyone around them talked animatedly about the things they'd seen, and Lorne metamorphosed into an endless series of animals as Mathew and Joshua tried to hike up the trail. Incongruous and woefully incomplete, the transformations were just momentary shadows of each other, like images in a kaleidoscope. Just as the poor old man was beginning to assume the shape and disposition of one animal, someone lumbering by with a necklace of cameras, slurping at their ice cream while they tried to keep track of children racing on ahead, would blurt out the name of another animal they'd just encountered and poor granddad would be mutating again. In the space of just a few minutes, while Mathew tried to guide him over the huge blue paw prints that staggered up the hill, his father was a goat, a grizzly bear, a white-tailed deer, a beaver, a muskrat, a lynx, and an elk. The only saving grace was that they hadn't been walking toward the Australian Pavilion.

Still, it had been enough for Mathew. He couldn't see the day getting any better. After a quick breath of air as they lay exhausted on the grass, he escorted his father back down the hill and out to the parking lot. People passing by glanced uncertainly and then snickered behind their hands when they saw Mathew steering his father along the trail with his palms cupped over the old man's ears. Although Mathew knew his father would have enjoyed the expedition, he was glad only Joshua had come today. Joshua was always a good listener. Tensely apprehensive, Mathew would talk to him when he could. About his fairy godmother. About separating. And maybe about Carol, too.

They went through several pavilions before Joshua tired and needed a lunch break. Mathew had forgotten to bring a snack in a disposable container, so he was forced to buy something at the McDonald's that dominated a grassy knoll. The little yellow arch blended in with the flora and fauna about as well as team loyalty and a professional athlete.

Mathew watched Joshua gnaw off another piece. "How's your hamburger?" At least he thought it was a hamburger.

Joshua said it was okay, which was the boy's way of saying *I'll eat it if I have to but don't ask me to talk about it again or I'll have to lie.*

They threw some french-fry-laced salt to the seagulls and geese that scavenged the ground for leftovers. Joshua seemed more interested in the people lolling around than the birds.

"What?" Mathew asked.

The boy shook his head, then gestured with his chin, giggling. "Look at that guy, Dad. Gross."

A fat man, two normal-sized men wide, was stuffing handfuls of food into a gaping chasm of a mouth. Some bounced down the hillside of his chin. Equally proportioned, his wife was obsessively trying to lick clumps of congealed milkshake from the bottom of her cup. The man's face and neck had been burned by the sun and he was perspiring profusely. His pants bulged down over the edge of the bench, his ass brandishing thick wads of black hair. He had hair on his shoulders too, and Mathew could see matted tangles poking out from underneath his t-shirt. Just looking at the man made him itchy. Mathew shivered, glad his own back wasn't covered in fur, and wondered, as he'd done countless times before, just how we ever got to be the pinnacle of the food chain.

When lunch was over, Mathew wanted to see the gorillas, but Joshua tugged at his sleeve and cajoled him along to the North American pavilion because that's where the otter exhibit was. As zoos go, the otters had a fairly large area to themselves. Still captive, they looked free. Kind of like government office workers in their little cubicles. The otters actually had access to two interconnected compartments. The one outside had been made to look like the edge of a river, complete with rocks, grass, trees, and plants. The one inside consisted of a large, glass-walled tank where you could watch them swimming and cavorting underwater. The two sides were joined by a little door the otters could hide behind when they got bored watching the people at the window.

Just a little after noon, it was feeding time for the uncaged, so Mathew and Joshua had the place to themselves. Joshua braced his hands against the glass. Spellbound, he quietly watched the sleek bodies spin by the window like miniature torpedoes fired from some distant submarine. He was sure one kept smiling at him beneath the outcrop of whiskers that sprouted from the sides of his face each time he glided by the glass or somersaulted back up to the surface. Father and son watched the otters swim and twirl by in fascinated silence for several minutes. *What a wonderful life*, Mathew thought. But he couldn't stop thinking about what he wanted to say, what had plagued his thoughts and dreams for so long. He cleared his throat twice, chewing over words made of glass.

"Joshua?"

The boy didn't look up but he could see his father's reflection in the tank. The smiling otter twisted by, swimming on his back, then spun around and shot past again like a tapered missile. Up, down, up down then around and around, trailing a path of air bubbles to the surface. "Otters are cool, aren't they, Dad?" He smiled at one he'd christened *Whiskers*. The other otter sat on a half-submerged branch, preening in the sun. "I wish I could be an otter for awhile."

Mathew forgot what he was going to say, because that's exactly what he'd just been thinking, too. Well not *him*, actually: the little voice. The little voice that was always there, always in the back of your mind, judging commenting, criticizing, debating, challenging. The one that wouldn't let *you* be *you*. The one it was almost impossible to turn off, just like his fairy godmother said. He should have bought one of the little Zen Gardens.

These otters are just like you and Lydia, Mathew. They're close, but they never touch. They're the same, but individual, too. They don't communicate, and if they do, it's just so they avoid swimming into each other. They look like they're having fun together but they're really on their own. They're not separate parts of a whole any more. They're in their own little world, and people looking in think it's fine. They accept the fact they've been thrown together somehow, that they share the same space and time, but they can't stop looking out and wondering what's on the other side of the glass.

Mathew gulped, and wished the little voice would go away, but it never did when you wanted it to. Breathe and let go, he thought. Breathe and let go. He thought his relationship with Lydia had slowly grown into something more akin to mating black widows. Necessary and probably useful in some esoteric grand scheme, but devoid of passion, need, and desire. He approached her tentatively, carefully now, arms raised defensively and always ready to run as soon as they came together.

Another torpedo fired by. The one on the log licked something from its paws. He didn't know where to look when Whiskers swam right at the glass. At the very last second the otter dived down, curled around, and shot back up to the surface, trailing bubbles.

Somewhere, his mind whispered. "I still love her."

The little voice wasn't placated. *"Sure you do. But not in the way you need to. Or want to. And in her own way she loves you too. But that doesn't mean you should stay together, does it? People are different at different times in their lives."*

A new playmate emerged from the little room that connected the two sides of the exhibit, floating on its back as its feet paddled the water like the wheel on a Mississippi gambling boat. *Whiskers* took a playful nip at the preening otter's tail. It barked vociferously, then teasingly flipped its bait back down into the water. *Whiskers* pretended not to notice.

"She's hardly ever home. It's difficult to work on a relationship if you don't have the time." Mathew looked around, wondering if he'd spoken out loud.

Perhaps things have changed for Lydia and she can't put in the time. Or the effort.

Whiskers whipped by the glass, his slender body sleek and rigid as an arrow. Turning, he made a long, slow arc around the tank and then glided up to the glass wall. He hovered motionlessly on unseen currents and stared right into Joshua's eyes. Joshua saw his own reflection on the otter's face so clearly he ran his fingers across his cheeks to see if he had whiskers or not. He stared back, transfixed, as the otter's breaths rose between them in a staccato pulse of tiny bubbles. Finally he turned away. Just as he did, the otter dove up, arched backwards in a graceful somersault, and sped off. He threw himself up onto the grass at the water's edge, then scurried into the hidden lair.

More and more people were gradually filtering down into the enclosure. Clusters of excited children pushed and shoved their way in front of the exhibits, elbowing the kids already there out of the way. Parents smiled blissfully and rammed overflowing strollers in beside their presumptuous little heathens so they could get a better look, too. Joshua watched *Whiskers* climb out of the water and haul himself up onto the grass, but he lost sight of his new found friend when some little thuglet flattened him against the glass.

"It's getting too crowded, Dad. Let's go back outside."

Clawing his way back from the window, Joshua took his father's hand, and together, they wove their way through the pressing throng toward the exit, fighting the current like shoppers on Boxing Day. They didn't speak again until they'd found a little empty grassy spot on a nearby hillock where they tasted fresh air and wet fur. Joshua scrunched down next to his father, plucked a slender stalk from the ground, and then absently wound it around his finger.

Mathew took a deep breath and let it out slowly, the things he wanted to talk about still there, festering and waiting for exposure, like a politician's secrets. A young man walked by pushing a three-seater stroller. Twins and one apparently a year or so older. Mathew couldn't imagine what that would have been like. He looked over at Joshua who was busily flicking foraging ants from the bottom of his shins. He'd rehearsed this speech a thousand times and envisioned the entire conversation in his mind just as many. But now, he didn't know where to begin. What to say, or how best to unravel his feelings. He'd always planned on having Lydia at his side when this moment came, but that was something he couldn't wait for any longer.

"Joshua --"

Joshua looked up at his father, shielding his eyes with a cupped hand and squinting in the sunlight that reflected off the pavilion's glass walls.

"Dad, can I ask you something?"

Mathew was thankful for another reprieve. "Sure Joshua."

"It's personal."

"That's okay."

"It's about mom."

Mathew felt his chest tighten. He waited, tensely alert.

"Well, you guys . . . "

"Go on, son."

Joshua undid the stalk from around his finger. His skin was lined with red gouges. "You guys don't really love each as much anymore, do you?"

Mathew tried not to look surprised. "Why do you think that, Joshua?"

The boy shrugged. He went to speak but waited until a man in a wheelchair glided by. "Just everything," he whispered.

"Everything?"

"You're not together much, and when you are . . . . " Another shrug. "I don't know. You're not *together*, if you know what I mean."

Mathew did. And it hurt. "Sometimes, as the years go by, people grow apart, Joshua. Your mother is a wonderful woman.

I love your mother and I think she loves me. But just because two people care about each other doesn't mean they should always spend their life together."

"Do you think you're going to . . . "

Another shrug. The boy was struggling with the words, or perhaps with what the words really meant. "Stay together?"

Mathew forced down a dry gulp, but Joshua went on before he had a chance to answer. There was a hint of false bravado to his voice. "It's not a big deal, Dad. Bobby Schroeder's parents are divorced, and Trevor Martin told me he's never met his dad. A lot of kids at school live with just one of their parents now."

Mathew nodded sadly. He'd hadn't really thought about that much before, because when he went to school, 'divorce' and 'separation' were two words he rarely heard. How had everything changed in one or two generations? And *why?*

Joshua undid the stalk. His finger was scored with red lines. "Are you still going to be my mom and dad?"

"Oh Joshua," Mathew stammered, slipping his arm around the boy's shoulders. "Of course we are. No matter what happens, we'll always love you. And we'll always be your parents, too."

And we'll always be your parents, too, won't we?

The idea was strangely disturbing. Mathew drifted back over the years. He was in the car again, thinking about the day Joshua had told them about living with his other parents in the Cape Cod house down by the subway station. He'd been thinking of becoming an architect. Building what others dreamed of. What would he have looked like now, if he'd still been that *other* Joshua?

"Joshua --"

The child's pupils dilated and his eyes glazed with the familiar mistiness that said he was slipping away somewhere else. That he was *being* someone else. *Becoming someone else.* His eyelids fluttered for a moment, he slumped forward, and his face melted into a monk-like mask of serenity.

But when the boy looked back up, Mathew sensed the transition was different this time. It wasn't . . . complete. Something in his eyes, the way he moved his head. It was like Joshua, the Joshua he knew, was trying to hang on, trying to keep a hold on his own memories, trying to have his own voice heard, while at the same time he was still changing into one of the *other* Joshuas.

"I didn't really have long with those parents in the Cape Cod."

"Joshua? What do you . . . .? "

"I know you're not my real father."

Mathew bolted forward. He felt like he'd been hit in the center of the back with a jagged brick. He tried to stay in control, to keep some semblance of composure. God, where was Queen Beatrice? After a numbing moment of silence, he struggled to speak.

"What do you mean by that?" It sounded even more ridiculous when he said it out loud.

The odd thing though, was he wasn't surprised that Joshua already knew. In fact, deep down, he always assumed he did. It was as if he'd always known Joshua was completely aware of their true relationship, but that they'd been silenced by some unexpressed covenant that prevented them from ever talking about it out loud.

"Joshua --"

The boy reached up and ruffled Mathew's hair. His voice was level and light, and for once, nothing betrayed who or what he'd become. "I don't mean that in a bad way, of course. Simply a biological one. In every other way you've always been a father to me. And you always will be. Even with all of the things you've had to deal with, you've always been as good as you can for me."

For some reason, Mathew wanted to cry. No, not cry: weep.

"How long?"

"Have I know?" His son smiled gently. "Always." Behind them, deep beneath a protective wall, one of the otters barked a long, eerie cry. "Your fairy godmother knows too, I bet."

Mathew nodded. *Probably.* "You never said anything."

"Why should I. And what would I have said? You saved me from some other life and took me in when I couldn't look after myself. You brought me up as your own son, and you've done your best to be and do everything a father is supposed to." He winked. "You've tried, and I couldn't have asked for anything more."

Mathew couldn't help smiling.

"I've always known you've loved me. And I've always loved you too. It doesn't matter whether you actually physically fathered me or not." He grinned. "You know, *the-old-index-finger-jabbing-through-the-round-hole thing your friend used to do?*"

Crowds streamed by. Mathew thought it odd that so many people couldn't go anywhere without eating. Something screeched in the distance, but the otters had stopped calling.

Another secret was out, so there was no point in hedging. "Joshua, do you know --." He chewed on his bottom lip. Of course he did.

Joshua leaned over and whispered conspiratorially, like a pirate telling his crony where the gold's buried. "I don't know *him*, but I know Carmalitta's my mother."

Another brick smashed the breath from Mathew's lungs. "Was it something we said?"

The boy said no. "There were lots of signs."

"What kind of signs?"

"The way you held me. The way Lydia tried so hard to make me feel special. How Carmalitta was always watching me, studying me, but how she was so afraid of getting too close to me. How Grandma was with Carmalitta when we were all together." Another shrug. "There were constant little hints, subtle clues everywhere. But that's not how I knew."

Mathew was reluctant to ask, but he had to. What was the point in turning back now if they'd come this far?

"Then how?"

Silence. And another change. The person Mathew was talking to, the one Joshua seemed to be clinging to, was slipping farther away, out of reach. The child looked thoughtful, reflective, unhurried. He seemed calmed and troubled at the same time. Saddened by happy memories, like the memories Christmas ornaments often call up.

When he finally spoke, his voice was softly ethereal, his words barely above a whisper. "Inside."

Mathew frowned. "Inside where?"

Joshua made a circular motion over his stomach with his hand. "Carmalitta used to rub me like this." He closed his eyes, remembered, felt it all again. "She always stopped with a little pat, so soft, so gentle." He showed his father.

"How could I not know her? I lived with her for so long, floating, turning, kicking, sensing, eating what she ate, drinking what she drank, tumbling in a sea of gentle waves, listening to her heart beat, her blood flow through her veins, hearing her whisper to me as I drifted off to sleep."

Mathew put his arm around the boy's shoulders and pulled him close. He looked down at his son. The boy remembered so many deaths, then why not that sweet time, too?

Joshua fell silent. He breathed slowly and deeply, and the liquid cloudiness gradually evaporated from his eyes. He was floating *up* again, but not all the way. Not all the way back to *Joshua*.

"I know it was a hard decision for her," Mathew said quietly. "And it's a decision adults have to make that affects a lot of people other than just themselves. I think she wanted to be your mother, but there were just too many things on her mind at the time that made it difficult for her to know for sure what to do. I know she's always loved you, though."

"I've always felt it." Joshua smiled, but Mathew saw a trace of sadness in the boy's eyes.

Mathew's eyes didn't cloud over like Joshua's, but he drifted back through the years with the same sense of floating restlessness. "She was going to get married. A nice young man, really. Intelligent, hardworking, not bad looking. But your mom -- Carmalitta -- well, she had these doubts about . . . well, about whether marrying a man was right for her."

Joshua reached over and touched his father's arm. "I know. I was inside her, remember."

Mathew sighed. "She didn't find out she was pregnant until after they broke up. She was confused. And I'm sure she was frustrated and afraid, too."

Joshua nodded solemnly and rubbed his eyes with the back of his hand. "I remember her being hurt and angry."

Mathew knew he was right. "So when she finally decided that she couldn't keep you, your mother -- Lydia -- and I thought the best thing would be to bring you home as our own."

"Why?"

Mathew shifted uncomfortably. "I'm not sure. It just felt like the right thing to do."

He uncurled his legs and stretched them out across the grass. The steady stream of eating passers-by had begun to ebb. A lot of them took the trail that led over to the African Pavilion, so Mathew pictured the lion compound in his mind. The edge of their vast pen sloped down into a gully, a moat without water, and there was a large fence at the top of the enclosure that angled in toward the compound, like the ones designed to prevent the soccer hooligans from pouring onto the field. But Mathew had watched the lions and tigers carefully. He'd seen the coiled power in their legs, the potent strength in their necks and haunches, the speed they could attain. Could they make it over that fence if they were desperate enough? He was sure they could. Many forms of death were easier to consider than being eaten alive by a lion. He wondered how many bites you'd actually feel.

"I guess it's still hard for her now," Joshua said, pulling Mathew back from his mastication. "Seeing me every day, watching me grow up as your son."

"Yes. I'm sure it is. But I think that in the long run, she knows she made the right decision."

"I just hope she knows it's not as important as she might think it is."

"In what way?"

Joshua shrugged. "Few decisions really are." He glanced up at his father and smiled, but his eyes betrayed a twinge of melancholy. "She'll have other chances, other choices. She always will."

Mathew shifted sideways and braced an arm back against the grass. He began to perspire and he knew it wasn't because of the sun. They were entering that other area again; the one he longed to know and understand but made him so distressed at the same time. *Joshua's memories*. The boy that still wasn't quite Joshua yet sensed his unease.

"Everything comes in waves."

Mathew thought about his fairy godmother. And about Carol.

"Picture a waving line, like a sound wave, perhaps." Joshua kicked at the grass with his heel until he unearthed a bare patch. He traced a pattern in the dirt with his finger, one wavy line that intersected with another parallel one, like ovals joined together at the ends.

"We meet, we come apart, we meet again. No matter what you talk about -- the seasons, the stages of a life, the flux of cultures, even the expansion and ultimate contraction of the universe -- the pattern is always there underneath."

Mathew clenched his teeth together so hard his jaw started to ache. Joshua touched him lightly on the arm.

"Cycles of death and rebirth. They're all around us." He retraced one line with his finger.

"We begin, we live, we meet, we die, but the cycle never stops."

Mathew felt dizzy. The blood in his temples began to throb. Nausea crept in.

"The image, or rather, the essence of the image, underlies everything. It's the symbol for infinity, for instance. And why do you think it just happens to be the same pattern as the double helix in DNA?"

An elephant trumpeted a mournful cry somewhere in the distance. Another answered back. Mathew stared down at the lines Joshua had drawn, wishing beyond hope he had the faith the boy did. Joshua reached down and blocked out half of his picture with the edge of his hand.

"Forget those decisions," he whispered, gesturing to the ground hidden by his hand. "And just look toward these." He swept his palm over the continuation of the intersecting waves.

Mathew's nausea withered away as quickly as it had blossomed. His body shivered, and he had the oddest feeling that he was very small and very large at the same time. Carol. His chest tightened painfully at the image of her name. Should he leave? Could he leave? And what would happen to all the time he'd shared with Lydia, with the rest of his family? His brow crinkled and he draped his arm around Joshua's shoulders.

The otter in the enclosure behind them barked once, then again. A young man in his early twenties that was walking up the hill stopped to swat a child on the rear. He wagged a finger at him threateningly as the boy coughed on tears. An old man checked his watch and looked up and down the path again, wondering what could have happened to them. Seagulls squawked overhead.

And then Mathew heard it. He stood up instinctively and quickly looked around, but he couldn't see where the sound was coming from. He heard it again and spun around toward the otter exhibit. People crowded around the concrete barrier that overlooked their grassy home. There -- just beyond the far wall that led into the warren beneath the exhibits where you could watch them swim.

When he looked down, Joshua was teetering like an unsteady bowling pin. His eyes fluttered, the color flushed back into his face, and a deep frown creased his forehead.

Joshua grabbed Mathew's pant leg, scrunching the fabric up into a ball.

"Joshua? What is it?"

The boy looked up, confused, uncertain, a glazed look in his eyes, but not *the glazed look,* a different one, like a ghost that's come to warn you about something but has outstayed it's time and is slowly dematerializing. Whoever he'd been for the last few minutes was trying to stay, trying to hang on to this time, this place, to stay in *this Joshua's* world for just a little while longer.

Fumbling with his words, he pointed behind them with his other hand without looking up. "Over there."

Mathew followed his son's direction. He thought he caught a glimpse of sunlight reflected off the rungs, but he wasn't sure. The sound was unmistakable, though: rickety old rusted wheels *click-clack-clicking* over the pavement.

Chapter Nineteen

10:09:16

I trid u a copel of tims yesterda; gues I lost in computr tag. Did u gt my mesages? We wer dow 4 an our. Il resend th mal agan in cas u coudnt receve it. I hav 2 sty lat bt Il try u agan wen I gt home. I mis u lots, an hop eveybody is wel. O, gess what? It looks lik wer geting th 'Transatlantic Transponders' acount. Major ot drain, bt ill b a rel fethr in my cap if I can gt them up and runing withot any probs. Anywy, lov an kises. Lol, Your Sheila.

***

Elizabeth, her eyes red, her face pinched, ushered in the next family. She could barely speak their names clearly. She gently closed the door as she backed out, her body sighing with relief that she wasn't the one that had to do this. Poor Carmalitta.

Mrs. Sinclair slumped down into one of the chairs but her husband, awkward and disoriented, stood behind the other one, arms braced rigidly against its back. Mrs. Sinclair daubed another tissue to her eyes. She held a wad of them tightly in her fist. Carmalitta had been on an emergency call with Dr. Emerson, the surgeon, and knew she was late seeing the Sinclairs, but the delay had been unavoidable. She wondered how long they'd been in the waiting room: Elizabeth didn't usually fall prey to the tears of her patient's relatives.

Carmalitta gestured to the empty chair. "Are you sure you wouldn't rather --"

Mr. Sinclair took his hand away from the back of the chair just long enough to dismiss the thought with a wave. Carmalitta was worried but didn't say anything. Mr. Sinclair was one of those ancient men no one could ever guess the age of that looked like they were ready to fall over any second and curl up into a tangled ball of dust and hair and cracked bone.

Once, Mr. Sinclair was average in height, with thick hair, strong hands, and a round face with a nose that was just this side of bulbous, but those years were gone. His wife was around seventy, her skin thin and transparent, the veins in her arms and calves throbbing with the irregular beat of her heart. Grey hair she hadn't bothered to dye in a long time, bony hands, and a wrinkled throat like the African women forced to wear neck rings probably have when they finally get old, their head bobs forward, and they have to take them off. Nice, average, everyday people who'd quietly lived out typically normal little lives. And now they were going to lose one of the things that had kept them going for the last few years, the thing that separated them from the darkness that was imminently pressing in closer.

Koala, or just 'Bear' for short on those few occasions he managed to step over the hidden threshold all animals know and make his owners cross, was a fifteen year old Maltese that did look a little like his namesake if you stretched your arms up and held him high above your head, his ears were back, and the lights weren't too bright. But "Koala" had some other special meaning for them that they'd never divulged. Blessed with a long and pampered life at the Sinclairs, Koala had finally outlived the feeble bones and mange-eaten skin that held his clumps of fur together. He was blind in one eye, never knew whether he was finished peeing or not, and could rarely keep the bulk of his meals down any longer. Koala had a tumor the size of a cupcake growing out of his back that forced him to limp, and each hobbling step he managed to take was a painful reminder to Mrs. Sinclair that everything God does must have some purpose, even if we can't ever understand it.

The Sinclairs were afraid to let Koala go, but they knew he'd lost any semblance of quality that made his life so special. They agonized over the decision for a month but still hadn't had the fortitude to take the poor animal into Dr. Emerson's for the final time. *The injection.* Running on pure emotion, they were, for the most part, beyond rational thoughts and explanations. Carmalitta knew they didn't see their own deaths in Koala's, but they had come to that debilitating moment when you realize you don't want to see your loved one suffer, but you don't want to see the thing you've loved so long close its eyes forever, either.

"Can I get you anything? Water? Perhaps some tea?"

Mrs. Sinclair shook her head. Her husband blinked *no*. The clock tick-tocked obscenely from the corner of her desk. Carmalitta wouldn't have kept it there if Miriam hadn't given it to her for her last birthday. It was shaped like a Panda, sitting on its haunches as it chewed a thick pawful of bamboo stalks. The face of the clock was imbedded in the Panda's stomach.

Carmalitta knew she could take Koala to Dr. Emerson's for the Sinclairs, but that wouldn't help them come to terms with their loss. Besides, it was important that they walk those final steps together. The dog would be frightened, naturally, but at least it had the opportunity to have its loved ones close by, holding him in their arms against the sterile steel table when the vet pushed the needle into his flank. The Sinclairs knew the procedure could actually be quite traumatic, but they both wanted to be there for that last whimper, scratching Koala's ears and rubbing warm hands over his back. What more could he ask for? What more could they give? But they had to get him there first.

Carmalitta leaned forward across her desk and folded her hands together. They'd been through all this before but she had to give them one last chance, one more time to summon the courage to do what they knew they had to do, or the dog's death would haunt whatever remaining time they had left to share.

"It hurts him to be alive now, you both know that."

Mr. Sinclair finally sat down, coughed and handed his wife a new tissue.

"You'll be able to be there with him, right at his side, holding him, stroking away his fear. A lot of animals never have that kind of attention and compassion when their time is close."

Mr. Sinclair gulped the dryness from his throat. He tried to speak, but stopped before whatever he was trying to mumble became audible.

"Nothing's gained by letting him have an extra day or two, because he's in pain. He's not comfortable, and he's not really aware of everything that's going on. I know you both love him dearly, but you have to be strong enough in that love to let him go."

Mrs. Sinclair sobbed softly and shook her head.

"Think about it. Please."

Mr. and Mrs. Sinclair got up slowly, each helping the other, and took a seat together on the long couch on the wall behind them. Leaning over so their heads were touching, they started whispering and whimpering.

Let him go. The words skewered memories Carmalitta didn't want to face. She glanced at the aquarium nestled into the wall unit behind the Sinclairs. There was a little castle in the bottom of the tank, complete with archer slits, a drawbridge, and a little plastic pennant on the top turret. Anachronistically nearby, a helmeted deep sea diver blew colored bubbles toward the surface. Two large, speckled goldfish leisurely swam in and out of the castle windows, lazily pursuing nothing but time. Their little mouths opened and closed in sequence with their gills as they glided effortlessly along the tank's walls, through the fake kelp, and then back around the castle.

Carmalitta pictured Miriam's condominium in the sky. *Their home.* In her mind she swam around it once more, gliding past her lover, the water warm and soothing against her fins. Around and around and around, in one window and out another, through this wall, skim over that one, float through the halls, thrash a tail, feel the current that waved through the little plants imbedded in the pink stones below.

Carmalitta tried to push the invading image away but she couldn't stop thinking about Jack and how close they were to being married all those years ago. Joshua was eight, so it had to have been about ten years ago now. She watched the goldfish glide beside one another before a quick swish of a tail separated them again. What had gone wrong? The same things that had initially brought them together, she thought. Jack was a wonderful man. Bright, articulate, sensitively strong, athletic, with a valuable career stretched out before him like a road to Rome. They both enjoyed music, art, knowledge, and reading, and practically everything progressed in their relationship like a fairy tale. They'd been together for almost a year before Jack asked her to share her life with him. Perhaps that was it. It wasn't getting married; it was sharing all that precious time together. One person, forever. And children. But with a *man.*

Nothing had incited so much distress and anguish in Carmalitta's life as that one simple question that was meant to be so reassuring. She couldn't decide what to do. She was close to Jack and she loved him very much, but deep down, she always knew something was missing. Jack was an attentive lover, a good provider, a supportive shoulder to lean against when the nights were too long. But there was more, wasn't there? There always seemed to be more.

Carmalitta drifted through the air bubbles and glided by the condominium again. It just hadn't felt right. But what did that mean? Something she could never verbalize because it was deeper than that, less tangible but an overpowering sensation that never let her mind rest. When she was truthful to herself and she was alone in her room and had pulled the covers up safely over her head, she confessed she'd been confused since early high school. No, confused wasn't the right word: it was more faithless.

She'd tried to fit in, she really had. She flirted with the boys in her class, went out on dates, kissed at the school dances, and helped fumbling fingers unclasp her bra in the back seat at the drive-in. But it never felt right. Stroking them to orgasm, she was there, but never really a part of it. Never committed, never involved. It was someone else touching the penis that throbbed against her leg, another person trying to moan when their nipples were sucked to a painful erectness. Her mind was always wandering, her dreams searching her visions for something else. Even after adolescence racked with ambivalence and guilt she still went out with boys. And later, men. But nothing changed. She didn't change. They simply couldn't satisfy that something, that need, that had always lay dormant deep inside her.

Even after the first naive and rather unsophisticated encounter with a woman who'd left her floundering and out of place like a swimming camel, Carmalitta tried to be with men once more. Again and again, and with a number of women too, but she never actually understood which sex she'd been experimenting with. Until Jack. Jack fulfilled her needs more than any other lover she'd ever had, but Carmalitta simply couldn't imagine spending her whole life with him. Or any man. Some part of her being cried out for something else, something she didn't understand: a sense, a hope, a feeling, a need. No matter how much she tried to dismiss it, she knew it was an invasive feeling that would torment her forever if she couldn't flush it away, like a Muslim bigot receiving a blood transfusion from a Jew.

The thing that finally pulled her back from the precipice of her emotional abyss was Miriam. Carmalitta knew at once that Miriam was what she'd been searching for. A look, a smile, a feeling in the pit of her stomach that calmed her deepest fears. They'd met two months before she was supposed to be married, and she'd stopped seeing Jack about a month after that. It was just after the date her wedding would have been that she'd learned she was pregnant. She never told Jack. How could she? In her own mind she'd hurt him enough already. But she wasn't alone with the new life inside her because Miriam never left her side.

One of the goldfish was hovering inside the castle walls. The other was nibbling microscopic bits of food trapped in the surface tension of the water. Despite Miriam's protests, fears, nightmares, tears, rantings, and three trial separations that tore them both apart, Carmalitta still decided that she couldn't keep the baby. It would be an unending reminder of Jack and the other life she'd left behind. She argued she had her career, of course, and wouldn't be able to give the child sufficient time or attention. That she wasn't married. That she didn't have any real maternal feelings whatsoever. But she knew they were just feeble excuses, misguided and defensive extrapolations of the truth.

What was she afraid of? Sometimes she still wasn't sure. She knew that in a generation there'd be scores of scientific and psychological studies available dealing with a gamut of issues concerned with children being reared in same-sex marriages. But there weren't that many now. There wasn't anything to read, nothing to fall back on, no self-help books crammed into the racks at the local bookstores that could tell her what to do.

Is a child better off with an adoptive family who loves it, or with a natural mother who's afraid, unsure, unwanting? When Carmalitta finally screamed one last time as she thrashed back and forth and her sweat-soaked head sunk down into the pillow as the last push tore the breath from her lungs, she knew she couldn't keep the pink, shivering mass of wrinkles at her side. One look, one kiss, that was all.

Mrs. Sinclair cleared her voice once more. Her eyes were red and puffy. Standing again, her husband gripped the chair back so tightly his knuckles had whitened.

"Doctor?"

Carmalitta came back from the fairy tale castle submerged in the tank. "I'm sorry. Yes?"

"Do you think you could possibly come with us? It would mean a lot." She reached over and touched her husband's hand. Again he tried to speak, but the words didn't come.

"Not just for Koala," Mrs. Sinclair whispered. "For us."

Behind them, the goldfish drifted through the moat that had claimed the entire castle.

"Of course." Carmalitta felt her gills ripple open, sensed the calming sea holding her up. Was that what it was like in the womb? "Of course I'll come with you."

Mr. Sinclair stiffened noticeably, and then relaxed. His wife dried her eyes and quietly blew her nose.

"We'll take him in tomorrow. I'll call Dr. Emerson and arrange everything. And --"

"Yes?" Mrs. Sinclair breathed through fresh tears.

"You're doing the best and most humane thing you can do. Never forget that."

The Sinclairs nodded. Carmalitta watched the goldfish slip silently around the tank, their little mouths opening and closing, their tails whisking the plants into dancing shapes, their fins pulsing ever so gently as they veered through the turrets and castle walls, together and apart, the same yet different, life one giant but very, very small little circle.

***

06:05:22

Θ watin 4 me whn I gt hom. I hd a realy bd felin tht somthin was rong. I dont usualy gt premonishuns so plese cal whe u receve this. ur makin me vere nervus. Is somthin rong? r u al riht? Any probs u dont want me 2 no abot? Somthin I did, or didn't do, by mistake? yur grandad oka? Im lonly, hurt, an woreed -- I luv my litle Cybernician, an this is th longest I havent ben abl 2 tak 2 u in months. Il b watin at my kybord 4 u. Lov and anxousnes, Sheila.

***

The line stretched out diagonally about twenty-five feet, from the back corner of the porch to the lowest limb on a thick maple tree that dominated the far side of the property. Hanging the wash outside to dry had always bothered Mathew. Whenever he saw a clothesline draped in shirts and pants and sweaters and socks fluttering in the breeze, the first thing he thought of was a dilapidated trailer park in the deep south, dotted with barefoot pregnant women, stacked cases of empties, rusted trucks, and mangy old dogs barking at nothing or sitting in the dust licking themselves.

Sometimes, it didn't. Sometimes he liked the freshness, the scent of *pure outside* that wrung the wetness from his sheets and pillowcases. It seemed far too personal to peg his underwear to the line, but other things -- off-season coats, sports clothing, towels -- seemed to grow brighter, more alive beneath the sun, when they billowed out like ship sails in a cool, bracing wind.

Lorne had tipped over his tray and spilled most of his dinner across the bed. The outside of the new comforter had been unsullied, so Mathew had just washed the inside shell. The spot was still there, but duller. Mathew didn't think his father would notice the blotch anyway, but if he did, he probably wouldn't care. Things always seemed so much easier to tolerate when they were clean. Mathew knew a few hours in the coldness of a bright, October day wouldn't do it any harm, so he draped it over the naked clothes line. The wire sagged, then bounced back up. The bright redness stood out starkly against the brown, dead grass.

Mathew hadn't been able to stop thinking about Carol all day. When he came back in, he went up to his room. On a whim, he pulled everything out of his closet until he found two dust-covered boxes buried beneath a pile of old shirts stuffed in the corner. A box of albums and a box of mementos. The things so hard to toss out. The things you want to keep, no matter what, but you don't really know quite why. Whistling softly to himself, he blew the layers of dirt away and carefully carried them down into the basement.

Mathew shivered when he pulled the first few albums from the box. As soon as he began fanning them out and glancing at the faded jacket photographs, he started hearing the old songs in his head. Drenched in memories, he couldn't have stopped the reminiscences from coming, even if he'd wanted to. There's something special about albums that you don't get with CDs: the crinkly plastic film that keeps the record clean, the cover, the detailed artwork and pictures of the band, the lyrics and notes that make everything seem so personal. The tangibility. You just don't get that with an MP3 or a downloaded song or something ripped from something else.

He thought it surprising that no matter how old you are or what era you grew up in, there are always songs that can touch you like nothing else can in quite the same way. The second you hear the first few bars of a special tune time stops, years melt away, remembrances erupt and pour out like lava, and dormant emotions rush to the surface the way newts race to the surface to breathe. Melodies are musical sorcerer-sirens that speak to the most guarded memories and the deepest secrets of your soul. Three or four notes and you can remember a dimension of things you'd thought you'd forgotten. A first date, a kiss between virgins ready to leave innocence behind, a dance, a lover's spat, a separation, a magical feeling or experience that overwhelmed you then and can still reduce you to tears now. The moment that song starts and plays your heart strings, you're there again, in another time, another place, in a body and mind that you think of when you picture yourself as you were back then. Not all songs have the power, but some certainly do. It doesn't matter if the memories are good or bad, because you don't have control over them anyway. You're just a feather on the breeze, a whisper on the wind.

As time goes by.

When Rick plaintively urges Sam to play *it* one more time, what thoughts and feelings from the past stop the blood in his heart and tear the light-filaments from his soul? The sweet softness of Ilsa's touch when Gestapo boots stomp heavily against the boulevard below? The way she leans up and closes her eyes when they kiss? The coldness of the rain seeping from his hat when the train leaves without her? Two simple bars that can shatter the world and bring back another life in a second.

Fanning through the dust jackets, each title reminded him of a particular time or place, and the lyrics of each song brought people back to life. Most of his memories were about Carol, but the first one he pulled out so gently from its jacket had been special to his father.

"Don't sit under the apple tree with anyone else but me,
Anyone else but me, anyone else but me."

What feelings did those lines engender in the men that heard them twenty or thirty or forty years after the last shells had blown their friends apart?

So many songs, so many memories.

"She loves you yeah, yeah, yeah, she loves you yeah, yeah, yeah."
"Silence is golden, golden, but my eyes still see."
"You ain't nothing but a houndog."
"Give me an "F". . . give me a "U"..."
"And she's buying a Stairway to Heaven."
"One o'clock, two o'clock, three o'clock rock."
"Love, look at the two of us, strangers in many ways."
"You are so beautiful, to me."
"One tin soldier rides away."
"Like a candle in the wind."

"I want to know what love is, I want you to show me."
*"All the leaves are brown, and the sky is grey, I've been for
a walk, on a winter's day."*

Mathew slipped a record out and poked the hole over the
spigot on the old turntable. He paused before he put the headphones on and cocked his head to the side, listening. Lost in the
music, he wouldn't be able to hear anything. What if someone
broke in to rob the house? What if a deranged psychiatric patient escaped from the Clarke Institute down on Queen Street
and pried the back door open, crept in, found one of the carving
knives in the kitchen, then tiptoed quietly down the basement
stairs, softly panting, the blade glistening in his upraised hand,
ready to strike and strike and slash and rip . . . ?

No. Mathew was fairly confident nothing like that was going to happen. He leaned back and looked up the stairs, called
"*hello*" out once (*as if the drooling, psychotic, blood thirsty
killer would actually answer*), and then put the headphones on.
When the needle lowered, the old phonograph circled and
scratched awake. He settled back into the chair and smiled.
Two bars, three, four, and he was floating away like a well-
travelled piece of driftwood on a moonlit tide.

When the first song ended there was supposed to be a few
moments of silence, but the record clicked noisily around. After
the pristine crispness of CDs and MP3s he'd forgotten what that
sounded like. Smiling softly as the next tune transported him
somewhere else, Mathew reached down into the treasures buried in the other box. It was filled with mementos. Pictures, rib-
bons, parts of trophies, dog-eared love notes, scraps of paper,
postcards, ticket halves, a menu, the label from a forgotten wine
bottle, pins, cards stuck back in torn envelopes, a feather, a
piece of some brick or something, and a yellowed plastic insert
for a wallet.

His legs trembled. They were all pieces of his life, fragments ripped from the past. And almost all of them had something to do with Carol. The tickets were from a concert they
went to at sixteen. Led Zeppelin, Maple Leaf Gardens. Like
everyone else they were half-heartedly frisked at the door, but

the cops didn't even bother to look back as everyone fired up joints all around them. Carol had worn new jeans, a beige tank top, and a leather necklace she'd made. She'd made one for Mathew, too, and he quickly searched the box. Nothing. His heart sank.

The piece of stone or brick came from the edge of the Rouge River where they used to go swimming every summer. Two years of playful friendship had passed before it had turned into something more, something deeper, and they kissed for the first time, stretched out on the grass beneath a late-autumn sun as a warm breeze crinkled maple leaves above their heads.

Mathew had to pry the pages of the billfold apart. The plastic was almost brown in spots and something had eaten a couple of edges away. It was filled with pictures, the little square, wallet-sized ones you get when school begins in the fall. The years were sequenced, and Mathew watched Carol softly mature as he flipped through the plastic sheaths. He knew what was written on the back of each one. He loved her more in every time-slice. Did she still have his, tucked away in some private keepsake box in the back of her closet? Or had they lost their meaning, replaced by other things and other pictures?

He fumbled with some of the letters. Most were hastily scrawled notes written while they were at their summer jobs, longing for the weekend when they could be together again. Carol had a special little way of signing her name. She always drew a little heart hanging from the upper curve of the capital 'C'. It was there, on every letter and every note she'd given him.

Another song, another flood of chain links tugging Mathew to the past. He tried to steady his fingers and slipped a few of the cards out of their envelopes. Christmas, Easter, Thanksgiving, 'I-miss-you-cards,' and the ones you send when you're hopelessly in love, 'just because.' An unseen hand gripped the muscles around his heart. He didn't realize his eyes were moist until a tear trickled down to the edge of his mouth and he tasted salt.

Where had his life gone? For the first time in a very long while when his thoughts became desperately consumed with Carol, Mathew didn't wonder 'what if?' He wondered, *why not*?

Mathew knew the psychotic murderer could be lingering on the bottom step right now, but for once he wasn't afraid. If death was to come, then what better time than now? He looked down into the recesses of the box, wondering, like an archaeologist who's unearthed one too many bones, just how much farther he should go. He started to pull his hand back, but something glimmered on the bottom and Icarus had to fly just a little higher, just a wing-beat closer to the sun.

Two rings. Gold bands with matching stones that had oxidized to a speckled green and brown. Ordered from the catalogue since jewelry stores were so daunting and expensive back then. His to her, and the other half of the circle. He held them in his palm, surprised at their lightness for all the weight they carried. Mathew took the larger of the two and slipped it on his finger. It was snug and he had to force it over his knuckle, but he managed to push it on before his finger turned purple. He realized he'd have an even harder time getting it back off. But he didn't want to.

The record kept spinning, the needle danced awkwardly through dusty grooves, his head filled with long-lost notes that lulled him to weightlessness, and Mathew squeezed Carol's ring between his hands until his fingertips went white.

Memories, pressed between the pages of my mind . . .

Chapter Twenty

Stuffed between twin Gothic columns on one of the narrow side streets that fed the main thoroughfare through Yorkville, the *Herodotus Gallery* was everything Eleanor needed it to be. Smaller, less ostentatious, and not quite as well-known as Peter Garfield's other venues, it was still a formidable brick in the infrastructure of the art world. High ceilings, indirect lighting, angled porticos, floors polished to a painful brightness, and whitewashed walls that reminded her of sunlit Greek mansions overlooking the Mediterranean. More self-consciously introspective than a novice priest, Eleanor immediately began to worry about her hair, her dress, whether or not she'd worn appropriate shoes, even her age. She was afraid to step farther in, to cross the threshold and venture down the labyrinth of interconnected hallways that stretched away from the main foyer.

Nailed to the floor, her eyes skimmed restlessly over the paintings and sculptures that lined the walls. Fortunately, she caught a glimpse of Carlos at the far end of the nearest hallway and her body sighed heavily. She could feel the blood draining back into her face. Much to their chagrin, Carlos bowed to a group of three young women that waited for his words like priestesses at Delphi, and glided without actually stepping to Eleanor's side. He took her hand and pressed his lips softly to her fingers. He'd combed his flowing mane straight back and wore a handsome suit of light blue silk that highlighted his eyes. A white silk tie and a blue ribbon that matched his suit held his hair back. This was true art, Eleanor thought.

"I'm so glad you could come," he whispered. "You look wonderful. Can I offer you some wine?"

Eleanor accepted his proffered elbow and Carlos guided her toward a hospitality table at the side of the room. A white-frocked waiter had already poured their drinks before Carlos ordered.

Carlos clinked Eleanor's glass with his own. "This isn't where Peter and I are planning to have the show, but I thought you'd like to see some of the work he represents."

Eleanor didn't know what to say. She looked around slowly, unable to even begin to imagine her work hanging on one of these walls.

"The exhibit I envision will be in its own room, naturally."

"Naturally," she agreed faintly. *Unbelievable.*

"Shall we?" He gestured to the main room with his glass, and escorted her toward the end of the gallery. His hand was on her elbow, and it burned. Carlos gestured with his glass as he spoke, like a symphony conductor emphasizing a particular passage.

"I prefer oils and sketches, but my heart has enough room for all of these."

Eleanor took a sip of wine. Was she wrong, or did *and you* dangle from his lips before he closed his sentence?

They stopped in front of the end wall. It was dominated by three large paintings obviously imagined into being by the same artist, but Eleanor didn't recognize the name typed on the little card beside the frames. Arranged in a straight line, each rectangular canvas was divided by a centered vertical and horizontal line so it consisted of four equal squares. The squares kitty-corner were painted the same color. The first picture was done in blue and orange, the second, in green and black, the third, brown and red.

"Karen Touliose. Such an elegiac tone, don't you think? You see how provocatively she captures the simplicity of spatial relationships by juxtaposing the panels with such divisiveness, although I would think some might say, ostensibly aggressive, lines. Alienation and cultural demarcation have always been central themes in her work. I don't mean to over simplify, but the image of the cross edges on a didactic confession. See there. The lines of the squares intersect with the same purposefulness as our spiritual lives slice through our corporeal forms. Truly amazing, isn't it?"

Tilting her head thoughtfully from side to side, Eleanor studied the squares and agreed. Carlos took a step back, closed his eyes, and merged even deeper with the images. Apparently weighed down by the overpowering sense of melancholy the pictures had infected him with, he took Eleanor's arm and moved on.

They passed a huge oval canvas that was completely blank except for a five inch circle in the middle that had been painted gunmetal grey. Carlos only paused for a moment, whispering that life was far too transient, time too precious, to allow one-self to be fettered by the chains of morbidity for any length of time. Eleanor glanced back as they moved away and looked closely at the oval again. Worried he might think her imagina-tion was sputtering, she refrained from telling him she didn't quite see the *mournful lack of substance, the confining aura of dimensionlessness,* that seemed to bother Carlos so deeply.

"Oh, but this," he effused, pulling her closer and moving his hand to the small of her back. Gentle pressure, but enough that she could sense each finger on her skin until it seared. He peered up over the rim of his glass at a narrow niche carved into the wall. Inside was a piece of chiseled soap stone Eleanor thought looked very much like a coiled spring. Perched on a piece of glass, the sculpture was illuminated from below, so slices of shadows splayed the top of the niche.

"Stunning," Carlos breathed. "Absolutely remarkable. He's only done two to date, that I'm aware of. Sabil Noorwanda. The other piece is over there."

Carlos turned and gestured to the opposite wall. Eleanor followed his gaze. The niche on the other side of the room seemed a little smaller, yet any nuances the sculpture may have possessed were too difficult for her to detect from that distance. But she still found them both deeply unsettling because they reminded her so clearly of something Joshua had brought home from school he'd made from plaster of Paris.

They toured the gallery for almost two hours. For Eleanor, it might as well have been a lifetime. Three glasses of wine had made her peculiarly light-headed, but she kept her feet firmly planted on the ground because Carlos was always touching her. Holding her arm, her elbow, tracing his fingers along her shoulder or down the center of her back. He only let her go to take a sip of wine or shake a hand when someone new was in-troduced, but there it was again, warm, supporting, tenderly possessive as soon as the glass was lowered or the person moved away.

When their inspection of the gallery was finished, Carlos went back to the side table and offered her another glass of wine, but Eleanor declined. He accepted one for himself.

"How would you feel if your work was up on a wall like these, and art lovers stood and talked and wondered and yearned for what you had done?" He flipped a straggling lock of hair back from his forehead. The gesture sent a tremor through Eleanor's knees.

What could she say? That every hope, every dream, every sleep-annihilating fear she'd ever had since the first time she put something down on canvas would finally come together in one glorious, tumultuous moment of ecstasy that would change her life forever? All she could do was shake her head. Carlos saw a tear bleed from the corner of her eye and brushed it away with the edge of his hand. She tried to move but he wouldn't let her look away. He held her with his eyes, his hand still gently resting on her side, motionless, his lips moving to speak but staying silent. He studied her eyes, her nose, her mouth, the smoothness of her neck, her lips again.

"Let go," he finally whispered.

"I can't."

"You can." He waited, his eyes darting back and forth about her face. "Think about what the gallery has to offer. What *I* have to offer."

"Oh Carlos. I don't think . . . ."

Carlos touched a finger to her lips and stopped her in midthought. He stepped closer and slipped his hand around her waist. A gentle pressure, but enough to pull her forward. He leaned down slowly, purposefully bringing his face closer to hers, his eyes never leaving her mouth. Closer, until Eleanor's eyes began to tear and he felt her body tremble. Closer, until she closed her eyes and tasted the warmth of his breath and melted into the strength of his arms. He kissed her ever so softly, brushing his mouth against her top lip, then the bottom, before letting their lips meet fully. A long kiss, light but not deep, yet one that let his cologne, the softness of his cheeks, the fullness of his lips and the beat of his heart burn indelibly into Eleanor's senses. When he finally moved away, she stayed there, hovering but not quite ready to fall, like a satiated hummingbird at a geranium.

"Eleanor, it's time."

"Yes," she whispered, panting, her lips parting expectantly.

"We'll take your car."

He kissed her lightly on the edge of her mouth. Eleanor touched her palm to her cheek and looked back up at one of the blank spaces on the wall. She realized she was crying. Had she been before? She was caught between two worlds, her head in the clouds but her feet stuck in quicksand. A moment later, she followed Carlos from the gallery.

***

Eleanor didn't see Joshua walking along one of the streets that bordered the edge of their neighborhood when she passed him at the corner gas station because there was simply too much going on all at once: she was busily scanning the crosswalk curbs for any sudden movement, thinking about her husband, wondering if it was time to change to her snow tires yet, trying to slow her heartbeat down, and just enjoying the delicate warmth of Carlos' hand on her thigh. She didn't even notice the frail old bag lady who was with her grandson.

About a quarter of an hour later, Carlos smiled appreciatively as Eleanor wheeled into the driveway. "What a lovely house."

Thank you sounded so shallow she didn't say anything. Eleanor never knew what to say when people commented on something she didn't have control over, like the house, a child, the weather, a spouse. When someone said 'oh, what a beautiful baby,' what were you supposed to say? *Yes, of course it is, I made it myself?*

"Please have a seat in the living room and I'll be right back."

"Thank you."

So formal. Eleanor didn't want to tell him *why* she'd be right back, why she needed the time. She felt like a teenager secreting a first date past the parents and into the parlor. She'd imagined her family being home, and had rehearsed her lines for each of them all the way back in the car. When she could think of anything but Carlos's hand on her thigh.

This is Carlos Montoya, my art instructor. He wants to talk to me about showing my work. How did that sound? Or how about -- *Please meet Mr. Montoya, my instructor. He wants to see some of my other pictures, but my portfolio case wasn't big enough to bring them all to school.*

She wasn't sure if she was relieved or not when she scanned the fridge, read all the notes, listened to the silence, and realized that no one was home. Just Cybernician: the gloves made his hands soundless against the keyboard, but she saw the telltale blue glow emanating across the upstairs landing. She took a deep breath and almost fainted. She steadied herself against the curved molding of the banister; sure she could hear the blood sloshing around inside her head. Had Lorne felt like that before the stroke, the first time he knew he was going to be with her?

She looked up and saw her own bedroom door. Why was she doing this? And what was it that she was really doing? She thought she should feel impassioned, empowered, adventurous, but she didn't. Intense guilt and uncertainty? No, that was missing too. She was beyond fear of discovery, yet still hopeful of some intervention that would take all the responsibility away and let her curl up on the couch with the cat and a cup of nice, warm tea. Herbal, so it wouldn't make her jittery.

"Are you all right?" Carlos was by her side, hands around her shoulders, leaning into her back, his breath wine-scented and warm.

"I guess so."

"You're afraid."

"A little."

"Of what?"

"I'm not sure. That's why I'm afraid."

Carlos pressed her body against the banister and gently undid the comb that held her hair back in a bun.

"You have such beautiful hair," he whispered, rubbing it with his cheeks. "Morning-mist grey, smooth, soft, and light, light as spider webs."

"Carlos, I --"

"Sshhh. I just want to touch your hair, the skin of your neck."

How could she push him away when this was all she'd thought of, all she'd ached for, for so very long? Her body trembled and her senses were on fire. Carlos kissed her neck, the edge of her throat, the soft skin of her ears. He wrapped his arms around her and drew her back harder into his chest. Eleanor looked up the stairs as her head was being tilted back, and in her mind's eye, she saw her husband thirty years before, raking the leaves on a day just like this in the tiny yard of the first house they'd managed to buy after they'd stayed so long in an endless series of basements and rented apartments. The rake was missing two teeth and the handle was cracked, but Lorne was smiling as he clawed the ground and pulled the crumpled leaves into tight little piles the wind couldn't blow away.

But where was he now? Where was he when she needed him so badly, when she longed to be touched and held and caressed and loved and told she was still living, still awake? She didn't know if Carlos had been right before or not: she couldn't picture herself in the same scene, the same time and place, with Lorne . . . *completely gone*. But she couldn't imagine it being any easier or any more difficult, either. She felt numbed by the inertia of ambivalence; no wonder people were afraid to make decisions, why *not-doing* was so much less stressful.

A life peeled back and she was in little padded slippers, walking up the long, steep staircase at home sometime before her father died, making her first foray up the stairs all on her own. One hand clung desperately to the spindles, the other, to Teddy. Mother crouched at the top, circling her hands and beckoning her forward. Her father was right behind her, arms stretched out to either side but not touching her, his leg braced near her back. Alone? Hardly.

This time she could feel the hands, one on her shoulder, the other in the small of her back. Two stairs creaked -- she thought it was her knees. She was glad there weren't any mirrors along the wall or the hallway. She took a labored breath when she reached the top. Carlos waited behind her, balanced on the top step, unsure of which way she'd go.

Forward. She stopped in front of her own door, and listened. Nothing. An investigating try at the one beside it: locked. Cybernician was working on something secret. She mouthed *the guest room*, and stepped quietly down the hall. She opened the door part way and slipped in quickly so the threshold didn't loom so great. She heard the door click softly closed.

Was there still time to turn back? Did she want to?

Eleanor pulled the drapes together across the little window. She saw the comforter down in the yard flapping and unfurling in the wind like a huge, red sail. Before she could even begin to convince herself that for once, if only for a moment, she needed something more than a man that peed the bed, Carlos was with her, folding her into his arms and smothering her neck and cheeks with eager kisses.

Was that a tongue, a tongue licking the beads of anxious perspiration from the hollow of her throat?

She couldn't remember, but knew it had to be. Something inside, something deep and dormant and hidden in a dark place she'd forgotten awakened and stirred, and she felt the rush of warmth she thought she'd never feel again.

I'm not just some old woman, she thought, allowing herself to be turned and letting Carlos' weight press her back against the wall. *Some desperate, pathetic, love-starved shell of what used to be that still needs someone to want them.*

Aren't I?

Her arms went up around Carlos' neck and she grasped him so tightly she thought she'd buried her fingers into his back. *Merge with your art.* She kept her eyes closed and tried not to think of anything: not Carlos' lips searching for hers, not the man in the next room staring blankly out the window, not what she looked like naked when she stepped from the bath.

Carlos reached down and put one hand behind her knees. A moment later she was floating, weightless, curled into his powerful arms. He laid her gently down across the bed and tucked the pillow up beneath her head. He lay beside her until her eyes opened again, stroking her legs and arms softly with his hands.

Eleanor stared at the ceiling and thought it looked rather yellow. Perhaps a fresh coat of paint . . . .

But Carlos brought a leg up over her, pushed his pelvis against her thigh, and pulled her back before she could escape. She felt like she was falling, but she felt like she was falling *away*. The room was quietly dissolving into a transparent haze, a muted shadow without a background. She felt Carlos' fingers on the buttons of her blouse and couldn't stop a low, guttural moan from erupting when he unfastened her new brassiere and her breasts tasted the light and a man's breath for the first time in so very long. She shivered when he leaned down and gently licked each nipple to a painful erectness, smiling when she realized her hands had moved without her knowing and were around his neck and head, kneading, probing, searching.

When his mouth released her skin she thought she'd died. Eleanor watched Carlos lean back and take off his shirt. His eyes never let her go. It was the first time since she'd been carried through the door and into the little two-room basement apartment on Sherbrooke Avenue, the one with the taps that made so much noise during the night, that she'd laid her hands against the chest of a man who wasn't her husband. She curled her fingers into the snow-white hair and her breaths deepened uncomfortably.

Carlos put his hands over hers and gently guided them down, down across his stomach, down over the manhood that thickened against his pants. Her fingers trembled. She'd never touched any one *down there* except her husband, and even those first few, tentative times had been in the safety of the dark. And now this man, this strange, wonderful man that loved her art and drank wine with her at the little piano lounge and walked so straight and tall was going to put his throbbing penis deep inside her. She stroked his length, felt him pulse against her hand.

My God, he's hung like a bull.

She wasn't sure if she'd spoken aloud or not. Murmured or yelled. She watched his pants flutter to the floor, his underwear melt away, the thing stab proudly up toward her, then felt his hands clutching at her dress, the cotton panties she wished had been smaller, the wet-warm folds of her inner sex. Eleanor sighed and convulsed with a shiver that made her hot and cold at the same time. She was kissing him again, writhing up to meet him, drowning in desire and letting the waves of lust fill her lungs and choke her deeper, deeper, deeper.

Outside, beneath her window, Lorne ran back and forth across the yard, his arthritic wrists against his forehead, his fingers raised like bony stubs, charging at the menacing red comforter as it waved and snapped and uncurled in the wind. One way, then the other. He stopped after each pass, pawing the ground with his feet, his back arched painfully forward, his breath in gasping spurts, and then he stomped once more through the leaves at his beckoning nemesis. No shouts from an unseen crowd, no sounds, no flashing daggers tipped with blood, no roses sent from above.

Just tears coaxed from the icy wind.

Chapter Twenty-one

Monday morning.

Again.

The weeks seemed to be passing by faster and faster, and slower and slower, at the same time.

The weekend was still a blur. And not a good blur.

It was the best of times, it was the worst of times . . . .

Mathew was at his desk, doodling some weird kind of endless design on his old-fashioned blotter that probably would have meant something to Dr. Stallworth, or maybe some convoluted image that would have been even more meaningful to his son, still caught in the spider webs of the weekend and thinking about what he'd talked to Joshua about at the zoo. And what he'd thought he'd heard before they left. Behind him, reflected sunlight glinted off the building's windows that surrounded him and choked his own office tower into semi-darkness like a boa's coils. He couldn't tell if it was cloudy or not unless he pressed his face right up to the glass, squashed his cheek, and looked up as hard as he could. Two pigeons nested in an overhang somewhere below his window, and every time they cooed he pictured them ruffling their feathers and puffing out their chests.

Mathew was still mentally and physically exhausted. Other than going to the Zoo with his son, they'd been some of the worst days in his life. And some of the best. Even after everything that had happened to his father and his world, the time he'd spent in the basement – the time with his albums and cards and letters and his memories of Carol – those few hours had been some of the most wondrous and happy moments he'd had in years. In decades.

For the first time in as long as he could remember, he had a sense of hope, a feeling that perhaps – just perhaps – he might see her and talk to again someday, and that everything – *alt-*

hough he didn't really know what that meant – might change. He'd slept with the little fake gold ring she'd given him all those years ago under his pillow, and for the first night in an unsettled and depressing age he couldn't define, he'd dreamed, dreamed without nightmares, without fears, without waking up in a cold and anxious sweat or tears on his face.

But he couldn't stop thinking about how his world had collapsed once more.

Well, twice more.

Two nights ago. *Was that all it had been?*

Carmalitta had been down in the kitchen arguing with him. No, not arguing: it had been more of an empathetic prodding of his denial. Lydia had left a message on the answering machine explaining she'd be gone for at least another week, that something *absolutely incredible* was in the works, and love and kisses to all.

Mathew was making dinner while his daughter listened to the tape. "I thought she might be back earlier."

"Oh Dad. Don't be so pathetic." She was apologetic before the word left her lips. "Sorry. I didn't mean that."

Mathew smiled and kept stirring the fettuccine. Had he already reached the point in life his children thought of him as an object of pity? He really thought it would've been later.

Carmalitta pressed. "She might not come back, you know?"

Mathew checked his sauce. It was slowly thickening, like his fear. He didn't want to admit his daughter was right. He added another touch of garlic to the swirling sauce.

"This is the longest she's ever been gone, isn't it?"

Nothing.

Carmalitta pushed herself up from the table and leaned into her father's back. She gulped and took a deep breath, then tentatively tiptoed into an area she was frightened of crossing, like a polar bear nearing the edge of a floe reaching out a paw to check the thickness of the ice. She was afraid of inching closer to the chilling water, but knew she couldn't stay where she was.

"If it wasn't for Joshua, you would have left a long time ago, wouldn't you?"

He shook his head. "Who'd look after Granddad?"

"He might be better off in a home." Carmalitta didn't really believe that. Who could be? And if you were better off there, what was it like where you were?

"Do you still love her?"

"Yes. Yes, I do."

"But you're not *in love* with her?"

Mathew couldn't feel the difference any longer. "That's not the issue."

"Of course it is."

"Times change, Carmalitta. So do relationships. What I needed before isn't necessarily what I need now. And I'm sure it's the same for your mother."

She acquiesced with a nod. "What is it that you need?"

Mathew swirled a wooden fork through the sauce, parting it like Moses' sea. He didn't answer. What did he need? Something that no one else could give him. Carol. Only Carol. And could she give it to him now, after all these years?

"Dad, maybe you should think about getting on with your own life."

"You mean while there's still some time left?" He smiled, not meaning to tease her. "I'm fine. Really I am. I respect what you're saying. But after you've lived with someone for twenty five years, it's hard to just wake up one day and let go, no matter what you feel. My priorities have changed. And I wouldn't leave Dad or Joshua."

"But I hate to see you so lonely, so unhappy."

He stopped stirring. "I'm not unhappy." He turned the sauce down. "And besides. Maybe once your mother makes something of a name for herself, she'll realize there are more important things than fame and careers. Things closer to home."

"God," Carmalitta said, shaking her head angrily. She was shouting now. "Don't be such an ass."

Mathew couldn't reply. The kitchen clock ticked obnoxiously loud. He stopped stirring, frowned, and cocked his head to the side. "What was that?"

Carmalitta covered her mouth. Too late. She knew her animals. "It sounded kind of like a disgruntled braying."

"Disgruntled braying? Where's Dad?"

"Upstairs."

"How long?"

Carmalitta didn't know. "Since Gram left, I guess."

They heard a crash. Then, *thud thud thud* against the floor. Another crash, then a loud bang that reverberated through the whole house.

"Oh, his poor knees."

Mathew knew the old man's knees were probably the last thing to worry about. It was easy to picture: Dad on all fours thrashing wildly around the room, desperately refusing to be corralled and lashing out with an endless series of high, quick kicks that kept everyone at bay. A snort, a whinny, another barking bray that must have hurt his throat, and then more thudding kicks with slipper-cushioned hooves.

Thud thud thud bang. He knocked something else over.

"What was that?"

"It sounded like Mom's little foot stool."

Hee-haw, hee-haw, hee-haw.

"The room's really taking a pounding."

"So's Dad."

A moment's silence. Then, *hee-haw, hee-haw, hee-haw,* and something else falling and tinkling into a thousand pieces as Mathew and his daughter raced up the stairs to help. By the time they reached his room it was in shambles. The mattress had been kicked off the bed and the little settee was on its side. Lorne had shattered his wife's favorite antique atomizer, and had literally destroyed most of the fragile keepsakes in his room with rampant kicks and head butts. There was glass everywhere; furniture knocked over, a lamp broken, one side of a three-sided dresser mirror shattered, the carpet ripped, the sheets ripped off the bed and torn apart. A drawer had been kicked right in and was barely hanging on its hinges. Fortunately, despite the glass, Lorne had come away relatively unscathed.

At least the old man was already settling down because the mule had slipped into his unconscious. Lorne was wheezing and completely out of breath. His legs shook uncontrollably when they lifted him off the floor and into his chair. Mathew pulled his covers back up over his legs and wiped the sweat from his forehead while Carmalitta dug the vacuum out of the utility closet. Except for the settee and broken drawer, they had the room back to normal fairly quickly. If only they could have done something for Dad that fast. How many more changes could his body take? *Or his mind?* They got him something to eat and drink, gave him a quick sponge bath so they could check for any injuries, and had him back in his chair by the window in no time at all, relatively calm, breathing fine, and looking outside for whatever it was he looked outside for.

They'd explained everything to Eleanor when she finally got back from her art class. She'd sighed and nodded, checked on Lorne, rolled his sleeves up over the little otters, thanked Carmalitta and Mathew mechanically for all of their help, then quietly walked into the bathroom, started a hot tub of water with her favorite bubble bath and skin softener that quickly steamed up the windows and mirrors, and then sat on the floor for almost an hour while she kept vomiting and flushing another part of her life away.

Mathew remembered the sound. The retching, the water swirling around the toilet, again and again.

His phone rang once more, but he didn't bother answering it. Undoubtedly, there would have been someone else on the other end of the line. He kept doodling. Outside, the pigeons were cooing. Were they angry, or were they mating?

He was pushing so hard, Mathew broke his pencil. *An ass!*

And then the next day, a *bull* for God's sake!

A *bull.*

It wasn't the deranged psychotic killer who invaded Mathew's tour through the ages and musical memories that cut him open, it was Joshua's scream. He heard the screech, he

heard it through the grapevine, not much longer would she be mine . . .

right *through the grapevine,* and he was instantly ripped from the Huey skimming over the river as tracer bullets lit up the night sky and back into his basement with Carol's dusty memorabilia and CCR blaring in the distance. He pulled the headphones off just as his son yelled again. He bounded up the stairs. Joshua rarely cried out like that unless he was in imminent distress of losing consciousness and not knowing who he was. Mathew knew he had to be fast.

But he also realized that it wasn't his son who was in turmoil or mortal danger as he reached the kitchen, it was his father. Joshua was yelling and windmilling his arm like a third base coach sending a runner home.

Joshua yelled, "He's a bull he's a bull he's a *bull!*" Mathew didn't even slow down to ask what happened. He dragged Joshua in his wake.

After Eleanor's – *her what?* – her tryst? her lovemaking? afternoon delight? her passionate encounter? when she got fucked? -- she'd driven Carlos back to school for his class that night. He'd kissed her goodbye so soft and sweetly it was hard for her to leave and go home. She pulled into the driveway just as Mathew and Joshua were tearing out the back door and into the yard.

Although they all seemed to see him at the same time, they all saw him in different perspectives, in various forms, in personal, didactic shapes.

There was no doubt that Lorne was a bull. His hands were still raised on either side of his head, his fingers splayed and sticking as straight out as he could get them. His feet pawed at the grass and fresh dirt. Half bent over, he snorted and coughed as he took aim again at what was left of the comforter hanging from the clothes line. He was covered in pieces of red down that looked like snow he'd torn from the cape that was still swaying in the wind.

The comforter was almost completely shredded. And so was Lorne. His chest heaving, he was gagging on whatever breath he could suck in. He was shivering, his bare feet slick with wet grass and trampled leaves. Tattered pieces of the comforter were wrapped around his hands and stuck to his head. His back was covered in feathers. Clumps of shredded polyester and red cotton balls blew across the yard, the lighter pieces rising like kites that were bobbing up and down on unseen currents.

When Eleanor saw him racing back and forth across the yard, stomping at the ground and then skewering the last vestiges of the comforter with his fingers, her heart felt out of her chest.

It took Mathew and Joshua about another half hour to calm him down and help him get settled, to get him to stop charging at the huge matador's cape, a swirling, blood-red cloak he could never really compete with, no matter how many times he charged it. He was wet and exhausted and every bone in his body ached when he'd finally collapsed to the ground with a loud moan, and let his son and grandson corral him into a shaking stillness. They'd wrapped him up in thick new blankets fresh from the dryer and gently guided him back to his room. His knees cracked with the cold, his breath made his chest heave, his hands couldn't uncurl. Groaning, he weaved back and forth on dirty, slippery feet.

Joshua went back outside. Refreshed by the cold, he tore down what was left of the comforter from the clothes line, ripped it up, and rammed it down into two of those big green garbage bags. He wandered around the yard, picking up all the pieces of the tattered comforter he could find so that nothing would remind the bull of the potential slaughter. Long cotton snakes slithered across the yard. There were red snowballs everywhere.

Inside, helping him upstairs, Mathew was surprised his father had actually made it through such a horrifying experience, because it was one of the most difficult, obstinate and aggressive animals Lorne had ever been. *That he knew of.*

Mathew and Eleanor took Lorne into the bathroom. They carefully undressed him, making sure they didn't aggravate the brush burns and stains and small cuts to his head and knees he'd endured in his primordial fight to the death. At least he'd won. *Or had he?* Mathew helped him into a warm bath, and gently washed away the dirt and blood from the cuts and scratches that made his body as red as the comforter had been. Joshua cleaned up all the pieces of foam and cotton from the bathroom and from his bedroom, and then re-made his grandfather's bed for the second time in as many days. After helping him into a fresh pair of pajamas, Eleanor made her husband a little something to eat. Lorne seemed agitated by the bed, so Mathew put him back in his chair by the window. Not too close, but not too far away, either. Lorne was exhausted. When Mathew stepped up close he could still see the red reflected in his father's eyes.

Raindrops slithered down the glass.

Mathew didn't hear the first knock, or the second, but he saw his door open a crack.

Mrs. Chiu peeked around the corner like a sheriff checking the street for desperadoes. Mathew told her to come in.

"I knocked, but I didn't hear you say anything."

"I guess I didn't hear. I was thinking about something." He didn't look like he remembered what it was. "What can I do for you?"

Mrs. Chiu stepped forward. She had a way of walking that invariably reminded Mathew of a dervish tiptoeing across hot coals. Small, slender, delicately proportioned with a wrinkleless face and a smooth neck, she could have easily passed for a woman half her age. She was fifty. Mathew wondered if she would have wanted to be twenty-five again if she knew all the things she knew now. She wore one of the light, non-invasive skin-colored surgical masks, and reeked of menthol lozenges. Unfortunately, it didn't usually help. Nor did the soap canisters, or the automatic door openers in the bathrooms. The "sick" building syndrome was getting more infectious all the time. Despite her defenses, the poor woman was highly susceptible, and still managed to catch almost every cold or flu bug that made the office rounds.

"New messages." She laid the little yellow papers softly on his desk. It looked like his fridge at home. Everything Mrs. Chiu did was done with a sense of control and sensitivity that Mathew always envied. She shrugged and frowned at the same time.

"These are actually just the last six or seven. There's been a lot more."

"From?" Mathew picked them up and shuffled them like a deck of cards.

"She won't say exactly. But --"

"Yes?"

"It sounds odd."

Mrs. Chiu inadvertently took a step back, and for once, a line of agitation creased her forehead. Mathew sat forward and folded his hands together. Mrs. Chiu lowered her voice.

"She says --"

Mathew waited patiently.

"She says she's your fairy godmother."

"I see." Mathew remembered she'd told him he wasn't supposed to say that any more.

"I didn't know what to tell her, but she keeps calling. She's quite insistent."

"Its fine, Mrs. Chiu. Probably someone just trying to play a joke on me."

"But --"

"But what?"

"She sounds so sincere." Mrs. Chiu looked down at her hands. "Enchanting, actually. She's quite pleasant to talk to, but hard to get off the phone."

I'm sure she is. "Just put her through the next time she calls, Mrs. Chiu. I'll handle it."

"Are you sure?"

Mathew said he was.

"Do you think she'll call again?"

Mathew's phone trilled. Mrs. Chiu looked down at the rows of buttons at the same time Mathew did. *His personal line.* Mrs. Chiu moved closer to his desk, but Mathew smiled and gestured that he'd get it himself. It rang again.

"It's fine, really."

Mrs. Chiu nodded and left. She glanced back once before she slipped out the door. No one else ever got calls from their fairy godmother.

Mathew took a deep breath before he answered. "Hello."

"My goodness you're hard to get a hold of," Beatrice announced.

Mathew heard the faint sound of her tinkling bracelet and wondered if she was wearing her crown. "Where are you?"

"Downtown, not far from your building. And I almost always wear my crown."

"In a phone booth?"

Beatrice clicked her teeth indignantly. "There you go again. You're always expecting things, aren't you?" She didn't give him time to answer. "I'm on my cell phone."

Mathew didn't laugh. "You have a cell phone?"

"Why wouldn't I? Everyone else does, and I'm a queen."

That made sense. "How did you get my work number? How did you even know where I worked?"

"Don't be so silly. I'm your fairy godmother. Anyway, I wanted to know if you'd meet me for lunch."

"For lunch?"

"Yes. The meal in the afternoon. You've had it before."

Mathew couldn't quite picture it. The mall was different. A fast food outlet would probably be reluctant to let her in. So then what? A park bench? A blanket stretched out on the sidewalk? Chairs by some dumpster?

"Well, I --"

"Good. How's one o'clock?"

"Well, I guess --"

"Good. There's a little place just off Dundas Street. *Eggspress*. You know it?"

Mathew mumbled yes. It was two or three doors up from one of the alleys that connected Yonge Street to the myriad streets behind. They served breakfast all day, and in the summer it had a little outdoor cafe set up on the sidewalk.

"Okay then. One."

The phone went dead and so did Mathew. He didn't want to look in a mirror because he knew his face would be white. He checked his watch. Ten to. He was meeting his fairy godmother for lunch and he'd have to take a short cut if he was going to make it in time. He looked down at his clothes and hoped they wouldn't get their food and take it back to the alley. What was he going to tell Mrs. Chiu? Private *business*. That ought to get the gossip flowing.

Hurrying from the office, Mathew was out of breath when he reached the alley. Police sirens wailed in the distance and a nearby church clock struck the hour. Mathew couldn't imagine living in an alley, even if it was spotlessly clean with all the amenities of home. It would still be an alley, like this one, lightless and stale, replete with smashed bottles, teetering stacks of garbage, and the sickening stench of rotting dumpsters. Behind one of them there'd be a dead body. Lydia, his blood-soaked wife, might be playing the dead body. The third one of a serial killer the newspapers were trying to keep quiet about so the police could hide his signature. Or *her* signature.

Cop one lifts up the edge of the sheet. "Another prostitute, Sarah."

Sarah (cop two) peeks under the sheets and nods. "He took his time with this one."

Cop three goes behind a dumpster to puke. Cop one smiles. Cop two lifts up the sheet a little more. The face is almost obliterated, but she has to remark the usual, "It looks like blunt force trauma.'

Cop three agrees, apologizing as he returns. "First one I've see like that."

Cop two (sympathetically) "You'll get used to it."

Mathew shuddered. He glanced around nervously, wondering where all the rats and cockroaches that feasted on the restaurant's leftovers went at night. What about the cats that roamed through all the garbage, the upended cans, the discarded pizza boxes crushed in half? Did they go home, slink through a window left open for them, and curl up on their sleeping owner's bed, still carrying the alley on their paws?

He didn't want to walk down the backstreet but he didn't want to be too late, either, so he shuffled forward like a pall bearer. It was only three or four steps before he saw her. Her back was pressed against the old shopping cart and her arms were stretched out defensively to the sides. The metal rungs glinted in the half-light. Four teens circled around her like a pack of wild dogs cornering a gazelle. One would take a threatening step forward then withdraw, just as his partner moved in and tried to snatch something from beneath the blankets. Beatrice kept backing up, and tried to keep them all in focus. She glanced back and forth at their faces, watching their eyes, sensing their intent. She tensed noticeably the closer they moved in, the smaller her little circle became. Mathew heard the jangle of her dangling bracelet.

The old woman's attackers were as individual as plankton to a whale. Hats on backwards, Clydesdale-dimensioned running shoes left untied, oversized pants that were so baggy they could be hiding another gang member inside. They appeared to be communicating through an endless series of secret head movements and patterned arm whirls that conveyed some esoteric meaning they all understood. Two Latinos, a tall black guy, and a white kid. All hard cases. One of them kicked a can out of the way and inched closer.

"Leave me alone," Beatrice said stiffly.

"'Leave me alone,'" the white kid mimicked in a falsetto voice.

The youths followed the lead of the tallest boy. They all started taunting the old woman at once, grabbing at her cart, kicking the wheels, lurching toward her in unfinished strikes, feinting back, lunging again.

"Wha'chu got der, hag?"

"Gimme evryting, you crusty old bitch."

"Give it up and we won't stomp chu."

"Beatrice!" Mathew yelled. He was surprised at the strength of his voice because his knees were shaking.

Beatrice didn't take her eyes off the boys. She warned him to stay back.

"Yeah, stay back you little shit or you gonna be next."

Mathew tried to stem the tremors in his legs and took another step forward.

"It's all right, Mathew. Don't do anything foolish."

Mathew took another step.

The Latino with a checkered bandanna turned. "I said back off, fuckhead."

Beatrice held up her hand. "Please. Just go. Just because I'm your fairy godmother it doesn't mean I'm some weak-kneed little leftist that can't protect herself."

Momentarily taken aback by what they *thought* they'd heard, the boys' faces splintered into laughter. But it only lasted a second before the hate returned to their eyes and they moved in again. Beatrice maneuvered her cart out from the wall so she could slip behind it.

"Yo momma. Wha'chu say? A fairy godmother? Well fairy this, grammah." The tallest boy made an elaborate panto-mime of unzipping his pants.

"No!" Mathew yelled, the cry reverberating eerily off the walls. Something scurried behind a nearby bag.

The leader turned again. "You ain't lis'nen, man. Fuck off or I do you too." He gestured something Mathew didn't under-stand. The other boys laughed.

Mathew was terrified and sensed bile rising in the back of his throat. He'd never been in a real fight before. He'd seen them at school, of course. But back then, a fight downtown at Jarvis Collegiate lasted as long as it took to bloody a nose or knock the other guy down. That was it. The invisible referee stepped in waving and counted one kid out. Someone won and someone lost, and whatever had been at stake was settled. It wasn't necessarily Queensbury Rules, but the code of honor expected in the ring was extrapolated to the street.

But the fights Mathew read about in the paper or saw on television weren't like that anymore. If someone was knocked down they were immediately swarmed and beaten senseless. Hit with sticks, clubs, knives, machetes. Back in high school, the fight was over when someone was on the ground. Now that was the cue to start kicking someone already unconscious in the head. Rules changed, he guessed. Or was it just that the people were different? It didn't matter. He didn't know what to do, but he knew he had to try and help Beatrice. He grabbed a piece of pipe sticking up between two garbage bags and yelled again.

"I told you to leave her alone."

The tall boy stopped Mathew in his tracks with a glare. "Dats it, man. You be dissin us fo da last time." He gestured with his head. "Chuckie." One of the other filaments of plank-ton, the second Latino kid with rings in his nose and eyebrows, separated from the group. "We gonna teach this boy some mannas."

Chuckie gestured to the pipe with an unconcerned nod. The taller kid shrugged, reached down into the endless folds of his pants and eased a knife from his pocket. He opened the blade with a quick flick of his wrist. Mathew felt his heart skip a beat.

Chuckie and the tall kid splintered away from their companions and slithered down the alley toward him. Mathew brandished the pipe threateningly. His attackers moved apart and slinked along opposite walls. Mathew pointed the weapon at each kid in turn, wondering who'd be the first to strike. Trying not to panic, he struggled to get a feel for the pipe's weight as the kids eased closer. He didn't know whether he should swing it like a club or jab it like a spear. He didn't have time to decide.

Chuckie lunged from the right. Mathew warded off the first blow, and the next, but then the tall boy moved in from behind and kicked him so hard in the side he lost all his breath. His legs buckled and he slumped down to his knees. Three quick, vicious kicks slammed against his ribs. He knew they were broken before he toppled over. Instinctively he tried to cover his head, but one of the boys yanked his arms back and rained several blows down onto his face. He tasted warm blood, heard Beatrice yell something from someplace very far away, and then saw the glimmer of metal beneath the fractured light. The knife descended for the second time before he even knew what was happening. He didn't feel the first stab, but his lungs gasped with the second and third. He heard a loud sucking noise, felt another kick, then listened as feet scraped away through the tumbleweeds of garbage.

Mathew's mouth filled with blood and his eyes started to flutter closed. He shook his head, tried to clear his vision, but the pain was overwhelming. Coughing up bloody phlegm, he imagined himself crawling forward and scratched at the pavement with his fingers. He tried to form Beatrice's name but the sounds wouldn't come. Just a gurgling noise and cars honking in the distance.

Mathew forced his eyelids open and blinked away the blood and tears. The last thing he saw was a confusing collage of intermeshed images he had trouble separating days later when he managed to crawl back out of the black oozing tar pit he'd fallen into.

Beatrice looked down the alley to where Mathew had crumpled and she knew she was losing him. But she didn't panic. She reached out and pulled her crown from under the corner of her blanket. She placed it regally on her head, adjusting it patiently like she hadn't a care in the world. She almost smiled when two of the boys started to laugh, but her eyes were fixed and determined. Her hand disappeared into the cart again, returning with two small dowel-like sticks before her attackers had time to move. The sticks fell apart and something glistened between them. Her bracelet? No, a chain.

The images Mathew remembered later were nauseatingly surreal. Beatrice spun around in a full circle, the sticks dangling at her side. Even if he'd been able to see them clearly, Mathew never would have known they were *nanchukas*. And he wouldn't have realized what they were, anyway. But somewhere, slipping in and out of consciousness like a seal through an ice floe, he was faintly aware of the damage they could do, although he still couldn't imagine Beatrice wielding that kind of power in the first place.

Mathew's two attackers were just reaching their comrades when Beatrice swung the sticks around her head and caught the kid with the bandanna in the shoulder. Even from where he was stretched out on the ground, Mathew heard the bone split and the punk's shoulder separate from the socket. The second kid's shock quickly turned to rage. The white boy with the hat to one side spun around on his back foot and threw all his weight into a sidekick aimed at Beatrice's head.

Beatrice moved effortlessly to the side and the boy's foot thudded heavily against the wall. The *nanchuka* sticks were in her left hand, spinning like propellers. She leaned forward, wrapped her right arm around the little gangster's exposed shin, and pinned his leg to her side. The propeller blades whirled closer. The first stick stopped spinning when it cracked against the front of the boy's knee; the second when it smashed into the back of his leg and tore out his tendon. The boy's mouth fell open with a stifled scream as he crashed to the ground. He pushed against the cart with his good leg, scurrying into the shadows like a three-legged crab.

Chuckie and the tall boy traded a quick look and moved in. Mathew struggled to keep his eyes open as the blood pooled beneath him from his mouth and nose. Beatrice stepped out from the wall as her attackers chose sides. She held the ends of the chain. Her arms moved like windmills and the sticks sliced through the air like little wooden rapiers. Chuckie wasn't so quick to move this time, but Beatrice didn't want to give him time to think.

She lunged between them, the sticks slicing viciously through the air, and turned to face the taller boy, the head of the snake. The sticks were moving so fast he could hardly see them, but he felt the air as they whooshed by. He palmed his knife back and forth between his hands, waiting for his companion to move into position and strike. But Beatrice sensed Chuckie move before the kid actually did himself. She turned and lunged at the same time, the sticks spinning wildly through the darkness like two skipping ropes whipping in opposite directions. They smashed into Chuckie's head and face, once, twice, three times, then again and again as the boy crumpled limply to the ground. He sunk to his knees, his hands trying uselessly to stem the flow of blood and skin from his face, and then collapsed forward with a stifled moan. His knife skidded across the pavement.

Mathew thought he heard a helicopter. Beatrice turned and wielded the sticks faster and faster until they hummed. The boy with all the piercings was sweating profusely. Without looking away, he reached down and grabbed the lid of a garbage can and tall kid's knife. Circling to his left, he kept jabbing the knife toward Beatrice's face to keep her back while protecting his side with the shield. She moved closer and the sticks clanged loudly off the metal lid.

Crouched down with his shield up like a gladiator, the boy faked another stab at Beatrice's head, then uncoiled his body and lunged, the blade aimed straight for her heart. But Beatrice deked to the side. With a stick in each hand, she yanked them apart and snapped the chain taut. She caught the boy's knife hand with the steel band of metal links. In one quick motion she crossed her arms, dropped to her knees, snapped the chain tighter again, and pulled the boy over her shoulder and onto the pavement. She stood back up immediately, his hand still trapped in the chain and his arm held rigidly back behind him in the air. He screamed as she jerked the sticks up and wrenched his arm back harder, tearing the tendons in his shoulder. She stepped in closer and aimed a ferocious foot sweep just beneath his elbow. One quick kick and his arm snapped in half.

Breathing heavily, Beatrice panted for air. A quick glance around the alley confirmed the threat was completely gone. Spinning them like a gunslinger holstering his six-shooter, she brought the sticks to a sudden stop and jammed them down into the waistband of her bulky overcoat. She hurried to Mathew's side. His body was still squandering blood excessively, and his breaths came in long, slow wheezes that were clipped at the end. His face was a hideous purple and his legs twitched to some unheard chant. He shivered uncontrollably.

"Mathew." Beatrice waited, and then whispered again. "Mathew. Can you hear me?"

No. But he did hear something. He just didn't know what.

***

A slow afternoon for a downtown bar, even for a weekend. Maybe it was the cold, or perhaps what had been on the news earlier. Commuter traffic crawled by the window, the cars' headlights muted by the hazy darkness of the lounge. Three or four people stood at the bar pretending to listen to each other; an old woman teetered on her elbows at the far end behind a row of shot glasses. The piano player was on break but no one seemed to realize he'd stopped masking the silence with his mournful chords.

Carlos pushed the case back under the little table with his foot. He ruffled out his car coat again, flicking beading water drops to the floor, and re-draped it over an empty chair. He wanted it bone-dry before they left. He sipped his wine, his stare unnervingly intense. Wet curls hung over his forehead.

"Your art improves each week."

"You're just saying that."

"I've told you before. I never 'just say' things. Words are expressions and I never waste them. I watch you more than you realize. More than you even understand. You must have felt that at the gallery."

I doubt it. But I do. I feel your eyes on me all the time. "I'm still having problems with color."

"Everyone does. Except Monet, of course. You're starting to see *inside* the color though, aren't you? *Behind* it. *Past* it, like I said you would."

"I'm trying to."

"Don't be so hard on yourself. You know I think you're one of the best students I've ever taught."

Oh, just to hear you say that . . .

Carlos reached across the table and extended his hand between their wine glasses. He had such delicate, warm skin. Perfect nails. Slender fingers. Especially when they were wet, and sweet, and tasted of him.

"And it's not just your art, your potential, that draws me to you. You know how much you captivate me. Entrance me."

Sometimes I can't bear you so close. Everything changes. Especially me. Even at times like this, when I know I shouldn't be here but I can't stay away. Oh God . . . what am I doing here? Losing one love to find another?

"Carlos —"

"Ahh, the light of innocence. You're even more beautiful when you blush. But why are you still so embarrassed? Is it because of the other night?" There was a mischievous glint in his eyes.

"I'm not sure."

"You don't feel the same things for me? You don't come to my classes simply to hear me ruminate about the creative process, to watch me extract *something* out of the other students, something that will never be more than chicken scratches in the sand?"

If you only knew how much! The nights I've spent, longing, wishing . . . "Yes, of course I do!"

"Then what is it? What makes you afraid?"

"That —"

"That what?"

"Oh Carlos! That I'll fall so deeply in love I'll never be able to breathe on my own again."

"I'll hold you up, and you will always have my soul's very breath."

"But if you don't —"

"Shhh. Has your painting taught you so little? The meaning is in the art, not the thing others see when you move on to a new canvas. The process, the *being* of each drawing. Let yourself *be* that expression of freedom. Let your experiences merge with your dreams."

"I . . . I know. And I'm trying, I really am."

"Do you? Are you sure? Can you forget everything that's going on at home?"

"I'm *trying*. You understand my past. You know everything there is to know about me. I've never felt this way about anyone else before. Even . . ."

"Sshhhh."

"It frightens me."

"I know, I can feel it. So there's only one thing you can do."

A gulp and threatening tears. "What?"

"Keep letting more of yourself go until there's nothing to hide behind."

Help me, Carlos.

"Be the wind, without a beginning, without an end. Invisible, flexible, curving around anything that stands in your way. Never looking back, and always, always going forward."

But I need something to hide behind.

Carlos pulled his hand away. "Come with me."

"Where?"

"A place not far from here, but far enough. You've seen it in your dreams."

"I —"

"Come with me. We'll go to the realm that only artists seek, that only painters and visionaries can create. Together."

"I'm afraid."

"Let the fear consume you, then let it go. Trust me, and this night will be like no other. You'll paint something wonderful after you wake up beside me."

Carlos smiled and brushed his hair back from his forehead. He counted several bills out onto the table as he stood, then reached down and picked up the little portfolio case.

"I enjoyed these new pieces very much. And now I want to enjoy you."

No smile. Carlos pulled his overcoat on and glided soundlessly toward the door. There was a moment's hesitation, and then the other chair scraped back from the table. A sigh, an anxious gulp that was louder than it was meant to be, and Tristan, his hands shaking, followed his mentor out into the rain-slicked darkness of the street.

Chapter Twenty-two

08:56:21
I got yur mesag this afternon. Thank u. I ws woried Id hav 2 cal th polic or somthin. Im so sory 4 th trobel an pain Ive caused u. I façade men 2 hurt u. Dream@Fangs is ded 4evr. Plese Cybernician, cal me. We cant thro a hole relationship awy 4 this. Plese! Forever yours, love you-know-who.

***

Other than the steady pulse of the Panda clock and the gurgling of the air tube in the aquarium, Carmalitta's office was silent. She'd closed the window blinds, and the only light left on was the little brass lamp on the edge of her desk. The file she'd opened and closed three times without reading it had been pushed to the side. Leaning on her elbows, she absently studied her Tablet Day-Timer, agonizing over tomorrow's entries. But they hadn't changed since the last time she looked.

The Sinclairs would be home by now, she thought. To what was left of their home. Dr. Emerson had been sympathetic and professional, as always, and Carmalitta had been as supportive and compassionate as she could, but the poor old couple had been devastated with Koala's death. Everything had seemed too bright for Mrs. Sinclair: the shiny examination table, the overhead lights, the silver equipment, the slender tip of the syringe, the animals crying out in the other room. She'd kept her sunglasses on the entire time, even though she had to keep tilting her head back so she could see beneath the rim. Mr. Sinclair had almost fainted twice but he'd managed to steady himself against the side of the table. It was Mr. Sinclair who held Koala when Dr. Emerson gently eased the plunger down that would close the little dog's eyes forever.

But was it really that bad?

The last few years of little Koala's existence had been filled with pain and suffering. The Sinclair's' own lives manifested with a continual sense of hopelessness, of sorrow, of an incessant inability to give their dog any kind of meaning. All they truly felt was guilt and sadness, of anything better, or perhaps even easier, for them and for their dog to leave his final paw prints upon. As if it might finally have meant something. Anything. Anywhere.

The Sinclair's stayed in the little room for about ten minutes by themselves. When they came back out they'd aged even more. They leaned against each other, each holding the other up, and shuffled past the reception desk without a word or a glance. Tears streamed down Mrs. Sinclair's face. She palmed Koala's little fake, diamond-studded collar between her hands like rosary beads.

What would they do now? It was undoubtedly too late for another pet. When the time comes for an old person, or an invalid, to leave the world behind, one of the things they always find most distressing is when they think about what's going to happen to their pet. They're not concerned about their apartment, the china doll collection, the collage of old photographs, the favorite chair, their clothes, or the little spoons that reminded them of all the places they'd visited over the years. Their greatest fear is what will happen to Toto or Muffy or Satchel or Rover or Cat. So Carmalitta didn't think the Sinclairs would want to start a new life with another pet when they both felt they wouldn't have the chance to take care of it for long, anyway. They wouldn't want to get attached to something else again when it was time for them to let go. The feeling was mutual, a dichotomy of sorrow, because they'd know in their heart of hearts, by not getting another pet, they understood their own time, and their own time with each other, was short.

Carmalitta closed her eyes. Miriam was behind her lids again, their apartment hiding in the shadows behind her, the wind-laced storm clouds that rolled across the Lake and scratched new threats in the sand. But Carmalitta couldn't think of the condominium without thinking about Joshua. She had a child and she'd let him go. There'd never been a time when she wanted to tell him everything about their relationship, about what had happened, more than she did now. She didn't know what to say or where to begin or whether it was really in his best interest for her to tell him anyway, but she knew she had to tell him the truth. Was it for him, or was it really just for her? She was too close to the situation to know for sure. What was her motivation? Guilt? A need to expunge herself of her secret so she could get on with the rest of her life? Did she need to be a mother, even if it was to one gender more than it was to another?

Somewhere far off in the distance, a phone rang, a shrill cry like in the old Bogart movies. Carmalitta closed her Tablet because she wasn't sure what difference it made if tomorrow came anyway. As long as the Sinclairs could still hold each other in the darkness and make love together in the coming light, and listen to each other's heartbeat. She was startled when the afterhours line trilled again. Was it the Sinclairs? She started to panic. She took a deep, slow breath.

"Yes?"

"Carmalitta? Hi."

"Joshua? Goodness, I was just thinking about you." *Was this an omen*? But her sudden smile quickly withered. Panic returned. The little alarm everyone has deep inside that tells you something's wrong rattled her senses. She tried to control her unease. "What is it Joshua?"

Carmalitta sank back into her chair and listened to Joshua's anxious account of what had happened in the alley. She watched the fish swim round and round the castle walls. She swiveled around to face the closed blinds. Moonlight seeped through the cracks.

"I see," she finally whispered, trembling. *Stabbed*. How hard it must have been for such a young boy to say that word. Her son. "Joshua, are you okay?"

"I think so. I'm kind of scared too, I guess."

"I know. Thanks for calling me. I know how hard it must have been. You're a brave boy."

That made Joshua feel a little better. An inside smile. Carmalitta had absolutely no idea what he'd been through over the years. Over lifetimes. Arrows in the back. Sliced by a fragment of a metal sword. Drowning when his galleon was pierced and rammed at full speed. The sickness from the wine he tasted for Belle, the love of that life. The heart that stopped the jeweled dagger meant for . . . .

Carmalitta didn't know whether to ask the question or not, but quickly decided she should. "How's he doing?"

"I'm not sure yet. They're not sure yet." Of all the times he wanted to morph into a physician or surgeon. But it wasn't something he just did. *It was someone who came back.*

"Don't worry, Joshua. I'll be home as soon as I can." A pause. 'I love you. I'm sure he'll be alright."

***

Thick and occluding, the conjured mist of some unseen wizard swirled the tiny bathroom into a realm without dimensions. Moist and warm, the steam banished the mirrors from sight. Lydia slipped deeper down beneath the bubbles until her entire body was hidden by the foam. She closed her eyes and listened to the bubbles crinkle. The hot water lapped against her skin, soothing her toes and gently caressing her back and shoulders.

Although Michael oozed power from every pore of his body, he'd been attentive and decidedly unguarded throughout the evening, so dinner had been wonderful again. The only person he'd patronized was the waitress who blushed every time he voiced his displeasure at some trifling detail or other. Yet other than a few perfunctory trailing hands, the producer had been the consummate gentleman. Was that good or bad? Lydia wasn't sure, but she didn't have time to dwell on such pointless digressions because all she could think about was Raphael.

Raphael Santoriago. Even the name made her skin tingle. She'd seen him on and off the set for days now, but she knew he was not the type of man that she could ever get accustomed to. Few people could really be described as suave, sophisticated, and urbane, but Raphael certainly was. His presence was overwhelming and magnetic. Tall, well-built, handsome, and charming without a hint of self-consciousness. Why should he be? He was one of the most revered talk show hosts in the country. In the world, for that matter. He had a gentle, disarming smile that turned Lydia's knees to quicksand every time she saw him. He actually had to hold out a hand to steady her when they were first introduced. She was sure he noticed, but she assumed he must be used to such flagrant manifestations of awe and respect. She moved her hand under the water and touched her other elbow. There, near the forearm. That's where he'd reached out and touched her, destroying the chasm between them, lifting her up to her toes with the slightest brush of his fingers until her spine felt solid once more.

Lydia sloshed forward, searched for the tap at the end of the tub, and plunged more water into her lagoon. She drifted dreamily over the last few days, not finding it strange in the least that she could remember every nuance of Raphael's words and gestures during the moments they'd been on the set together. Naturally, she'd been ruefully intimidated at first, but Raphael possessed an uncanny ability to put the people surrounding him at ease. He seemed to be able to bring out the best in everyone. In a rare moment of silence, he'd even leaned over and quietly explained to her what the best boy and the key grip actually did. God, he was so patient.

Lydia pulled handfuls of foamy bubbles over her shoulders, under her chin, and down across her chest. She felt her breasts, content with the hard fullness she'd struggled so very hard to maintain. She touched her nipples, tentatively at first, but then less uninhibitedly, teasing them with gentle circles of her palms then squeezing them erect between her fingers.

Even his voice was enough to drive her mad. Deep and resonant, with just a playful hint of an accent that was hard to place. She looked down and rolled her nipples with her thumb and forefinger. Had he noticed her? Really noticed her? He'd been direct with his criticisms but equally forceful with his accolades about how she was doing, the way in which she was bringing her part to life.

Lydia's hands dove back beneath the water. She stroked her calves, behind her knees, and then walked her fingers gently over her thighs. She spread her legs and an island of bubbles floated up toward her breasts. The warm water rushed in, and she swirled it against her sex by moving her hands like fins. It pulsed through her hair, the soft folds between her legs, awakening a desire she hadn't felt in a very long time. She tried to think of her husband, but Raphael's face kept nudging him away. *Oh Mathew, what happened to us?* Her hands trailed up and down the inside of her thighs and she sunk down a little deeper into the water, her goose bumped nipples poking through the little islands of foam. *Raphael.* She rolled the name across her lips, tasting its sweetness with her tongue. She saw his eyes again when he'd told her she was doing so well, that it was indeed a pleasure to work together. *Why can't love be the same as desire?* Her hands moved down between her legs and she shuddered.

But the phone rang and shattered her dreams. Fuck. She couldn't ignore it in case it was someone from the set. Rubbing her thighs together, Lydia stopped floating and returned to earth, her sex rampantly red and wonderfully sore. She sloshed over to the edge of the tub and tugged the receiver from the wall.

"Yes," she answered softly, sweetly, still squeezing her legs together. But it wasn't someone from the set. An *operator*, for shit's sake.

"What?" she answered curtly. "Who?" Speak louder, woman. "Who? Well yes. Yes, put him on."

She tensed apprehensively. Dread flushed the color from her cheeks, and her nipples eased back to their normal size. Why would *he* be calling?

"Mathew?"

No, it wasn't Mathew. Wrong voice for the body she imagined. The woman said it was her son.

"Joshua?"

"Mom?"

Static on the line. The operator asked something obtuse.

"What? Yes, of course I'll take the fucking call, you stupid woman. Joshua, is that you?"

"Yes, it's me."

"Heavens, what are you calling me out here for? Do you know what time . . .?"

Instant panic and fear, the kind that lines your forehead with cold sweat, and cramps your stomach like diarrhea. Lydia pushed herself up higher in the tub, frowning, shaking. Why would Joshua call? Something didn't feel right.

"Are you okay, Joshua?" she wondered slowly. She hoped she was talking to *Joshua,* and not someone else.

"I'm fine," he breathed, his throat harsh.

"Then why . . . God, Joshua. Is everybody else . . . .?"

"Mom," he replied softly, fighting the tears.

"Oh, Joshua – "

"Dad's been stabbed."

Chapter Twenty-three

Lorne was mesmerized by something in his lap. He'd bunched his blanket up into piles that billowed over his chest, and his hands were hidden inside the folds. Were his otters playing? His eyes were half-closed, his breaths light and constrained. He looked more tired than he'd been in a long, long time. He was looking out the window: no, he was looking past it, past whatever was out there in the darkness. Perhaps he was listening to the thickening rain. Eleanor was at her dresser, her settee wobbling on a broken leg, and one of her drawers unable to close. She had a little cotton ball in one hand and a moisturizing cream in the other. She wondered how much time she'd spent over the years looking at herself in a mirror. Had it ever helped? With one mirror broken, she saw her reflection twice in the angled panels, but she knew she was really seeing the woman *behind* her, the transparent one that looked just like her and was always there in the background, reminding her of the things she wanted to forget or questioning whatever she did. That woman's face was young this time, free of wrinkles, pain, and false hope. Twenty years ago? Thirty?

Eleanor closed her eyes and pictured Lorne in the backyard once again, stomping at the ground, fingers raised like horns, charging back and forth at the bright red comforter waving in the wind.

Another time. Lorne was with her, the other Lorne she had before this one, the one who worked so hard all day and then came home to help redecorate the little bungalow they'd scraped the down payment for on Sherbrooke Avenue, the Lorne that was more than a husband then, the one who kept whistling or humming no matter how tired he felt, the one always smiling, teasing her about this or that or about something he'd seen on the Spadina streetcar that morning, while he slathered more paint around the roller and told her how very, very beautiful she was in her old sweater and kerchief spotted with three different flecks of paint. His hair tumbled down over his forehead, and a slash of blue streaked one side of his nose.

Why do you remember some things and not others? Memories are transient and inconsistent; what you recall doesn't depend on whether you want to be able to summon a particular time and place back again or not. Eleanor thought it a little unfair she couldn't choose the things she wanted to remember and simply forget the things she hated being reminded of.

She stared through the woman behind her at the statue of her husband. He'd been so loving, so kind, so industrious. Nothing more had pleased him than simply being able to please her. She watched him wash and wax the dented Hillman, build Lego robots with a Mathew it was hard to recognize, pace back and forth when he was worried about his job, straining to keep his broad shoulders beneath the umbrella as he waited for the streetcar, add another tome to his animal books, towel himself dry after a shared shower, and sleep that restful sleep curled into her side that cocooned them after they'd been together like no one else had ever been together before.

Eleanor couldn't remember when he hadn't been by her side. He'd been there when Mathew was born, at a time fathers were rarely offered the chance to be in the delivery room when their wife's last scream echoed into the baby's cry. When she'd lost her job at the big Eaton's department store, and when he sat so patiently beside her at the school concert when Mathew tried his best to play the violin. And later, when her own mother had died, folding her into his arms and kissing the tears away. But what did all that matter now when she didn't have any one to kiss away her tears? What did all those other things mean?

"Lorne?"

It was difficult talking to someone you weren't sure could hear or understand you. Like people bedside at the hospital whispering to a relative in a coma. Did the still shape swaddled in sheets snapped too tight hear anything at all? Did they understand? Dream? Where were they?

"Lorne? I never meant to hurt you."

It sounded so puerile: she wouldn't have felt so bad if she *had* meant to hurt him. But *had* he been hurt, or had he just been another animal that day, oblivious to all the other things that were going on around him?

"I need things too." She put the moisturizing cream down. "I can't just stay here all the time. I look after you as much as I possibly can, but I can't stay locked up in this house all the time either."

She gestured to the room with a nod. Finished with the cotton ball, she tossed it into the garbage and picked up her brush. Her reflection watched stoically.

"I feed you. Bathe you. Wash your clothes, take you for walks, read to you, shave you, put you to bed and help get you into the chair in the morning. Clean you up if you've been – she knew it was silly, but she whispered anyway – some animal or another."

She looked at the spot on her dresser the atomizer he'd given her so long ago had been, until a mule's kick had sent it crashing to the floor. She stared, and then glared, at the statue behind her, the image fractured in the broken mirror.

"What about me, Lorne?"

She waited. "Well? What about me? Just because you're – you're wherever you are, it doesn't mean my life's over, does it?"

She felt the tears coming: half sad, half angry, part sorry, part guilt, but tears, still tears. "It's not as if I know things will change, that things will get better, because I know they won't. This isn't some dream we'll wake up from."

The reflection of *her* reflection was staring at her in the mirror so she looked away. "I can't go on like this, day after day after day. I know . . . I know you're the man I married, the man I loved all my life. The man I still love. But you're not the same man, are you? Are you?"

Nothing. Either the rain thickened its beat against the window or Eleanor had lowered her voice again.

"I don't know where you are, and I'll be damned if I'm going to live out the rest of my life wondering where *I am*."

Nothing.

"Sorry. I know it's not your fault."

But it's not mine, either, God damn it!

"You know (or do you?) how much I like to paint. That's why I started the lessons in the first place. Not just to get out, although that was part of it too. To meet people, to talk, to just be outside. To socialize. But it was also because I really wanted to work at my painting. I never really had much of a chance when I was younger, and this is – this is probably my last chance. I want to do *something*. Something before my life's over."

Eleanor's reflection grew a little lighter when her *real* body started brushing her hair. She tried to think how Lorne would have been if *she'd* been the one the stroke skewered. Would taking care of her have been enough for him? She stared at her husband, then quickly tried to think of something else. She was brushing her hair so hard her scalp tingled.

"If you --." She paused, chewing on words with syllables made of crushed porcelain. "If you had *died*, then I think I might've felt different in some way. There'd be closure, if you know what I mean. I'd grieve, remember, grieve some more, and little things would always remind me of the wonderful life we had together. But now –"

No, I'm not blaming you, or saying I wish the stroke would have taken you completely. "It's just that I see you sitting there all the time, and sometimes – sometimes it's worse than having you *not here*. I'm always seeing what I can't have, what was, but will never be again."

The house must be dry: the longer Eleanor combed her hair, the more it fluffed out with static. The woman behind her was still; her hair curled delicately around her face. Eleanor felt like some penitent confessing to a screened-in priest, although she could count the times she'd been at church (other than for weddings and funerals), on two fingers.

"It started innocently enough. With the painting. Painting – I don't know – lets me bring out things I don't think I could say or do normally. It lets me express myself, I guess. *A window to the soul*. And the more I worked at it, the happier I felt about what I was doing. It even made things here easier to cope with, because – because I had something else, too. Can you understand that?"

Nothing. The rain was getting stronger. A new comforter was draped across the bed between them like a flag over a coffin.

"And when Carlos noticed my work, I was thrilled. There I was, some old grandmother that had never taken serious lessons before and he thought *my* work was the best. *Mine.* Yes, I was flattered, but there was certainly more to it than that. I was proud. I was *doing* something that *meant* something, and someone else appreciated it. Someone else saw the worth in it, too."

Saw the worth in me.

Eleanor stopped brushing her hair. She was startled to see that the *other* grandmother was sitting on the bed, rubbing her hands over the comforter.

"He talked to me quite a bit about my work, and the more he showed me, the better my painting became. We'd talk during class, and then after, too. First, it was just about art: techniques, colors, little tricks to try, shading, how best to use this-or-that, mental exercises to help me unleash my talents. I didn't really think he was *interested* in me; I thought he was just trying to encourage me and bring out my best work. But later . . . later I knew it was more than that."

Thirty years loving and being faithful to the same man; she'd almost forgotten what flirting was. The signs, the signals, the feelings, the mystery. But it hadn't taken long to remember. Eleanor wondered how other people started, what it was they said in the beginning, when they were ready to confess.

"After a while we started talking about *personal* things. Painting is an expression of something inside. And if you're confused, worried, or if you're keeping things bottled up, your flow of creativity stops. Carlos knew things were blocking my creativity, that I wasn't using my imagination and insight as I should be. So he started talking to me about it. About what was holding me back."

The statue had been holding her back. But had it? Eleanor was having a harder time rationalizing everything than she'd expected. It wasn't her husband that made her so uncomfortable; it was the young woman sitting so thoughtfully on the comforter.

"We talked about how everything had been before. Before I wanted to paint. You know: school, jobs, fears, marriage, children, dreams, the things I was proud of and the things I wished I'd done differently. Hard times and good times. Family and friends. The things I'd always thought were important. You."

Eleanor finally put the brush down. Strands of hair shimmered in the half-light and the back stood out defiantly from her head. She thought she heard the faint reverberation of distant thunder but it might have been Lorne's stomach. What would it have been digesting, anyway?

"The more we talked the more I opened up. I guess that's natural, isn't it?"

She glanced up but didn't pause for an answer; she thought his hands must have been baking beneath the blanket. They'd be red and swollen now after the beating they took outside trying to tear through the cape, then inside, when they were hooves.

"I finally told him."

More thunder. No, it was the pounding of her heart. "I finally told him about the stroke. How my whole world changed in a second at some point during an evening that had started just like all the other evenings, after we kissed when you came home from work, and I started making dinner while you watched some documentary or another, and then I heard Mathew shouting for help, and I came in and heard you trying to say something but I couldn't figure out what it was, and I never heard you say anything else again."

Yes, I guess it changed your life, too.

"Carlos was very sympathetic, very understanding. He let me go on and on about everything: the shock, the hospitals, the trips to the rehab clinics, the nurses at home, the care-giving classes, selling the house and moving back home with Mathew, and the fear – no, the terror – the first time you became *something else* and you moved and we thought we'd seen a miracle but we quickly realized that miracles were for other people and this was just a part of the same curse, a little postscript to the affliction.

"And once I started talking, everything I've held in for so long just kind of poured out. I felt emotions I hadn't experienced in a long, long time. I guess the proverbial floodgates opened, and it was – I don't know – overwhelming. Yet the strangest thing though, was that the more I talked about what had happened and what I felt, the better my painting became. I didn't actually notice it at first, but Carlos did. He saw things I still couldn't see myself."

Eleanor closed her eyes and listened to the rain roiling against the window. Slithering sheets that even looked cold. She didn't want to look at herself sitting on the bed. *No, no miracles.* Were the people that strokes sliced in two different in some way from those that were touched by miracles? Could both befall the same person?

Eleanor opened her eyes again. Her reflection on the bed was standing, moving nearer, reaching out to her. The woman's hands touched her head, her shoulders, then reached farther, deeper, *inside*, and she drew herself closer, closer, until the outline of their bodies touched and the woman grew dim then disappeared into Eleanor's back.

Eleanor shivered. "You know in all those years, I was never unfaithful to you at all."

A half-smile. "I looked – who doesn't? And I didn't really mind if someone flirted a little with me either, at a party or something. As long as it wasn't serious and there wasn't any touching involved. But I never – never – even considered being with anyone else than you. I never needed to, and I never wanted to."

Eleanor's throat was painfully dry. For a moment, she thought she heard something in the adjacent guest room: her own voice, the wind slapping the window, Carlos' heavy breaths, the scratching creak of the box spring.

"But I needed something. Someone to touch me, someone to tell me that I mean something, that I am something."

Outside, the rain slowed to a stagnant pulse. Tears streamed down the pane. And then the wind came again.

Eleanor covered her face with her hands. "Can you understand that? I – I just couldn't take it anymore. The loneliness. The sense that I was living and dying at the same time. The fear of being alone, but not *alone*. That *I* was the one in a coma, or who'd had the stroke."

Lorne's hands were folded into a little peak beneath the covers, like the way you make a church. The bedside lamp framed his head in light against the window.

"And then the other day . . . "

Eleanor's palms were wet and she realized she was crying. "Oh Lorne! I didn't know you were here! No, maybe I did. I thought you might be out with Mathew. I can't remember now. But I didn't think you'd *hear*, that you'd *know*. Oh God, I never would have come here, to the house, if I'd thought you'd be aware of what was going to happen. But I've seen you sitting there for so long, not moving or saying anything, away, wherever you are, and I thought you wouldn't even understand that I was here anyway. And it wasn't until later – *after* – when I got home and I saw Mathew and Joshua running into the backyard, and I heard you, and then I saw you -- ."

She turned and stared down at the comforter through a veil of tears. "I never thought you'd *know*."

Eleanor sniffled and wiped her eyes with the back of her hand. "And I still don't know if you did. I still don't know."

She thought her husband shuddered. She cupped her hands around her face, surprised at how heavy her skin seemed. There was a quick knock at her door. Before she could answer, Joshua peered around the corner. She knew something was wrong before the child spoke.

"Gram?" Joshua sputtered through fresh tears.

"Dad's in the hospital. He was stabbed."

He rushed forward. Eleanor opened her arms and folded the child into her chest.

Chapter Twenty-four

Surfacing.

Yes, that's what it was like. Holding your breath underwater for as long as you can, until your lungs are ready to burst and you feel like peeing and your eyes are going to pop out of your head, and then swimming up toward the surface, sure you're not going to make it. Seeing the sky, the clouds, shards of sunlight dancing on the waves. Everything's hazy, out of focus, but the closer you come to that fragile space-slice where the water meets the air, the shimmering world beyond slowly clears. You burst through, your body still beneath the waves but your face is in the other dimension, gulping deep, luxurious breaths that make you dizzy and bring fresh blood all the way down to your toes.

Yes, surfacing. It's just that it kept happening over and over. Mathew kept sinking back down under the water before he had the chance to breathe. Up and down, in and out, rising and sinking. Not unconscious, but not aware of whether he was awake or not. Was he dreaming? Sleeping? Or had he already died? How did you know if you were in a coma or not? Where were the sounds coming from: the past, or above? It was as if a thin membrane of plastic had been stretched out across the world and he'd run right into it, face first but not completely through, so he was an indentation on one side and half a mask on the other, trapped somewhere in the suffocating realm in between.

He kept hearing things. Feeling them, too. Sensing them without his senses. But he couldn't tell if he was just dreaming them or not, because he didn't know who *he* was or where *he* might have been in the first place. Mathew thought he woke up completely once, a day or a year or a lifetime ago. He hurt all over. Smelled asphalt and warm blood. His chest burned, his stomach felt like it was ripping from the inside out, his lungs scratched with sand. Someone was there. His fairy godmother? Perched beside the bed, hovering, reaching out and holding – what? – his hand in hers? Joshua was with her, the Joshua he *knew*, his son, the one he'd *hidden for someone else,* the one who'd died more times than he had teeth, murmuring, stroking his forehead with his palm. Had they talked? He wasn't sure, but he would have sworn his guardian angel had whispered to him. If he'd really opened his eyes he'd closed them at once though, because the first thing he thought he saw was the inside of a coffin, a bag of someone's blood hanging on a metal bird feeder, and two clear tubes snaking out of his nose like transparent fangs. A sterile whiteness and lights too bright? Was this what he was supposed to walk towards?

Our father . . .

He tried to call for help but didn't because he couldn't remember how to speak. Waking and sleeping, day and night, pain and flying, silence and the echo of his throbbing blood all swirled together like bat wings and toad warts in a bubbling witches brew.

Later, whenever *later* was, Mathew remembered dreams. What he thought were fragments of dreams. Scenes without sounds, nothing complete, just fleeting images and half-recognizable pictures that came and went each time he came nearer to the surface, each time he almost stopped smothering and broke through the plastic membrane separating the worlds.

His foot was trapped between a pair of boulders. Helplessly, he watched Joshua running and falling, porcupine quills quivering in his back. He heard the pounding of hooves across a barren field. Not horses, but giant otters pulling chariots. The warriors raced by hurling keyboards at archers that kept popping up like meerkats all over the field.

A horde of bees buzzed around an old woman's corpse. But just as they started stinging her head and body, she leapt up from the ground covered in diamonds and sprayed them with mace. Falling like rain, the attackers writhed all over the ground, blood spurting in fountains.

Sometimes. Half of a play came back in identical reruns. He saw a pirate trying to corral a wild goat in the middle of some sandy arena while an obese young girl in coke-bottle glasses looked on from the stands, writing furiously while everyone around her yelled *ole*.

Ow! He told them where the gold was buried but they cut him open anyway. One bright light, first in one eye, then the other. A huge, glistening blade dripping with blood. He saw himself on his wedding day. But the faces of all the women, including the bridesmaids, the guests, his mother, Lydia – were all Carol's face. Even the minister wore her mask. He hurried through the sermon, prompted by spears of ferocious gladiators who jabbed him in the small of his back. Then he was in bed with a young girl. Carol. His wife –Lydia?–or Carol?–was standing beside them, watching, notes in hand, urging Mathew on and telling him what to do better.

He talked to Carol all the time. I never stopped loving you. *I know. And I never stopped loving you, Mathew. Even when I was married I thought about you every day. I'll pray with you now. Too late. Too early.*

It never felt right with someone else, did it?

Not at all. You don't know how many nights I'd lie in bed thinking about what you might have been doing at that moment and wishing I hadn't lost you.

Dreams and more dreams, mixed with a cacophony of sounds and sensations that ceaselessly infiltrated the realm he'd been banished to. Cries, things clattering to the floor, blow darts from hidden pygmies digging into his arms, train wheels over rusted tracks, sirens, soldiers stomping past, angels whispering. More pain.

Mathew didn't know when his nose escaped and poked through the surface of the water, but when it did and his face finally shredded the plastic wrap, the first thing he saw clearly with his senses intact and knew wasn't a dream, was Carol.

"Where am I?

"Toronto General."

"I'm on a soap opera?" *Wasn't that Lydia's job? Was she playing a doctor or a patient?*

"No. You're in the hospital."

Well that explains the tubes, Mathew realized. The *blip blip blip* in the background, the sheets snapped so tight he couldn't move, the sterile smell. The way his penis hurt.

He tried to lift his head from the pillow and winced. The dream looked so lovely. "You're all I've been thinking about. For years. But why are you here?"

"Because you're here. Do you remember what happened?"

Mathew closed his eyes and watched the film unravel on the back on his lids. Just parts. But every time he watched it he saw something he hadn't recognized before. A tube. No, an alley, Beatrice, the thugs' attack, his stomach falling out, sinking in the blood, his fairy godmother moving like the old Chinese women he often saw in the park doing their exercises, wheeling something between her hands that sliced screams into his attackers. Her attackers. Scooping up the blood and trying to push it back in.

"Beatrice? What happened to the old woman with the bracelet? My fairy godmother?"

"She's fine. She got you here just in time."

"Just in time? For what?"

"You lost a good deal of blood."

"Yes." Mathew remembered that part. That and the feel of the knife tearing into his stomach. He couldn't picture what his insides looked like. He didn't want to.

"You're going to be fine. You need time to rest. The doctors say you'll heal up nicely."

Mathew tried to look down. "I was stabbed."

"Yes."

"Did they hit anything important?"

Carol smiled, her face almost radiating. "Just you."

"How long?"

"Have you been here? Almost three days."

"How did you –"

"I saw it in the paper."

"In the paper?"

"The local crime beat. I came right away when I saw your name."

"Thanks."

"I couldn't stay away. I was really worried."

"Did they catch them?"

Carol nodded. They'll be laid up a lot longer than you."

Mathew pictured the sticks swirling through the air. He could almost hear their hum. He looked up at the IV stand and watched someone else's blood drip down into his veins. Carol saw him flinch.

"Some of it's mine," she whispered. "Joshua's, too."

"Joshua?"

"He's donated twice. He's quite a little character, isn't he?"

"Yes. He is."

"He's come in before when I've been here."

"You've come before?"

"Every day."

"I really have been out of it. What about your husband? What if he finds you here?"

"I wouldn't care. We've been separated for years."

"I'm sorry." *No I'm not.*

"Don't be."

She glanced uneasily about the room. Outside in the hall, the intercom crackled awake and summoned two doctors with a secret code. Surgery, or a meeting with their investment banker?

"Tell me," Mathew asked. He didn't like looking up through the tubes. All he could think about was hiding under Kafka's bed. The blood was backing up in one of the tubes taped to the back of his wrist. He gestured for some water. Carol slipped her hand behind his neck, eased him forward, and helped him take a small drink. The coolness burned. But not as much as the wonder of her gentle touch. Her skin on his.

"There's really not much to tell."

"No, not that. I want to know everything about you." *All I've missed.*

"About my marriage?"

"Yes."

"I met him a couple of years after we stopped seeing each other."

Mathew winced. *Stopped seeing each other.* It still hurt to hear the words.

"We started off okay, I guess. But there was always something missing. It never felt completely right."

Mathew remembered being at home. He thought about Lydia and all the times he'd stared out the front window watching the days change and thinking the exact same thing.

"I loved Ronald, but – but I never really stopped thinking about you. That we should have stayed together. Got married, the whole thing." She twirled an imaginary ring around her finger.

Mathew felt tears well in his eyes. "Carol –"

"No, don't say anything. I shouldn't have said that now."

"Yes you should."

"You're still married."

"Marriage doesn't always mean love."

He dug a hand free from beneath the sheets. Carol reached over and took it between her own. He was holding hands with the woman he'd loved forever. He shivered. "I think about you all the time, Carol. I've never stopped. Even when I heard you were married I couldn't ever get you out of my mind." One of the monitors punctured the awkward silence. *Blip blip.* "When did you separate?"

"Almost three years ago."

"Why?"

She shrugged. "A lot of reasons. I think I stayed so long because of the children."

"What do you have?"

"A boy and a girl. Both off on their own. Two of the nicest people you'd want to meet."

"They would be if you raised them."

Carol squeezed his hand. "Once they left, I realized how empty everything seemed, how little Ronald and I had in common. He's not a bad man, and, all things considered, he was a pretty good father. But I –"

"What?"

"But I just couldn't ever feel the things for him that I felt for you." Carol's eyes reddened. She pulled her hands away, but Mathew reached up as far as he could, his hand and arm quivering. She took his hand again. He wished he would have been stabbed years ago.

"That's what I always felt, too," he breathed. "My wife – Lydia – is a wonderful woman in her own way. We've had our ups and downs, but it's been pretty steady for the most part. It's just that I can't love her like I loved you. Like I love you."

Even though he felt guilty uttering the words, an enormous weight lifted from Mathew's body. He wondered at first if he'd died and his soul had left, but he could still feel the soft warmth of Carol's hands around his. The weightlessness was there because he'd finally said it. Admitted the secret to the world that he'd been guarding for so long. His skin tingled. Stitches itched everywhere.

Carol was crying. "I never stopped loving you either, Mathew. Whenever I was doing something, whenever something happened, I always imagined what it would have been like if —"

"It had been with me?"

She nodded and sniffled.

"It's been the same for me, Carol." Eyes moist, he turned and watched the monitor's blue lines bleep across the screen. "It's been the same for me. And a night's never gone by that I haven't prayed for you. Your happiness, your health, the wellness of your family. Even if I wasn't a part of it."

"Oh Mathew." Carol leaned closer and pressed her face against his cheek. Their tears mingled, and a thousand sights and sounds and feelings and emotions washed over Mathew's senses like waves sinking a capsized boat. She turned and kissed him on the edge of his mouth. She was softer than the silky skin on the end of a horse's nose.. She leaned back and wiped her eyes.

"I'd better go."

"Please don't."

"What if your wife comes in?"

"I want you to stay."

"I can't. If I stay I won't want to leave."

"I don't want you to leave. I lost you once and I won't lose you again."

"Oh Mathew. You don't know what you're really saying."

"Yes I do. Please."

Fresh tears. "I have to go."

"But you'll come back?"

She nodded.

"Promise?"

Carol leaned down again and kissed him lightly on the forehead. "I promise."

She looked deeply into his eyes. "How are you feeling?"

"Like I've got my life back. Oh God, Carol. There's so much I want to tell you."

She blushed. "No, I mean physically? Are you in pain? Do you want me to stop at the nurses' station and get you anything?"

"Thanks, but I'm fine. Just seeing you again has given me everything I've needed. A life – a life to live for."

Carol wiped away her tears, leaned down, and kissed Mathew on the cheek. She smiled as she stood up and gathered her things. She hovered at the side of the bed for a moment, like a mourner at a funeral, wishing there was something more she could do, something more she could say, then turned and left. It was all so sudden! Carol paused again at the door, choked on a tear, and quickly slipped out into the hallway. As the door swung silently closed, Mathew realized he could hear his heart pounding somewhere in his chest. He looked at her chair, imagining her there again, sensing her with every single fiber of his being.

And then his eyes fluttered closed, the blood dripping through the tubes started to hurt again, he felt he was drifting down and away, and an inky blackness curled around him like Merlin's mist and he felt himself falling back into the other unknown world again.

He started to cry.

***

"Beatrice?"

Mathew's eyes had fluttered open again. She was sitting on the chair beside the bed, flipping through a six year old magazine, her face practically glowing. She was wearing her heavy overcoat, but it was the first time Mathew had seen her without her cart.

"They wouldn't let me bring it in, so I had to leave it outside."

- 312 -

Mathew nodded dully.

"It's safe."

Something bit at his memory, some scene from some alley swallowed part of his consciousness: swirling sticks, gangsters crying and yelling and running, a blade sticking out of his stomach. Yes, the rickety old cart would be safe. Even from the people standing outside the hospital, one gown facing the front, one gown facing the back, dragging along a pole with a couple of monitors and intravenous bags dripping into their arms, feverishly intent on getting a few more cigarettes in.

"So you're finally awake. You're not looking too badly now, actually. But you certainly had me worried there for a while, you know."

He looked around the room. Everything seemed different, but the same. He flexed his nostrils. The tubes were gone. He could swallow. Tubes taped to his wrist carried something into his blood. Had they really all been there before?

"How long have you been here?"

Beatrice shrugged. "An hour or two. Today."

"You've been in before?"

"Stop asking everyone that. Don't be silly, of course I have. We've talked a few times already. But you kept slipping back out of reach." She lowered her voice and gestured toward the hallway. "Out of reach for *them*, I mean. I just didn't want to bother you because I knew you had to conserve your energy. You lost a fair amount of blood."

She leaned back from the bed, pushed one of the little picture-buttons, and lowered the side rail a bit. "So how are you feeling?"

He answered truthfully. "I'm not sure."

Beatrice saw the look in his eyes. "What?"

"I had the weirdest dream."

"When?"

"Who knows? Before. I don't know when. Carol came to see me."

"The Carol of your dreams?"

"Yes." Mathew looked confused. "I woke up and she was sitting right where you are. We talked. About us, I think. It was like we'd never been apart." He shook his head. "I guess it was you, then."

"Nope."

"'Nope' what?

"It wasn't me. She came out just as I was coming in to check on you your first day here."

"Carol? How did you know it was her?"

"I'm your fairy godmother. And even if I wasn't your fairy godmother I still would have known it was her, just by the way she was looking at you. The aura that held you both inside like a soft, cotton-candy cocoon. And no, we're not talking about auras today. You have to save your strength. You're not out of the proverbial forest yet."

"The proverbial 'woods.'"

"What's proverbial to you might not be what's proverbial to me."

Mathew still looked frustrated. He couldn't think of anything proverbial about confusion. "So she was *here*? And I talked to her?"

"Uh-huh. A couple of times. As I said, though, you kept slipping in and out like an otter through kelp. I had a lovely chat with her yesterday."

"You actually spoke to her?"

"It's rather difficult to chat without speaking, Mathew."

"What did you talk about?"

"Gee, I don't know. The rising political tensions in Senegal? The escalating arms race in Pakistan and India? Third world poverty and its relationship to HIV? East Asian doping and DNA restructuring to create super athletes for the Olympics?" Beatrice shook her head and clicked her teeth. "We talked about you. You and her. What was. What is."

Mathew still found it hard to believe. He was sure it had all been a dream, the thoughts and images and feelings just feathers on the wings of morphine. "So when I thought I woke up and talked to her, I really did? I'm not imagining that?"

"Not in the least."

He groaned, and his body came up a bit. Beatrice put her hand lightly, oh, ever so lightly on his shoulder and eased him back down. Her touch felt better than the morphine.

'Don't move too much, Mathew. You have some Franken-stein stitches down there in your stomach. That one little fart got you pretty good."

"Frankenstein stitches?"

"The crisscrossing kind, like the ones that hold Lon Chaney's face and head together in those old movies." She leaned over conspiratorially. "Would you like to see them?"

Beatrice almost seemed excited. She reached down for the edge of Mathew's gown, but he shooed her hand away.

"No, I don't want to see them. I don't even want to think about the stitches or being cut or stabbed or anything."

"Are you sure? You just have to lift up the edge of the bandages. They did a really fine job. You wouldn't believe it, but one side actually looks a little like the . . . "

The realization sunk in. "You've already seen them?"

"Well, of course I *peeked*. I'm your fairy godmother. That's how I knew one part looked a little Frankensteinish. I showed Carol, too. She couldn't believe this one part either, but she thought it looked. . . . "

"*You showed Carol*?"

"Oh, don't be so silly and protective. Some of the wounds were wider at the bottom, so they had to sew you out in a "v", just like when you had your appendectomy. Remember? Carol saw all your appendectomy scars, didn't she? She just wanted to make sure you were okay and that everything was healing nicely."

Mathew nodded dully. Yes, she'd seen his other physical scars, too. He'd been thirteen or fourteen when his appendix burst. He'd got an infection, and was in bed for over a month. Carol had come over every day after school to bring him his homework, keep him up to speed on all the school gossip, help him with his calculus, and to just sit on the side of his bed and talk. He remembered how anxious he used to get when he looked at the time and knew she'd be coming over soon. He missed her before she got there and after she left. It was some of the best anxiousness he'd ever had. God, did he miss it. He didn't realize how much he really loved her.

Beatrice smiled. "Never forget that you're not the only one hurt here, Mathew. She needed to know you were okay. She was really worried."

If roles were reversed, Mathew thought, he'd want to make sure she was alright, too.

"Don't you remember what she brought you in the other day?"

"Carol brought me something?"

Beatrice pulled the curtain to one side, then carefully wheeled over one of the narrow storage trays that can fit across the bed so it's easier for the patient to be able to eat. Something large almost covered the table. Groaning again, Mathew lifted himself up a bit. He frowned and smiled at the same time. It was one of the Zen gardens he'd seen in the store next to the laundromat. The ones with the little rakes and stones. The physical effort drained him and he collapsed back down.

Beatrice touched his forehead, and the pain and the wrinkles disappeared.

"I don't understand."

"Why do you think I made you choose that particular laundromat, Mathew?" She winked and laid her finger alongside her nose.

"Because you own the store?"

"Exactly. And I wanted you to see it. I told Carol about the Zen boxes one day when you were sleeping. She went in the next morning and bought you this one. She thought it would help you relax when you were healing."

Puzzle pieces started coming together for Mathew.

"You told her about owning the store? About the laundromat? Why I was there? About the comforter?" He gulped. "About being . . . . "

"Your fairy godmother? Of course."

Mathew winced.

"She took it just fine," Beatrice said. "But then again, she's a lot more open than you are. Always has been. And she wanted something – a path – *a symbol of a path* – that you might be able to work on together. Before it's too late. Just like your son tried to tell you at the Zoo."

His mind was muddled from the pain and the drugs, but Mathew knew Beatrice was right. Saw it. Felt it. Sensed it with every atom in his soul. He remembered the picture Joshua had drawn in the earth and sand at the Zoo, the one of the interwoven strands of DNA, and how lifetimes are braided together in the same way, like the overlapping rhythms on an EKG monitor, the double helix, or the birth and death of a star. Or just birth and death.

His voice was soft, almost painfully sore. He'd need another shot soon. "The scar . . . not the bad one . . ."

"To close the odd shape of the knife wound, the doctor stitched one part closed in a crescent shape. Right in the middle of the half-circle, at the very top, you have a little birth mark that looks like a heart."

A "C" with a heart hanging down from the top.

Mathew's eyes closed. Behind his lids he saw that symbol on almost every important card or note or letter that he'd seen in the dusty box he'd pulled from his closet just the other day.

He felt the tears coming. Beatrice stopped them. "Here, have some water. Your throat will feel better." She bent the straw towards him, but it took a few seconds for him to actually get it between his lips. Pieces of conversations were slowly coming back through the mists of his memory. Carol. Her hand on his face. Laughing when he tried to draw straight lines in the sand. The questions about happiness.

"Has – has anyone else been in to see me?"

"You really don't remember much, do you?" Beatrice giggled, dangling her bracelet. They sounded like chimes. The door opened and a nurse poked her head in.

"Not now," Beatrice said sharply. The young girl disappeared immediately. "Your mother came for a few moments. So did Carmalitta and Miriam, although I wasn't here then. Other than Carol, Joshua has been in the most. He was really quite upset about the whole thing. They weren't going to let him in until I had a word with them." She winked.

"Is he okay?"

Beatrice nodded. "He's been injured pretty badly a few times before, remember. Fatally. He's an incredible young man. Old man. You know what I mean."

Mathew gulped the dryness from his throat. "So you know all about . . . . "

Beatrice waved him into silence. "Of course I do. He's my little tightrope walker through time."

"Your –"

"So, when he's not *Joshua*, he knows how you feel. He's quite used to physical and emotional pain. I must say, though, he was quite taken with Carol."

"Oh God. They met, too?"

She smiled and glanced up at the IV stand. "They've both given blood."

Mathew looked down at the festering bruise where the needle disappeared. "You did too, didn't you?"

"Why do you say that?"

He frowned. It was a feeling he'd never be able to put into words. "Something feels different. Inside."

She stroked her hand lightly across his forehead. He was flushed with warmth. "You'll feel better in a few days, don't worry."

"Beatrice?"

"Yes?"

"Thanks. For getting me here. For saving me in the alley."

She dismissed the thought away with a flip of her hand. "It was my fault, Mathew. I had to do something. I really didn't think you were going to get hurt so badly. It was just supposed to be a nick."

Mathew's head was spinning. "What do you mean, 'supposed' to? Are you saying the attack was planned?"

"Of course not! How could you think such a thing? I'm your fairy godmother."

She was practically shouting. Mathew was relieved he had a private room. Beatrice recovered quickly and calmed down.

"Sorry," she said. "I don't usually misjudge things quite so badly, though. You never know when you're dealing with these young hoodlums of today. I guess I'm half-human after all." She smiled a broad grin that melted years away from her face.

"No, you weren't meant to get hurt. But I did bring you to the alley. You had to go there if you didn't want to be late for lunch. I didn't think those gangbangers were going to turn on you so quickly, though. And Mathew —"

"Yes?"

"I really appreciate what you did for me. It took a great deal of courage to try and come to my rescue like that."

"I didn't do anything." His eyes misted over, and he saw her in the alley again, wielding the sticks and disabling her attackers. "What were those things you had?"

"*Nanchuka* sticks. You can never be too careful when you roam around in some of the places I do."

The image was unsettling. Comforting, but unsettling.

"But why did you want me to come into the alley if I was going to get hurt?"

"I told you, you weren't supposed to get hurt so bad. I really didn't foresee you getting knifed. But I needed you in the alley."

"Why?"

"So you'd be injured enough to stay in the hospital overnight."

"But —"

"So you'd get your name in the paper."

He shook his head.

Exasperatedly, Beatrice tapped a finger against the side of her head. "So Carol would see it and come."

Mathew stared blankly into Beatrice's eyes. It was the first time he realized they didn't have a definable color.

"This was all so we could meet?"

"Don't be silly. You've known each other for years. No. You saw me in the park that time so you could meet Carol again."

"The park?"

"Right. That way I wasn't such a shock when I saw you at the laundromat."

Mathew shuddered. His chest tightened painfully, and he had an almost overwhelming need to scratch under his bandages.

"Fairy godmothers often have to use rather circuitous ways to bring things about, Mathew. We're certainly not as powerful as you probably think." She winked. "But powerful enough, I dare say."

Mathew wondered, if he had the choice, would he have wanted to be stabbed just so he had the chance of seeing Carol again? He knew the answer was yes.

"Do you remember what you talked to her about, Mathew?"

He squeezed his eyes into a squint. "A little. I hope I thanked her for the Zen Garden."

"You did. And a lot more than that, Mathew. I can see it in the energy all around you. Close your eyes, and remember."

He did. Carol. She was on the chair beside the bed again. She was everything he'd always imagined her to be. He saw her eyes, felt the gentle touch of her hand, her lips against his cheek. Somewhere deep inside his head, he heard all the words he'd said to her again. He told her about the albums and the box of memories, the cards and special little notes and *just-because-you're-you* letters. He told her that he wanted her to stay. That he didn't want to leave ever again, and that he had never stopped loving her. His body trembled. His stitches tickled and he felt pressure in his lower back. He knew it was going to be a long time before he'd be able to stretch or bend over comfortably.

"Your body remembers everything, Mathew. Soon, you will too." Beatrice leaned across the bed and pressed her palm against his side. Her touch was warm and energizing.

"Beatrice?"

"Uh-huh?"

"What do you think I should do?"

"Whatever your heart tells you to do, of course. You should rest now." She trailed her fingers gently over his face, like a blind person reading Braille. Her voice was soft and hypnotic. "Close your eyes, and sleep. And when you sleep, remember. Remember what it's like to be in love. When you wake up, let go. Make something with your Zen Garden."

She tugged his blankets up over his chest, smoothed them out, and took the hand without all the tubes taped to it between her own.

Her breaths were soft and shallow, her heartbeat as slow as a hibernating cub's. She let his hand drift gently down to the bed, and watched him for several minutes until sleep had claimed him once more. She moved one of the stones, a pink heart stone, from one side of the Zen box to the other, next to a piece of quartz. Beatrice picked up one of the little rakes, swirled the tines around, and made an image in the sand. She traced it again, and again, gradually deepening them until the lines were perfectly balanced and deftly shaped. She sat back and smiled. A symbol. *But of what?*

Mathew was breathing heavily as Beatrice stood up and moved back away from the bed. Somewhere, somehow, he could hear her bracelets jangling, the chimes ringing. When he dreamed, he dreamed of Carol. Then, and now. He had the most incredible sensation that the wound inside his stomach was already healing.

And so was the large hole in his heart.

Chapter Twenty five

"What was it?"

Mathew struggled with his senses. The clawing effect of the painkillers still lingered, the way fear persists when the person you testify against is released from prison.

"I'm not sure. It might have been eggs and some kind of sausage, but I wouldn't swear to it."

"At least you're eating better." Carol stopped trying to analyze whatever was left on his plate and wheeled the breakfast tray away from his bed. "More juice?"

"No thanks. What about –"

Carol shook her head. "They said no coffee yet."

Even the word made his stomach grumble. His senses cried out for caffeine but his whole body yearned for Carol so much more. He stared into her eyes. Beatrice was right: he'd remembered everything while he slept, and when he'd awoke, he broke through consciousness with a fierce longing that made his stomach wound seem like nothing more than a scratch.

"What?" Carol asked, behind a smile.

"Nothing. Just looking. I still can't believe you're here."

"Believe it," she whispered. She stroked his cheek with the back of her hand. "I see you've been working on your Zen garden. It's coming along quite nicely."

He'd put it on the moveable tray he ate his meals on so that it was easier to reach. He'd left the lines Beatrice had drawn alone, and started his own little design in the other corner.

"You have new flowers," Carol said, glancing at the ledge beneath the window. Her eyelids fluttered. "The large mums there are from – Cyber-

"Cybernician."

"And the other ones are from your wife."

Mathew nodded. "She's not coming?"

Carol handed him the plant. He freed a little card wedged atop the fork of a plastic stick.

Sorry about what happened. Hope you're doing better now. Will come back as soon as I can. Spoke with doctor – says you'll be fine. I begged, but they won't let me go right now because of scheduling. Will come if you really need me. Thinking about you. Take care and rest. Love, me.

Carol put the plant back on the ledge.

"She's busy filming out on the coast," he explained. He realized he didn't have to.

Carol changed the subject. "When's the doctor coming in?"

"He's supposed to see me before lunch."

"Do you think you'll be able to go home tomorrow?"

He nodded. "Or the next day. As long as I rest and take it easy." He reached a hand down and laid it protectively over the wad of bandages that covered his side.

"It still feels weird," he mused. "Like something's missing inside."

"Well, I'd be happy to come and take care of you."

"That would be great. What about your work, though?"

"I've already asked for a leave of absence, so it's not a problem."

Mathew's smile quickly faded. "But if Lydia –"

"Shh. We'll worry about that later."

We'll worry about that later. The w*e in we'll*. It sounded so nice Mathew felt his eyes tear. But before he could speak his door opened. Beatrice staggered in, practically obscured behind a bouquet of colored balloons. They all said *congratulations* or *happy birthday*. When Beatrice set them down beside his bed and peeked through the tangled strings, Mathew realized she'd chosen them on purpose. She returned his smile.

"Morning." She winked at the balloons. "And it's good to see you're learning, Mathew." She turned to Carol and smiled. "How wonderful it is to see you again. How's our little patient doing?"

"Much better. He might be going home tomorrow. The following day at the latest."

"And you'll stay with him, of course?"

"Beatrice –" Mathew stammered.

"Of course," Carol replied emphatically. "I'm not letting him out of my sight."

Mathew felt his face blush.

"Good. He needs you."

"We all need someone," Carol said quietly.

"Don't you just love it when a hero comes to your aid? And, speaking of heroes, look who I found wandering through the halls." She gestured to the door, puffed out her cheeks, and made the best horse sound Mathew had ever heard.

The first thing Mathew saw was Zorro's swirling cape. The second thing was Joshua. Masked, plastic sword at his side, dark pants, a purple sash, and his black rubber rain boots.

"Daddy!" the boy cried, rushing to the side of the bed. He acknowledged Carol with a smile and a quick hug. "You look a lot better today. "He turned to Beatrice. "He's going to be okay, isn't he?"

She nodded.

Joshua looked down warily at the sheets that covered his father's stomach. "How are you really feeling? Bet it hurts."

"I'm feeling better now that you're here. Just ride in to town?"

Joshua nodded, then stared at the bandages bunched up under his father's pajama bottoms. "I better show you how to sword fight, Dad." One hand aloft, he made a few quick stabs, parries, and lunges with his sword.

"Maybe you can show me when they let me out of here?"

A broad smile. "When are you coming home?"

"By tomorrow," Carol announced happily.

"Great. I'll get you the best practice sword I can find, even if I have to take it from a King's Guard." He slashed the famous 'Z' into the air.

"How's everyone at home?"

"Faring well," Zorro replied.

"Good." Mathew's smile weakened. He was deeply worried about his father.

Zorro turned in a flash and brandished his sword when Mathew's door opened again. The doctor stopped in mid-stride when he saw Beatrice standing next to the famed swordsman. Mid-forties, short, with a scientist's mane of unruly hair and glasses that seemed a little too thick, it all took him back for a moment. But he'd worked his share of shifts on the late night emergency ward, and after a quick head-shake he recovered and reassumed an air of practiced indifference.

"We'll need a few minutes alone, thank you," he said, dismissing everyone as he unfastened his stethoscope. Always the queen, Beatrice shuffled Joshua and Carol from the room, glad that she never wore her mantel with the sanctimonious self-importance that infected so many physicians.

Mathew instinctively recoiled when Dr. Armstrong approached the bed. He could hear his own heart beat when the doctor listened to his chest.

"Huum."

Mathew hated it when physicians said *huum*.

"Let's take a look, shall we?"

He never liked it when they referred to him in the plural form, either, but he dutifully undid his pajama top and tugged his bottoms to the side. Dr. Armstrong peeled the bandages away. Mathew was relieved when he didn't mutter *huum*.

"We're looking much better, now. Simply fine."

"Will there be much of a scar?" Mathew ventured.

Dr. Armstrong looked hurt. Hurt, or insulted. He pointed down at the wound. "Not with *that* stitching work, I dare say."

"That's good," Mathew whispered. He'd always felt self-conscious about scars, even though he only had two, and neither one was really very prominent unless he actually told you where to look. He didn't know how many he had in his stomach. Other than the one that looked like Carol's signature.

"How are we feeling?"

I don't know – how are you feeling? "Not bad at all. Although –"

"Fine. Simply fine." Dr. Armstrong resealed the bandages. "I'll have someone change the dressing later. Any pain?"

"Not when the medication kicks in. But when I –"

"Good." A quick watch consultation. "I'll stop back later, but I don't see any reason to keep you here more than another day. I'll arrange to have you come in and get the dressings done

again in a few days, just to make sure we don't get any septici-
ty. I'll write out a script for you, too."

Mathew didn't say anything because he didn't want to be
interrupted again. Dr. Armstrong jotted something down,
flipped his little notepad closed, and left without a word. Beatrice brought the others back in before the door closed.

"Tomorrow for sure," Mathew said proudly.

"Good clean steel, then," Zorro noted. "No infection. I
thought I was going to have to round you up some maggots."

Mathew was more than pleased he wasn't going to have to
have a bunch of little bloodsuckers crawl across his stomach.

"I'll take Joshua home, Mathew," Beatrice told him, leaning down and touching his forehead. "Get some rest – you feel
a bit warm."

"Okay. And Joshua? Look after your grandmother, all
right? And granddad?"

Joshua nodded, then bowed deeply with a flourish. "I await
your presence on the 'morrow, good sir." He kissed his father
on the cheek then looked up at Carol. "Beatrice and I are going
to Darnelle's for a chocolate shake. Want to come?"

"That would be lovely. I'll just say goodbye to your father
first."

Beatrice put her arm around the boy's shoulder and drew
him from Mathew's bed. He glanced back as they left and
winked.

Carol sat down on the edge of the bed and stroked
Mathew's cheek with her hand. "They're quite a pair."

"They certainly are." Mathew realized he'd forgotten to ask
if Beatrice had gone to his house to pick up Joshua or if they'd
already been out together. How did she know where he lived,
anyway? But he didn't let his worry fester because he was beginning to understand that fairy godmothers implicitly know
much more than they ever let on.

"Will you be all right on your own for awhile?"

"Sure. But I'll miss you."

"And I'll miss you too. I'll come back later. Can I bring you
anything?"

Just your smile. "A magazine less than a decade old would
be nice. And a coffee."

Carol laughed and kissed him lightly on the forehead. "I'll find you something to read." She didn't have to ask what because she still knew all the things that interested him. "Rest, like Beatrice says." She stood to leave.

"Come back."

"I will."

"And bring me a coffee."

She blew Mathew a kiss.

"A latte, then."

She shook her head and ducked past the door as it swung closed, just as Mathew called out 'or a cappuccino!'

He sank back into the pillows she'd carefully propped up behind him. He looked at the plant on the window ledge, then down at his bandages. Little blotches of blood and yellow ointment had seeped through to the surface. The area around the bandages was still all painted sterility red. What a wonderful wound, he thought.

It had opened him up in so many ways.

***

Two days later, Carol picked Mathew up after breakfast. Despite his protestations, the nurse on duty insisted that he be rolled out in a wheelchair, which immediately put him on the defensive and made him feel worse than he actually did. Even though Carol drove as carefully as the traffic would allow, the ride home was a little more uncomfortable than Mathew hoped it would be. Each turn made him grimace and every pothole that caught her tires jiggled his stitches. He sighed with relief when she pulled into the driveway.

"Is anyone home?"

Carol knew who '*anyone*' was. "No, your daughter left a message on the fridge saying Lydia will still be out on the coast for a few more days."

Mathew looked uneasy.

"I'll go if you want."

"No, don't."

Despite his daily shuffles around the hospital corridors, it still hurt to walk, and Mathew took the front steps gingerly. He felt better as soon as he stepped inside his own house.

Carol dropped his little valise in the foyer and hesitantly waited to be invited further in. Mathew forgot she didn't know where his room was.

"Upstairs, to the right," he smiled, ushering her in.

She picked the suitcase back up before he could. *Nice house* sounded a little awkward and silly, but she said it anyway. Not quite the way she would've done it, she thought, and not the way Mathew would probably have done it, either. Simple, direct, functional. Carol frowned at the blue light that scattered the dust motes in the hallway.

"Cybernician's screens," Mathew whispered. He hesitated at his own bedroom door before he pushed it open. He gestured to the dresser. "Maybe you could just –"

"Sure." She opened it and took out his things. His clothes still smelled of hospital. She smiled when she saw he'd brought his little paper slippers.

"Where do these go?" She had his toiletry case. It seemed strangely intimate.

"Ensuite." Mathew pointed to the far door, wondering if they'd ever really been apart.

"And your pajamas?"

They were draped over her arm, and for the briefest of moments, Mathew thought he was going to cry.

"The hamper over in the corner's fine," he whispered. He wasn't sure why he felt the need to whisper. He sat down heavily on the side of his bed. *Their* bed. He didn't realize how much the little trip home had taken out of him until he stretched out and lay down. Carol found the extra pillows everyone always keeps in their closet and stuffed them behind his back until he was comfortable. She fussed with the covers like a teenager taking care of their first clandestine pot plant.

"What's that noise?" she asked.

"The hum? My son's equipment. He works quite a lot."

"So I've heard. Can I get you anything?"

Just what's left of my life back. "No, this is great. I'm sure I'll be fine."

Carol stood at the dresser and tried not to wring her hands together.

"Will you stay a moment?" Mathew asked, patting the edge of the bed.

She sat down and the room disappeared. Mathew's side ached, but it didn't matter anymore. They looked into each other's eyes without speaking. Finally, Mathew took her hand.

"Oh Carol. You don't know how much it means to me to have you here."

"It's where I always wanted to be. Where I always should have been."

***

The days passed with the comforting regularity that comes when time loses its meaning. There wasn't anything pressing to do, but the lack of commitments seemed to fill up the hours nicely. Mathew read, took short walks up and down the street, listened to more of his old albums again, tried a few crosswords, rested, caught up on a couple of movies he'd been wanting to see, and tried his best to design his own Zen garden. Nothing mattered though, and he drifted through the days like clouds through a sky, falling into a routine only when he wanted to.

The only thing he really needed to do every few hours was peel back the bandages and look at his wounds. It was a macabre fascination, one that bordered on the feeling so many people have when they passed an accident and slowed to look even though they didn't really want to. Mathew studied the stitches so carefully he knew which ones were ready to dissolve next. He watched the color change, the skin begin to scar, the tiny hairs near his navel sprout back once more.

Except for the moments he looked at the knife wounds that had sliced his life in two, Mathew shared most of his time with Carol. They didn't do all the things together, they were just *together*. They talked, laughed, played cards, or just put some heavy sweaters on, sat on the back porch, and watched the afternoon sky blush with the setting sun. They had a lot of catching up to do but they weren't in any hurry.

Carol slipped effortlessly into the life of the family. After several hospital visits, and then subsequently making sure her father was well looked after at home, Carmalitta went back to her usual routine and spent most of her nights at Miriam's. Carol, then, was able to stay for most meals, which, although she didn't admit it right away because of her thoughts about Lydia, relieved Eleanor of some of the tremendous pressure weighing her down. Carol wasn't a gourmet cook by any means, but she was still able to teach Eleanor a few things in the kitchen. Sharing recipes and a listening ear, they traded memories and stories about Mathew. Carol was somewhat surprised about how much Eleanor actually remembered about her relationship with Mathew when they were back in school. Little anecdotes that Carol had forgotten, stories that made her eyes tear. It was Eleanor who confessed she was amazed when they didn't marry. She liked Lydia – she loved Lydia – but she knew in her heart of hearts that Mathew had never managed to love his wife as much as he had his sweetheart.

Carol sensed Mathew's mother appreciated the company. It was good to have someone near she could talk to or simply stand beside and work in silence, because no matter how hard she tried, Eleanor still hadn't been able to stop visualizing her husband charging back and forth at the comforter flapping in the breeze. The guilt was as razor-sharp as the blade that had ripped through Mathew.

Granddad had changed that day. So had Eleanor. Everyone else could see it, even though they couldn't quite verbalize how, or in what way. Lorne was quieter, if that was possible. His eyes barely moved and his blood didn't make the veins on his hands stand up like it usually did when they were folded together in his lap. He wasn't eating as much and nothing beyond the window seemed to interest him in the least. In fact, he didn't even want to look at the world any longer. The strangest thing was that every time Eleanor came into the room, his blanket was crumpled up in a pile on the floor beside his chair.

Chapter Twenty-six

"You know what I think we should do?"

Mathew closed his book. "What?"

"We should go on a day trip."

"A day trip? Where?"

Carol had obviously been considering the idea before because she didn't hesitate. "Niagara."

Mathew pictured hordes of rain-speckled tourists scrambling closer to the edge so they could get their picture taken right where the water plunged over the lip of the Falls, and cringed. That meant a bumper to bumper drive through the acrid shroud of smog that blanketed Hamilton, an anxious foray over the huge bridges that spanned Lake Ontario in towering arches, a constant battle for parking when they reached the Falls, and overpriced food in a carnival atmosphere that never ceased to depress him. People with so many cameras dangling in front of their chests that they looked like African marriage necklaces. The inevitable and never-ending rainbow. Like most of his friends and neighbors, he'd stood in the eternal mist and marveled at the fall so many times already he didn't really want to fight the maddening crowds or listen to the cameras whirl any more or inhale the fumes from the tourist buses until he coughed. When he coughed his stitches still hurt. And the barrage of articles about body parts being found along the shoreline. Carol recognized the trepidation in his eyes.

"No, not there. To the new butterfly exhibit."

Butterflies. Mathew had read about the pavilion in the newspaper. "Sounds lovely."

"Yes. It's supposed to be quite beautiful. And they say that if you wear something bright the butterflies will land right on you."

"Great," Mathew said, his interest piqued. It was rather like the way his fairy godmother had dropped onto his shoulder and into his life. "Maybe we could stop in for one of the winery tours, too."

"Sure. We can make it an overnight thing."

An overnight thing? That meant a hotel. And a hotel meant . . . . "When do you want to go?" Mathew asked, already beginning rudimentary plans of their itinerary. Lydia wasn't expected for at least another three days. Two days with Carol all to himself. What could be more wonderful?

"How about tomorrow? Do you think you'll feel well enough for the drive by then?"

Mathew wanted to check the wound but thought he better wait. Everything was healing quite nicely, just as Beatrice had promised. "I don't see why not."

"Good. Then I'll drive. That'll make it easier on you. And we'll stop whenever you need to. I'll pack later because we'll only need a few things."

Carol turned back to her book. Mathew watched her read. He loved the way she frowned and moved her lips ever so slightly as her eyes led her mind on. He tried to remember back to one of his public school science classes, the big picture of the butterfly's growth stages taped to the wall.

Larvae, chrysalis, cocoon, butterfly. The thing emerging, wings unfurled and ready for flight. He felt like one, too.

Mathew turned back to his book but he couldn't concentrate. He was filled with the nervous excitement that comes whenever you plan a getaway.

***

Mathew stopped outside Cybernician's door. Unable to remember the last time he'd seen his son (he'd been pleasantly sedated since he came home, and he thought he'd seen him, but wasn't really sure when), he wanted to say goodbye before he left. He knocked once, then again. The keys stopped their incessant rattle, and a moment later Cybernician cracked his door open. Still wearing his hat, sunglasses, and gloves, he beckoned his father in with a wave. The only light in the room was the blue tinge emanating from the computer screen.

"I saw your light. Still working?"

Cybernician nodded.

"I'm going away for a day."

Cybernician didn't turn away from the screen. "I heard."

Mathew watched his son's fingers float across the keyboard. How long had it been since he'd stopped being a child, that he'd grown into a man? He tried to picture what he might be like in ten years, then fifteen, but couldn't. He even found it awkward to think of what his son looked like ten years before. He knew he hadn't been born with those gloves on, but now, while he watched him work and images fluttered to life on the screen, he wasn't so sure. He couldn't figure out if his son was happy or not. He thought he was. But then again, people always seemed to mumble things like that when they were being interviewed about their neighbor's murder-suicide the night before. *He seemed pretty happy. I always thought they were a pleasant young couple. No, they were nice and quiet and stayed mostly to themselves.*

Sensing something was wrong, Mathew finally broke the silence. "How's Sheila?"

Cybernician's fingers stopped in mid-air. The room was filled with the modem's hum. He slunk back into his chair, his hands still raised, ready to type. A moment passed, and then they floated down like leaves in autumn.

"Why?"

Mathew frowned. "Nothing. Just thought I'd ask."

"Sorry. She's fine."

Fingers back on the keyboard, left hand on the mouse. Even in the blue light Mathew saw that his son's hands were shaking. If he squeezed the mouse any harder it was going to break. The cursor danced erratically.

"Cybernician –"

"I said she's fine. I'll probably get her in the morning."

"Can I help with something?"

Mathew waited, watching the cursor flee invisible bandits across the screen. He couldn't remember the last time he had a father-to-son talk with Cybernician. With Michael. The last time was probably years ago, when his son used to go out, Mathew called him *Michael*, and he had to broach the whole issue of unprotected sex. Cybernician had been ready to start

university, and everyone knows that at university you're supposed to have sex, especially if you missed it in high school, so
Mathew thought he should say something before his son left.
Gone were the days Mathew had grew up in, when gonorrhea
and syphilis were the things you had to worry about. Crabs, if
you were really stupid. Uncomfortable and embarrassing, they
were still treatable. But now, sexually transmitted diseases were
deadly. One mistake, one chance that shouldn't have been tak-
en, one single lapse of discretion could ultimately cost you your
life. Mathew remembered how tense he'd been, how he'd agonized at how to begin and what to say.

Watching him type, Mathew knew he shouldn't have worried so much. Not about what to say: about his son. If he'd ever
met anyone that had *virgin* written across their forehead, it was
Cybernician. But Mathew realized that wasn't really such a bad
thing after all.

He tried again. "Do you want to talk about it?"

Cybernician kept typing one-handed for a moment while
the little arrow performed some esoteric, ritual dance. When he
finally stopped and turned around, he was silhouetted in blue.
Even behind the glasses, Mathew could see the restlessness in
his son's eyes.

"We had a fight."

"Everyone argues, Cybernician."

"Not like that. A big one."

"About?"

"I don't think we're sexually compatible."

Mathew tried not to show his confusion. From everything
he'd managed to piece together over the past couple of years,
Sheila seemed a lot like Cybernician. Quiet, reserved, highly
terminal-oriented. And he knew his son had never actually
physically met the woman of his dreams. So how could he
know they weren't compatible once they flicked their monitors
off?

"How could you know that?"

"Because she's something I'm not." He lowered his voice
because the word still hurt. "Unfaithful."

Cybernician fidgeted anxiously for several minutes, then
blurted everything out. Mathew listened while his son told him

the whole sordid tale of following Sheila across the Net. When he was finished, Mathew was still waiting for him to get to the unfaithful part. But Cybernician had already slunk back into his chair, his hat tipped over his forehead, fingers drumming against the mouse pad.

"You've been together for a couple of years now, right?"

"Two years, ten months."

"And is this the first time –"

"Yes."

"I think you're overreacting a little, Cybernician."

The young man shrugged.

"We all have needs, right? Isn't it a little bit like having a last fling at your bachelor party or something? I'm not saying you're actually with someone else then, but – you know."

Mathew stared at his son and realized Cybernician didn't know.

"There are often strippers at those types of parties, and they get rather close. From what I hear. The girls tease the groom-to-be, that sort of thing. It's always hailed as the last chance you have to see a naked woman before you're married."

A glimmer of understanding flickered across Cybernician's face. He frowned. "What she did was different."

"Perhaps. But she wasn't unfaithful to you any more than you are to her when you fantasize about other women, was she?"

Cybernician's cheeks reddened, but his face was still framed in blue.

"It's just my opinion, Cybernician. But for what it's worth, I think you're making a big mistake."

He didn't look up.

"She means the world to you. Am I right?" Mathew felt Carol there beside him, leaning into his shoulder. Cybernician nodded.

"Then don't throw everything away, because it's not very often that you ever get a second chance with someone you really care about. Believe me son, I know."

When Cybernician glanced up, Mathew did something he hadn't done in a very long time: he reached out and put his hand on his son's shoulder. He squeezed, gave him a little pat, then turned toward the door. He spoke over his shoulder.

"I've heard laments from two different people. One guy at work remarried at sixty-three. A few years later he got quite ill and I went to see him in the hospital. One of the things he regretted most about his life was that he hadn't met his *second* wife *first*. If he had it to do all over again, he would have wanted to spend all those years with the woman he was with now."

Mathew stared at the door. He heard his son shifting in his chair.

"And the other one?"

Mathew's eyes closed for a moment. "His wife died just a few years after they were married. She was twenty-eight. He remarried two years later. He had a wonderful life with his second wife: kids, a nice home, cottage, the works. But he told me one night that he would've given up everything if he could've had his first wife back."

Mathew listened to the modem's hum. The bluish tinge to the room suddenly shattered when the monitor timed out and a new screen saver materialized. Colored origami designs folded back and forth across the screen and the door was flecked with a shimmering rainbow.

Mathew turned as he opened the door. "Don't be either one of those men, son."

***

"You got everything, Dad?"

He nodded. "I think so, Joshua. Can you carry the case out to Carol's car?"

The little valet was already on his way.

"Do you know where you'll be staying?" Eleanor asked, always the mother.

"Mathew felt his cheeks redden. "We'll get a couple of rooms anywhere we can."

Eleanor smiled. She thought about the last time she'd made the pilgrimage to the Falls with Lorne. They'd stopped at a little kiosk where you could get dressed up in period costumes and have your picture taken. They'd chosen their clothes from the

Old West. She, a dance hall girl with a ruffled dress and feathered hat; he, a gunslinger with a black leather vest and studded holster. He'd tried his best to sneer but he didn't look very ruthless. She wondered if the photograph was still tucked away in one of the drawers upstairs. Like Lorne was tucked away somewhere.

"Careful you don't exert yourself too much, Mathew. You're still healing."

Healing? No. I'm a butterfly. "Tell Carmalitta we said goodbye." He lowered his voice. "And don't worry about Dad. Okay?"

Eleanor nodded. "And if Lydia calls, I'll look after it."

"Thanks. We'll be back around lunch tomorrow. What would you like me to bring you back, Joshua?" Mathew exhaled a laboured breath as he sunk down into the passenger seat. He knew he was going to have to take it easy.

The boy smiled. "Something silly."

"Will do," Mathew smiled.

He rolled up the window and waved as Carol backed out of the driveway. The sky was an icy blue and the wind was light. A few straggling clouds, but nothing that threatened rain. Mathew figured they'd be on the highway at the cusp between the morning and lunch time rushes, so, barring any annoying delays for the routine broken water mains or jack-knifed tractor trailers, it would be relatively smooth sailing across the city.

He remembered Carol was a cautious driver who hated tailgaters, and the irresponsible drivers who kept cutting in and out across the lanes. It never ceased to amaze her just how many vehicles came without directionals. She liked to maintain a fairly constant speed in the slow lane, and just enjoy the drive. She hadn't changed. They weren't actually going to sail across the highway. It would be an easy, relaxed cruise, which suited Mathew just fine. He'd tried to save his fairy godmother's life, he'd been stabbed, he'd been stitched, and he was with Carol once again, after all these years. What could be better?

Carol was humming softly to herself. Mathew looked at some of the other drivers that hurried past them. As soon as eye contact was made they quickly looked away. Why did they look over for in the first place? Did they really expect to see someone they knew? He glanced up at the overpasses whizzing by above them, and smiled. His father used to tell him to duck whenever they went under a bridge. For once he didn't think of what would happen if the girders collapsed. Dad. Mathew hoped his father would be all right. Trembling, he reached over, took Carol's hand, and smiled.

***

Breathing in the autumn's redolent chill of the river, Mathew and Carol decided to make one of the numerous wineries that dotted the edge of the Niagara Parkway their first stop. Since it was relatively late in the season there were only two or three other people around, so they had the guide all to themselves. They walked through the vineyards studying the grapes, then had a brief tour of the buildings where the wine was pressed, stored, and bottled. Mathew learned about different grape varieties, how they're planted, when they're harvested, and how they should be aged. Vintages, corking techniques, and the intricacies and painstaking demands of barrel making. He even became acquainted with *botrytis cinerea*, and tasted what delicious sweetness the fungus known as noble rot could engender.

A brief tasting was offered after the tour ended. Although it wasn't mentioned significantly during the excursion, Mathew knew the Niagara Region produced some of the finest ice wines in the entire world. When their inspection of the labelling machine concluded, he hurried back into the winery so he could treat Carol to the sublime sensation of ice wine. He was quite disappointed to learn there wasn't any left. The sales clerk explained that although a certain number of bottles must be kept for domestic consumption, most vintages are bought up in advance by Asian and European markets. Dejectedly, he bought a Vidal to share with Carol later on. But he couldn't stay sad for long. How could he? The only reason any of it really mattered was because Carol was there beside him, her hand in his, their shoulders touching, their thoughts one. They carefully paced themselves so that he didn't put a strain on his stomach.

After a light lunch at the Prince of Wales Hotel in the heart of downtown Niagara-on-the-Lake, Carol drove them back along the Parkway to the butterflies' new home.

Surrounded by the Botanical Gardens, the walkway leading into the exhibit was a blaze of colour. The intermingled scent of tens of thousands of flowers overwhelmed Mathew's senses and tickled the back of his throat. Was this what Eden had smelled like?

The exhibit was fairly crowded but the line-up to get in was mercifully short. As Mathew pushed the door open and squirmed through the plastic barrier, he stepped into a world of oppressive heat that nearly took his breath away. Domed in glass and cloaked with thick trees and climbing vines, he felt like a bug or a beetle in a giant terrarium. By the time he'd taken a few tentative steps inside Mathew was perspiring and his hair was matted with humidity. His clothes felt damp and heavy and his soaked shirt clung to his back like an addict's need. Yet despite the intensity of the heat, he knew at once that Carol was right: it was irresistibly beautiful.

He sat down on a large rock and looked around, letting his body acclimatize to the heat and humidity. It was hard to breathe. There were butterflies and moths everywhere: not just one or two, here and there, but thousands. Mathew had no idea there'd be so many. The trees enveloping him were filled with glimmering specks of rainbows. The butterflies came in all shapes, sizes and colors, and some even changed shades and patterns when the sun peeked through the glass ceiling and touched their wings. Four or five huge specimens were feeding at a tray of rotten fruit right beside the walkway. Entranced, he watched them eat and drink, their fragile wings fanning nearby leaves with just the lightest trace of a breeze.

Shuffling forward, Mathew watched countless butterflies gliding and drifting overhead and realized that it was like being in the jungle. He couldn't imagine living in some Brazilian rain forest beneath a canopy of trees, hunting barefoot, his face painted to match the foliage, a poison-tipped spear in his hand and God knows what hanging in the branches above his head. He wondered if Joshua had ever lived in a place like this.

The butterflies were all around him, swirling like prismatic snowflakes, but Mathew knew deep in his heart their beauty was short-lived. Most of the butterflies would die within a month. His soul ached. Is this how Dorian Gray felt the first time he tried to hide his picture?

Looking up, he saw a little iridescent blue butterfly land on a rock outcrop near the glass ceiling. As its delicate wings unfurled, he remembered a magazine article his father had shown him about native boys on the cusp of manhood. As adolescence ended, so did innocence: at twelve, each boy in the village undertook a ritual rite of passage. For seven days and nights they had to survive out in the jungle on their own, hunting, foraging, building a place to sleep, dreaming and listening to their ancestors. But before the week began they were initiated into adulthood: each boy was circumcised by one of the elders. Mathew couldn't really understand what bleeding from *down there* had to do with being a man. He couldn't imagine running through the jungle at night, insects hovering in clouds and snakes coiling around tree limbs, as he ran through the underbrush. It had to hurt if some palm frond or thick vine whacked you *there* when you were running, didn't it? He tried not to think about it and quickly caught up to Carol.

She was standing in front of a little waterfall that cascaded down into a pool, with perhaps fifty butterflies of all shapes and sizes and colours dancing around her hair and shoulders. He moved beside her and wrapped his arm around her waist. A warming sensation of tranquility rippled over him in waves. Carol hadn't seen or felt it, but a tiny wisp of the deepest purple Mathew had ever seen hovered above her head then landed gently on her shoulder. Another one landed beside it.

It almost made him cry.

***

It had been a glorious day. The only exacting part came after dinner when Mathew and Carol had to find a place to stay. It was somewhat difficult to choose between hotels because there wasn't anything to choose *from*. Mathew's only unshakeable consideration was that the hotel didn't display a *good food* sign.

They finally decided on one of the places they'd seen dominoed together from the highway.

The Cottage Hotel. Mathew pushed the door open and sighed. Other than a surgeon's gloves, few things are more sterile than hotel rooms. The only thing that made this compartment any different than any other he'd ever been in was Carol. Why did they always look the same? Granted, there was only a modicum of space to work with, and there were just so many ways a simple array of functional furniture could be arranged. But did it always have to be so nondescript, so utterly uninviting? If the hotel owners wanted you to stay, then why didn't they go out of their way to try and make the room aesthetically pleasing? Or at the very least, welcoming? Look at the things you could do with a Zen garden.

There was a dresser down one wall. Its banal veneer top was punctuated with a swivel television, an ice bucket, an envelope of stationery, and even though it was a non-smoking room, an ashtray. Directly opposite were two identical single beds with a little table in between. The window was covered with plain drab curtains that had a black backing to diffuse some of the light since they couldn't be drawn closed in the middle. A closet without a door, a round table framed with two tub chairs, and a tiny, dreary bathroom that wore the ingrained scent of a thousand other travellers.

Mathew poured them each a glass of wine and settled into the chairs with Carol. They reeked of ancient smoke and he could feel a spring poking up under one thigh. He glanced outside. Like all hotel rooms, their window faced one of the parking lots. Cars squealed around distant corners, and a group of people argued over by the building's front entrance. He tugged the drapes closed as far as he could, trying to keep the outside world *where it was.*

Out of the corner of his eye, Mathew glanced uncomfortably at the nearest bed. So did Carol. For the first time since he'd found her again, Mathew felt uneasy. He knew why.

"The butterflies were amazing," he said over his glass, eyeing the other bed and trying to think of something else. "I still can't get over the colours and how they all seemed to swirl together."

"Yes, they're unbelievable. And they're so soft and light. I've never felt anything like that before."

They sipped their wine. Equally sensitive to the need for a diversion, Carol pulled a little plastic bag from her purse. "I hope Joshua likes this."

Looking inside, Mathew grinned. "I'm sure he will. After all, he did say 'silly'."

Strolling arm in arm after dinner, they'd stopped and had their picture taken at one of the little sidewalk shops jammed together on Clifton Hill. The set-up was simple: at the rear of the shop there was a large backdrop. The picture was of the water plummeting over the edge of the Falls. In the foreground there was a real wooden barrel you could stand inside. The barrel teetered precariously on the brink, seconds away, it seemed, from plunging into the misty abyss. Accustomed to dealing with giggling, self-conscious newlyweds, the kiosk owner waited patiently while they tried to decide who should be in front. Prodded on by a gaggle of tourists, Mathew took the back.

Mathew and Carol had done their best to feign fear and surprise for the photographer, but the inscrutable lens of the camera had captured something different, something deeper: Carol looking up over her shoulder, her hand on his atop her shoulder, and Mathew staring down, sharing her smile, unspoken whispers sparkling in their eyes.

When Mathew tucked the picture away, the silence was awkward, impatient. Carol shifted uneasily and stared at the farther bed. "Mathew, --"

"I can't do it, Carol." He stood up and started pacing. It was a confined, narrow walk, and he had to be careful not to trip on the little suitcase. His stomach started to hurt a little bit. Or maybe he just thought it did.

It had been on their minds all day, and had become more potent the longer they were together and the closer evening came. Mathew desperately wanted to be with Carol, and he could see it in her eyes that there was nothing she wanted more than to offer her soul to him.

"I can't," he whispered again. He stopped pacing and sat down on the edge of the bed. The people outside were still arguing. "You know how much I want to be with you."

Carol reached over and took his hand.

"But no matter what I feel, I couldn't do that to Lydia."

"I understand, Mathew."

He stared down at the wine and swirled it around. "Will you wait?"

"Of course," Carol smiled. "It's because you've always thought that way that I've loved you all this time." She put her glass down and shifted over onto the bed. "You wouldn't be the man I thought you were if you'd said anything different."

The hours passed by gently, filled with thoughts of flowers, butterflies, snippets from old songs, feelings desperately needing to be felt again, smiles, hugs, kisses.

Sleep finally beckoned. Mathew had turned the lights off and scrunched down under the covers of the bed farthest from the window. Carol hesitated at the bathroom door, scanning the room with the soft light behind her so she could see where she was going to walk. A flick of the switch, the room blackened, and Mathew heard her tiptoeing across the worn carpet. But the pulse of her steps didn't go far. She stopped at his bed. She pulled the covers back and slipped down beside him. Her feet were cold and she burrowed into his side.

Mathew tensed for the briefest of moments, then relaxed. She snuggled in so closely he couldn't tell where her skin began and his ended. It was like two new-born puppies squeezed into their mother's side and asleep at the same teat. Their bodies fit perfectly: it was as if she'd never left his side. She wrapped her legs around Mathew's and entwined her feet with his. He felt the soft warmth of her hips against his, and the gentle slope of her shoulder where it pressed into his side. She used his shoulder for a headrest and draped her arm across his chest.

Footsteps padded along the hallway beyond their door. Mathew heard the crunch of a metal bucket being scraped against a bin of ice, and then the footsteps padded back down the corridor. A distant door closed and the world seeped away. The voices beneath the window faded into a monks' chant, white noise that filtered everything else into a pleasing tone of nothingness.

Carol snuggled deeper into Mathew's side. They were so close he could hear and feel her heartbeat pulse against his own chest. Her breathing was light, just barely above a whisper, then slowly deepened into the long sighs that foretell dreams are coming. Melting together, Mathew bathed in the delicate warmth of Carol's body. He remembered it so well, yet every touch awakened thoughts and sensations he never knew he had. His fingers moved instinctively, stroking and caressing her hair, and he felt more relaxed then he'd felt in years. He whispered *I love you*, and closed his eyes. The last thought he remembered the next morning was how wonderfully puerile the whole idea of sex seemed sometimes.

***

Mathew and Carol didn't talk very much on the drive home. They didn't have to. The only thing that was on Mathew's mind was what he was going to tell Lydia, and later, his family.

Despite the traffic and a minor delay for an overturned truck, they made fairly good time back. Carol pulled in the driveway just after lunch.

"Are you coming in?"

"No. I've got some things to do at home."

"Are you sure?"

"Yes."

"Dinner, then?"

"That would be great." She leaned across and cupped her hands around Mathew's face. "I love you." She kissed him softly on the lips.

"And I love you too."

"You still feeling okay?"

Mathew touched his side. "Fine. I hardly feel anything there at all."

"Good. I'll get your bag, though."

Carol opened the trunk and retrieved Mathew's valise. "Oh, and don't forget Joshua's gift." Carol tugged the plastic bag free from a pile of others.

Mathew glanced at their picture again.

Memories, pressed between the pages of my mind . . . Faded photographs, touched with lines and wrinkles . . .

"Drive carefully, Carol. I'll see you tonight."

Mathew hugged her tightly to his chest, unwilling to let her leave. Finally, Carol drew back, kissed him once again, and got back in her car before she changed her mind. Mathew watched her until she turned the corner at the bottom of his street, then picked up the valise and walked carefully up the porch steps.

And then he stopped, frowned, and cocked his head from side to side.

What was that odd sound coming from inside the house?

Chapter Twenty-seven

Eleanor liked having Carmalitta home for lunch. Since Mathew and Carol weren't expected until a little later, she needed the company. With some time left unaccounted for due to a late cancellation, Carmalitta was equally glad for the diversion and had welcomed the chance to dine at home for once. The morning had been quite distressing. She'd talked to the Sinclairs for an hour. Plagued with denial and guilt, they'd called in a panic. They'd done what they thought was best for a loved one, but now, they were finding it difficult to live with their decision. And their guilt. It took her a long time to calm them down, and the conversation had left Carmalitta despondent and self-doubting. She knew the ambivalence of giving up something for love far too well.

Love. She was absolutely dying to meet the woman who'd secretly held her father's heart for all these years. She was ambivalent, naturally, because of her mother. She didn't want to see either of her parents get hurt. At the same time, however, she knew quite well that they hadn't really had a close, loving relationship for years. They'd been companions and shared a home, that was about it. And they'd raised Joshua. As much as he needed raising. Other than the personae episodes, he seemed to be progressing quite nicely on his own. Carmalitta had actually thought at various times over the last few years that they were going to separate. She hoped they hadn't stayed together just for Joshua's sake. He hadn't needed them to be together to become what he was.

At her insistence, Miriam had rearranged an afternoon session and had come to lunch. They both knew how much they needed to talk. With the decision about the condominium still pending, Miriam had become more aloof and testy as the days passed. Defensive and unnaturally curt, her words were often tainted with acrimony. Carmalitta sensed there was an ultimatum in the offing, and although she found the pressure almost unbearable, she couldn't blame her lover, either. Miriam had waited long enough.

Perhaps, Carmalitta thought, Miriam wouldn't have to go back to work at all this afternoon. Maybe they could go for a stroll down the Boardwalk, and then stop at one of the bars dotted along Queens Quay. Have a drink, watch the planes take off from the little island airport, listen to the waves tumble beneath the pier.

Joshua was at the kitchen table, working on one of those puzzles where words are hidden inside a matrix of scrambled letters. Carmalitta was leaning back against the counter, raiding the piles of vegetables her grandmother was cutting and tossing into a big salad bowl.

"So," Carmalitta went on, picking at a slice of wet lettuce, "it was a difficult decision for them." She looked at Joshua, then Miriam. "Decisions about love usually are."

Miriam shredded more lettuce a little too vigorously. Eleanor kept dicing the carrots. Carmalitta took one. "I still find it surprising how deeply some people feel about their pets. To the Sinclairs, there wasn't anything that caused them more distress and yet offered them such a world of happiness than their *odga.*" She wasn't sure how sharp granddad's hearing was, and she hadn't wanted to take the chance he could hear them in the kitchen.

"Then they're like most people," Miriam mumbled cryptically.

"Hardly," Carmalitta replied. The day's strain was still in her voice.

Prying another leaf apart, Miriam disagreed. "Nothing divides us more."

Carmalitta liberated a piece of cucumber. "I feel sorry for them. It was a life-changing decision for them to make."

"Isn't it always? What are you really trying to say?"

Joshua sensed an argument coming. He closed the puzzle book and tried to slip off the chair, but Miriam had already stepped from the counter and was blocking his way.

Carmalitta frowned. "What do you mean?"

"I mean, Carmalitta, what's really on your mind? What decision are you trying to make about love?"

Carmalitta was taken aback. "Why would you even think something like that?"

"The Freudian slip. It's not like you."

"When?"

"You said *odga*. I think you meant *ogda*. You said, 'there wasn't anything that caused them more distress and yet offered them such a world of happiness, than their *God*.'"

Carmalitta shook her head. "No. I said *ogda*."

"No you didn't."

"I was talking about the Sinclair's pet," she said curtly. "Their *ogda*."

"What are you getting so defensive about? I just pointed out that the first time you said *odga*, not *ogda*, which was a little surprising. You're always talking about animals. It's a mistake you wouldn't normally make."

"And I didn't." Flustered she turned and stared at Joshua. "What did I say?"

"I wasn't really listening," he said softly, trying to look smaller.

"Well, I didn't say it."

"You did. I heard it distinctly. From what you've said before, I'm sure you're right and God does a play a very important part in the Sinclair's' lives. But their dilemma wasn't with God. It was with their *ogda*. It just seemed odd that you confused those words, that's all. Admit it. You made a mistake. You don't have to be right all the time."

"I meant *dog* and I said *dog*," Carmalitta said with the quietly controlled tone she always used when she didn't expect to be contradicted. It was the same one her mother evoked when she was being dismissive.

"Fine," Miriam said, struggling to maintain her composure. "I was simply bringing something to light. But perhaps you may want to consider whether or not some unresolved conflict might underlie the slip. And your reaction to it."

Miriam turned back to the lettuce. Eleanor's *chop chop chop* echoed off the cutting board. Carmalitta looted the carrot pile again and stared at her brother. At her son. Was Miriam right? Did she have a conflict with love? Always, she thought. Always.

Upstairs, Granddad was sitting on his behind, his back straight and his forelegs stiff against the floor. One rear leg was curled back under his front paws; the other was bent upwards and stuck out awkwardly at his side. Leaning down as far as he could, he licked furiously at his crotch. He couldn't quite bend around far enough, but he *knew* he desperately had to lick himself *down there*. His tongue darted out like a cobra tasting the air. He kept stretching over harder and harder, struggling to get his head down farther and his leg higher up, until he slipped past his balance point and fell over onto his side. He yelped indignantly and thrashed back up to his feet. He brought one of his back legs up and violently scratched his side with his foot. It wasn't quite the same as licking himself but it would have to do. He stopped a few moments later. Sniffing the air, he stood immobilized on three paws for several seconds, a ferociously determined look in his eyes, alert but apparently quite contented.

An overpowering urge smothered him. No gray line here: just *not having to go* and *having to go*. Fortunately, the bedroom door was ajar. Bounding down the stairs, Granddad raced to the front door and started jumping up and down. Quick, frustrated barks punctuated mournful whimpers. He *really* had to get out. He circled the front hall round and round, as if he was chasing his tail. Stop, bark, jump, look up, whine, wag his butt. Stop, bark, jump, look up, whine, wag his butt. He kept frantically looking around, hoping his antics had summoned the attention of one of the larger two-legged animals, but no one came. He listened, sniffed, moaned. Still nothing. Where could they possibly be? He *really* had to go now. *Really.*

The dog lowered his head and scanned the perimeter of the hallway. Where had he done it before? He saw two spots – one at the edge of the hallway near the kitchen, and the other by one of the chairs in the living room. The carpet was soft, fuzzy and warm, but his flanks had been smacked with the rolled up newspaper even harder that time. He looked at the edge of the hallway. But oh, the carpet felt so nice, especially in the winter when snow stuck to his bum-fur. Decisions, decisions. The hallway, where he wouldn't get in so much trouble, or the luxurious, feathery carpet? Cottony toilet paper, or ice-cold linoleum?

The poor dog was beside himself with uncertainty. He looked at both spots, stopped long enough to scratch himself again with his hind leg, then started barking so hard and loud he thought he'd swallowed his tongue. But the French doors on the kitchen stayed closed. A few quick circles, another jump, a begging whine, and a flurry of scratches that took the paint off the front door. Then a long, eerie growl, like a monkey's warning from deep in the heart of a rain forest that a leopard was near.

He took one step toward the edge of the hallway and stopped, his front leg raised in mid-stride. A condescending sniff, and he trotted off into the living room. He hunched over, undid his fly, tucked his head down into his neck like a vulture, and grinned. The dog pranced back into the foyer just as Eleanor pushed the kitchen doors open. The second he saw her face his head dropped and he slinked down closer to the floor.

"I thought I heard something. What are you doing down –"

The cues were unmistakable: Eleanor immediately knew her husband was a dog. She also knew what it meant when a dog's eyes melted and it tried to cover its head with a front paw. A quick glance into the living room confirmed her suspicion.

"Oh, bad dog," she said.

The dog cringed. It wasn't the 'bad dog' that caused the psychological damage, it was the lowered voice and the disappointed tone.

"That's a bad dog."

Granddad recoiled and backed sheepishly away. He tried to make himself as small as he possibly could and slithered along the wall. Eleanor took a step closer, then stopped. It was always easy to see your own mood by watching a pet's behaviors. She knew it wasn't his fault. The dog was looking away like all dogs do when they don't want to be seen. Eleanor felt guilty. But before she could bend down and gently stroke his back, the front door opened.

"Hi," Mathew called.

The dog sensed its chance and took off before the old woman could move. Scurrying on all fours, he raced past her outstretched hand and along the foyer, nearly knocking Mathew down.

"Don't let him –"

Startled and instinctively trying to protect his side, Mathew couldn't take in everything in time, and didn't move quickly enough to stop him. The dog made a beeline out the door before it closed.

"Hurry," Eleanor yelled. "Grab him before he gets away."

She was after him in a second. Mathew dropped the valise, turned, and followed his mother outside. But they were too late. Running on just his hind legs, Granddad was already halfway down the street when Eleanor reached the curb. She screamed at him to stop, but the dog rounded the corner at full speed and didn't even pause to look back.

Mathew's father was gone.

Chapter Twenty-eight

"Shit, shit, shit."

Eleanor stomped erratically around the kitchen, her fingers combing through her hair.

"It's all right," Mathew said, putting his hands on her shoulders. "He'll be back"

Eleanor shrugged him away. "No. No he won't. I can feel it. He's not coming back."

"Don't say that."

"He's changed. You don't see him the way I do. He's been different since –"

"Mother –"

Tears welled in her eyes. "Since *then*. I can see it in his eyes. He wanted to run away, and now he has his chance."

Joshua came into the kitchen shaking his head. "I couldn't catch up with him," he panted, still half out of breath. "I lost him before I got to the corner."

"See," Eleanor cried. "See. He's gone. He hates me and he's gone."

"He doesn't hate you, mother. Now listen. Joshua and I will take a walk around the block, see if we can spot him. Maybe he's just . . . maybe he's just out running around. Okay?"

Eleanor sniffled.

"Carmalitta?"

"Sure, Dad." She glanced at Miriam, reached out, and took her hand. Their simmering argument was forgotten. "We'll check around, too."

"Good."

"Why don't you take the car?"

"No, it'll be too hard to see him."

"But your stomach – "

"It feels fine. We'll grab the phone though, and call you if we see him. Don't worry, mom. We'll have him back before you know it."

Refusing to be consoled, Eleanor didn't nod this time. "Find him, Mathew. And when you do, tell him I'm sorry. Tell him —"

"Shh. You can tell him yourself. But I'm sure what happened has nothing to do with this. Now come on, we need your help. Why don't you put the kettle on? Dad will probably like a nice warm cup of tea when we get back. His bones will be pretty sore."

Mathew gave his mother a reassuring hug. Joshua came back in, brandishing the phone.

"Relax. We'll be back in no time." Mathew touched his side. He'd have to walk as quickly as he could but he'd have to be careful, too.

Eleanor looked out the kitchen window and watched them walk down the driveway. They consulted for a moment, then disappeared in opposite directions. She leaned against the counter, her arms quivering, and didn't try to stop the tears.

***

Eleanor couldn't stay still. She pogoed around on some invisible stick, lurching off balance when the phone rang, and then later, when it didn't but she wanted it to. *Needed* it to. The house seemed unnaturally close, soft yet stifling, like the plush silk inside a coffin lid. She thought the rooms would have felt empty but they didn't. She sensed her husband's presence every place she went; not just in his room, over by the window, but in the kitchen, too. In the family room, where she'd last seen him. In the basement, where he used to like to go before the stroke to sift through old boxes of things he'd kept forever. She felt him in the dining room, and saw him in her mind at a forgotten Thanksgiving leaning over the table and sniffing at one of her home-baked pies. He was everywhere, clinging to the walls like a spectre lost between worlds.

Restlessly searching the house, she didn't know what she was looking for. She carried his blanket around for a while then laid it back carefully across his chair. Pacing, she passed the kitchen phone three times before she finally picked it up, and struggled to punch in *his* number. It was her own fault, she knew that. But she needed to talk to him, to tell him she was sorry but her chest had been ripped open and her heart turned inside-out and that she wasn't ever going to see him again. No answer.

Eleanor haunted every corner of the house. She paced the hallway, sat on the stairs, hovered in the doorways, lingered thoughtfully beside knick knacks that dotted walls or tables. Finally, weary and jaded, her feet thick and ponderous as an elephant's, she crumpled down into one of the kitchen chairs. She leaned over the table, laid her head against her folded arms, and let the tears come again.

***

Granddad loped casually along the sidewalk on his hind legs. He paused every few feet to sniff a pole or check out the garbage stashed at the curb for the next day's pickup. To everyone else, he probably looked like a slightly disheveled, eccentric old man who had to keep stopping so he could catch his breath. An old man walking the street in a bizarre fashion was no longer an anomaly. The vacant stare and frenetic behavior was commonplace since the funding cuts to the hospitals had taken effect and the psychiatric patients had been passed along to over extended community outreach programs. There was no place for the dollars to go. Granddad ambled down the sidewalk like he owned the world, weaving in and out and around the clusters of people walking towards him. Even when he stopped by a bakery window, growled, licked his lips and scratched his side, no one seemed to notice.

He was hungry, though, there was no doubt about that. Every time the little bells tinkled and someone stepped out of a grocery store or bakery, he glanced up expectantly through half-closed lids with a mournful look in his eyes. But no one gave him anything, so he finally pranced on. Luckily, he caught the scent of something inviting in the distance, and found it in the next block. A hot dog vendor.

The man behind the cart barked out his wares. Heavyset, with a high forehead and thick, Neanderthal eyebrows, he was a good three or four heroin addicts wide. Granddad saw something in the man's eyes and cautiously approached the cart from downwind. He backed away when the man turned and saw him, pretending to be interested in the mailbox chained to a nearby post.

"Can I get you a dog?"

Dog? Where? Granddad looked quickly around. All he could see were legs.

"How 'bout a nice ballparker with everything on it?"

Granddad winced and looked down at something on his paw. He hoped it wasn't more gum. The hot dog vendor shrugged, turned away, and tried to catch the eyes of other hungry passersby. With a Mr. Bean-like concocted disinterest, Granddad inched closer to the cart. Always watching the man, he reached a tentative paw out to the nearest wiener tumbling over the metal rollers. But the man turned just as he was ready to snatch it away.

"Hey!"

Lurching backwards, Granddad bared his teeth, growled, and the hairs on the back of his neck bristled. The hot dog vendor stared for a moment, and then his angry frown relaxed. He'd seen the posters that littered the windows and were stapled to telephone poles all around the city. Someone was always lost now: patients, old people with Alzheimer's, forgotten children, and grandparents who hadn't realized senility had stalked them like a murderer and strangled their memories. The hot dog vendor had an uncle who'd been recuperating at Sunnybrook Hospital over on Bayview Ave. Convinced that spies had infiltrated the hospital and his cover was blown, his uncle had yanked out an IV and catheter, and then escaped. They found him wandering in Edward's Gardens two days later, dazed and confused, and still wearing the hospital's little paper slippers. They were two of the longest days in the vendor's life.

The man made up a hot dog, wrapped it nicely in paper, and offered it to Granddad. The dog was tensely alert and didn't move.

"Here, take it," he whispered, gesturing with his eyes. One look at the man's face and Granddad knew he was safe. He stepped closer, took the proffered meal so that it barely touched his lips, and then tore off down the street with his tongue hanging out of his mouth. The vendor was sure he'd seen the old man try to smile. Gulping the hot dog down in a nearby laneway, Granddad couldn't remember when anything had tasted quite so good.

***

"Anything?" Eleanor asked hopefully. She'd half-risen from the table, but sank back down despondently into her chair when she saw the look in Mathew's eyes.

"Nothing yet."

She glanced at the clock. Three hours had passed. "Where's Joshua?"

"Digging out some of the other street maps in the garage."

"How far did you go?"

Mathew shrugged. "Down to Queen and almost over as far as the Parkway."

Eleanor's hand went to her mouth. She hadn't even considered the possibility that Lorne might have gone that far. Could he have run out onto the road or something horrible like that? Been hit by a car? Was he lying beside some curb, bleeding from a broken leg?

"We went to most of the neighbors around here you both know. We thought he may have gone some place he understands as being safe."

And I guess that wasn't with me, Eleanor thought. "You tried the Standfields."

Mathew nodded.

"The Tomlinsons? The MacGreggors, the Yeungs? What about Mrs. Mewbury?"

Mathew said he'd visited each of the people she'd named, but none of their friends had seen Granddad. In any guise.

"Mr. Willcox? His dog died a couple of weeks ago. Maybe Granddad might have wanted to use the house he built for Hercules."

"We checked there too, Grandma," Joshua said, coming into the kitchen with an armload of maps.

"But there wasn't a trace of him," Mathew added. "Where's Cybernician?"

Eleanor gestured upstairs with her chin. "He made some posters with Granddad's picture on them after you left. He's printing more of them up and contacting everyone he knows. He's trying to set up some kind of social network or something to alert everyone in the area."

"Carmalitta and Miriam?"

"They're still not back yet."

"Maybe they've got some good news," Mathew offered encouragingly. He hoped it sounded more convincing to Eleanor than it did to him.

"Can I get you some tea, Grandma?" Joshua dumped the maps on the kitchen table and was already getting the kettle out. Eleanor nodded dully with a forlorn, *what does it matter anyway* look in her eyes.

Mathew started studying the street maps. Where were the most likely places a dog would go? Where would *he* go if he was a dog? Carmalitta and Miriam came home just as the kettle roiled to a whistling boil. Shaking her head at the anticipated question, she rubbed the tension from the back of her neck and nodded when Joshua offered her a cup.

"Where did you go?" Mathew asked, spreading out one of the maps. Like always, there was a small tear down one edge, on a fold, right near the middle of the page.

Carmalitta peered over his shoulder, got her bearings, and pointed. "Here, then here, and down here. Then we went to the park."

"Kew Beach?"

"Yes. We checked the restaurants, change houses, the bike rental shops. Nothing. We talked to as many people as we could, especially the ones walking a dog. She turned to her grandmother. "I'm so sorry."

Eleanor reached over and took her hand. She tried to smile.

"You guys didn't have any luck either?"

Mathew said no and quickly outlined the areas they'd searched with a highlighter.

"I think we really should get in touch with the police," Miriam whispered gently.

Even though it was something she expected and realized was the best course of action, Eleanor jumped. Having the authorities joining in on the search immediately made everything more urgent, more final. Maybe it already was.

"I'll go as soon as I grab something to eat," Mathew told her.

"I'll come," Joshua offered. Carmalitta wanted to go, too.

"Maybe someone should stay here," Mathew suggested, subtly nodding at his mother. "In case he comes back. Or if someone calls, we'll have to be able to follow it up right away."

"I can look after that," Eleanor said.

"I was just —"

"I can look after that," she interrupted forcefully. She turned and stared out the kitchen window. "I'm sorry Mathew. I — I just wish he'd come back."

Mathew moved closer and took her hand. "He will, Mom. You'll see."

"What if he's hurt? What if he's been hit by a car and he's lying in a gutter, scared and coughing up blood? What if —"

"Shhh. Calm down, Mom. That's not going to do us any good. We have to stay positive."

Eleanor dabbed her eyes with a crumpled tissue. "Yes, I know. You're right. It's just that I keep imagining him in trouble. Oh, Mathew. What if he's run away for good? What if he's never coming back?"

I wouldn't blame him at all if he didn't, she thought. Eleanor pictured the 'bull' repeatedly charging back and forth at the red matador's cape that had been teasingly provoking him in the wind. She'd been taunting him inside the house too, from less than twenty feet from their bedroom where he sat helplessly perched by his window. The second he'd heard the word 'dog' he had his chance, perhaps the one he'd been looking for all this time.

Joshua moved behind his grandmother's chair. He put his cup down and started stroking her neck and shoulders with his hands. Tired and weary, she sank back and closed her eyes. But she jolted forward so hard she banged her knees against the underside of the table when the phone cried its shrill ring.

Mathew took a deep breath before he answered, catching it on the second ring.

"Yes?"

"Mathew. Good, you're home. It's Carol. I just got your message about your father."

Mathew turned to the room. "It's Carol." Eleanor exhaled a suspended breath.

"Have you found him yet?"

"No."

"I'll be right over."

"You don't have —"

"Yes I do. Are you going out again soon?"

Mathew didn't want to mention the police out loud. "Yes."

"Then I'll be there in time to go with you. And Mathew?"

"Uh-huh?"

"Don't think for a moment we won't find him."

"Okay."

"I mean it. How's your mother holding up?"

He looked back at the table. Her hands were trembling with the weight of the tea cup. "Yes, everything's fine."

"I understand. I'm on my way. Mathew?"

"Yes?"

"I love you. Remember that."

I've never forgotten for a moment. "I will. I won't leave without you."

Never again.

***

Mathew heard himself chewing throughout their dinner. He felt his jaws move up and down, his teeth grind, the food roll from side to side as it got smaller and smaller. He was disturbingly conscious of where his tongue was, how it pressed against his gums or the back of his teeth. The food was bland, beyond tasteless, and he had to struggle to keep his throat open long enough to drink his milk. After a few obligatory remarks, the stillness wasn't tense or awkward: it was sadly reflective.

Where was his father, and what was he doing right then, at that exact moment, while his knife and fork clattered desultorily against his plate?

Carol arrived just as they were finishing. Mathew shook his head to the unvoiced question as Joshua showed her into the kitchen.

"Coffee?"

"No thanks. How are you doing, Eleanor?"

Without turning away from the sink, Eleanor shrugged and mumbled she was fine.

"You don't mind going to the police station?" Carmalitta asked quietly.

"Not at all." Carol looked at Mathew. "I'll do anything I can to help."

Carmalitta gulped down the last dregs of her coffee. "Thanks for coming to help, Carol. Oh, this is Miriam." The women nodded to each other. Introductions could wait: there was more pressing business at hand. "We're off too."

Miriam nodded. "We'll try Ashbridge Park this time."

Mathew put a hand on his son's shoulder. "Joshua, you stay and man the fort, okay?" The boy looked at his grandmother and took the hint. "Sure."

Mathew took Carol's hand. "Then let's go."

***

Mathew was glad Carol was with him because the police station intimidated him more than most things. He knew you never went there for fun: either you were in trouble or someone else was. He stopped across from the front entrance of 51 Division, checking the totem pole of parking signs twice to make sure it was legal to park where he was. Few things were more embarrassing than getting a ticket in front of the police station.

Mathew hoped the inside of the precinct would have looked like one he'd seen on countless television shows so that something, however small, would seem familiar, but it didn't. Despite the weather, the air conditioner was on full blast. People hustled by, apparently oblivious to the chaos that reigned all around them; prisoners being escorted in, parents seated on benches, crying or staring blankly over half-finished coffees, ambulance attendants meticulously filling out forms, reporters, and of course, police officers everywhere. Mathew didn't like hearing the incessant drone of their radios or the clanging of the handcuffs dangling from their belts.

Mathew took Carol's arm and followed the signs to the front reception desk. The bullet-proof glass made him even queasier. He spoke into the grate of a round hole, wondering if his voice was being magnified on the other side. Nothing happened. Carol gave him a nudge, but before he cleared his throat, an officer looked up, waved for him to wait, and then approached the counter a moment later.

A woman. Tall, well-built, any hint of femininity hidden by the bulky paraphernalia she had to wear. No wonder the place was kept so cool.

"Can I help you?"

Her voice was lighter than Mathew expected. Was she the good cop in the good-cop-bad-cop routine? Looking up into her eyes, Mathew knew he'd tell her anything she wanted him to.

"I've come about my father," he whispered.

"Speak a little louder please," the woman demanded, turning her ear to the grate.

"I've come about my father," he repeated.

"What's the problem?" She shuffled some forms together and checked her pen by scribbling furiously on the edge of a page.

Mathew didn't like the idea of being on file. Once one governmental arm or bureaucratic agency knew even the slightest thing about you, your privacy was completely and irrevocably dissolved. But he needed to find his dad. "He's gone."

"Gone, as in dead?"

"Gone as in missing."

"How old is he?"

Mathew had to think. "Seventy-three."

"Has he ever gone missing before?"

"No." The biggest gun he'd ever seen was holstered to her hip. He was sure that if Dr. Stallworth had been there doing knee bends, he would have undoubtedly mouthed some reference to penis envy or a sublimation of repressed hostility.

"Did you have a fight?"

"No."

"Nothing out of the ordinary happen?"

Mathew shook his head. He wasn't sure whether he should mention the 'dog thing' or not.

"Health problems?"

Mathew gulped and looked at Carol. "Kind of."

"Kind of?" She stopped writing.

"He had a stroke a few years back and he's not as sharp as he used to be." Mathew pointed a finger at his own head.

"How long exactly has he been missing?"

Mathew checked his watch. "Since lunch."

"I see." The woman jotted something down, then shuffled the papers together.

"Wait right over there on the bench. I'll have someone come out and talk to you as soon as I can."

Mathew turned and guided Carol to where they'd been directed. Everything around them looked clean but he didn't want to touch anything, just in case. Despite his fear and concern, he still felt the whole thing was rather exciting. Secretly, Mathew hoped to catch a glimpse of some prostitutes. Always a token presence at any police station, prostitutes meant vice and vice meant street-wise detectives immersed in the clandestine world of sex and drugs. He wasn't disappointed. He couldn't help staring at two women handcuffed in a little holding area. Blushing white, he shook his head when one of them blew him a kiss and asked if he wanted a date.

Not everyone appeared as friendly and nonplussed with the routine as the hookers. Some people looked completely out of place, while others had a seedy, shiftless look in their eyes that suggested it had just been a matter of time before they finally ended up here. As Mathew glanced around the foyer, he couldn't help imagining the heinous crimes some of the people must have committed. The young man with a bowl cut was probably a break-and-enter artist. Armed assault suited the biker-type over at the coffee machine. Which one was a murderer? Mathew's nervous excitement was tinged with dread, because it was people just like this, people he saw every day hustling along the sidewalk or riding the streetcar on his way to work, that actually *were* involved with those kinds of crimes. He wasn't going to let Carol out of his sight.

A chill tingled up his spine when he noticed a man leaning back against the wall on the other side of the foyer. He was huge, with the neck of a football lineman and the body of a wrestler. Half-day's growth of beard, a scar that edged his hairline and down to his right eye, and hands like meat cleavers. Mafia, Mathew thought, trying not to stare. A hired assassin.

Mathew was staring down at something on the floor when two black, patent leather shoes stepped on what he was trying to see. He looked up. And up. *And up.* It was the Mafia hit man. How much did it cost to have someone whacked? He'd heard it could be as little as fifty dollars in places like New York and Detroit. Mathew forced himself to stand. When he looked straight ahead, all he could see was the man's bulbous Adam's apple.

"Detective Larken," the giant said quietly, extending his hand. Mathew took it tentatively. He figured one good shake from this behemoth and he wouldn't be able to drive home.

"Mathew," he said, praying his voice wouldn't crack. "And this is Carol."

"Husband and wife?"

Mathew said no, and smiled at Carol. But it certainly sounded nice. She seemed to know what he was thinking, and blushed.

"May I sit down?" The detective gestured to the bench. Mathew didn't think it was going to be able to bear his weight, but he shuffled over and gave him as much room as he could.

"So your father's missing?"

"Yes. Since lunch."

"And he has some health problems?"

Mathew wasn't sure what to say.

"I know this is difficult," Larken offered softly. "But believe me, it happens every single day, and it certainly isn't anything to feel embarrassed about. For you, or for him."

Mathew nodded.

"As the population ages, we get more and more of this all the time. People are always walking off on their own. To something, or just away. Anything that you can tell me might help."

Mathew took a deep breath and told Detective Larken everything. The man barely raised an eyebrow when he recounted the whole *Dad-changes-into-animals* part. Larken scribbled down his own notes, nodding when it seemed appropriate. Mathew was surprised at how easy he found it to talk to a man that just moments before he thought was a mob enforcer.

"And how long can he –"

"Stay as a dog? We're not sure. But I do know it's never been this long before."

"Do either of you have a recent picture of him?"

Mathew dug one out of his wallet, and then gave Larken one of Cybernician's posters as well.

Detective Larken studied the image for a moment, then attached the photographs to one of the forms he was filling out. Mathew saw it in the man's eyes: he'd seen a hundred just like it before.

"The problem we have," the officer began gently, "is one you're probably already aware of."

"That you have to wait a certain amount of time before you can do anything?" Carol asked.

"Exactly."

Mathew frowned. "How long?"

"The time frame is generally twenty four hours. Normally, and I'm not just saying this to be overly optimistic or just to get your hopes up, the people in these situations usually turn up by then. We often find them wandering the streets, lost and confused."

That's half the population, Mathew thought. The detective watched the cloud pass over Mathew's face. He reached out and laid a huge hand on his shoulder. "We usually find them safe and sound."

Carol took Mathew's other arm. "So there's nothing you can do until tomorrow?"

Larken shook his head. "We'll forward the photograph to the papers, though. They're quite helpful that way, and they'll have it out in the morning edition, with a little blurb about what he was wearing, where he was last seen, that sort of thing. I'm sure he'll come home or he'll be spotted. But if not, call me."

He handed Mathew a card. "I've got all the information so we'll be able to start whatever procedures are necessary as soon as I hear from you. Hopefully, they won't be necessary."

The detective stood and the bench creaked. "Go home and get some sleep. I'm sure he'll turn up. They usually do."

They usually do. Mathew pictured teeming hordes of dazed seniors, psychiatric sleepwalkers, street kids and overmedicated outpatients roaming the streets, all tangled together and bumping into one another, desperately trying to find their way home.

Mathew pocketed the card with the officer's number, wrapped his arm around Carol's shoulders, and left. He moved to the side when three burly cops dragged a manacled, writhing teen in through the front doors.

* * *

The first night was the worst. It always is for an animal on its own for the first time.

Cloud-filaments snaked across a troubled sky. A light wind whisked Styrofoam cups and little clumps of debris along the sidewalk like tumbleweed. No stars, and it was getting colder. Granddad sniffed the air. If it rained there was a small chance it could turn to snow. Huddled in a doorway of one of the only shops he'd seen without metal bars on the window and door, he peeked out and glanced up and down the street. Bundled against the approaching cold, a lot of people were still out crowding the sidewalk. Most ignored him, but not everyone. A young woman stopped and stared, shook her head, and tossed something round and shiny onto the stoop by Granddad's feet. He picked it up as soon as she left, but it was hard and inedible so he pushed it away.

Night thickened. He was still trying to decide what to do when an odd but half-familiar scent transfixed his senses. He sat up straight, hands in front against the ground and feet tucked in beneath him, and waited anxiously as the smell wafted closer. He knew he'd been sensed, too. The smell grew stronger with every beat of his heart.

A moment, two, and then the dog stepped into view: a small terrier that had seen better days. Probably worse, too. It

- 365 -

woofed indignantly, surprised at its own mistake. Granddad could see the terrier had obviously been expecting something else, something just a little more hairy, perhaps. They exchanged uneasy stares, then Granddad leaned closer and sniffed. The terrier let him smell his face, then stretched forward and inspected granddad's throat and neck with his own nose. Granddad shifted up so he was on all fours and the terrier climbed up onto the stoop. Still a little wary, they smelled each other's hind quarters and privates. Granddad wondered if his nose was as cold as the other dog's. The terrier seemed a bit confused. He couldn't tell where Granddad had been or what type of dog he was. He wasn't even sure if he was a male or a female. The only thing he knew for certain was that Granddad wasn't in heat.

The terrier finally sat down on the stoop next to Granddad. Heads turning at the same time, they watched the pedestrians hurry home and the cars inch by like metal snails. A few minutes passed, and then the terrier crawled back down onto the sidewalk. He stopped and looked over his shoulder at Granddad, then glanced up the street. He obviously knew where he was going, but Granddad didn't want to seem too needy and unworldly, so he waited until the terrier started walking away. Leaving the sheltered warmth of the doorway behind, he stepped off the stoop and trotted off after his new friend.

Granddad followed the terrier to a narrow alley off Yonge Street, just south of Dundas, where the crowds thinned out considerably. The two dogs stopped at the edge of the laneway and sniffed the air. Neither detected a threat. The terrier lifted a leg and marked a garbage can. Granddad yanked his zipper down and followed suit, then cantered off happily.

But the terrier jolted to a sudden stop, his body rigid, one paw frozen in mid-stride. Granddad crept up beside him and followed his companion's gaze. Another quick check of the myriad scents that contaminated the alley, and then he saw it too. Instinct took over. The dogs crouched down low to the ground, watched, and waited.

Three men huddled around a makeshift bonfire spewing from a rusted, metal can. Flames licked its edges and streams of grey-black smoke spiraled up into the night. Their faces muted by the flames, the men moved back and forth, stamping out the cold, coughing, slapping their shoulders and muttering strings of disjointed curses. They'd hold their palms to the heat for a moment then rub their hands furiously together. They only drew their hands away long enough to take a swig from a bottle half-hidden in a paper bag and then pass it on to the next shadow.

The dogs watched for several minutes before they sensed the coast was clear. These ones were no different than they were, just lonely animals searching for warmth and a little glow of light. Granddad raised up when the terrier did. Trying to stay invisible, they inched closer to the wall and slinked down the alley. They both stopped when a man looked up. One of them said something, the other laughed, and then they all turned back to the crackling flames.

The terrier quickly found a place between a dumpster and a stack of garbage bags piled up against the wall. He started clearing it free of debris with his nose, and Granddad moved in beside him to help. The terrier watched Granddad sniff the spot then circle it indecisively several times before finally feeling comfortable and settling down. Leaning into each other for warmth, they listened to the sounds of the street at the end of the lane. The terrier yawned, licked a pebble from his paw, and watched the sparks from the fire dance up into the night.

A red and blue light circled the end of the alley for a moment, then was gone. Granddad scratched an irritating itch, and then nuzzled the terrier's neck. He was just about to put his head down and curl into his paws when another sparkling light caught his eye. He looked down to where the men gathered, but sensed it wasn't their fire he'd seen. He squinted in the darkness, and stared. And then he saw it again. Softly at first, then stronger. Bright, pulsing, palpitating, like a huge candle flame hovering in the air. He watched it for a minute before it flickered into nothing. Granddad put his head on his paws and sighed. The crackle of flames quickly lulled him to sleep.

***

It was the first time Mathew had really *wanted* to see her, to have her there, with him, beside him, and her absence punctured him with an emptiness he hadn't felt in a very long time. Where was she? Didn't she know he needed her? Was she scrounging in some dumpster, or protecting her cart in the back of the mission on Spadina she went to when it was too cold to sleep outside? Or was she just pushing her way through the downtown streets, searching the curbs for some treasure everyone else had missed and waving at her subjects as they parted to let her pass?

Mathew couldn't believe she'd deserted him. Where could your fairy godmother go when you finally admitted you needed her? Did fairy godmothers run out at the most inopportune times, too, just like everyone else? She was a bag lady, for God's sake.

What could have been so important?

Chapter Twenty-nine

The night threatened a deeper cold that would bring a smile to pharmacists all over the city. All their cold medicines were neatly arranged in rows down the shelves, along with the extra soft tissues, the lozenges, cough syrup, the sinus remedies, the countless bottles of aspirin, and teetering pyramids of vitamin bottles. Extra strength soap canisters and industrial potency masks were already stacked in anticipation. All they had to do was wait: Mother Nature and the new Asian or Hong Kong flu would do the rest. The moon was tucked behind the buildings and the sky was thick with restless clouds. The wind carried a damp chill that knotted old bones.

"*Sshhhh, ssshhhhh*. It won't be long now."

Beatrice shifted sideways and pulled the stack of blankets farther over onto the grate. The subway rattled by underneath, *click-clack-clicking* hurriedly over the tracks and blowing gusts of warm air into the night. Like a sauna, it steamed up the rusted metal rungs of the grate just nicely. She heard a distant siren and the pile of clothes next to her seemed to move by themselves.

"Here, let me do that," Beatrice whispered. She straightened the mound and dug out a wider air hole in the jumbled pyramid of discarded sheets and cardboard. "Better?"

A tiny voice echoed up out of the cocoon. "Yes. Yes it is. Thank you. But I'm still so cold."

Beatrice tugged another blanket free from her cart and added it to the pile. She patted it down softly and tucked it around the grate the way a preschooler paper-Mache's a light bulb. She knew it wouldn't help much, but she fussed with it until it looked right, the way an embalmer tries to make a face look better than it did before. In a moment she'd have to take them off again, anyway. Her friend was burning hot one minute and icy cold the next. At least she'd stopped coughing up blood and her eyes weren't oozing yellow pus any more.

"What time is it?"

Beatrice smiled. She'd known the woman who belonged to the little birdlike voice for longer than she'd had her bracelet, and she'd never once been interested in the time before. But most things are more interesting when there's not much of them left and your last mask has to come off.

Beatrice looked down at her bracelet. "Early in the night."

That seemed good enough to satisfy Denise. She snuggled in closer to Beatrice's side. "I want to see."

Beatrice pulled the swaddling covers back just enough to expose her friend's eyes and mouth. She kept an old scarf wrapped around the woman's forehead and chin, trying to keep in as much of the warmth as possible. She held an extra thick blanket over their heads.

Huddled together under their blankets like crusty old Mexican farmers taking an early siesta, they peeked out from their canopy and watched the people hurry by. They were at the edge of an alley, framed by two buildings that deflected some of the wind. Their backs warmed the bricks. Beatrice smiled when another train passed by, reheating their grate.

Denise watched coat-bottoms swirl by. "Hudson's Bay."

Beatrice nodded.

"Bianca Nygard."

Another nod. Denise had an uncanny ability to know where clothes originated just by catching a passing glimpse of a hem, a sash, a collar, a button.

"Daillards."

"Are you warm enough."

"Warm as I'll ever be." She laughed at her own joke.

A man walking by tossed a couple of dollars down onto one of their blankets. Beatrice didn't pick it up.

"Perchance . . ."

Beatrice smiled. 'Perchance' had always been Denise's way of asking if there was anything left in the bottle to worry about, and, if there was, how about passing it back?

"Kept it right here for you. But take it easy, there's not much left."

Beatrice held the bottle to her friend's lips. Two gulps, no more. She wiped the rest from Denise's chin before the dribbles started to freeze. Scarred with dry cracks, her lips were puffy and a light, almost transparent blue. No, it wouldn't be long now.

"Fairweathers."

The little voice almost hummed. She heard a commotion farther down the street, near the corner, but she couldn't move forward enough to see. Besides, she didn't want to disturb the blanket-nest Beatrice had woven for her. It was like the bower birds made to attract a mate. They strained to listen: it sounded like someone was trying to hang on to something they didn't want someone else to have. But it also could have been a prostitute struggling with her punter in one of the dingy little stairwells.

The woman coughed so hard she almost shook her head off. Beatrice checked the scarf for blood or phlegm: nothing. At least the worst was over and the bottle had numbed her pain. That's why Denise had wanted to leave the shelter and spend whatever time she had left outside. There wasn't anything anyone could have done for her now, and since she'd always felt safer outside, she'd asked Beatrice to take her to one of her favorite stretches of sidewalk.

Beatrice listened to Denise's withered lungs grasp for breath. She was beginning to miss her already. They'd shopped through the dumpsters together for years, and spent more Christmases at the Mission than she could remember. When one of them visited the soup kitchen alone, a volunteer always asked where the other one was. Two peas without a pod.

It was Denise who'd given Beatrice one of her most prized possessions, one of the first priceless baubles that decorated her bracelet. It was a little coin she'd found, some thick foreign piece with the centre cut out that Denise had originally worn as a ring. Despite the weather, it had never changed color at all. Beatrice always made sure it dangled right over the coarse home-stitched suicide scars that lined her wrist.

Beatrice re-covered their feet with the edge of the blankets and smiled at her friend. Denise was somewhere between fifty-five and sixty-five. Even if she knew for sure she wouldn't tell.

What was left of her hair was bone-white. It was hard to imagine how tall she'd once been because she'd shrunk down so much into herself it looked like her head came right out of the hollow between her shoulders. She had small, pinprick eyes and just the merest slice of a mouth. Without her glasses she could have been mistaken for a mole.

Denise was one of Beatrice's closest friends, and she was one of the only people who knew what Beatrice *really* was. And Denise had always kept her secret safe.

It was years before, but only two streets over from where they were huddling for warmth. They'd been tucked into a door opening behind the Eaton's Centre, between the parking lot and the little church that had been overwhelmed by the concrete walls of the shopping mall. The mall had been built so close to it that it had completely enclosed the ancient church on three sides, effectively putting religion back into its proper place.

The clock at St. Timothy's United had just struck 2:00 A.M. The police were still playing 'shuffle the transients', and the last buses were heading to the depot to get washed and debugged. Denise was halfway through a second bottle. Something had been bothering her all day, but she'd kept it to herself. And then suddenly, after a long, rumbling burp for a preamble, she tore open her heart and let her soul peek out. Barely stopping for breath, she told Beatrice about *her other life*, about who and what she'd been before a combination of ill-timed events sucked her into a void with the grip of a giant squid and she'd woken up five years later to find herself on the streets.

So long ago. And now, toasting herself on the grate, Beatrice couldn't remember what Denise had said. A teacher? A housewife? A clerk, or was it a cleric? It didn't matter anyway. That night Denise cried for something she couldn't remember she even had. Beatrice had never seen her so unhappy. She sensed Denise was teetering on the edge. So, even though it was blatantly antithetical to 'The Code,' (and Beatrice, if anything, was a stickler for being obsequious to 'The Code') Beatrice told her friend her secret. Her *big* secret.

Denise didn't seem as surprised as Beatrice thought she would. But then Denise had always known there was something special about her friend. She listened thoughtfully, nodding when something touched some hidden chord or frowning when something didn't seem quite right. She sat quietly for several minutes after Beatrice finally drew her story to a close. She took a long drink and pondered everything that had been said.

"And that's how you became a fairy godmother?"

Beatrice nodded.

"And why you wear the crown?"

"Because I'm Queen, yes," Beatrice shrugged, acknowledging the weight of responsibility. "Queen of the fairy *godmothers*. The fairies have their own queen."

Denise shook a thin, deformed arthritic finger at her friend, and winked. "I'd always thought there was something different about you. Something extraordinary."

"There's something very special about everyone, Denise."

"Does this mean you're *my* fairy godmother, too?"

Beatrice smiled and shook her head. *The innocence of mortals.* "No. Fairy godmothers don't get to pick."

"Oh, I see."

"But you have your own, you know."

"No!"

"You do."

Denise looked quickly around. Around, and for some reason, *up*, immediately figuring that *up* would be the best place to look if you wanted to see your fairy godmother because she assumed they probably hovered like hummingbirds. But she didn't see anything, not even a hazy, disintegrating trail of magic dust. Just a cruiser's light ricocheting around the walls above their heads.

"You'll see her when you really need to."

Denise sank back down and the sparkle disappeared from her eyes. "Does everyone see their fairy godmother?"

"Not everyone needs to. And not everyone wants to, either."

Denise nodded slowly, but she didn't really understand. *Who in their right mind wouldn't need to?*

Denise never mentioned it again after that night. They never talked about it unless Beatrice brought up the subject, which was rare, since fairy godmothers are intrinsically quiet and unassuming. It only came up when it had to. But even though it was something they didn't mention very often, it was something that tied them together like nothing else could ever have done. A symbiotic secret.

Another train whooshed by below. Beatrice heard the debris scatter in the train's wake. The tracks screeched a metallic cry. More steps approached. Denise struggled to look up and out of her cocoon.

"Oh my, London Fog. Haven't seen one of those in ages."

Beatrice thought most of the coats looked the same, but she didn't have Denise's discerning eye for detail.

"Bea, I'm really getting cold. Do you think there'll be another train by shortly?" Another harsh cough that racked her limbs.

Beatrice didn't have the heart to tell her two more had just passed beneath their grate. "Soon, Denise. Soon it won't seem so cold."

"What about my things?"

"What . . . what would you like me to do with them?"

Denise pushed her chin down deeper into the scarf. "Maybe –"

"Yes?"

"Maybe you could look after them. Give the things you don't want to someone who might really need them."

"Yes, I can do that. Don't worry. I'll find good homes for all your stuff." Beatrice wiped her eyes with her coat sleeve. She didn't think Denise had more than a bag or two crammed under her mattress at the shelter but she'd check around, just to make sure.

Boots squelched by and more coats flapped in the wind, but Denise didn't say where they'd come from. Her eyes had closed and her face was shriveled like a prune. Shivering, she seemed to be thinking very hard about something.

"Beatrice, someone else is here."

Beatrice looked up and down the street: commuters, shoppers, beggars, a couple of dogs, a bus inspector checking something on a sheet down at the intersection. A couple of rummies.

"No. *Someone important.*"

Beatrice closed her eyes, too, and smiled. Yes, there certainly was. A new one she'd never had the pleasure of meeting before. They opened their eyes together.

"Oh Bea. Can you see --?"

"Yes, Denise. I can." *Just not in the same way you're seeing her.*

"She's . . . she's coming closer."

Beatrice nodded respectfully. Denise gasped.

"I don't know how to say this, but I think I'm seeing right through her? Is that possible?"

"It is. What do you see, Denise?"

There was a moment's silence. Two taxis careened by, narrowly missing a pedestrian. Deep in the alley, a cat clawed at a paper bag.

"I think she looks a little like my sister."

"You never said you had a sister."

"I didn't remember having one until just now. She died when I was very little. Jennifer." Trembling, Denise coughed so hard she could barely catch her breath. "She's coming closer, Beatrice. The light. I'm afraid."

"You don't have to be."

"She's so tall. Much taller than I expected."

Why do people always assume we're short?

"I can't tell how old she is. She could be any age. Or all ages. But she's wearing a beautiful scarf, just like my grandmother used to wear. And a hat, a hat with flowers. An Easter bonnet like they wore on spring walks down along the boardwalk. Oh my, she's so lovely. And her eyes!"

Beatrice felt the woman approach. Denise lifted a hand from inside the blankets just enough so she could rub her eyes. "Beatrice?"

"Yes?"

"What should I do? Should I say something?"

But by the time Beatrice had started shaking her head, Denise's breath had lightened and a delicate, longing smile shimmered on her lips. She closed her eyes and tilted her head to one side and then the other the way a dog listens to an owner's intonations. She made little gurgling sounds like she was trying to talk. She frowned, listening attentively, her blue lips always moving soundlessly. Minutes passed, and three subway trains rattled by beneath the grate. The cat was still.

Denise collapsed back down into the cocoon of blankets like a puppet cut from its strings. Her face was a blotchy red and her hair was matted with sweat. She gulped, almost choking. The dullness had returned to her eyes and she stared down vacantly at the cracks in the sidewalk. But Beatrice knew she wasn't afraid any more. She didn't have to ask her friend what the woman had said because she could see it in Denise's halo.

A pair of boots stomped by, prefaced by the *tap tap tap* of a cane.

"Sears."

A shiver, a whispered breath, and then nothing more. The blankets smelled like cinnamon.

Beatrice leaned over and pulled the ragged pile of covers closer, hugging her friend tightly to her side. She thought it unfair that Denise's last word, her last breath, would have been about someone else's coat. Surely there were more important things to exhale with your soul. But then again, Beatrice knew there were far worse things, too. And besides, who was she to judge?

Another train rumbled by.

Chapter Thirty

Grey fingers of thickening clouds reached across the sky, clawing at the night and scratching the skyline into shreds. A wind that was neither bitter nor cold slithered against the window like a hungry snake. The pane pulsed.

Joshua let the drapes fall closed. "I hope he's all right."

"So do I." Mathew pulled his son's covers up and sat down on the side of the bed.

"I'm sure we'll find him in the morning," the boy said, trying to sound brave.

"Yes," Mathew said. "Me too."

Mathew didn't want to leave, and Joshua didn't want to let him go. The boy scurried down beneath the blankets but his eyes stayed wide open: there'd be no sleeping tonight. Mathew looked around his son's room. Nothing suggested the presence of a child: no trophies, team pennants, jumbled mounds of discarded clothes, or magazines spread-eagled on the floor with candy-wrapper book marks. Just a desk with a computer and three shelves lined with books. Mathew remembered hearing some of the ones down at the bottom: *Thomas the Train, Whales at the Seaside, Ollie the Otter Goes Home*, and *Tales of the Buccaneers*. He realized there weren't any stuffed animals around, either. He wondered if Beatrice had some favorite toy, some special friend, tucked down in the bottom of her cart? Did Carol have one at home? Could he have given it to her? Could he be it?

"Dad?"

"Uh-huh?"

"You love Carol, don't you?"

Mathew feigned a smile. He wanted to say something, to try and explain his thoughts to his son, the whirlwind of emotions and feelings about Carol and Lydia that constantly swirled through his head, but the words wouldn't come. Somewhere beyond the window a siren sliced through the night. Oh God, he hoped his father was safe. Carol. Lydia. What could he say? Fumbling for a way to begin, he stopped before he started. When he turned back to his son, he saw right away that Joshua wasn't listening any longer. The boy was falling *away*, away down deeper into the bed. When his eyelids stopped fluttering, the boy's face had glazed over with an unfamiliar mask. His skin almost glowed. When he spoke his voice was light and melancholy, his expression maudlin.

Whomever he'd become looked around the room with sad, appraising eyes. "The room was smaller than this one. A fan with cracked blades hung from the ceiling, slicing the heat apart, pushing the sweat deeper into our skin. It wobbled as it circled, moaning with each turn, droning like a hummingbird, whisking the world outside away into a pulsing silence. The little room was damp with humidity and the sweetly moistened scent of lovemaking."

Mathew gulped, then whispered. "Who are you?"

"Maria. Maria Gonsalves Orestes."

It was the first time Joshua had remembered being female. It threw Mathew for a moment but he recovered quickly.

"And you're in –"

"A small village on the coast, about an hour from Lisbon."

Portugal. "Are you in your own room?"

Joshua nodded. "I could hear life in the narrow little street below the window. Flower carts creaked over the battered cobblestones as the vendors pushed them home. The fishermen down at the pier were yelling back and forth while they fixed their nets and readied the boats for tomorrow. Waves bubbled foam against the beach, and the leaves of the acacia trees whispered secrets in the warm wind."

The boy smiled wistfully. "A box full of delicate bougainvillea lined the window sill. A sea-breeze fluttered through the curtains, and the bed sighed. I clutched the edge of the mattress, pressed my face into the pillow, and leaned away from Paulo. I stretched back, arms behind my head like I was falling from a hilltop, and I let him move again. He whispered the way he always did when he was inflamed, quiet murmurs flushed with longing, with need. I rose to meet him, urging him to an even closer intimacy by the rhythm of my hips.

"I remember him wrapping his arms around me, his face nestled against my neck, enveloping me and folding himself into me the way the velvet petals of a rose close together in the final flicker of dusk. I knew him so well: the cadence of his heart, the tightness in his muscles, the warmth of his skin, the closeness of his blood. I cried out with passion. He tensed, and for the beat of an eyelash he was strangely still and somehow far away. And then we moved and shuddered together, skin on fire, breaths deliciously short, and hearts pounding frantically to the excited rhythm of love."

Joshua stared up at something he seemed to see in the shadows that flickered across the ceiling. "A tingling tremor rippled through my body." He shook his head and his eyes narrowed." And then – and then my mind, my body, my soul were filled with the memory of my husband."

Paulo wasn't her husband? Mathew fussed with his son's covers but didn't say anything. A light draught seeped from somewhere.

"After Paulo fell asleep I lay there for hours, staring at the ceiling. Night had fallen, teasing the narrow walls and iron-ringed balconies with shadows. The smell of dinners seeped from the other tiny apartments, filling the air with the essence of the day's fresh catch. Everything took me back. I was there again, with him. A lifetime ago."

Mathew breathed *when*?

Joshua's frown relaxed. "It was a night very much like that one, long ago before my skin had started to sag and little wrinkles had begun to tug at the corners of my eyes."

"What was his name? Your husband?"

"Luis. Luis Avealar Orestes. We met on a boat ride. A tourist boat of all things, the ones that circled the rock statues offshore while sunburned passengers sipped white wine. I had gone with my parents. Mother had lived in the Azores all of her life but never had the audacity to buy a ticket for a tour on a ferry. But she'd fallen ill, and my father bought us fares on the most splendid sightseeing boat he could find for an afternoon cruise at the end of summer."

Maria smiled.

"What?"

"Mother had been so excited she'd even bought a new hat, a jaunty little straw affair like all the women in Lisbon were wearing that year. We almost didn't go because Miguel, my father, was so worried about her. He was afraid the activity, the crowds, the intense afternoon heat that baked the beaches, or even the gentle rocking of the ferry as it leaned from side to side in the waves would unsettle her. But in the end, as always, after pounding his fist over and over again into his palm, he acquiesced and agreed to go."

Maria closed her eyes: she was on the sightseeing boat again, and Luis was walking towards her.

"I saw him before I even turned. I knew I'd always been waiting for him. I was a struggling poet and I sensed his life rhymed with mine. Luis did something he'd never dared with a stranger before; he walked up beside me and took my hand without speaking. We held each other's gaze. Then he apologized for his boldness, asking my forgiveness for his insolence and intrusion. He wanted to know where my parents were so he could find father and try to explain his actions, even though he didn't really understand them yet himself. But he never let go of my hand."

Mathew thought he heard a dog bark outside. He strained to look out the window. Nothing. It was always safe to blame things on the wind. "What did he look like?" Mathew wasn't surprised he'd asked because he felt like he needed to know.

"His face was smooth and handsome, his nose slight, his lips soft and full. His eyes were sapphire blue, and he had long, jet black hair that hung down over his shoulders. He had a lithe, athletic build, and his skin was hairless and clay-red. He had a boyish charm that could melt the coldest heart."

"And you fell in love?"

"Is there love at first sight? Yes. Love is like a spirit, nourished with hope, tempered with emotion, preserved with understanding and time. One look in his eyes and I knew I'd be committed to him forever. He was everything that my mother loved in my father; kind, gentle, honest, soft-spoken, articulate, erudite but always willing to learn. He laughed easily and possessed a natural sense of humor, a teasing character that bordered on mischievousness."

Maria blushed. "We spent the entire cruise together, the whole day and well into the night. Then the next day, and the day after that. That summer, and every day of the fall as it surrendered to winter, and then spring too, when the balboa trees grew thick and tall.

"Mother lived another season, just long enough to see us married. Lost and lonely, father died of a broken heart a few months later. At first it was hard to be alone, but we had each other, and we were never apart. Every Sunday afternoon after church we'd walk hand in hand, down along the spider web of piers that anchored the fishing trawlers to the seaside. Weeknights we'd tend the little patch of grass behind the apartment we used like a garden. Or we'd just sit out on the tiny balcony overlooking the street and read until the night slowly darkened our pages. I think it was the closest I've ever come to loving selflessly."

Mathew knew the feeling.

"And it wasn't long before we realized we were going to be parents ourselves."

Mathew looked at his son. It was one thing to envision him as a young woman lost in love. It was quite another though, to imagine him pregnant and giving birth. Transfixed, he leaned over closer and brushed a straggling hair from his son's brow. *From Maria's.*

"How did you feel?" he asked a little uneasily.

"Nothing could have made us happier." Joshua closed his eyes, smiling at the memory.

Mathew waited patiently for a few moments before he whispered. "Where are you? Maria?"

There was a stiff silence.

"The sky beyond the window was grey-black and thick with shadows. It was starting to rain. The first few tentative drops splashed against the window sill, wet-staining the little earthen flowerpots on the ledge. Luis had been so proud. He wanted to make a special trip into the city one Saturday morning late in the fall when the nights were slowly growing shorter. Something felt wrong though, and I told him not to go."

"To Lisbon?"

"Does it matter?" Maria took a deep, labored breath, and apologized with a glance. The memories were hurting. "He wanted to choose something special for me and our child-to-be. He looked up old acquaintances and finally, through the friend of a friend, found the man he'd been searching for; an aged jeweler who had made his own parents' wedding bands so many years ago. Luis went to the shop just before nightfall. He shared a bottle of wine with the stooped old man and drank to his parents' memory. He ordered two things before he left; one was a gold locket for the child, engraved with his family's crest; the other, an eternity ring for me. Two interlocking heart-shaped diamonds set so they'd be touching forever." Maria closed her eyes and listened to the waves tumble over the seashore down at the end of the street. "He never made it back to his hotel alive."

Mathew tensed. "What happened?"

"Luis left the jeweler's shop quite late, just before the crows would awaken the farmers on the outskirts of the city, and walked back to his hotel through unfamiliar streets. He was too surprised to move when the world suddenly ripped open all around him."

Maria gulped. "Whistles pierced the night. Bright orange lights flashed in a circle and the air filled with horns and blaring sirens. A security vehicle with some type of governmental insignia appeared from the intersection Luis had just passed, careening around the corner, a police car in front and behind it. They made a sharp turn right in front of Luis as he jumped back onto the sidewalk, and he realized at once the little convoy was being pursued.

"Two motorcyclists screamed out of an adjacent side street, the riders bent over for speed as they tried to cut the other vehicles off. They wore khaki pants like the army used. Camouflage bandannas concealed their faces beneath their eyes, and the dark striped scarves of the Separatists covered their heads. One man rode behind each driver, automatic weapons slung over their shoulders and brandished at their side.

"The ambushers roared past Luis. Two more suddenly appeared out of nowhere up ahead at the next intersection. They jolted to a stop right in the middle of the road, blocking the convoy's escape route. They opened fire as the first cruiser tried to swerve around them, shattering the windshield and mutilating the driver and his companion. The second police car cut around the government vehicle, shielding it from the gunfire. Someone screamed at the driver to turn around and go back.

"But the other two motorcycles were right behind them, spraying the street with a hail of bullets that ricocheted off the cobblestones and tore great chunks of plaster from the walls of the nearest buildings. They stopped beside the car and each of the attackers unloaded his weapon into the back seat. Then someone signaled. The back two bikes joined their companion at the intersection and sped off into the darkness of the night."

"Who was the man in the car?"

"The Finance Minister. His body had been raked so badly with bullets he was almost unrecognizable."

"And Luis?"

"He was struck by a stray shot that bounced off one of the cars. The coroner – " Maria struggled to choke down a dry gulp. "The coroner said he was dead before he hit the ground."

Mathew shuddered. Maria turned her head and stared out her bedroom window. Her eyes teared, but she had the stoic look that comes when you finally accept the fact that the past is never really finished.

"It was a double loss, because the pain of his death made me lose the child, too."

Mathew looked away.

"Twenty four years passed but nothing changed. I still loved Luis with all my heart. And then I met Paulo, and something inside told me I had to go on. He was a kind man, strong but gentle, his face and hands weathered by life as a fisherman. He was fair and honest and was always trusted in business. A good friend when you needed one. And he loved me very much. And I loved him, too. But I never loved him as I did Luis."

Maria trembled beneath the blankets. It was times like this that some invisible scorpion stabbed her in the chest and reminded her so conclusively that time would never stitch close the tear in her heart and the rip in her soul.

"That night when Paulo and I finished making love, I couldn't stop thinking about Luis. Lying there in the dark, I kept remembering the times I'd been with him. The passion before, the tranquility after. The touch of his hands, the warmth of his skin, the sensation of his lips. And I recalled the things I'd said to Luis, my lover of all time, the things only those in love ever say. The special things, the things murmured with utter abandon, without thought, without guilt, without knowing where the words and hopes and dreams and wishes ever really came from."

It had been a long time since Mathew had said those kinds of words. Or heard them, either. He remembered the special little name he called Carol in those intimate moments . . . *after*. "But why –"

Maria stopped him with a raised hand, her fingers shaking like an expectant junkie's. "I realized then that after twenty-four years, in another lifetime, I'd said some of the same things in the darkness to the man beside me. Paulo. Moans, whimpers, urgings, praises. And yet I'd sung these same exaltations, uttered these same cries, murmured the same pledges I'd just whispered to Paulo to Luis when our acts of love lengthened the night into daybreak."

Maria shook her head thoughtfully and wrapped a loose thread from the edge of the blanket around her finger. "And then I saw him."

"Luis?"

A nod. "He was there, sitting on the sill, framed by the window, his hands wet from the rain, his long black hair tussled by the sea-wind. He was mouthing some soothing thought I couldn't quite hear. I thought –"

"What?"

Silence.

"What, Maria?"

"I thought he was asking me to forgive him. To forgive him for his love of all time."

Fresh tears. "He was soaked with rain. Blood pooled at Luis' naked feet, and I watched it trickle toward my bed. When I looked back up, he was gone. I remember burrowing into Paulo's side to stop shivering. I heard him breathe and felt the pulse of his blood through his veins, and then I started crying, crying like I'd never cried before."

Mathew licked the dryness from his lips. The bedroom was deathly still. Maria undid the thread and her finger pulsed with little red and blue lines.

"Never underestimate the things love can bring," she whispered, pushing herself up on an elbow, "because they last forever."

Mathew nodded, then brushed the same stubborn wisp of hair from Maria's brow. He saw Carol's face leaning over his bed at the hospital. "It's only now that I've seen her again that I know I've loved her all my life."

Maria's smile was bittersweet. "You can see it in your eyes, the way you breathe when she's near."

"But that doesn't mean I don't love Lydia."

"You must admit to yourself that it is a different kind of love. I loved Paulo very much. But no matter how long I was with him or how close we became, I knew in my heart I'd give everything up in a moment if I could have Luis back again. And that's not saying anything bad about Paulo. It doesn't denigrate my love for him, or weaken my feelings in any way at all. It simply means that I knew my love for him could never equal the love I had for my husband."

Maria sank back down onto the bed. Mathew fussed with the covers, then looked out the window while another siren punctured the night. There was always so much trouble in the world. He thought of the police station: Detective Larken, the prostitutes, the woman that had to be protected by bulletproof glass. What would he give up to make the world right? Everything, he thought. His job, his house, his life. Everything.

Just not Carol.

He shivered. Where was that draught coming from? When he looked back down, Maria was leaving, drifting away from the lines of his son's face, receding and leaving something new, like a tide revealing the freshness of a beach. Joshua blinked repeatedly, and Mathew could see the child was surfacing back up through a lifetime of years. He leaned down and kissed him lightly on the forehead. The child's face scrunched up as he yawned. Mathew went to speak but the boy's breaths were deepening and he was already succumbing to the siren's call of sleep.

A while later, Mathew realized he was sitting in the dark, but he couldn't remember who'd turned off the bedside light.

***

As Mathew was coming back down the stairs, Carol was in the foyer, searching the closet for her coat.

"Is he asleep?"

"Yes. Are you going?"

"I think I should. It's been a long day for everyone, but I'll be back first thing."

Mathew took her coat and draped it over his arm.

"You don't have to go."

"I know. But I do. We're from the old school, remember?" She leaned over and kissed him lightly on the nose.

"You could stay in the guest room?"

"Would you want me to, Mathew?"

He shook his head. Carol wrapped her arms around his waist. "I couldn't stand being that close and that far away at the same time."

"No," he realized. "Neither could I." Mathew glanced back upstairs. "Joshua was talking to me about someone else he's been."

"I thought so." Carol watched Mathew's eyes. "I could tell by your face. Who was he this time?"

"A Portuguese woman who lost her husband when she was very young. A good man who happened to be in the wrong place at the wrong time." Mathew took Carol's hands between his own. "He says I shouldn't let you go, that the chance of a lifetime's love doesn't come around more than twice."

"He's right," Carol whispered.

Mathew helped her on with her coat, his arms burning when he hugged her against his chest. When they kissed the floor fell away and he knew he could begin to dream again. He watched her walk to her car from the front window. She stopped, waved, put a hand over her heart, then got in and drove away. Mathew kept looking until the car turned the corner and Carol was out of sight. How long was it until tomorrow? How much time was left?

***

Hoping Eleanor had found some rest in sleep, Mathew tiptoed past her door on the way to his own room, but her soft sobs betrayed her fear. He knocked lightly and she asked him in.

Still dressed, she was sitting in her husband's favorite chair over by the window, the blanket crumpled up over her knees. She had a box of Kleenex in her lap. Mathew sat down on the floor with his back against the bed, surprised at how different everything looked from such a simple change in perspective. He listened to her breathe and waited patiently for her to speak.

"You know I love Lydia, Mathew. But —"

Mathew held up a hand. "You don't have to say it."

Eleanor nodded. "So Carol didn't want to stay?"

"It didn't feel like the proper thing to do."

"But you really wanted her to?"

"Yes. I did. I do."

Eleanor offered a half-smile. "Don't let it hurt you, Mathew." She looked out at the darkness and watched the shadows of the trees shiver in the wind. "I remember you together. Once you're in love like you two were, you're always in love."

Mathew thought about what Joshua had said. *Maria.*

"Do you think we'll find him, Mathew?"

"I know we will." He leaned over and touched his mother's arm. Even through her sweater she felt cold.

"I hope —"

"What?"

"I hope he wants to come back."

Eleanor wrung her hands together underneath the blanket. "What if he doesn't? What if we find him and he doesn't want to come back here?" She gestured to the room with her eyes. "To this? To me?"

Lives upon lives upon lives. Who had Mathew been before? Who had he been with? He didn't know, but he was certain that Carol had been there in some form or another, too.

"He'll want to come. You've always been in love."

She glanced up and smiled. "Yes. Yes we have, haven't we?"

Silence.

"Find him, Mathew. Please."

***

The voice on the other end of the line was sleepy and not just a little confused.

"Mathew?"

"Yes. It's me."

"Where are you?"

"In the kitchen," Mathew replied.

"What time is it there?"

Mathew glanced at the clock. "Just after two, Lydia."

"In the morning? So it must be – almost eleven here. What are you doing up so late? Is something wrong, Mathew? God, you haven't gone out and got yourself stabbed again, have you?"

"No, I'm fine. It's not me."

"What's happened?"

He explained everything: how Eleanor had brought Carlos home, how his father had transformed during dinner and run away, that they still hadn't been able to find him, the police station, the posters and fruitless searches. Well, almost everything.

"And the police can't do anything until tomorrow?" Lydia wondered how many times she'd heard that during a taping or, while she was sitting in the back of the set waiting to be murdered.

"No."

"So what are you going to do now?"

"Try and get some rest and then start fresh in the morning."

"Do you think the posters will help?"

"I hope so. His picture should be in the morning paper, too."

"Someone will see him, surely," Lydia said hopefully.

"I'm more worried about him tonight."

"Yes. Yes, you're right. Listen. I've got a rehearsal in the morning. But if you need me back there, if you think I should come home –"

"We can manage."

"But maybe an extra pair of eyes could make all the difference in the world."

"Can you really afford to miss the rehearsal, Lydia?"

Silence.

"Lydia?"

"Well, not really Mathew. I'm still not the one they shoot the scenes around, you know. But if it's something like this, something that really seems quite important, then maybe they could let me have some time off."

"I'm sure we'll be fine," Mathew answered. "I just wanted you to know."

"Well, if you need me, call. Really. Please."

"I will."

"I hope you find him. And I hope he's all right."

"So do I, Lydia. Thanks."

"Mathew?"

"Yes, Lydia?"

"I hope you're all right too."

"I am."

"And Mathew?"

"Uh-huh?"

Silence.

"Lydia?"

"I just wanted to say I miss you."

"I miss you too."

"Don't worry. No one stays lost forever."

No, they don't. "I'll call you as soon as I hear anything."

"Good. Yes, please do. And –"

"I'll say hello to everyone for you, Lydia."

"Yes, good. No. What I wanted to say –" But Lydia realized that some things were always best left unsaid. "Give Dad a kiss for me when you find him."

"I will. Goodnight, Lydia."

"Goodnight, Mathew."

Mathew put the receiver down carefully, as if it was made of glass. He hung on to the phone, dangling like the bunched up cord, his head braced forward against the wall and his legs quivering as twenty-seven years swarmed over his senses like an enveloping mat of army ants. They ate everything in sight: memories, forgotten kisses, birthdays, houses, jobs, births, touches in the middle of the night when lightning crackled and thunder shook the world. The ants swarmed and Mathew surrendered. He was devoured, skeletonized, nothing more than a carcass stripped bare and humbled in their wake, a stick figure held loosely together with filaments of hopes and dreams.

***

Hands in his pockets, Mathew stared out through his reflection in the front window. The wind had picked up considerably, swinging the hydro wires that stretched from the street to the corner of his eaves like skipping ropes. The sky threatened icy rain. The shifting clouds had thickened and massed together, like a battalion before battle. The street was still, the neighbors safely locked away inside their houses. For once, the curb on the other side of the road wasn't lined with an unbroken chain of cars.

Mathew wondered where Beatrice went when there was a storm. Where was his father? Inside somewhere, he hoped, safe and dry. A bus splashed by. A moment later, Carmalitta wheeled her car into the driveway. She glanced quickly at the sky then jogged up the porch steps. She'd seen Mathew's silhouette in the window and joined him in the living room.

"It's going to team," she whispered.

He nodded and stared at the clouds. He couldn't remember what they were made of. Something you could pass through, but not touch or hold on to. Clouds must be made of life.

"How come you're still up?"

"I couldn't sleep."

"Any news?"

"No, nothing yet. What have you been doing?"

"After we checked the park, Miriam and I went around to some of the places I knew Granddad liked to go before, when he went out."

That seemed like an awfully long time ago, Mathew thought, recalling another era. "He used to like walking along Queen Street, looking in all the windows and traipsing through the used bookstores."

"Yes, we checked there. Then we drove around some of the old neighborhood churches, and stopped in to see some of the people he used to be friends with."

Mathew wondered what that meant: *used* to be friends. What broke the bond? "We'll just have to start fresh in the morning."

"His picture should be out by then."

Mathew nodded. "The police will make it an official case in the afternoon."

"Hopefully that won't be necessary and he'll be back safe and sound."

Carmalitta wrapped her arm around Mathew's waist. She was so tall now, he thought. His mouth went dry when he re-membered her as a little girl: skinny, sun-bleached hair, her round face blotched with freckles she absolutely hated.

"Let's hope so."

They stood quietly together, waiting for the rain. An edge of the moon peeked out from between the clouds for just a mo-ment, then was gone.

Carmalitta sighed. "I had a long talk with Miriam tonight, too, while we were looking for Granddad." A short pause. "I've decided to buy the condominium with her."

"That's great, Carmalitta." Mathew almost managed a smile. "What made you change your mind?"

She thought of the Sinclairs and how she'd helped them take little Koala to the vet. How they held him in those last few moments, how they wouldn't let him go, how they walked away from the clinic, each one trying to hold the other up.

"I've been frightened and guilty far too long, Dad."

"What about Joshua?" he asked gently. He felt Carmalitta squeeze him a little tighter.

"I'm going to tell him the whole story. Everything."

Mathew nodded, but didn't speak.

"He's been with me every day, but I've never really been his mother. And I want to be a mother to him now."

"Miriam?"

"She's behind me all the way. I don't know if I could have done this without her." She breathed a heavy sigh of relief. "I should have listened to her a long time ago."

"You're listening now," Mathew whispered.

"I just hope he understands why I made the choice I did."

"Now, or then?"

"Then. Both."

"I'm sure he will." Mathew saw his reflection smile.

"The only other thing I'm concerned about is how he'll see you."

"Maybe as an extra father. A friend. As long as we still see each other, everything will be fine. He'll never stop being a part of me."

"I hope not."

Mathew wrapped his arm around Carmalitta's shoulders and pulled her close. She smelled of strawberries. The first few tentative drops of rain splattered against the window. The ones that hit the outside sill echoed dully and bounced back up with tiny splashes. Somewhere in the distance, the sky rumbled like a moaning cow. The rain thickened quickly, then tapered off for a moment, then condensed again, streaking the window with winding rivulets that ran like tears. The tree branches crackled in the wind.

Where did lost dogs find shelter, Mathew thought? In the same places people do?

***

The little terrier was having a dream when the first thunderclap rippled through the night. He yipped, frowned, shook, then curled up into a cowering ball. Granddad awoke when the next boom rumbled down the alley and reverberated against the dumpster. He lurched back into a half-sitting, half-kneeling position. He was dry, except for his front paws, because one side of the dumpster's lid had been left open and they'd used it as their awning. The rain battered their metal roof and drenched the stacks of garbage bags that helped shield them from the wind.

Granddad looked down. His forelegs were shaking in time with the terrier's. He scurried backwards on his haunches, his front paws braced against the rain-slicked pavement. The last few wisps of smoke smoldered from the men's fire in the can. Granddad sniffed: he could smell two of them, but even the faint trace of the third man was gone. Another dog was somewhere nearby, but he couldn't see it.

A fresh burst of lightning whitened the world, ghoulishly silhouetting the buildings that framed the alley. A mounting bass-beat of thunder rose to a crescendo and made Granddad's heart pound wildly against his chest. The terrier scurried back farther until his behind was pushed into the larger dog's side. Tail against the wall, he used Granddad's outstretched forelegs as trees and hid as best he could. Granddad rested his chin atop the smaller dog's head. Whimpering and shaking, the terrier nuzzled him back. Even though their flanks were dry they both smelled of wet dog.

Granddad raised up a little and glanced down the alley. His pupils had dilated, but he still couldn't see where the lane met the street. He sensed the other dog was awake now, too. Filled with nervous tension, he had an overwhelming urge to stand, shake, howl, and run. He could barely contain himself. He didn't know where he wanted to go, what he thought he should do, only that he needed to race off into the pulsing shroud of rain as fast as he possibly could. He cocked his ears when tires slipped and squealed in the distance. A jagged bolt of lightning peeled the darkness away for an instant. A resounding crack, a rumbling boom, and the alley tumbled back into the blackness of a bottomless pit. Sinking back down between the garage bags and the dumpster, Granddad nudged the terrier closer with his head.

Chapter Thirty One

Headquarters had been established in the kitchen. Stacks of coffee cups were pyramided in the sink and computer graphs of the surrounding neighborhood were strewn across the counter. An underlying sense of controlled chaos, of frenzied purposefulness, pervaded the room. Carmalitta, Miriam, Eleanor, and Joshua were hunched over the kitchen table, studying the maps. Upstairs, Cybernician was posting messages about his grandfather all over the Net. Carol was resting in Mathew's room. After being up most of the night, she needed a quick power-nap if she was going to be any use the rest of the day.

Mathew excused himself and went to the door, not realizing until he got there and reached for the handle that he hadn't heard anyone knock. The doorbell hadn't chimed either. But he knew someone was there. *Dad?* The police? He opened the door carefully.

Beatrice.

She'd left her cart on the grass beside the front porch, her things safely tucked away inside. Despite the deepening cold her hands were bare, but her cheeks were alive with a flush of sun-warmed redness. She peered around the corner past him.

"Well, aren't you going to ask me in, Mathew? For Heaven sakes. You knew I'd show up, didn't you?"

His mouth finally closed. Yes, he thought, I guess I did. He went to take her coat but she waved him away.

"I hardly ever take it off," she reminded him in a whisper.

Mathew recalled how impotent he'd felt the day before when his father had first made his dash to freedom. He frowned, almost angry. "I needed you."

"I know. A lot of people do. That's why I'm here."

"Yesterday. I didn't know how to get in touch with you."

"You didn't try hard enough."

"Where were you?"

Beatrice touched her bracelet. "With a very dear friend."

Mathew's flash of frustration dissipated faster than a terrorist's guilt. He sensed the darkness her eyes were trying to hide. "Your friend. Is he --?"

"She. And yes. Yes she is." Beatrice pretended to be concerned with a strand of hair that dangled over her forehead. "But now it's time to concentrate on finding your father."

Mathew agreed. He didn't even bother asking her how she could have possibly known. She was his fairy godmother, after all. "Any suggestions?"

His fairy godmother shrugged. "I'd check the places a dog would normally go first."

That made sense, since Mathew had considered the same idea himself. But where would that be?

"Parks, children's backyards, senior's homes, alleys."

Mathew winced, remembering the fight in the alley near the Eaton Centre. He hoped his father hadn't spent the night in some destitute back street.

"Why check where seniors live?"

"Because they're an easy mark. Slink around on the back step, whine a bit, look real sad, and you'll get a meal for sure. Dogs and stray cats know it even better than those dishonest home renovators, or the glib con artists who target the aged." Beatrice tapped her nose with her finger. "Keep an eye on the streets nearby, just in case. But I wouldn't count on the fact he's stayed close to home. He left because he was so hurt."

Mathew remembered how distraught the bull was when he'd finally managed to calm him down and brought him back inside.

"I thought we'd go in teams again."

"Makes sense," Beatrice said. "You cover more ground if you're alone, I should know. But two pairs of eyes are always good to have around. Don't leave the teams together, though."

"Why not?"

"It'll breed boredom, more of a lax attitude. Pick a few rendezvous points, and when you trade information, trade partners as well. Everyone will get a fresh perspective, and they'll be more likely to stay focused and alert."

Mathew didn't realize recon planning took so much attention to detail.

"Beatrice?"

"Uh-huh?"

"I'm sorry. About your friend."

"Yes. Thank you. So am I. But it was her time, you see. And in the end she was really quite blessed."

"In what way?"

Mathew's fairy godmother smiled. Her subjects never ceased to amaze her. "And don't worry, Mathew. We'll find your father. I know it."

Nothing Mathew could have heard would have been more reassuring than that. He took a deep breath and showed her the way to the kitchen.

It's odd the way some things are accepted. Like faith. And love.

The conversation didn't falter, it stopped dead. Everyone seemed to look up at once. Later, when they had a moment to talk about it amongst themselves, everyone in the kitchen seemed to have seen something a little different than everyone else. The way everyone in a crowd at a hockey game sees a penalty or a play differently. Or descriptions of an accident. Mathew watched their faces. No one seemed startled. On their toes, but not startled. They appeared more curious than anything else. Curious, and perhaps a little unsettled. Confused. Wondering. But already half-accepting, veiled with a sense of hope.

Mathew didn't know what to say. How would he introduce her? What would he tell them about her? Joshua was aware of who, and what, she was. But the others? Where would he even start? He shouldn't have wasted the time even thinking about it. Beatrice shuffled toward the table, drawing everyone in with her eyes, jingling the bracelet at her side the way a hypnotist swings a pendant.

"I'm Beatrice, Mathew's fairy godmother."

A giggle froze in the back of Carmalitta's throat when she realized the woman was being completely serious. After all, this was the person who'd taken her father to the hospital after the fight in the alley. That's all Mathew had said about her.

"You must be Carmalitta. It's nice to meet you. You helped a friend of mine a long time ago."

Carmalitta paused with uncertainty. What owners would she have counseled that might have known this woman?

"Oh no," Beatrice corrected her. "A patient."

"A patient?"

"Uh-huh. A black lab. Sonny."

"Sonny? You know him?"

"Quite well. He's still doing very nicely. And from what I hear, he doesn't go in the house any more at all."

Carmalitta looked pleased. She had the strangest desire to ask the old woman who told her: the owners, or the lab? She stepped to the side, gracious and smiling.

"This is –"

"Miriam, I know." Beatrice turned to Miriam, apparently staring at the space all around her. "You're a healer of some kind."

"A physiotherapist," Miriam replied, returning Beatrice's smile. She'd grown up in a privileged world where destitute people were generally ignored, but she felt herself drawn to this woman in a way she'd never experienced before. "Why do you think --?"

Beatrice kind of waved to the room as a whole. The power is all around you, generating outwards." She pointed at Miriam's chest. "But there it's most strongest." She turned back to Carmalitta. "You have it to, but it's different, because you have to deal so much with death."

Beatrice stepped closer, gesturing back to Miriam with her eyes, and lowered her voice. "Don't let this one go, Carmalitta. It's about time you two finally bought a place and settled down. The market's just right for it. So don't sell your stock in that transformer company." She winked at Miriam, who flashed her a secret 'thumbs-up' sign from down at her waist.

Without taking a breath, Beatrice moved over to where Eleanor was still standing by the sink. Eleanor hadn't stopped staring at the old woman since she'd come in. Did she recognize something? She wasn't sure. But if she had to trust someone she'd never consciously seen before, this would be that person.

The women locked eyes. Eleanor was searching for something in the older woman's face. "I remember you," Eleanor whispered without looking away. "Mathew told me about you."

Mathew was positive he hadn't mentioned Beatrice by name to anyone other than Joshua.

He'd been vague about the specific details of what happened in the lane way near the Eaton Centre.

"Your husband will be fine," Beatrice told her confidentially. "And never forget how much he loves you."

Eleanor gulped.

"No matter what. Know it in your heart. And he knows you love him too."

Eleanor suddenly felt warm. And calm. "It was a long time ago, wasn't it?" She nodded at Mathew but kept her eyes on Beatrice. "With him. With Mathew."

A statement, not a question. Eleanor nodded at some private thought, her mind whirling. The years tumbled by, the past roared forward. Faster, faster. "Mathew was only about three," she remembered. "It was when he had pneumonia, wasn't it? It was touch and go for a while and I was scared we were going to lose him."

Beatrice smiled.

"He had a fever, I remember that. He woke up sweating in the middle of the night, yelling and kicking the covers away."

"He was a little frightened, too," Beatrice whispered.

"He cried out. I went in again to check on him, and he started telling me all about his fairy godmother, and how she'd come to see him. How she touched his forehead and told him everything was going to be fine."

Eleanor frowned, but she was smiling, too. "And in the morning his fever broke. I knew I'd never forget that night. Forget you. Although –"

"Although?"

Eleanor shook her head. Disbelief is always so strong. Easier, but strong. "When he was ranting and raving, he described you quite clearly. I knew I'd recognize you if we ever met. But I always pictured you much younger, somehow."

We all look a little bit alike, Beatrice thought. She leaned closer and whispered behind her hand. "It wasn't really all that much." Her eyes sparkled.

Mathew felt the kitchen tip on an awkward angle. Had Beatrice really known him when he was a boy?

Joshua's voice poked a hole in the silence. "Thanks for coming to help."

Beatrice turned, her face beaming. "A marauding group of archers in close pursuit couldn't have kept me away," she smiled.

Eleanor was swept away again with a tide of confusion. "You know each other? You've met Joshua?"

Joshua didn't speak. This wasn't the time to mention they'd been walking down the street together when his grandmother drove past with Carlos.

"We've run into each other a couple of times," Beatrice replied. "At the hospital." She winked at Joshua. "We got to know each other quite well, didn't we?"

The boy grinned.

"And I met Carol there as well."

Returning from her rest, Carol rounded the corner from the hallway just as Beatrice was saying her name. Perfect timing, like a magician's sudden appearance.

"Beatrice. How wonderful." Carol gave her a lingering hug. "It's so good of you to help."

"You never know what brings people together, do you?" Beatrice was looking down at her bracelet, but everyone in the room knew she was talking to them. Again, they couldn't quite put it into words when they talked about it later, but it was as if Beatrice spoke to everyone individually while she was talking to them as a whole. She quickly pulled them back from their reflections. "Has your son learned anything yet on the computer, Mathew?"

"Cybernician? No, not yet. He's still trying to get the messages out and follow up on any leads." Mathew turned to the group. "Beatrice thinks we should concentrate our search on a few places in particular. Senior's homes, for instance."

Carmalitta nodded her agreement. "Traditionally they're an oasis for any kind of stray. If we're lucky, someone might have even taken him in last night."

Eleanor teetered for a moment and had to steady herself against the sink. The thought that Lorne had been out the whole night, all on his own without a proper bed to sleep in, stabbed her through the heart. Had he found some unused dog house? Or had he kept moving, afraid to stop and curl up in a doorway, tired and sore and panting for breath?

"That won't help at all, Eleanor."

She looked at the old woman and nodded.

"Well then," Mathew said. "Let's get back to work."

They all began poring over the maps, animatedly pointing things out and making notes. Mathew paused a moment later, thinking he'd heard a hesitant knock at the front door. He dismissed it. But a few seconds later the doorbell chimed and everyone froze. Mathew wondered aloud who it could be. The first thing he thought of again was the police. Beatrice shook her head to confirm *it's not about him*, and the rescue team immediately continued planning their strategy. Mathew volunteered to get the door. The shape on the front porch stepped back as he opened it.

"Hello. You must be Mathew." The young woman extended her hand shyly. Sunglasses, despite the overcast sky, banal, 'nothing' clothes just so she wouldn't be naked, and flesh-tone gloves. "I'm Sheila."

The first thing Mathew thought about was grandchildren. Would they be born with gloves on? But what would that matter, anyway? He stepped forward and hugged her as if she was a long lost daughter that had just returned from being shipwrecked on a desert island.

"I'm sorry about your father. I've come to help."

Mathew pulled back and nodded. "Thank you."

She paused, and appeared to be summoning up another bout of courage. Mathew hadn't stopped to realize how difficult this must be for her until he studied her face.

"Is —"

"Yes, he's here," Mathew smiled. "Come in." He looked into Sheila's eyes and knew what his fairy godmother would have said. That his father had run away on purpose so these two parts of a whole could finally be brought together.

"Mathew? I'd like to wait here."

So he'd have to come out. "Sure. I'll get him."

Forgetting the pain in his side, Mathew bounded up the stairs, then knocked softly on his son's door.

"Yes?"

"I think you should come out for a minute."

"Can't. I'm trying to post some messages on the Net about Granddad, and I keep trying Sheila, but I can't reach her. She's got a program that could help."

"I think you should take a break."

"No time. The faster I get these messages –"

"Cybernician."

Mathew's tone was unnaturally insistent. Cybernician's fingers stopped in mid-air. Had someone already found granddad? Had something happened to him? He straightened his hat, adjusted his glasses, flexed his gloves, and unlocked the bedroom door. Mathew's face didn't look as distressed as he'd expected.

"Come downstairs."

Following his father to the foyer, Cybernician was afraid to ask any questions about his grandfather in case Mathew answered them. He was startled when Mathew paused in the hallway and gestured to the door.

"Someone's here for you."

"Here? For me?" Cybernician shook his head. "This really isn't the time to be fooling around. I should be –"

Mathew pointed his chin at the door the way the spectre of Christmas Future gestures at Scrooge's tombstone, then turned and went back into the kitchen.

Cybernician frowned. He looked down at the space separating him from the front door and then carefully tiptoed over a bed of hot coals. He reached out a trembling hand, his glove moist with perspiration. When he opened the door he almost fainted.

"Hello, Cybernician."

He felt like he'd been pushed from a helicopter. His knees buckled, his mouth fell open, and a flush of warmth rippled through his chest. He tugged his glasses down the bridge of his nose.

Cybernician mouthed her name and she whispered hello once more. He mouthed hers back, surprised he didn't hear his own voice. The mirage took a step closer. Cybernician reached out and touched her arm the way a soldier checks to make sure the motionless figure on the ground is really dead. The illusion was real. He touched his own face, overwhelmed by the emotions and feelings that bombarded his senses. He rocked back and forth on his heels for an instant, then lunged forward and took her in his arms. He whispered her name over and over through his tears.

Sheila was crying, too. She held him like someone pushed through a window who desperately grapples for the ledge, the only thing holding them between this world and the next.

They stood entwined on the front porch until the frantic beat of their hearts finally began to slow. Cybernician would pull back just enough that he could see her face, then cocoon her in his arms again. He couldn't speak but knew he didn't have to. Every nerve in his body was alive, every impulse jumping synapses for joy. Exhausted by the sheer strain of his emotions, Cybernician finally guided her inside. They laughed, they cried, they listened, they talked so fast the room spun. Their questions and answers came faster than political alliances when money was at stake.

The conversation rose and fell in such furious bursts they both had trouble breathing. They had so much to share. But Cybernician knew this wasn't the time. No matter how much he wanted to stand there with her, talking, looking, feeling, Granddad was still out there somewhere, all on his own.

"Come on."

When they went into the kitchen, Sheila nodded at Mathew.

"This is my grandmother, Eleanor."

Sheila held out a gloved hand. Mathew could tell by his mother's eyes that she hadn't expected Sheila to be so attractive. Eleanor let go of her hand and hugged the girl warmly.

Carmalitta stood up, moved around the table, and introduced herself. She hugged Sheila, too. "This is my partner, Miriam." Miriam nodded hello.

"And this," Mathew said, ushering the boy forward, "is Joshua."

Joshua offered a slight bow, then shook her proffered hand. "I'm glad you came. You're all he ever talks about."

He nudged his brother in the ribs. "I liked the way you sang *'Happy Birthday'* at the restaurant."

Cybernician's face went a deeper crimson than Sheila's did. Joshua smiled. He turned around and took Carol's hand. "This is my father's best friend, Carol."

"I've heard so much about you," Sheila said. "I know Cybernician appreciated all you did for Mathew in the hospital."

Carol stared at Mathew, her eyes sparkling. "I don't know who saved who."

"And this –" Cybernician fumbled over the words. He was looking at Beatrice and realized he didn't know who *this* was. Confused, he glanced at Mathew for help.

"Beatrice," Mathew explained. "She's my fairy godmother."

"Your fairy godmother?" Cybernician repeated uncertainly. The second he had the chance he was going to flood every search engine imaginable across the Net for 'fairy godmothers'.

"Well, actually I'm the queen of the fairy godmothers," Beatrice added quietly.

Cybernician exchanged a quizzical glance with Sheila. What difference did it make who she was, as long as she was here to help?

"It makes a big difference."

Startled, he peered intently at her over the rim of his sunglasses.

"Because when you believe in me, you're a little closer to believing in yourself."

"Mathew saw her when he was a little boy," Eleanor said. "She saved him then and she's going to help us now."

Help us now. There was a collective sigh. Everyone's thoughts turned back to Granddad. Eleanor sat down at the table and perused the maps. So did Carmalitta and Miriam.

"Wait," Beatrice suggested. She turned to Cybernician. "Doesn't the other compass leg have something to show us?"

Cybernician almost fainted. How could she possibly have known . . . .? Never mind. Mouth agape, he traded a cryptic stare with Sheila. Maybe she *is* his father's fairy godmother.

"What have you got? The program?" Cybernician's voice warbled pitches like a teenager's, although everyone pretended not to notice. He still couldn't believe he was talking to her in person. *Outside* his room. She nodded. "Sheila's brought something that may help us find Granddad," he said, still staring at Beatrice.

"It's a disc," Sheila said, pulling it from her purse. She started explaining, but Mathew and the others lost her completely after the first few words. Carmalitta admitted she had no idea what the young girl was talking about. Sheila remembered what Cybernician had told her and put everything in non-computer literate terms.

"I've been working on this program for months," Sheila explained.

"She first started developing it because of all the Alzheimer patients she heard about that kept roaming off," Cybernician interjected proudly.

Sheila nodded. "They're always wandering away. Very few of them even realize they're missing. Many can't remember their name, where they live, or how to get in touch with their family. Even when someone's recognized and you approach them, you're never sure how they'll react because you can't be certain they know who they are themselves. Posters, pictures placed in the newspapers, and things like that help of course, but it's cumbersome and time consuming. I knew we needed something better."

"What have you got?" Eleanor wondered.

Sheila palmed the disc between her hands. "This will give everyone on-line information about your father. Vital statistics like height, weight, eye color, hair, that sort of thing. What he was wearing when he left."

There was an awkward silence.

"But that's not all. It also contains his medical history and psychological data as well. That'll help point people to where he might have gone. I've digitized a lot of photographs, too. Once the information's downloaded, we'll have a whole network of interconnected computers – I mean people – looking for him. It's not unlike people putting up posters on telephone poles and things like that, only it's much faster, easier, and has a far greater reach. We should be able to find him in no time at all."

She looked around hopefully.

Carmalitta glanced at her grandmother. "What about his behavioral symptomology?" she asked as delicately as she could.

"That's all here too," Sheila replied. "And the best thing is, all the information can be updated with a key stroke. Everyone looking for him will understand who, and what, they're searching for."

"Can you download the information into the police files?" Joshua asked.

Sheila said she could. "And I can access their data base as well. If it's information you need, we've got it." She waved the disc in the air.

"And the system works?" Eleanor asked hopefully.

"There's always intangibles," Sheila admitted. "But we've used the program successfully a number of times. There are still a few bugs, but we're getting there."

Mathew slipped his arm around Carol's waist. "When can you get started?" He noticed a tear in the corner of Eleanor's eye.

"As soon as Cybernician takes me upstairs to his room." They both blushed again. "To his computer," Sheila added quickly.

Cybernician had already started towards the stairs. He stopped after a hurried step, reached out tentatively, and touched Sheila's arm. She was still there. His heart missed a beat, he smiled, then quickly ushered her up to his room. It felt exactly like he dreamed it would, like he'd done it a thousand times already.

***

The brainstorming continued for another half an hour. Mathew knew they needed more time, but time was a luxury they didn't have. Every minute inside was sixty seconds that his father was wandering the streets alone. He drew a few last boxes of lines over part of his own map, and then gathered up the charts and street guides. He didn't bother trying to fold them together properly because he knew he couldn't get them back into their little rectangles if he tried. He rechecked the notes on his clipboard and called out the assignments and pairings.

"Carmalitta and Miriam, you'll take the area directly north, up to Bloor Street."

They nodded and gathered up some extra posters.

"Eleanor, you should go with Carol. Check all the places Mom and Dad have gone in the past. Friends, their favourite stores, that sort of thing."

Carol took his hand, kissed him on the cheek, then grabbed her car keys from the counter.

"Joshua, you're with Beatrice. Focus on the backyards nearby. And the park, if you have time."

"You're going on your own?" Beatrice asked.

Mathew said yes and checked his watch. "How about meeting at eleven?"

"Where?" Carmalitta asked.

Mathew winked at Beatrice. "*Eggspress*. We'll change assignments then."

There were hurried murmurs of assent as the tactical teams collected up maps, coffee cups, fact sheets, and street guides.

"Don't forget to keep checking in with Cybernician. He'll be manning the base and can update you on everything. Questions?"

"What do we do if we find him?" Miriam asked.

"*When* we find him," Beatrice corrected.

"Get in touch immediately with everyone else," Mathew reasoned. "And get Carmalitta there as soon as you can. She'll be able to reach him if anyone can."

Carmalitta nodded. "It's unusual for him to stay in his transformation shape for so long, so if you see him, be very careful what you do and say."

Eleanor looked unsettled. "Should we try to get him to change into – into something more manageable?"

"No, definitely not." Carmalitta was adamant. "It would be extremely risky from a psychophysical point of view, especially if he's been acting out as a dog for this extended period of time."

There was a moment's silence. Everyone seemed to be picturing what it was they were likely to encounter and no one wanted to speak. Beatrice's bracelet jingled like wind chimes. She'd backed away from the others and was quietly barking out orders into her phone.

"Who was that?" Mathew asked when the phone disappeared back into the folds of her coat.

"My own team," Beatrice whispered. She waved Mathew's question into silence. "Computers are a little complicated for me so I have my own underground network instead. Street people. Beggars, squeegee kids, the homeless, the raving lunatics, all the people with nowhere to go or no one to take care of them. They're everywhere, and they're more important than most people ever stop to realize. They can be mobilized in a moment for something like this. It's my Alzheimer's network."

Eleanor wiped her eyes and whispered *thank you*.

Mathew rechecked his watch. "Let's go."

The teams dispersed. The morning clouds had thickened. In the last hour, the sky darkened another shade and a breeze that was neither warm nor cold slithered through the street like a hungry iguana. Mathew hoped the rain would hold off and that the temperature wouldn't drop any more. His father certainly wasn't dressed for the cold.

Just as everyone was getting into their respective vehicles, an orange and black cab careened around the corner and jolted to a rocking stop at the end of the driveway. The rear door popped open, and as the driver ran around behind the car and jettisoned a small suitcase onto the sidewalk, a woman stepped gingerly out from the back seat.

Lydia.

Mathew's heart stopped. He looked at Carol, who was just revving the engine to life. Lydia waved, hand aloft like a queen, and picked up her luggage. She seemed confused, like she was trying to take in everything at once: the house, how Mathew looked, the trees that hadn't been bare the last time she was here, Carmalitta running down the driveway, the battered old shopping cart on the grass. She smiled uneasily and took a few baby steps forward. Carol drove past her as Lydia reached the edge of the sidewalk. Lydia frowned but waved again.

"Lydia." Mathew stepped forward and took her bag. "I didn't know you were coming home."

For a second he stood still in front of her, the space separating them a pulsing field of energy, like two magnets turned with their negatives toward each other. It only took a moment to become awkward. He finally leaned closer and kissed her on the cheek.

She did the same to him. "I wanted to help with your father."

"Thanks."

"Any news yet?"

He shook his head.

"I know you'll find him."

"I hope so."

Lydia pulled back and looked him up and down. "How are you coping?"

"Pretty good."

"I'm glad." She reached out and delicately touched his side. "And you're recovering nicely?"

Another nod. Lydia chewed on what she wanted to say. "Mathew, I wanted to come back when you were in the hospital. I really did. But there was just so much going on, and I knew it was the one big chance I've been waiting for, and –"

He stopped her with a finger to her lips. "It's okay, Lydia. I understand."

"Joshua kept telling me you were fine, that everything was okay."

"Really, it's all right, Lydia."

She smiled uncomfortably. "I couldn't stay away now, though."

Mathew didn't know what to say.

"Mathew – I hope I'm not too late."

"No, we're just starting out again. We're going in teams."

"I didn't mean that." She looked down at her suitcase. "I mean with us."

Mathew smiled sadly. His was beginning to feel that his heart couldn't take much more. He leaned closer and gave her a hug.

Lydia wanted to go on, to say all the things she'd rehearsed on the flight home, to unleash the torrent of feelings and confessions and fears she'd dammed up for so long. But she looked at Mathew's face and plugged the cracks as best as she could. "Who was that with Mother? The woman who drove off in the car?"

Mathew returned her stare. He didn't want to hurt her or make her unhappy in the least. He'd never lied to her and he wasn't going to start now.

"Carol."

"Carol?" The face seemed oddly familiar. Lydia searched her memory for some association to the name.

"She came to help me find Dad."

When Lydia placed the face her heart skipped a beat. "Carol? From school?"

She knew it was before Mathew answered. And she remembered what Carol had always meant to her husband. She steadied her legs but couldn't stop her stomach from crashing to the ground. She bit at the corner of her lip.

"We met again when I was in the hospital. Lydia –"

It was her turn to stop his thoughts with an upheld hand, and she tried to sound brave. "Come inside, Mathew. Tell me what I can do to help."

You already have, he thought. Mathew took his wife's arm and guided her up the driveway, but as soon as they started to move he felt her steps falter. The next shock was just settling in. Mathew looked into her eyes: she had the glazed appearance of someone who's fallen through the looking glass and still has the shards in her face. Carol was driving away with Eleanor. Fine. But Cybernician was actually *outside,* on the porch. With a *woman.* Lydia had seen Sheila's picture on a screen saver once and recognized the young girl immediately. But what was she doing here? It was what she'd always hoped for but it still seemed oddly disquieting. She went to speak but Sheila was already going back inside.

Cybernician outside. But just as that thought was slowly becoming acceptable, Lydia's eyes settled on Joshua. She pointed a quivering arm toward the child. He was standing beside the porch with a disease-infested *bag lady.* Lydia looked up at Mathew and started to swoon.

He reached an arm protectively around her waist. "It's all right, Lydia. Everything's under control."

"Control?" She tried to sneer, but the disgusting old woman cloaked in rags was staring right at her.

Mathew tried to explain everything as quickly and as gently as he could as the others hurriedly took up their assignments. But time was an issue and he was a little more vague in spots than he would have liked to have been. Lydia listened as attentively as she could without taking her eyes off the old woman. She tried to keep up with what Mathew was saying, but she felt like she was skydiving without a parachute. Every time he excitedly explained something else, Lydia thought she'd jumped out and freefell again. Over the course of the next few frenetic moments, Lydia took more dives than a South American soccer player. When Mathew finally stopped to take a breath, Lydia had one question in particular that she needed answered. Carol could wait. She actually expected Carol, or someone quite like her. But she couldn't understand what Mathew was saying about the old woman standing by the shopping cart with her arm around Joshua.

"She's your fairy godmother?"

Mathew nodded. "Actually, she's the queen of the fairy godmothers."

"I see." Lydia looked at her husband's face. Perhaps he was still on some type of medication for his stomach surgery. Lydia remembered some of the things she'd read about from people who'd had near death experiences. Maybe Mathew had come too close to the other side and the old woman was a way of dealing with his fear.

Mathew saw the trepidation in her eyes. "I know it's hard to understand, Lydia. I didn't at first either." He turned and glanced back at Beatrice. "But I do now."

"Your fairy godmother," Lydia said quietly. She immediately thought about Raphael. Certainly he could use something like this for one of his shows.

"We don't have time to waste," Mathew told her. "So —"

The front door opened and Sheila stepped back out onto the porch.

"Good, you're still here Mathew. The police just called. They want you to come in. Hi Lydia." She handed him some papers. "Cybernician just updated these pictures. Maybe you should take enough so the police can circulate them, too, while I'm installing the program."

"Sure." He turned to Beatrice. "You and Joshua go on. I'll take Lydia to the station and meet you as soon as I can."

"We'll be somewhere on the block," Beatrice said. She winked at Lydia.

"I'll find you," Mathew said. "Come on Lydia. I'll fill in as much as I can on the way."

Fill me in, Lydia thought? *Only if you can stop me leaking first.*

***

The first thing Granddad realized when his eyes fluttered open was that he had to pee very badly. He yawned, licked his lips, rolled and staggered to his feet, then stretched forward so his head was on the ground and his rear was pressed high into the air. The little terrier was gone. Granddad trotted over to the other side of the dumpster and urinated on the garbage bags. He stopped in mid-flow, moved over, and sprayed another couple of stacks, just to be sure. When he ambled back to the make-shift den, he remembered the second thing he'd realized as he woke but had forgotten immediately because he had to pee so badly. The scent was unmistakable: fresh baked bagel and cream cheese. He shoved his paw under a piece of cardboard and dragged the enticing thing out. It was the top half. A human's mouth imprint marked one edge, and he knew at once it had already been gnawed in half by a dog. He licked his lips. The terrier was certainly street-wise and knew how to eat.

He was almost finished breakfast when the other dog trotted back up the alley. Granddad jumped up, whined, offered a few fake, playful growls, then licked the terrier's privates in thanks for the bagel. The little dog's tail wagged happily.

Chapter Thirty-two

Lydia was a little more threatened by the police station than she thought she'd be, since everything seemed more urgent when it was real. There was a different woman at the front desk, but Mathew was directed to the same bench he'd sat on the day before. The prostitutes held overnight were just leaving but Mathew didn't notice. His hands were shaking. He'd already signed all the forms, so he was worried about what the police might have wanted. Had they found his father? Was he all right?

He didn't have long to wait. Detective Larken called and beckoned him over from an adjacent doorway. "Thanks for coming in."

"I brought these new bulletins," Mathew said. "And some extra fact sheets."

Detective Larken shuffled them all together. "Thanks." He looked at Lydia.

"This is my wife. Lydia."

Larken took her hand. Did she know about the woman from yesterday? "I need your help, sir."

"But I thought I signed all the paperwork yesterday. You said that if –"

Mathew stopped when he looked into Larken's eyes.

"We've located someone who fits the description of your father," the police officer said carefully. "We need to know if it's him."

Mathew frowned. Larken quietly paraphrased what he meant. "We need someone for identification."

"Where is he?" Mathew asked excitedly. He peered into the room behind the officer's back. Nothing. "Does he know we're here? Can we see him?"

Larken sighed. This was never easy. "He's downstairs."

Mathew started rising. "Well let's go then. Has he eaten? Is he --?"

Lydia reached over and took Mathew's arm. She remembered all the police scenes she'd done, the mutilated bodies she'd portrayed, motionless on the metal gurney, the top of the "y" incision just visible beneath the white sheet. "Mathew, the morgue is in the basement."

His legs buckled but he managed to regain his balance before he stumbled back down onto the bench. The room was spinning out of control.

"We found him early this morning," Detective Larken said softly. He studied Mathew's eyes. "Do you think you're up for this?"

Mathew thought about all the times he'd seen someone identify a body on television or in the movies. The little curtained room, the metal table, the sheet pulled back just enough so you could see the person's face. He took a deep breath, and nodded, but he knew he could never really be ready.

Larken guided them downstairs. Two flights, but the longest descent Mathew had ever taken in his life. They stopped in front of a screened off window at the far end of the hall and a white-coated technician introduced himself. Mathew didn't hear his name. The man gave his customary speech about what to expect, although he knew as well as anybody else that nothing can prepare you for the moment when you first look into the dead person's eyelids.

Mathew stepped closer and clutched Lydia's arm as tightly as he could. The technician knocked on the window and the curtains parted. The little room looked too clean, too white, to have anything to do with death. Someone else in the room waited awkwardly for a second and then draped the sheet back from the body's face.

Mathew gulped and leaned forward against the glass. He looked again. And again. He mumbled something incoherent.

"Pardon, sir?"

"That's not my father," Mathew whispered. He wasn't sure why he was crying. Lydia patiently struggled to pry his fingers away from her arm. She leaned closer and hugged him until he stopped shaking.

"Are you sure?"

"Positive." Mathew looked again. It wasn't Dad. But it was someone else's father, someone who was probably sitting at home worried sick about where he might have been, someone walking the streets like he'd done and hopelessly fearing the worst.

The technician drew the sheet back and the curtains winched closed. Mathew couldn't stop thinking about all the lonely people he saw every day in the streets, the doorways, the edges of the back alleys. He felt Larken's hand on his shoulder.

"Thank you. We had to be sure. I know things like this are quite difficult, so I didn't want to say anything on the phone."

Mathew nodded and exhaled a long, slow breath.

"So. Nothing yet?" The officer took out his little notepad.

Mathew shook his head.

"We'll get right on it, don't worry. I'm sure we'll find him soon."

That's what he said yesterday, Mathew thought. He kept picturing the body on the metal table and for some strange reason couldn't help worrying that it might be cold. Couldn't they cover it up with something else? A warm blanket or something?

"Are you all right, sir?"

Mathew surfaced from the quicksand. "Yes."

Larken ushered them back upstairs. "Thanks again for the photos and updates. I'll get everything circulated right away. Stay in touch, okay?"

Mathew tried to smile and shook the officer's hand. Larken had the soft grip of a large man who's always worried about his own strength.

"Do you mind driving?" Mathew asked Lydia when they reached the car.

"Of course."

Slipped down into the passenger's seat, Mathew blinked repeatedly, but he couldn't stop everything from looking fuzzy and distorted. Without any prompting he started his story again as soon as Lydia pulled out of the parking lot, filling in as many blanks as he could remember. Beatrice at the laundromat and the mall. The fight in the alley. Joshua's recent memories and changes. Carlos, and Dad tearing up the backyard as a bull.

Carol at the hospital. The incredible lightness he'd felt when the butterflies settled on his head and shoulders. How sad he'd been that he hadn't been able to get closer to Lydia.

When they reached home, they circled the neighboring blocks twice before they finally saw Beatrice and Joshua. They rounded a corner just as Joshua was climbing over the chain-link fence in front of the MacGreggors. The MacGreggors used to have Eleanor and Lorne over at least twice a month for euchre tournaments before the stroke, although they hadn't seen them now in ages. Why is it that when someone dies the one who's left isn't invited out as much as they were before? The MacGreggors had a dog so it was worth a try, but Mathew could tell by Joshua's face that the boy's search had been fruitless.

Lydia pulled to a stop beside the curb.

"Anything?" Mathew asked, getting out.

Beatrice shook her head. "We've checked most of the houses Joshua says his grandparents frequented in the area, but we haven't caught a glimpse of him yet."

Joshua took his father's hand. "What happened at the police station?"

Mathew told him. Joshua stared up sadly at Beatrice. "Someone's always lost, aren't they?"

"But not for long," she replied gently.

"Well," Mathew wondered. "Where to now?"

Beatrice checked her watch. Lydia couldn't picture her in the alley whirling the *nanchuka* sticks.

"It's not time to meet up with the others yet, so maybe we can –"

A loud shrill ring cut him off.

"Excuse me," Beatrice said, checking the inside of her coat. She turned away and flicked her phone open. Joshua silenced Lydia's expected question with an *of course she carries a phone* kind of shrug.

Beatrice listened intently. "I see."

Silence.

"Yes. I'm on my way. Pull back and take the perimeter. Under no condition should he be approached, unless there's a problem. Yes. In a few minutes."

Joshua and Lydia couldn't tell anything from her expression and waited impatiently for her to finish.

"Well?" Lydia asked as soon as Beatrice snapped the phone shut.

"He's been spotted a couple of times. One of my subjects followed him to the U.N."

Lydia looked puzzled. "The U.N? That's in New York, isn't it?"

"Yes. But I don't mean that one. I mean Toronto's multicultural hub. The subway station at Yonge and Bloor. We probably have more countries represented there than anywhere else in the world."

"I see," Lydia replied. But she really didn't. She hadn't been down in the subway since high school. Back then, no one was ever pushed out onto the tracks, the trains weren't marred with graffiti and the gangs didn't battle for turf in the underground labyrinth. "Well, let's go then."

Beatrice stopped her with a glance. "I think I better go alone."

"For Heaven's sake, why?"

"He might feel unsettled by a lot of attention."

"We could stay back and wait for you at the entrance or something," Mathew offered.

Beatrice shook her head. "He might not have changed yet," she whispered. "It might be safer if I did this one on one."

Mathew reluctantly agreed but his eyes betrayed his concern.

"Why don't you take Joshua and Lydia home with you," Beatrice said.

"But how will you and he –"

"Don't worry about us, we'll be fine."

"We'll call the others," Joshua said, taking Beatrice's hand.

"Good. Have them meet us at home."

Lydia was still uncertain. "But what if –"

"I'll call you if I need any help. I promise."

Mathew looked at Lydia. "You can't get anything more reliable than a fairy godmother's promise."

"No, I guess not," Lydia agreed. Although she was still a little uneasy about the whole fairy godmother stuff.

"We'll be back before you know it," Beatrice said. She laid a finger alongside the bridge of her nose. "Go home, and next time don't take the Gardiner home, remember."

Mathew smiled.

"Why can't we take the Gardiner?" Lydia wondered.

"Don't ask," Mathew said, winking at Beatrice. "We'll see you back at the house. Good luck."

Beatrice shuffled off along the street. She paused just long enough to call back over her shoulder.

"Oh, Mathew. You should know by now that luck has nothing to do with it at all."

***

Even though it was one of the only places she could move around without drawing unwarranted attention, Beatrice had never liked the subway. The air was thick with an unventilated dankness that made her wheeze. The crushing throng of people was always moving, and the interconnected tunnels were plagued by a droning, numbing hum that infected everything, like the oppressive humidity that follows a summer storm. The ubiquitous smells curdled her nostrils: the old women's' thick colognes, the pungent halos of dope smoke that clung to the high-schoolers, the sweat from the factory workers, the pristine freshness of the newly anointed who were secretly meeting someone on the way home, and the body odor from the transients strewn about the floor.

As she stepped off the escalator, a train rattled out of one of the tunnels then jerked to a screeching stop in a hissing shower of sparks. A heated wind followed it through the cavern, scattering dirt and debris across the platform. Beatrice couldn't see Mathew's father right away, but she sensed he was there. Bulldozing her way through the crowd, she smiled broadly when she finally saw him.

Lorne, not a dog. He'd changed back. Crumpled down against the wall, he was sitting alone at the farthest end of the station. Framed by the blackness of the tunnel, his knees were drawn up to his chest and he was staring straight ahead at one of the huge billboards that broke up the monotony of the walls.

No, Beatrice realized, he wasn't alone. The terrier was with him, cradled in his lap and scrunched up under his jacket so that just his head was poking out. He looked like the little alien that ruptures out of John Hurt's chest during the dinner scene just when Sigourney Weaver and the rest of the crew think the horror is finally over.

It took Beatrice several minutes to maneuver to where he was sitting because the station was thick with commuters and her crown didn't mean as much down in the bowels of the city as it did up on the street. Beatrice huffed and shoved her way over to his side then slunk down the wall beside him. After a few tentative sniffs, the little terrier feverishly struggled to lick Beatrice's face and neck. He couldn't settle down until she scratched his chest and tucked him back inside Lorne's jacket.

Silently, Beatrice shifted forward and stared into the mouth of the tunnel. Distant maintenance lights pricked the darkness. She looked back along the platform. The throng of impatient commuters was so dense it was difficult to distinguish faces. Beatrice watched the people jostle for position, pushing forward, oozing and squeezing into opened gaps the way an oil slick creeps up a beach. The tide surged and thickened with every blast of the warning whistle.

"Everyone has been very worried about you. They've hardly had a moment's rest since yesterday."

The old man stared straight ahead. Beatrice reached over and rubbed the terrier's ears.

"Did you take good care of him?"

The little dog wagged his tail against Lorne's chest. *Thumpity thumpity thumpity.*

"Good. I'm glad you didn't let him stay alone. Thank you for your help." She leaned down closer and whispered to the terrier. "He might not have made it without you."

The terrier whimpered and licked her hand. Another incoming train ground to a stop and its thick metal doors winced open. When the people inside were expunged out onto the platform they were immediately swallowed up by the aggressive mass that festered around the doors. A staccato pulse of whistle cries ripped through the tunnel, the doors slammed closed, and the cars lurched ahead. The unsettled crowd inside toppled backwards, then rocked from side to side as the train picked up speed and disappeared.

"Eleanor is especially upset. She understands how you feel, believe me. But she didn't mean to hurt you, just like you never meant the stroke to hurt her."

Lorne studied some esoteric sign hidden in the poster.

"She needs you, Lorne. She really does. You have to try. If not for yourself, then for her."

Beatrice's soft urgings were abruptly drowned out by a sudden commotion at the other end of the station. Two or three screams, then whistles, shouts, raised voices, frenetic movement, and the thundering roll of rubber shoes pounding against the concrete floor. Beatrice craned her neck forward, carefully balancing her crown. Transit security and several police officers were dragging a disheveled man away. Eyes wide and blood seeping from the corner of his mouth, he jerked and writhed against his captors like a trout dangling from a fisherman's line, kicking his feet out at anything he could reach. The news burned through the anxious crowd like a brush fire through a parched forest. He'd run up behind a young girl and tried to push her onto the tracks for no apparent reason whatsoever. Beatrice fingered one of the keepsakes on her bracelet and shook her head.

"It's horrible, isn't it? The unexpected violence. The tragedy of its randomness, its meaninglessness." She turned to Lorne. "But you can never tell how close you are to the things that separate you from this world and the next, can you?"

The old man flinched.

Beatrice leaned closer and shared a secret. "He actually saved her though, you know."

Lorne's eyes narrowed.

"Oh yes." Beatrice watched the paramedics wheel the girl away on a gurney. "Look at the light all around her. It's different than the one in the alley last night, isn't it? She's been thinking about how lost she is, how meaningless her life has been for quite a while, I can tell. But that push, that one little shove right out into the face of nothingness made her realize she really wants to live. She's going to be just fine now."

Beatrice reached over and smoothed Lorne's wisps of grey hair across his head. "And so are you."

Another train rumbled into the station on the track behind them. Beatrice noticed that everyone was staying far back from the yellow warning lines near the edge of the platform now, although two boys kept daring each other closer.

"Eleanor has always loved you. You must know that."

The terrier nuzzled his friend's throat.

"She's having a hard time coping without you. You're there, but you're not there, and I know she finds that difficult to deal with. I know you understand how that feels, too."

Beatrice tugged her coat open and fanned some of the heat away with her collar. "People often think they need things they really don't. And they often need the things they don't think about."

She reached down into the folds of a half-torn pocket. She mumbled *my, what's this* as she pulled a cookie out and offered it to the terrier. The dog took it gently and disappeared deeper into Lorne's jacket like a kangaroo diving into its mother's pouch. Beatrice looked up and down the platform. Darkness at both ends with a few moments of light in the middle that keeps them apart. How poetic.

"If you can't forgive her, you've never really loved her as much as you thought."

She felt him stir.

"You have to try harder. For you, and for her. I know it hurts and I know how frustrating it can be. But you have to try Lorne, because that's all you have left. There isn't anything else."

The terrier smacked his lips and got another cookie for his trouble. The two trains that had been backed up because of the emergency a few minutes before clattered into the station. Bored passengers traded places with fresh pall bearers.

"Go to her, Lorne. She needs you."

The terrier looked up imploringly but Beatrice shrugged. "I don't have any more." He snuggled back down into his companion's side.

"Come back." Beatrice whispered it again like a spell. "Come back."

Lorne's frown melted. Beatrice laid a hand over his heart. "First here," she said softly, staring into his eyes. She pointed up at the ceiling. "Then there."

Mathew's father gulped.

"Think of all the things that have come before, and all the things that can happen again."

Lorne looked down at the terrier and almost smiled.

"Come. It's time to go."

Beatrice rose with the grace of a ballerina, but no one close by seemed to notice. She steadied her crown, reached down, and helped Lorne slowly to his feet. His bones creaked obscenely. He leaned against the wall for a moment while fresh surges of blood reawakened the muscles in his legs. He smelled of alley. He wrapped his arms around the terrier and shuffled along the platform. Beatrice took his elbow and guided him through the crowd. No one touched them or stayed in their way, and the people that suddenly moved to let them by seemed surprised by their own behavior when they passed. Lorne and Beatrice appeared to have a little pathway all to themselves. When Lorne stepped gingerly onto the escalator he cocked his head from side to side. Beatrice knew he was listening to the light, ethereal song that her bracelet chimed.

Chapter Thirty-three

Everyone was festered in the driveway. Cybernician and Sheila were sitting with their backs against the front door, hats tipped forward and knees drawn up to their chests like migrant workers taking a siesta. Mathew was pacing up and down the driveway while Carol tried to keep Eleanor calm. It was Joshua that saw them round the corner first.

"Look Dad. There they are!"

Eleanor's breath caught. She cupped her hands over her face and mouthed a hurried prayer. Mathew stopped pacing and looked up. He saw his father clearly, but part of his body was occluded by a soft, pulsing light. When he came a little closer, he realized the light was Beatrice.

Crying, Eleanor rushed down the driveway and along the street to meet him. She flung her arms around his neck and buried her face against his chest. Sobbing and choking on excited breaths, she reached over and hugged Beatrice to her side.

"Thank you," she whispered through her tears. "Thank you so much. For everything."

Beatrice smiled and took Mathew's hand as he ran up to meet them. She held a finger up to her lips.

"He found me," she whispered behind a wink.

Eleanor finally let her husband go and Joshua took her place.

"I missed you Granddad. Lots and lots." He felt the terrier move against his cheek. "Look," he cried. "Granddad's got an *uppypa*."

"A puppy?" Eleanor said, turning back. She couldn't believe she hadn't felt it when she was hugging him so tightly. She gasped and quickly covered her mouth.

"It's all right," Beatrice said gently. "You can say it."

Mathew peered over into his father's jacket. The terrier peeked out, unsure of what all the fuss was about. Eleanor was laughing and crying at the same time. She heard someone running up the street behind them.

"What is it, Gram?" Carmalitta called.

Eleanor was in tears. "He's got a little puppy. And I said *'puppy'* and nothing happened. And –"

"Eleanor?"

She turned and looked at Mathew. "Yes?"

Mathew shrugged and shook his head. "I didn't say anything."

Eleanor was rigidly still. "I heard you call me."

Beatrice smiled and Granddad whispered once more. "Eleanor. Can I keep him?"

Only the little terrier's head poked out of his jacket. Eleanor couldn't move. She looked at her husband, at Mathew, then Beatrice. She couldn't believe what she'd heard.

"Can I keep him?" Granddad breathed again. His throat was sore and a little scratchy, but that would pass with use.

Eleanor's eyes filled with tears and Carmalitta caught her just before she collapsed. Eleanor struggled to regain her balance as the world spun out of control beneath her feet. She choked on her sobs and hugged Lorne as hard as she could. Trembling, barely able to stand, she rocked back and forth against her husband's chest as the terrier licked the tears from her cheeks.

***

Dinner was a rather tumultuous affair, the noise deafening, because it's always such a wondrous time when someone who's lost is found. It was the camaraderie of warfare. If there was even a brief lull in the conversation, Mathew didn't notice it. The only time he tensed uncomfortably was when Lydia, after a moment's hesitation, sat in the last available seat next to Carol. But it wasn't long before the women were adding their own fuel to the bonfire of anecdotes, reminiscences, and laughter.

Eleanor's face was flushed with contentment. She rarely left her husband's side, and made a deliberate show of leaning closer every time he tentatively tried to mouth a few words or ask a question. Much to Joshua's delight, the little terrier

- 424 -

scrambled beneath the chairs, eagerly accepting whatever was surreptitiously offered from above. Dinner, talk, wine, dessert, more wine, and coffee. And Mathew's father answering as many questions as he could with a soft *yes* or shake of his head.

Mathew didn't want the evening to end, and he was saddened when Carmalitta leaned over and whispered she had to leave.

"I'm staying at Miriam's," she said. "Now that Granddad's fine, we're going to go over the condominium designs and get our offer all ready for tomorrow."

Mathew nodded, and held his daughter's hand. "And Joshua?"

"I thought we'd have him for an overnight on the weekend. We've got an awful lot to talk about."

Carmalitta kissed everyone good night and gave her grandfather a long, lingering hug she was reluctant to let go. She kissed Beatrice on the cheek and playfully pushed Cybernician's hat down over his eyes.

"Dad," Cybernician began, readjusting his hat.

Mathew cut him off and smiled. "Of course Sheila can stay."

He couldn't tell which of them blushed a deeper red. Eleanor whispered *thank you* through fresh tears and watched them go upstairs, arm in arm, head to head.

When Carol started tidying up the dishes, Eleanor went into the kitchen to help. She took Lorne with her because she didn't want to let him out of her sight. Beatrice asked Joshua if she could have a private word with him in the living room. He nodded and followed her down the hall. Mathew, finishing his wine, struggled to calm his heart and the tears he felt welling behind his eyes.

"I'm glad everything's turned out so well," Lydia said. She glanced around the dining room and had trouble remembering the last time she'd eaten in here.

"I should be heading back tonight," she continued quietly, checking her watch.

"You don't have to."

She looked at the empty chair beside her. "Yes, I do."

Silence.

"Lydia –"

She held up her hand and struggled with her own tears. "We'll talk later. Okay?"

Mathew nodded and reached over for her hand. He'd forgotten how small Lydia's wrists had always seemed.

"Lydia –"

But she stopped him again. "It's no one's fault, Mathew. I've always loved you and I always will."

Mathew kissed her fingers.

"But I really do have to go. We'll sit down and have a nice long talk when I get back. Just the two of us."

"Are you sure?"

She nodded.

"Will you be all right?"

"I'm going to try," Lydia smiled faintly. "And as I said, I've got to get back. Frank got me a new part in a continuing series, so it'll keep me really busy." Her head and heart pounding, she was giving one of the strongest performances she'd ever given in her life.

"That's great. What is it?"

Caught off guard in the lie, Lydia pretended to search her memory. "A soap, but I really can't recall its name. It's brand new, and destined for the top. Ever since the Raphael thing I've been getting so many offers I can't keep up with them all. Oh, and those shows I did with him will be aired next month. I know you don't like those kinds of talk shows, Mathew –"

"I wouldn't miss it for the world, Lydia."

Lydia hoped Mathew couldn't hear her heart pounding against her chest.

"You know what? I can tape it. Your first really big shot at everything you've ever wanted to do. I'm so proud of you, Lydia. So proud."

Lydia blinked away the tears. No acting now. "Thank you." She sat back, released Mathew's hand, and desperately tried to control her breathing. A half smile.

"Perhaps you'd call me a taxi while I go upstairs and throw some things together."

"Sure. Can I help?"

"Thank you, no. But perhaps –"

"Yes?"

"Perhaps you'd come outside and wait with me."

Mathew's chest tightened painfully. "Of course," he whispered.

"I'll just go in and talk to Joshua for a minute first."

Mathew shuddered as Lydia pushed the French doors open and the woman that he'd shared so much of his life with walked down the hall toward the family room for the last time.

***

They were standing shoulder to shoulder down at the end of the driveway when the taxi veered around the corner. Lydia tugged Mathew's collar up more snugly over his throat, then fixed his scarf. Mathew didn't know what to say. Neither did Lydia, so they just stood quietly together, arms wrapped around each other, their faces touching, their bodies shivering from everything else except the cold.

The taxi rolled to a stop by the curb and Mathew put Lydia's bag in the trunk. Trying to hide the tears, he turned and shuffled slowly back toward the house. The stab wounds were nothing compared to this pain. The front door opened and Beatrice hurried down the driveway past him.

"Lydia," she called. "I wanted to say goodbye." She took Lydia's hands between her own.

"That was a very nice thing to do, Lydia. I know it was hard."

Lydia looked puzzled.

"What you said to Mathew."

"But you were in the other room. How did you hear –" Lydia didn't bother finishing the question. She tried to smile. "Who knows? It could happen. I have to stay positive, you know." She sniffed back a tear.

"He still loves you very much, Lydia. And you shared a world of memories. Don't ever forget that."

"Yes. Yes I know." Lydia looked past her and up at the house. "And I know I'll always love him."

"We can't always love the people we need to most in the way they need us to," Beatrice whispered.

Lydia's eyes sparkled with tears. "And Joshua?"

Beatrice smiled. "He'll be fine. He'll be flying out to see you work before you know it. She touched her bracelet. I can feel it right here." She let go of Lydia's hands and struggled with one of the clasps on the charms.

"My fingers are a little thicker than they used to be," she admitted with a blush. The clasp finally flicked open and she pried one of the little ornaments loose. It was a butterfly. She studied it thoughtfully for a moment then gave it to Lydia.

Lydia shook her head and started backing away. "Oh no, I couldn't."

But Beatrice was already pressing it into her hand and closing her fingers around it. Lydia looked into the old woman's eyes and knew there was no point in protesting.

"Thank you."

And then Lydia did something she never would have done before. She kissed Beatrice warmly on each cheek. Beatrice held the door as she climbed into the back of the cab. Lydia looked wistfully up at the house again.

"Another time," Beatrice said softly. Lydia nodded.

"And that's for you."

Lydia was just about to ask what Beatrice was talking about when her phone rang. She quickly scrounged through her purse.

"Yes? Frank? Oh, hello? What? What? They want me for *what* part? Really! Oh my God, of course I can!"

She was still speaking as the taxi spun away from the curb. Lydia tried to get him to stop but the taxi's tires were already peeling asphalt from the street and shooting little sparks of stones in its wake. Tears in her eyes, she scrambled up into the rear window and waved frantically as Beatrice slowly disappeared into a little dot in the distance. Lydia would have sworn that little dot was glowing.

***

Mathew waited until the taxi careened around the corner and then walked back down the driveway. Standing beside Beatrice, he looked up at the sky. "It's going to team."

Beatrice held up a finger to the wind. "Not for a while."

"Beatrice?"

"Uh-huh?"

"I don't know what to say."

"Then don't say anything. Too many people speak before they think."

"I want to thank you for everything you've done."

"You already have."

Mathew looked puzzled.

"It's hard working on your own. You've helped me bring a lot of people together, Mathew. And you've been at my side when I've steered them toward fulfilling their dreams." Her face broke into a broad, unabashed grin. "You won't mind if I stop in every now and then, would you?"

He shook his head. "Of course not. You'll always be welcome here." He glanced back at her cart. "And anyone else you'd like to bring."

"And Joshua?"

"I can't imagine him letting you stay away. I have this funny feeling you already know he'll be looking for you."

Beatrice grinned broadly. "Well, the thought may have crossed my mind. I'm sure he'll know where to find me."

Mathew checked the sky again. If Beatrice said it wasn't going to rain yet, then it wasn't. But he still didn't like thinking about her alone at night, wandering the streets and pushing her old rickety cart down half-lit back alleys.

"Beatrice, you could stay here tonight, you know."

"Thank you, but I really must be off." She touched her crown. "The weight of responsibility and all that, remember."

Mathew nodded.

"Perhaps you'd be kind enough to drive me home, though."

"Home?"

"Yes. Home. The place where I live."

Mathew didn't feel the wind any more. "But I thought you just lived –"

"On the street? Don't be ridiculous. I'm a queen, and royalty doesn't live on the street. No. I like the street, and I spend as much time outside as I possibly can because that's where my special subjects are. But I don't live there. I live at home. In a house."

It all seemed a little incongruous to Mathew. Didn't she live in the alleys, the doorways, the bus shelters, the missions? He couldn't picture her in a house. In, or out. While her neighbors washed their car down on a sweltering summer afternoon, did Beatrice hose off her cart in the driveway? When did she cut her lawn, water her plants, shovel the snow, or carry in her groceries? No matter how hard he tried, Mathew couldn't envision his fairy godmother sleeping in a real bedroom, on a real bed with actual covers, with a night table and a bedside lamp and a headboard and maybe even a television in a corner armoire.

"I don't have an armoire," she whispered, shattering the silence.

Mathew wondered if she parked her car in the driveway at night.

"I keep it in the garage," she sighed. "So it doesn't bother some of the neighbours."

Mathew couldn't even begin to imagine what her house might have looked like.

"Well, do you mind giving me a lift?" Beatrice put a hand to the small of her back and stretched from side to side. "It's been an awfully long day."

Mathew agreed. "Of course. I'll grab my keys."

Carol was waiting in the foyer. "Isn't Beatrice coming in?"

"No. She wants me to drive her home."

"Home?"

Mathew smiled. "That's what I thought. But she actually has a house and lives somewhere."

"I never realized that fairy godmothers were so complex."

"Maybe it's just their queen." He smiled and kissed her lightly on the cheek. "I'll be right back."

She stopped him, leaned up, and kissed him on the mouth. "I'll be waiting."

That was one of the most comforting things Mathew had ever heard in his entire life.

Beatrice was standing by his car when he went back out. He held her door open, carefully ensuring her crown didn't poke through the roof as she tumbled in. It took him a few minutes, and he had to arrange a multitude of odds and ends, but he managed to get her cart in the trunk. It was close, but it didn't quite fit. He had to use a rope from the garage so that the trunk wouldn't bounce up and down while he drove. He didn't want to lose anything: he was just beginning to realize how special so many of the things she carried around might have been. When he was finished and everything was tightly secured, he slipped behind the wheel.

Beatrice looked out the window and watched the people pass by like fence posts on a country road. Her crown was askew and her bracelet jangled with each pothole. Mathew kept staring at her out of the corner of his eye. What could he possibly have said to her? Now, after all this? After what she'd done. A memory kept creeping into his consciousness, but he couldn't quite retrieve it. But then suddenly, it was there. He pictured the intravenous stand in the hospital, and Beatrice's blood flowing into his veins. It made him feel warm all over, and words superfluous.

He had no idea where he was going. Beatrice led him farther down into the city through a maze of interconnected back streets that would have confused a rally navigator. If he'd been coming from another direction, in another time and safely hidden away in a different frame of mind, Mathew might have been able to see where he was going. But he couldn't. You often don't know where you're going until you get there. Every time Mathew thought he might be getting close to her street, Beatrice issued a new set of directions the way a captain talks to a helmsman who doesn't have a firm grasp of nautical-speak.

"Turn left here."
"Right up there."
"Right again."

Mathew watched the houses change the deeper he wound through the labyrinth of side streets. The lots seemed to get a little smaller while the homes got bigger. Years passed. These ones dated from the thirties and forties. Brick sides with stone fronts. Narrow and tall, with thick wood trim and hydro wires that ran from the street to the corner of the eaves. The streets had towering, majestic trees with interlaced limbs that met high above the road with the ones on the other side. A nice place to grow up, Mathew thought.

"Yes, it was. "Beatrice stared straight ahead.

"You lived around here all your life?"

"As soon as I was married. I had my family here." Her eyes glimmered with sadness. "They're gone, though." She wiped her eyes with her sleeve and stared out the window. "It's changed quite a lot." She smiled. "But not necessarily for the worse."

"The houses are lovely."

"Everyone used to take a great deal of pride in their homes. Most still do. It wasn't a case of keeping up with the Jones', or anything as trite as that. But everyone wanted the people who passed by on their nightly walks to look up and say, 'my, that's a nicely kept home, isn't it?'"

Mathew started to speak but Beatrice interrupted.

"Keep going until you hit two more sets of lights, and then go left. As soon as you make the turn, get over in the right lane because the next street's mine."

The next street's mine. Mathew still couldn't imagine Beatrice having a street. He'd assumed the entire city was his fairy godmother's street, and he couldn't quite get over the fact that she lived somewhere; that she had an actual address.

"The next right. That's the one."

Mathew signaled, which seemed to confuse the driver behind him, and made the turn. An intoxicating rush of unease blitzed his senses. Something about the street felt oddly familiar, but he didn't think he'd ever been along this road before. Yet the houses drew him like iron filings to a magnet and tugged his thoughts together in jumbled clusters. He slowed the car to a crawl. Each house he passed made him feel more tense and expectant. Beatrice though, seemed relieved. She was home.

"There, the one just a couple in from the corner. That's it."

That's it.

Few paired words had ever struck Mathew with such terror. And in some way he couldn't describe, that much happiness, too.

He eased the car into the driveway. When he stopped, he slouched down behind the wheel and stared up quietly. The world was spinning so wildly Mathew had to reach out and touch his dashboard to make sure it was still there. To make sure *he* was still there. Long forgotten words from a day he remembered all the time melted into his consciousness like dollops of butter on a hot pancake.

Yes, he did see it now, after all these years. Mathew looked at the positioning of the dormer windows, the gingerbread lattice work, how the porch jutted out to give it a façade of greater depth. The architectural signs were unmistakable, although in all fairness, the model was actually based on a facsimile of a traditional Cape Cod design.

Joshua's Cape Cod.

Meet our Author

Donald Owen Crowe

Donald Crowe holds an Hons. B.A. and B. Ed from the University of Toronto. He enjoys an eclectic range of literature, and has a special affinity for Shakespeare, Dickens, and the great writers of the late eighteen hundreds. He also admires the nuances of Spanish and European writers. He divides his time between Ajax, Ontario and Estero, Florida.

www.ingramcontent.com/pod-product-compliance
Lightning Source LLC
Chambersburg PA
CBHW070800030726
47504CB00003B/629